W9-BXR-586

MIDNIGHT HORIZON

DANIEL JOSÉ OLDER

LOS ANGELES·NEW YORK

In loving memory of Baba Craig Ramos

Printed in the United States of America

First Edition, February 2022

10 9 8 7 6 5 4 3 2 1

FAC-021131-21351

ISBN 978-1-368-06067-7

Library of Congress Control Number on file

Design by Soyoung Kim, Scott Piehl, and Leigh Zieske

Visit the official *Star Wars* website at: www.starwars.com

STAR WARS
THE HIGH REPUBLIC

The tragic events of the Republic Fair have galvanized the galaxy. The Jedi and the Republic have gone on the offensive to stop the marauding NIHIL. With these vicious raiders all but defeated, Jedi Master AVAR KRISS has set her sights on LOURNA DEE, the supposed Eye of the Nihil, and has undertaken a mission to capture her once and for all.

But unbeknownst to the Jedi, the true leader of the Nihil, the insidious MARCHION RO, is about to launch an attack on the Jedi and the Republic on a scale not seen in centuries. If he succeeds, the Nihil will be triumphant and the light of the Jedi will go dark.

Only the brave Jedi Knights of STARLIGHT BEACON stand in his way, but even they may not be enough against Ro and the ancient enemy that's about to be unleashed. . . .

STAR WARS TIMELINE

THE HIGH REPUBLIC

FALL OF THE JEDI

THE PHANTOM MENACE

ATTACK OF THE CLONES

THE CLONE WARS

REVENGE OF THE SITH

REIGN OF THE EMPIRE

THE BAD BATCH

SOLO: A STAR WARS STORY

AGE OF REBELLION

REBELS

ROGUE ONE: A STAR WARS STORY

A NEW HOPE

THE EMPIRE STRIKES BACK

RETURN OF THE JEDI

THE NEW REPUBLIC

THE MANDALORIAN

RISE OF THE FIRST ORDER

RESISTANCE

THE FORCE AWAKENS

THE LAST JEDI

THE RISE OF SKYWALKER

PROLOGUE

CORONET CITY

"I'm going in," Prybolt said.

Ovarto shook his woolly horned head. "Client said not to go in."

The hounds growled and scanned the empty street, sniffing with those huge nostrils. One of them, Serenata, pulled toward the door, yanking Prybolt forward a step. The others seemed to grumble amongst themselves, then followed.

The building was one of those weird cylinder-shaped ones that seemed to pop up out of nowhere like mushrooms all around the Syllain District and then disappear just as quickly. This one had been painted bright orange (ugly), had strange metal markings on it (creepy), had no windows (bad), and as far as Prybolt could tell, had only the one door, which Minister Nomar Tralmat—Coronet Father of Finances, the man Prybolt and Ovarto were pledged to protect—had entered exactly twenty-two minutes earlier, with various insistences that they not follow or check on him under any circumstances.

He had sworn he knew what he was doing, that he was safe, that he just needed them for security to and from the meeting, not during. And no, he wouldn't tell them what the meeting was about, or who was there; he'd already been explicit about the need for secrecy when he hired them. It was probably some coordination for the upcoming Finance Ball—an annual performance of unvarnished excess that marked the beginning of open-market trading. Didn't matter, really—and Prybolt knew better than to ask too many questions. But still, to keep someone safe, a bodyguard shouldn't be kept totally in the dark.

Nomar Tralmat was a human, and humans, in Prybolt's experience, were notoriously reckless when it came to getting themselves murdered or horrifically mangled or exposed to ghastly diseases. They just couldn't be relied on to follow even the most basic precautions; all they did was throw themselves in front of blaster fire or into massive explosions or off cliffs, and no matter how obviously deadly the situation was, it was still the bodyguard's fault if they died.

"Crash says sometimes the client doesn't know what's good for them," Prybolt said, "so we have to know instead."

"Yeah, well"—Ovarto lit a death stick, even though you weren't supposed to smoke on the job, and sighed some smoke up into the night—"sometimes even Crash is wrong."

That was obviously not true, and it was clear Ovarto didn't believe it, either. Crash, who was Prybolt's best friend and ran Supreme Coronet City Diplomat Protection, was no exception to the "humans are reckless" rule; in fact she was the chief example of it. The difference was, she also somehow excelled at not dying and making sure no one around her did, either. And no one could think of a time she'd been wrong.

The hounds snorfled loudly against the door. They were large, imposing creatures, all white with hunched torsos and beady, malicious eyes squinting out from round protrusions on their skulls. Squirming tendrils dangled from their jaws. All in all, the hounds gave the impression that they could tear someone to shreds without much bother. This was in part because they absolutely could and would. But they'd also been bred to look that way—a handy trick that ensured they didn't have to actually shred anyone most of the time; people just kept their distance.

Prybolt loved the hounds with all his heart. They were the truest friends he had besides Crash, and they always knew when something on a job was off.

Like right now, for instance. The hounds, still at the door, seemed to confer for a moment, and then they all craned their necks and released an eerie keening noise.

Prybolt appraised the building again. "Okay, yeah, I'm not the only one that doesn't like it. And to be precise, I hate it."

Other things Prybolt hated at that moment:

—The way his voice sounded like it was pleading
—The way his long, Grindalid body felt squished into his ridiculous protective suit, every muscle on each of his many arms burning with complaints about the long night they'd had
—How, between the rows of towering buildings around them, another Corellian dawn teased the edge of the dark horizon

These types of shenanigans were exactly why his family had pleaded with him not to go into this line of work.

"Let the humans and their other sun-loving friends devour and destroy each other," Mother Fastidima had begged in the cool darkness of their underground nesting pool. "Your place is here, away from all that. A whole underground empire awaits you. You don't need to scrunch up your body into those silly fabrics. You don't need to live in fear of disintegration in that cruel Corellian sun, my sweet pupalette."

But Prybolt had known what he wanted, and it wasn't to spend his life hiding in the shadows with his hundreds of other nest sibs. "I'm not a pupa anymore," he'd said, sounding, he knew, very young and ridiculous. "And anyway, you just don't want me to be in danger all the time because if I die you'll have to avenge me and that might upset the delicate political balance you're always going on about!"

He'd spat out the words with a ferocity he hadn't realized he felt, and they'd found their mark—Mother Fastidima reared back like she'd been hit. "That's!" she gasped. "That's!" Water slopped down her chin tendrils and splashed into the pool below as she stammered.

But she couldn't quite deny it, because it wasn't entirely false.

The Garavult Clan had protected the underground water systems of Corellia for centuries, and their legacy was one of both honor and vengeance. To strike down a Garavult Grindalid meant incurring the wrath of all seven hundred and forty-eight Garavults, which is exactly why it almost never happened. That blood oath outweighed any of the petty politics of the time, and Prybolt knew it as well as Mother Fastidima did.

But that wasn't all there was to it. His nest mother also wanted him close because she loved him.

Prybolt had sighed, already out of the dark water and heading for the tunnel that led to the surface. Sometimes winning hurt more than losing. "I just want to see more of the city I live in than the sewers and tunnels. And I want to protect people. I'm good at it!"

And he was—even Crash had admitted it, and Crash rarely gave compliments. He'd already mastered moving in the protective suit, and he easily grasped the intricate and delicate art of becoming one with a crowd while staying close to a client on the move. He understood violence, the chaos and suddenness of it. Weapons posed no problem—every Grindalid came up studying a variety of defense techniques with different staffs, blades, and blasters. The hounds, of course, adored him, so training and working with them was no problem.

And, most important, he knew when to trust his gut.

And right now, as the night ever so gently gave way to dawn around them, Prybolt's gut was telling him something very wrong was happening on the other side of that door.

"I'm going in," he said again, and this time he meant it.

Ovarto shrugged, flicking away his death stick. "Your funeral."

"Beeta, Serenata, Sibak. At ready." The hounds obediently stopped their investigation and stood on either side of Prybolt.

He touched the control panel by the door. It slid open to reveal . . . another door. A muffled beeping went off somewhere inside: alarms. Prybolt hit the touch sensor on the second door, and that one rumbled to the side with a rusty groan.

Several figures moved through the dim room within. What light there was came from the center, where Nomar

Tralmat was on his knees, nose bloodied, face desperate. Above him stood a tall woman with red skin and the long folded ears of an Er'Kit poking out from either side of a strange gas mask. She had a blaster rifle slung over her shoulder; the fierce bayonet on the top glinted in the flickering lantern light. And she looked like she was winding up for another hit.

Get between the threat and the client.

That was all there was, all that mattered.

Prybolt launched forward with a single command to the hounds: "Eat." The woman raised her rifle just like Prybolt hoped she would—because that meant it wasn't aimed at Tralmat. Prybolt pivoted to the side, adjusting his stride to accommodate the shift in balance, as blaster fire roared out.

"Ayeeee!" Ovarto yelled from the doorway, and then all two meters and one hundred kilograms of him crashed noisily to the ground. One of the hounds squealed and fell—Beeta, maybe. The others sprang forward.

Before either Prybolt or the remaining hounds could reach her, the woman threw something at the floor and it burst with a flash. Sibak and Serenata squealed, and a foul yellow smoke billowed into the room, covering it almost instantly.

But there was only the client and the threat, the client and the threat. Or, probably several threats, but that woman was the most important one. Some smoke wouldn't stop Prybolt. It couldn't get through his breathing apparatus and coverall suit anyway. He crossed the floor in three bounds and hurled himself toward where Tralmat had been just a moment before, shivering on the ground. He felt an arm, a shoulder.

"Come on!" Prybolt yelled, pulling the man to his feet.

Sudden, searing pain tore through Prybolt's thorax just as the woman's gas-masked face appeared in the mist.

That bayonet.

He sidestepped the next swipe, the huge blade swishing through the yellow cloud where he'd just been, then spun forward, allowing his own momentum to power a devastating uppercut. It connected with the woman's mask, sent her spinning back into the fog.

Up ahead, a doorway slid open to what looked like a small antechamber lit by the breaking day. This building was full of secrets! There'd been no sign of another entrance on the outside. Didn't matter. It was a small blessing, and Prybolt would take full advantage of it. He hefted Tralmat, who was coughing and sputtering, onto his shoulder and made for the light.

Turned out the doorway had opened to let in reinforcements, but Prybolt was counting on that. Two more masked raiders hurried in only to get hit with Prybolt's blaster bolts. He ran past their squirming bodies and out into the street.

He let Tralmat down gently—the man seemed mostly okay besides the bloody nose and coughing from whatever that chemical was—and started pulling him along. "You have to come with me," Prybolt said. "Quickly."

Tralmat looked around, wide-eyed. "Come on!" Prybolt urged. Any second, someone was going to burst out of the misty darkness, blaster bolts first more than likely. "We have to go . . . *now*!" Why was Prybolt so out of breath? He hadn't exerted himself that much, and the gas shouldn't be affecting him with . . . the suit.

He glanced down, already pulling Tralmat into an awkward, stumbling run. The woman's bayonet had torn a serious gash in his protective suit, scraping his carapace. But it wasn't the wound or the gas that was sapping his energy so suddenly; it was the sun.

"We have to . . . we have to go," Prybolt wheezed, still clutching Tralmat's arm. "I can't . . ." It was the client; it was only the client. All there was was the client. But if Prybolt didn't make it, no one would be left to protect Tralmat. "I need . . . shade . . . darkness . . . something."

A sharp, crackling burn erupted along his left flank as the day grew brighter and a gentle morning breeze pushed the torn fabric of his suit aside. "Come on," he moaned. "Come this . . . this way."

But when he looked back, Tralmat was gone, probably snatched by one of those raiders, and the masked woman was walking calmly out of the mist toward Prybolt.

"Client," Prybolt grunted, as if that would somehow make Tralmat reappear on the street beside him.

He stumbled around a corner, his gloved fingers wrestling the comlink out of its belt holster.

"Crash," he muttered into it, hoping he'd hit the transmit button. "Crash . . . Crash!"

She would know what to do.

"Come in, Crash . . . I . . ."

The Er'Kit woman was probably already behind him; she had to be, raising that rifle for the shot that would end him.

Prybolt pulled out his own blaster and spun around, firing wildly.

The street was empty.

The sun kept rising.

"Crash!" He pushed forward. Somewhere, there would be an open door, an entrance to the tunnel system that was his true home, the darkness that would embrace him, protect him. Then he could heal and go find his client. He could make this right still.

"Crash, it's Prybolt. I . . . I messed up. There's . . ." What were those attackers? They all wore the telltale gas masks of the Nihil, but there was no way the Nihil were on Corellia—that was an Outer Rim problem. They were reckless, sure, but not fools. They'd never risk coming this deep into the Core of the Republic, the heart of the galaxy.

It had to be imitators, or a cartel of some kind trying to cover its tracks by pretending to be Nihil. That was it.

"Nihil," Prybolt rasped into the comm. "Dressed like Nihil. Gas masks, and gas . . . but . . . I don't think . . ." Didn't matter. They'd figure it out. Crash could figure out any problem, so she'd work out this one. Prybolt just had to stay alive to help her do it.

He rounded another corner at a stumble and ran straight into the red woman in the gas mask. She leapt back, too fast to track or attack, then her rifle seemed to come dancing out of the sky toward him as she lunged forward.

All he could do was fall backward, but he wasn't fast enough; the blade shredded the whole front of his suit wide open, and then the ground rushed up behind him and he slammed down so hard all the air left his many lungs.

None of that mattered nearly as much as the sizzling that screamed through his whole torso, though. All his smaller appendages were probably wriggling as they burned. Daylight—that bright, blinding poison—poured through everything, flooded over him and sent frantic searing warnings all through his nervous system.

"I've always wanted to see this happen," the Er'Kit woman said with what sounded like delight in her voice. She stood over him with one booted leg on either side, and if he'd had any strength left, he would have happily kicked her, blasted her, *anything* to get that smirk he was sure she was making off her face.

But none of his body parts were responding the way Prybolt wanted them to, and almost everything was made out of bright, unrelenting light, and then light became the world, and then there was nothing at all.

PART ONE

ONE

STARLIGHT BEACON

"Ram? What's the matter?"

"Hm?" Ram Jomaram looked up from the tiny reactor core he'd been taking apart and putting back together for the past . . . he'd lost track of how long. The flickering hologram of his master, Kunpar Vasivola, blinked back at him, concern in his wrinkled old eyes. "Nothing," Ram said, and went back to fiddling.

"*Vakateebakbak!*" one of the small furry Bonbraks—Tip, probably—yelled from across the room. *False statement*, basically, which normally would've riled Ram up, but he couldn't be bothered. What was the point?

"Your little friend is right," Master Kunpar said. "I've

known you your whole life, Ram Jomaram. And I know when something's wrong, even if you refuse to admit it."

"I . . ." Ram stood and pulled his goggles up to his forehead. His Padawan robes were covered in grease, as always—no matter how many times he washed them, the stains stayed where they were.

"It's just . . ." He'd fully intended to explain himself when he opened his mouth. But then, as had happened so many times recently, the words dried up and evaporated. Maybe language just couldn't encapsulate what he felt and he should stop trying. But then he'd keep hearing about how he was stubborn from Master Kunpar and the Bonbraks and anyone else who felt like piling on, too, probably. V-18 was gone as usual, otherwise he'd surely join in. Since they'd left Valo, Ram's droid had spent most of his time rummaging through Starlight's scrap bin, looking for new upgrade parts.

Ram shook his head, trying to clear it. "I don't know," he finally said.

The old Ongree nodded sagely, stroking his face tentacles like he always did before saying something incredibly wise that would take Ram about eight years to untangle the meaning of. "That's a good start!"

Ram scoffed, picked up the rusted metal casing around the core, then released it, letting the Force hold it midair in a slow spin. "It's like . . . I've faced down Nihil, right?" he said, watching the core instead of his master. "And the Drengir.

I've been shot at, almost eaten. Arrested. Had things exploding all around me more times than I can remember . . . and that's just in the past couple months!"

He wasn't even exaggerating. Ever since the Nihil had attacked the Republic Fair on Ram's home planet, Valo, he'd been trying to stay alive and keep balance in a galaxy that had seemed to go from peaceful to war-torn overnight. In the midst of that battle, Ram had met Lula Talisola, a Padawan from Starlight Beacon, and she'd been so poised in the storm of fighting—somehow a compassionate warrior and the very essence of what Ram imagined the Jedi were supposed to be—he'd realized he had to do whatever he could to help make the galaxy safe again, just like Lula was doing.

So he joined her and her friend Zeen, who was Force-sensitive but not an actual Jedi-in-training like Lula and Ram, when they returned to Starlight, and he'd been with them ever since, running missions and making more friends than he'd ever thought he'd have in his life—and almost getting killed in every way imaginable (and a few more).

But somehow, none of that was the problem.

"It's been a very difficult time for the whole frontier," Master Kunpar said, "but especially you young people caught up in the fighting." He shook his old head sadly. "It shouldn't have been like this."

"But that's not it," Ram said, trying not to let the frustration he felt singe his voice. After all, if he couldn't find words or meaning behind what was wrong, how was his master supposed to? Ram sighed and the tiny core casing clattered to the desk.

"*Fraka-botá!*" yelled the other Bonbrak, Breebak. That was a Bonbreez word that was best left untranslated.

"Sorry," Ram called. He looked back at the holo of his master, scrunched up his face, and spat out the words without thinking about them: "The problem is the opposite. I *don't* feel anything, not right now. Not even when we got into battle. I don't feel fear, I don't feel sadness. I'm not excited when we win. I barely even . . ." He shook his head, letting the words turn to dust again, wishing the thoughts would, too.

"Go on," Master Kunpar said kindly.

"I barely even feel good when we save people."

Ram wasn't sure when it had started, this terrifying emptiness. During the attack on the Republic Fair, it had seemed like he felt all the emotions possible at the same time. Lonisa City, *his* city, was under attack; people were dying all around, and it seemed like the Nihil had come to stay. He was heartbroken and terrified, *and* he was meeting new friends, friends he was pretty sure he'd have for the rest of his life—he just wasn't sure how much longer that would be. And together they had really made a difference, restoring planet-wide communications so the Republic could organize its counterattack. Death and destruction were all around, but they'd been part of the solution, and it had felt amazing to be able to help.

And then at some point after he'd arrived on Starlight

Beacon, somewhere amid all those explosions and rescues and shootouts—a change had happened inside him. It felt like someone else had taken over his body. Someone cold. "I know we're supposed to be unattached and all that," Ram said. "But this feels like . . . something else."

"Mmm," Master Kunpar said, eyes closed. "You are striving for balance, young Ram."

"I guess. But what do I do?"

"Keep searching, Ram. Don't stop."

"*Ramamalamaaa!*" Zeen Mrala sang, sliding in through the open door and executing a near-perfect pirouette across the room. "We have a mee-eeting!"

Zeen had grown up among people who hated and distrusted Force users, so she'd kept her abilities secret for most of her life. Then her home planet, Trymant IV, was nearly demolished by an Emergence from the Great Disaster and she'd been taken in by the Jedi. She'd helped Ram and Lula fight off the Nihil when they attacked Valo, and Ram had felt close to her ever since. She was a relative newcomer to the space station, just like him, and she always knew how to cheer him up. Unlike Ram, she somehow managed to always look fashionable and clean, whether she was wearing her flight jacket and had blasters strapped to each hip or was in the sleeping robes Lula had loaned her or, like now, had on just a casual flowy robe over a sleeveless shirt.

"Yeah," Ram said, already putting the reactor core parts away in their box and getting up.

"Is that my favorite Mikkian?" Master Kunpar said, his little holo form squinting as Zeen sailed past with a graceful lunge.

Zeen laughed, popping back up over Ram's shoulder; her head tendrils brushed lightly against his cheek. "Hey, Master Kunpar! How many Mikkians do you know?"

"Enough to have a favorite!"

Zeen beamed and got back to her dance.

"You know, you can take a break if you need to," Master Kunpar said, turning back to Ram. "Come back to Valo, help the rebuilding effort."

Ram nodded, but he knew that wasn't going to help him find balance. The very notion of going back home made him nauseous. There was so much happening out here that the Jedi needed his help with. "Thanks, Master Kunpar."

"A break would be absolutely *wizard*!" Zeen said, using Ram's favorite word for when something was completely amazing and the best possible thing ever. She only did that when she was trying to make him feel better. Zeen winked at Master Kunpar, who stared blankly back at her over the holo connection.

"What's *wizard*?" the old Jedi asked. "That something you kids are saying these days?"

Zeen looked scandalized. "Ram! I thought that was something people on Valo said!"

Ram had to laugh. "No, I totally made that up. Isn't it wizard?"

"All righty, I'll just be going now," Master Kunpar said. "May the Force be with you both."

"Can't believe you made up a whole slang word and didn't tell us," Zeen said, clearly using the Force to elevate her flying cartwheels a little higher. "You okay?"

Ram shrugged off the compliment and the question and picked up his holoprojector. "You're such an amazing dancer, Zeen. Can I take a holo to send back to Valo?"

"Of course," she said, twirling. She stretched her arms wide. "Send it out to the whole galaxy! Haven't you ever dreamed of being a star, Ram?"

"Absolutely not," he said, sidestepping to keep her in view.

"I have. I don't think I'd really love it, but I always wanted to try, just for a day or two. Be like those fancy singers on the holos, with the whole galaxy cheering." She pirouetted again, then spun into an elaborate bow.

Ram applauded.

"I've always thought maybe in another lifetime, I would've been a famous star!" A sad smile crescented her face; then she looked away. "But that's not for me, not really. . . ." She shook off whatever fantasy she'd gotten lost in and directed a sharp glare at Ram. "Don't think I haven't noticed that you dodged my question."

"I . . ."

"Hey!" Lula Talisola popped her head in from the hallway. "They just upgraded this to a mission briefing. Something happened on Corellia. We going or we dancing?"

TWO

CORONET CITY

Alys "Crash" Ongwa picked up the comlink and growled into it, "Are you in position, Barchibar?"

She didn't mean to let her irritation out like that. She usually tried to reserve obvious signs of anger for especially dire situations. But really: everything had felt pretty dire since the night Prybolt and Ovarto had gone missing.

And if Prybolt were here, she wouldn't be growling at this overgrown screerat to make sure he was in position. Prybolt would've just been in position; he would've been anticipating attacks from all angles, including above and way down below, just like Crash had taught them all to do.

"Almost there, Crash," the reply crackled through the comlink.

Crash managed not to throw the device off the rooftop. "Almost? What does that mean? No ETA, no coordinates, just *almost*?"

"Sorry, Crash!"

What kind of name was Barchibar anyway? Made your tongue feel prickly just saying it. Who named their kid something that sounded that much like *barf*?

"Okay, in position!"

"Yeah, yeah." Crash had already launched out over Diadem Square in her small skiff. If her people were choosing sloppiness, she needed the only eyes she trusted on the scene: her own. She pulled her bright pink hair back into a loose bun and got up on tiptoe for a better view.

"Commence ruse procedures, Master Crash?" 10-K8 piped up.

"Gah!" Crash yelped. "I forgot you were there."

The short mushroom-shaped droid was excellent at being forgotten about—which was why Crash usually used her for intelligence gathering. That and she was the only one around who made Crash look even remotely tall. Without Prybolt, the team needed a second set of, well, everything, running logistics and support. But Crash must've been extra frazzled if she'd forgotten someone was right behind her.

Prybolt had to be okay, and he had to come back. That was all there was to it. If Crash had to bring him back by sheer force of will, then that's what it would be. His final message hadn't offered much hope, and the fact that both Ovarto and Tralmat, the client they'd been protecting, had vanished, too, well . . . No, Crash wouldn't give up on her best friend. If anyone could survive a situation going south, it was Prybolt. They'd probably just gone to ground or something, waiting for whatever it was to blow over.

And anyway, there was no way that whatever was left of the Nihil would dare show their faces on Corellia.

But whatever had happened, it was pretty clear someone had hurt Prybolt and Ovarto. If they were okay, they would have reached out by now. And given the shadiness and sniping of Coronet politics, that someone had probably been gunning for their client, the Father of Finances, and Prybolt and Ovarto had just been in the way—obstacles to be removed. And that brought Crash once again to the worst part of it all: whoever had done it was almost definitely one of her other clients, someone she was sworn to protect. Just about had to be. Her crew was responsible for every major politico in Coronet City.

Keep them all at arms' length, Crash's mom, Baynoo, had told her when she turned the company over to Crash the previous year. And situations like this were exactly why that advice mattered so much. Crash was working for people who would snuff out a life for more power without blinking an eye.

She had taken that advice, and her team had kept all their clients safe from each other, until now. And that was bad enough, but the fact that people she cared about had apparently been hurt, too, meant she *had* to find those responsible and deal with them.

And find them she would.

"Mind the huge hulking beast thing!" 10-K8 warned.

But more important, Crash had to stay focused! Today she had her reputation to restore, and a complex public drama to arrange that would require all her attention. She swerved the skiff hard to the left, almost dumping 10-K8, and managed not to smash straight into the huge Savrip standing on a rooftop.

"What's that big ridiculous lump of reptile doing just standing on a rooftop anyway!" Crash demanded, once they'd spun around and were a safe distance away.

"Uh, what you told him to?" 10-K8 suggested.

"Oh?" Crash blinked at the massive creature, who had barely even noticed the collision they'd just avoided. "Ohhh, that's Tamo!"

"Caf," 10-K8 said dryly, passing a steaming mug to Crash.

She took the drink and sipped it glumly. "Ah, yes. Thanks."

"Mmm-hm. Anything you want to talk about?"

Crash shook her head. "I just miss my friend, is all. And I can't . . . seem to . . ."

"Keep your head in the game?"

Down below, crowds streamed into the wide-open boulevard, just like Crash had planned.

The holocams loved Svi'no Atchapat, in part because light seemed to dance off her in dazzling, colorful beams. That was mostly because she wore jewelry and even sometimes blouses made with thousands of tiny mirrors, Crash knew, but it helped that Svi'no also radiated stardom. Also, she was a Taymar, so she had naturally glittery blue-green skin and flowy tendrils. And she could literally float, so it basically looked like a majestic melodramatic wind followed her around everywhere she went.

Crash didn't care about all that. The two girls had met five years before, when Crash's mom was running things and Crash was just an awkward twelve-year-old tagging along and learning the ropes. Svi'no was twelve at the time, too, and already performing shows with her family music group in sold-out venues, and even though Crash had already met dozens of famous people by then, this strange floating girl seemed legendary on some other level; so Crash had felt, for maybe the first time, a little starstruck. But then Svi'no had turned out to be funny, easy to talk to, and, most important, just as mischievous as Crash, and they'd become instant best friends.

Their friendship had waxed and waned over the years, but recently it seemed like an unpronounceable distance had opened between them. Crash figured it was probably just a product of growing up or Svi'no's superstardom or Crash having to manage a whole company or whatever, and tried not to take it personally.

"Client on site," Barchibar reported over the comlink.

The holos had reported Svi'no Atchapat's rumored appearance because Crash had told them to. And it worked: chatter on the holos became whispers on the streets, whispers turned into yells, and theories and daydreams and on and on forever until the whole of Coronet City shined with the excitement of seeing their beloved daughter, their cultural ambassador. It had taken only a day for the whole thing to reach critical mass: by that morning, the talk of every neighborhood was whether the secretive pop star would actually make a rare public appearance, in Diadem Square no less!

And so they came, and they came in droves. Of course they did! The street adored Svi'no Atchapat—when she was just a little kid, someone had taken holo footage of her singing along to the clanking of factory machinery as her family built star cruisers in the shipyards.

She'd been doing it since before she could walk, and she'd learned from her grandma, who used to sing the same songs as a girl. It was an old music—they called it Galan-Kalank, after the sounds of the gears and turbines that provided its rhythm—but Svi'no had transformed it into something that sounded brand new, too, and it took the galaxy by storm. Soon her mom and dad and all six brothers had fabricated portable instruments out of their grease-covered machinery, and they took little Svi'no on tour, bringing Galan-Kalank to amphitheaters and music halls from Chandrila to Coruscant.

They all still worked in the shipyards between gigs—it

was family tradition, after all—and that only gave the music group an even deeper sense of authenticity and lore. The Atchapats had changed the galactic music game, put Coronet City on the pop-cultural arts map, and given Corellia, for once, fame that was about something more than making great starships.

And so the entire overcomplicated ruse was going as planned.

But it didn't feel like it, because Prybolt was still gone, and so was Ovarto, and they were both probably gone for good.

Crash rubbed her face and growled. "Yes, keep my head in the game."

A cool, heavenly tone rang out, something like the bells of Coronet Cathedral but . . . alive. A second note shimmered into the warm summery sky, wrapping harmonic waves around the first. The crowd fell silent, awed. Svi'no had come to dazzle them, and she did not disappoint. When the beat dropped in time with a third majestic, gold-tinged note, everyone went wild.

Crash closed her eyes and allowed herself a slight smile. "At least one thing is going—" A sharp pop cut through the cheering and excitement, and suddenly everyone was screaming. Then three more pops.

That wasn't supposed to happen!

Crash's eyes opened wide. "Wasn't our fake assailant supposed to have a knife?"

Down below, Tangor, a silverback Wookiee from Crash's

team, had already wrapped around Svi'no and was moving quickly through the rippling crowd. Good.

"Thermal detonator!" Barchibar yelled over the comm. "Gotta be!"

"I need info, not wild theories," Crash barked, hitting the thrusters on the skiff and looping around to get a better view. "Stop yelling, Barchi. Report in, one by one."

"Air-Eleven," Fezzonk's gruff voice announced. "Got nothing but runners and screamers. No suspicious rooftop activity. Nothing doing in the skies."

"Good, good," Crash muttered, sipping more caf. Then some more.

"Tunnel Team Twelve," Smeemarm said in that creepy whisper she always used. "All clear."

Down below, no smoke rose, nothing had shattered. Everyone was running for cover, but no one seemed to know which direction to go.

Tangor roared in Shyriiwook that she had the client covered and was heading down Loomar Alley toward one of their designated safety points.

"Droid cam scans show no sign of any malevolent forces on the move," 10-K8 said calmly. "Besides our own, of course."

Tamo! Crash glanced back at the empty spot on the rooftop where they'd almost run into the hulking beast a few minutes earlier. "Where's the Savrip right now?"

Something wasn't right, and it wasn't with her team. The absence of Prybolt was a gaping hole in her operation, of course—one she was increasingly thinking she might have to get used to for good—and Barchibar was useless, but that was nothing new.

"Tamo's heading down to the plaza like he was told to," 10-K8 reported. "He's just a little slow because we gave him a big breakfast to keep him happy."

"That's good, that's good," Crash said absently, vaguely aware that such sloppiness could've caused huge problems in any other circumstance but for once not caring at all.

Because something . . . wasn't . . . right. A bang—several bangs!—but no smoke and no casualties could mean only one thing. Sabotage of the most theatrical kind. And there was only one person in Coronet City as adept at creating unnecessary drama for profit or pettiness as Crash herself.

"Dizcaro," she snapped, her competitor's name a curse in her mouth.

"You think?" 10-K8 gasped.

"Dizcaro knows we're down, knows what's at stake. *Of course* he'd organize a distraction to keep us from our big comeback." She paused a half beat as the plan sizzled across her brain and took shape. "But we can still save this."

The comms came alive with a series of overlapping messages:

"Ready, Crash."

"Tell us what you need."

"In position and prepared."

"*Hrraaarrrckkkshrark rghaaagh!*"

"Let's do this!"

Crash took a breath, taking in the bliss of a mostly competent team at the ready. It would take a miracle, but impossible wins were what she did best. "Ten-Kayt, get Malfac Orfk on the comms for me. Tangor, swing Svisvi—errrrr, the client, rather—back around toward Diadem Square."

"*Shrawrr rargh!*" the Wookiee pointed out discreetly.

"Tell her it *is* part of the plan," Crash hissed. "Because it is now."

"Orfk is on the comms," 10-K8 said.

"Orfk!" Crash said with a wicked grin and elaborate hand gestures even though it was just an audio connection. "Have I got a story for you!"

"Get to the point, Crash," Malfac snorted. "You already blew one story for me today—got camera crews ready to cover a legendary live concert, and suddenly it's a mass casualty event!"

"Mass casualty? Please. Everybody looks fine to me. Anyway, how 'bout I give you a heartwarming humanoid-interest story instead, starring the star of stage and holoscreen herself."

"I'm listening."

"Swing a few droid cams back over to the square and you'll get an exclusive."

"When?"

Crash lifted her macrobinocs, zeroed in on the elaborate fountain, then swept beyond it to Tombtok Road, then

Loomar Alley beside it, where Tangor and Svi'no Atchapat were making their way through the shadows. "In five . . ." she said.

"Five what?" Malfac snarked. "Minutes? Hours? Days? C'mon, Crash—"

"Four."

"Wait! Seconds? Are you nuts?"

"Three, and on the next number I'm calling that lowlife Taljo Stant at the Coronet Independent Media Network you hate so much so he can scoop you."

"I'm on it! I'm on it! Sheesh, Crash!"

"Two."

A whole squad of droid cams whizzed through the sky, past Crash's skiff toward the plaza. She waved gingerly at them and flashed a winning smile.

"I'm not seeing any—" Malfac hissed into her earpiece.

"Just wait."

For a few moments, the droid cams hovered in the empty plaza, grabbing footage of the fountain, the litter left by so many people leaving so fast, the random storefronts.

Crash held her breath.

She exhaled silently as Svi'no Atchapat floated out from the alleyway, all by herself, an absolute picture of grace and fragility.

The Savrip couldn't have timed it better if she'd begged him to. Looking a little slow and ungainly, apparently from his extra-large breakfast, Tamo rumbled out from a building on the far side of the plaza, a huge rusty blade swinging from one of his giant green hands.

"Yaaaargh!" Tamo roared, selling it a little too much maybe, but it would do.

"Shooting stars of Bolbotarp!" Malfac yelped.

Crash just smiled. Any second, Tangor would come barreling out, too, and beast would clash with beast in an epic battle over a desperate starlet. Iconic!

Except now Tamo was only a few meters from where Svi'no floated, trembling and screaming for help, and Tangor was nowhere to be seen.

Crash disconnected the link with Malfac and jumped on the team comms. "Tangor! Where the kark are you?"

Only static came in reply.

The huge Savrip leapt, landed on the fountain, and then swung into the air at Svi'no, shattering the stone statues as he went.

"Smeemarm!" Crash yelled. "We need you *now*."

"Already . . ." A utility hole popped open between the singer and the beast. The long, strange wiry top of Smeemarm's body appeared, her arms raised to her face, where a long tube protruded from her mouth. Smeemarm jerked forward, and Tamo howled, slapping his neck, then collapsed into a heap on the pavement.

"Whoa!" Malfac squealed, popping back into her earpiece. "Whoa! Whoa! Whoa! Did you see that, Crash? Did you know that was going to happen?"

"*Know?*" Crash said, managing not to sound breathless. "How could I know? I was just trying to get you an exclusive interview with a galactic superstar!" She disconnected the link on him.

"Nice work, Smeemarm," she sighed. "Go play it up for the cams, and be sure to mention you work for the one and only Supreme Coronet City Diplomat Protection. The only way to stay safe . . ."

"Is if we keep you that way!" everyone said at once over the comms.

Tangor stumbled out of the alley, clearly high as an atmosphere probe, and sat in the ruined fountain, shaking her big Wookiee head like she was trying to clear it.

"What happened to her?" 10-K8 asked.

"Same thing that happened to Tamo, from the look of things," Crash said. "Tranquilizers. Except Tangor can probably take a higher dose, since she's had so much practice."

"You mean—"

"Dizcaro." Crash scowled. "Gather the team."

THREE

STARLIGHT BEACON

From now on, *I'm putting us first.*

Reath Silas had said those words over a year before, and he was pretty sure he'd spent most of his time since then trying to figure out what they actually meant.

It was just the type of riddle that the old Masters loved to interpret and disagree about—the straightforwardness on the surface only served to conceal enough layers of meaning to get lost in. Who was *us* to a Jedi? Was it the Order? The Republic? The whole living galaxy? And even if there were a simple answer to that (there wasn't), what did it mean to put something first? Was the only way to sacrifice your life? Was adhering to the commitments of the Order its own sacrifice?

Somewhere in that labyrinth of possibilities, there lay a single path, and that path would lead him to become the Jedi Knight he was always meant to be. He was sure of that much. He just had no idea how he was supposed to find that path.

Also: he was probably late to meet his master, Cohmac Vitus, for yet another training session.

He glanced up at the time. Okay, he was *definitely* late.

Reath stood up, packing away his studies, and let out a long sigh, looking around at the stacks of information around him.

If someone had told Reath Silas a year or two earlier that he would come to think of a space station in the middle of nowhere as home, he would've had a good chortle and then gone back to his only true home: his studies.

Of course, when a Padawan laughs, the Force laughs harder. Surely some smug old sage had said that; Reath would have to check which.

He wasn't sure when it happened, exactly. It was less a moment, more a gradual understanding. Somewhere amid all that fighting for his life, surviving battles against Nihil and Drengir . . . his heart had reoriented itself toward this strange dot in the far reaches: Starlight.

He'd been a Coruscant boy through and through. It was the center of the Republic and, more important, the Jedi Order.

The temple archive there was the most extensive in the galaxy, and Reath could've easily spent the rest of his life soaking it all in and died a very happy old man full of obscure knowledge.

Which was probably why he'd ended up out here instead, and somehow enamored with this station deep in the frontier—because the galaxy was constantly outdoing itself with new ways to prove Reath Silas wrong.

He stood up, his body as restless as his mind, and walked idly through the displays of relics and old carvings, running his finger along the wooden cases.

It was here, in this most unlikely of places, that Reath had found a place to call home. And somewhere in there lay a piece to this puzzle he'd been toying with endlessly: *From now on, I'm putting us first.*

Because on Starlight, he had found a new understanding of *us*: a community.

On Coruscant, he'd enjoyed the company of his fellow Padawans, sure. They were kind, no question, and the cohort collectively enjoyed their fair share of inside jokes and training woes.

But he never quite clicked with them, either, not in that effortless way they all seemed to have with each other. He'd resigned himself to that—he preferred keeping to himself mostly anyway, and it wasn't like his feelings were hurt.

On Starlight, though, he'd somehow, against all odds, made friends. Good ones. Great ones. People who had risked their lives for him as many times as he had for them. People he trusted deeply. He'd come to understand himself not just as a solitary recluse spinning through a vast galaxy of information, but as a part of something much bigger than himself—an *us*.

He stepped out into the hallway, waved at Master Monshi, the little furry engineer Jedi, and allowed his thoughts to guide him in a slow stroll toward the training room.

But that wasn't the only *us*. It couldn't be. There was the rest of the galaxy. Reath had been fighting for it, almost dying several times, for more than a year, and he didn't feel any closer to an answer, a path.

He could still feel the sheer terror of waking up on the Gravity's Heart, a Nihil hyperspace weapon, confused and groggy and mostly helpless, surrounded by allies and enemies both. Without any effort at all, he could call up the sense of dread that the creeping darkness of the Drengir caused, those spiny branches springing toward him from the shadows of the Amaxine station.

None of it had shown him what it meant to put *us* first. None of it had gotten him anywhere but more lost.

It seemed like every time he tried to make a move, every time he got closer to figuring out his path, something exploded or someone tried to kill him.

Or, worse, someone he cared about got killed.

His first master, Jora Malli, had died fighting the Nihil, along with so many others—too many to name.

He just needed a moment to breathe. To be. And then the path ahead would be revealed to him, he was sure of it.

THREE

The familiar smell of sweat and incense surrounded Reath as he stepped into the training room.

"You're late," Master Cohmac Vitus said, and then spun forward, his practice blade dancing through the air toward Reath.

FOUR

STARLIGHT BEACON

A shimmery image was rotating on the holotable when Ram walked into the briefing room with Zeen and found a seat beside Lula. He couldn't make out what the projection was—someone in a full-body suit, maybe? Its gradient and resolution were both very low quality, and Ram had to fight the urge to go fiddle with the controls to make it clearer.

Kantam Sy and Torban Buck were conferring quietly in the middle of the circular room, along with a few other Masters, and they all looked serious.

"What's going on?" Ram whispered to Lula.

She shrugged. "Some weird message from Corellia."

Corellia! That was the one place in the galaxy Ram had *always* dreamed of visiting. So much of the planet was shipyards and factories and more shipyards and turning gears and moving machines and . . . they just . . . they built things there! So many things! All kinds of things! Machines especially. Ships mostly! Coronet City had lots of skyscrapers and fancy dignitaries and a famous nightlife, yeah yeah yeah, but at the feet of those tall buildings, and all along the outer reaches of the city: conveyer belts, assembly plants, cranes, metal.

It was heaven, basically.

And to top it off, the legendary Anzellan engineer Shug Drabor was reportedly overseeing the construction of several more MPO-1400 *Purgill*-class star cruisers right there in the Santhe Shipyards in Coronet City. That was the same kind as the *Halcyon*, which had recently towed Starlight Beacon. Ram would've given his left arm to get a glimpse of Shug at work.

Zeen didn't seem to notice that he'd completely disappeared inside a churning, creaking fantasy world. "Core World Jedi," she said, "they love tossing anything that smells even slightly like a Nihil our way."

Ram stifled a laugh. One thing Zeen could be counted on was telling it like it was with no elaborate courtesies or pretensions at politeness. Ram liked that about her. Zeen's best friend from Trymant IV, Krix Kamarat, had gotten so upset about Zeen being a secret Force user that he'd run off and joined the Nihil and risen in their ranks to become a ruthless raider whom Ram, Zeen, and the others had been trying to track down and stop for the past what seemed like forever.

A whole mess, basically. Ram couldn't imagine dealing with that kind of betrayal—his best friends were basically the Bonbraks and whatever mechanical thing he was working on. But Zeen managed to face it all with grace and a sly smile, and even though she wasn't technically family, all the Padawans and, well, everyone on Starlight, basically, loved and took care of her like she was. Plus, she'd proved herself over and over in battle and had come to be recognized as one of the task force's best assets.

"Welcome, everyone," Master Kantam said, their sly half smile crescenting across their light brown face. "I'm afraid we don't have any news on the whereabouts of Krix Kamarat or his raiders."

"Aw, man, forget this!" Zeen got up and pretended to storm out, and everyone cracked up. Their long friendship and sudden rupture had made her feel somehow responsible for Krix's reign of terror, and all the Padawans knew she was the most pressed about finding him. But at least she could joke about it.

Zeen sat back down next to Ram with a chuckle and let the laughter die down before yelling, "Kidding!" which made everyone giggle again.

Ram had absolutely no idea how one even began to be brazen enough to make a room full of Jedi laugh like that. It seemed scarier than going into battle; although, the way he'd been feeling lately, maybe that was a good thing. Maybe that was exactly what he needed to snap himself out of this weird, no-feeling feeling: to put himself out there!

"So, when you're all done having fun . . ." Kantam said, but Ram could tell they weren't really bothered. Magic! He would never have dreamed of a scene like that playing out on Valo, where formalities ruled the day and the utmost respect had to be observed at all times. Or at least, the illusion of respect. Ram wasn't totally sure which was which, but he didn't think they were the same thing.

"We got a message from Minister Fendirfal, a Republic liaison on Corellia," Kantam said, all business once again. "She was passing along something that she seemed to feel was"—Kantam appeared to swallow down a smug aside—"more of our department."

"What does Minister Fendirfal think our department is?" Lula Talisola asked, her defensiveness clearly only partly in jest.

"The Nihil," Master Kantam sighed. "Of course."

The interior regions considered the Nihil to be an Outer Rim problem, even though they'd once effectively shut down hyperspace lanes to the whole galaxy and were proving a more formidable enemy than anyone had imagined. The Nihil had also captured a Jedi Master and turned him to dust, and no one had figured out how yet, so Ram felt like the whole galaxy could stand to be a little more concerned about them, even if they were in retreat.

"But wait," Lula said. "The Nihil are scattered and nowhere near Corellia, right? They know enough to stay away from the Core planets."

"Well . . ." Kantam walked over to the holoprojector, where the frozen image of the person in the full-body suit still rotated slowly. "Probably not, but that's exactly why we must look into the situation. If there *are* somehow functioning Nihil cells in the Core, well . . . we need to know about it. The Coronet City temple got this from a source and wanted us to see it." They pushed a button and the flickering image came to life, stumbling forward in a frantic tangle.

"Crash," the man panted. "Crash . . ."

There was something odd in the way he moved. Ram couldn't quite put his finger on what, but even through the flickering bad reception, he could tell that whoever this was, he wasn't comfortable in his own skin.

"Crash!" the person said again. It looked like he was in a city street.

Master Torban Buck, a huge, imposing Chagrian with light blue skin and a tendency to speak in the third person when he got excited, stood up and paused the recording. "Why does this strange man keep yelling *crash*? Is he perhaps creating his own sound effects?"

"I think it's someone's name," Lula said.

"What kind of a name is *Crash*?" Torban puzzled.

The room went quiet. The Chagrian was well-known among the Jedi for his nickname, Buckets of Blood—he'd given it to himself in honor of his healing skills, hoping, perhaps, that people would hear he was coming and take heart, because soon buckets of blood would be returned to their bodies! It seemed to Ram like that probably backfired spectacularly more often than not, but since they were usually going into battle with Master Torban, it worked pretty well at striking fear in the enemy.

This was it! This was Ram's chance! *Who would ever give himself a new name to let everyone know what he's good at?* The words waited, ready. But was it "give himself" or "give themself"? And should it be "new name" or "nickname"? And what if it hurt Master Torban's feelings and he never spoke to Ram again?

"Why in the stars would someone pick a dramatic new name for himself?" Master Torban boomed.

For a moment, everyone blinked at him, probably trying to figure out if he was aware of the irony.

Then the huge Chagrian broke into a grin and winked; giggles and snorts erupted all around. Ram wasn't sure if Torban had been trying to kid around from the start or had just realized the humor of it from their reaction—you could never really tell with Buckets of Blood—but either way, the moment was gone.

Probably for the best.

Kantam cocked an eyebrow. "May we continue, Master Buck?"

"Of course!"

"Come in, Crash!" the man in the recording pleaded. "I . . ."

The man spun suddenly and unleashed a spray of blaster fire on the street behind him. The room around Ram got suddenly quiet. This person was clearly running for his life. "Crash! Crash, it's Prybolt. I . . . I messed up. There's . . . Nihil . . . Dressed like Nihil. Gas masks, and gas . . . but . . . I don't think . . ." The holo blipped out of existence, leaving an eerie silence in the briefing room.

Lula was the first to speak. "It can't be! Can it? The Republic is everywhere in the Core. Why would the Nihil risk going so deep into enemy territory?" The whole room suddenly seemed alive with chatter and worry.

"They are notoriously reckless," Master Torban pointed out. "And it's paid off. They may have suffered massive casualties at the Republic Fair, but they still considered it a tactical victory. And in many ways, it was."

"Also," Master Kantam chimed in, "we still don't know what happened on Grizal, or how they turned Master Greatstorm to dust."

That quieted everyone down. In response to the attack on Valo, Republic forces had overrun a Nihil outpost on Grizal, and they'd rescued a kidnapped Jedi—Loden Greatstorm—only to have him suddenly reduced to a pile of dust by . . . something. No one knew what, and the witnesses were all in too much shock to make any sense of it. The whole incident had become a dark cloud hanging over the Starlight Jedi. Most of them had stopped talking about it in group settings—there wasn't much to say once they'd cycled through enough rounds of "What could it have been?" and come up short, again and again—but Ram knew it still haunted many dreams. Then Masters Terec and Ceret had almost been killed by the same mysterious creature. They whispered about it late at night when they couldn't sleep, and imagined, and wondered, and then they slept and those wonderings became nightmares, horrific beasts and armies of empty-eyed sorcerers and impossible chasms of darkness growing wider and wider.

"Krix is our primary target. I'm not sure diverting resources to a Core World makes sense when we're so close to catching him," Lula said, sounding, Ram thought, very much like a full-grown Jedi Master.

"Why doesn't Minister Fenwhatsherface look into it?" Zeen asked.

"Fendirfal," Lula corrected with a smile. "But, yeah! Or pass it to the Corellian Jedi?"

"My sense," Kantam said delicately, "reading between the lines and based on my grasp of Core World politics right now—which is incomplete, I admit—is that the Corellian Republic administrators feel like this situation is dubious at best. They described the source as—let me see . . ." They pulled up a memo on their datapad. "'A chaotic and probably criminal element, although technically an honest business-woman. Adolescent and untrustworthy in the extreme.'"

"Also," Master Torban added, "with the Jedi from that temple neck-deep in the union dispute on Gus Talon, they probably don't have the resources to investigate this."

Ram was familiar with how certain worlds felt like they were more important than other ones, based on obscure things like how close they were to the center of the galaxy, what crops they grew, how many suns they had—you name it—and how that sense of entitlement led to actual real-world consequences, like which resources went where. Valo was a planet many called a backwater; most of the Outer Rim planets were. And while Chancellor Soh had been doing her best to correct those imbalances—the Republic Fair itself had been one attempt, however doomed—the longstanding feelings of superiority and inferiority remained in many.

Their intentions were probably good; they had other problems to deal with, from the sound of it, and the whole galaxy had united to help Valo and other planets repair the damage from the attacks.

But the truth was, the Nihil were everyone's problem, even if they'd been scattered, and even more so if they were strong enough to show up in the heart of the Republic.

Ram tried not to let all that grumbling enter his voice when he stood up and said, "I think we should go check it out."

Everyone turned to look at him, and for a moment, Ram wondered if he'd forgotten to put on his robes or something. Then he realized it was because he rarely said much in public meetings, much less made big declarations about what should be done.

"I agree," Master Kantam said. "It seems unlikely there are Nihil there at all, but even if they have established a presence on Corellia, I doubt it'll be large. I'll join Padawan Ram on a short exploratory mission. Lula." They locked eyes with their Padawan, Lula Talisola, who looked as calm and determined as ever. "Can you join Master Torban to take leadership of the task force to find Krix while I'm away?"

That was a big deal! Two other older Jedi—Obratuk Glii and Tabakan Pak—were standing nearby. Kantam had exchanged meaningful looks with them both before saying it, which meant they'd all talked it over already.

"Of course." Lula didn't even hesitate, Ram marveled. Everyone knew she would be knighted at any given moment, though, and this was probably part of her final trial before that happened.

"I'll go, too," Zeen said, standing and putting a firm hand on Ram's shoulder. "To Corellia. It'll just be a short trip, right? And I should probably take a break from hunting Krix anyway."

A look passed between Lula and Zeen that Ram wasn't sure he understood—something like sadness and recognition. Then Lula nodded.

"Very well," Kantam said. "I'll see if Master Cohmac and Reath will join us, as well. Where are they, by the way?"

"In the training room as always, probably," Master

Torban said with some concern. Cohmac and Reath seemed to be training constantly when they weren't on missions these days. They barely showed up to briefings at all anymore.

The Padawans were already rising, heading back to their chambers and practice halls.

"I'll find them," Ram said.

Kantam nodded. "Good. And then: to Corellia!"

FIVE

STARLIGHT BEACON

"Again."

Reath, already sweaty and panting, lunged again.

Master Cohmac blocked Reath's first strike, dodged his second, and then they fell into a fast flurry of parries and jabs, the silence easy between them, gentle.

Reath would ask Master Cohmac for advice. This time he really would. The lost feeling had been rising to a fever pitch in Reath for the past few weeks, the sense that he was somehow staring directly at the road he was supposed to take but still not seeing it. Masters were who you were supposed to go to with those problems—that was the whole point! But somehow, he hadn't been able to bring himself to ask Cohmac for guidance.

Cohmac's quick intake of breath was the only alert Reath had that he was about to get hit. Thoughts, thoughts, getting in the way once again. He lunged out of the way as his master's wooden saber whooshed where his head had just been, then he spun into a counterattack, whacking Cohmac's arm just below the shoulder.

"Hrgh!" Cohmac grunted, clutching the welt quickly forming on his light brown skin.

"I . . . sorry?" Reath said, clenching his teeth. "I shouldn't have hit so hard."

Cohmac waved him off. "No, it's not you. That's not it. You didn't overdo it. That's why we're using practice blades. It's . . . it's me, that's all."

For a moment, they both stood there, breathing, neither looking the other in the eye. Reath was acutely aware of his master's swirling tangle of emotions, the strange heaviness Cohmac had seemed to carry since . . . well, since they'd met, really, but whatever it was, it seemed to be getting larger, heavier, with each passing day.

And maybe that was why Reath hadn't figured out how to bring up his own troublesome thoughts. It seemed like Cohmac had enough to worry about.

"You're getting better," Cohmac said, his grimace finally creasing up into a slight smile, just visible behind the curtain of black hair that hung over his face.

"Am I?" Reath had never cared for fighting, but he was good at it, for the most part, and he'd come to relish the practice sessions that Cohmac kept insisting on, more and more frequently these days. He had learned to take comfort in the press of that sweat-soaked mat against his skin when he'd tumble forward to avoid a strike, the flash of his body as he whirled past the wall-length mirror, the gentle, obnoxious trill of that Hydraxian pipe music they always had on at a low murmur to keep the mood calm.

It was absolutely not him, and maybe after all he'd been through, finding solace in something totally different was exactly what he needed.

Cohmac, on the other hand, did not look happy. "Again," he said, winding his head to each side until horrific popping noises sounded.

"Master . . ." Reath said. Maybe his tone, his solemn face, his posture would somehow say it all for him, and he wouldn't have to explain any further what the problem was.

"Again, I said." No such luck. Cohmac's voice was a raspy growl. It didn't imply an actual threat, Reath knew by now, but the sheer ferocity and determination the older Jedi had to . . . what? What was he trying to get out of all this exertion and what had honestly become an exercise in futility? Reath was simply getting better and better, and Cohmac was not. So all this amounted to was a never-ending, increasingly awkward cycle of Cohmac getting his ass kicked.

On the other hand, Reath was enjoying it, probably more

than he should have been. "All right, Master Cohmac," he said, swinging forward, practice stick raised.

"Ah, hey hey hi!" The gymnasium door slid open, stopping Reath in his tracks, and Ram Jomaram stepped in, waving uncomfortably. The poor kid had been off Valo for a few months and still didn't seem to know how to just exist comfortably around other people—he was happiest alone in his room, tinkering with random machines and chatting with those little Bonbrak creatures he'd brought along with him to Starlight. That, of course, made Reath love him like a brother. Reath wasn't alone in that, though. It seemed like pretty much everyone on Starlight wanted to adopt and protect Ram as their little sibling. Meanwhile, Ram just wanted to fix things and break them again.

"Padawan Ram," Cohmac said, looking momentarily revitalized and even flashing that rare full-toothed smile. "What did you fix today?"

"The reactor core for a microbionic conduit selector!" Ram said, beaming proudly. Then he reconsidered. "Well, it's not actually fixed yet. But we're working on it!"

"That sounds, ah, dangerous, possibly?" Reath suggested.

Ram shrugged and let out a slight chuckle. "Not as long as we keep it away from lithium bicarbonate and fluxor solution!"

"You are a very rare and special individual," Cohmac said without a hint of condescension.

Ram clearly recognized it for the genuine compliment it was and nodded his appreciation.

"What can we do for you today?" Cohmac asked.

"Corellia," Ram said.

Cohmac and Reath both blinked at him.

"We're going! Well, we hope you'll join us! Master Kantam and me, that is. Er, I. Master Kantam and I. Hope you'll join us! Oh, and Zeen!"

"Corellia?" Reath gaped. He had *just* decided that the only hope for any answer to finding his path lay in remaining on Starlight, at least for a little while. He had finally found a place to call home, finally stopped dreaming of life in the center of the Republic.

The Force laughed harder, though.

Now he was being sent right back into the Core.

Cohmac tilted his head. "What in the stars for?"

"It's a transmission the Republic people sent . . . this person Crash and then someone who . . . saw, maybe saw the Nihil?"

Already, Reath could see the heaviness roll back over his master like a cloud.

"I'll talk to Kantam," Cohmac said, grabbing his satchel and heading out. "Thanks, Ram."

For a moment after the door slid closed, Ram and Reath let the gargly Hydraxian pipes warble through their achy dirge.

"Have you ever—" Ram started just as Reath said, "Do you want to spar?"

They both smiled, then Ram said, "Yes, I do, actually," and pulled out his lightsaber.

"Whoa, whoa, we could just use the practice sticks." Reath laughed, but then thought better of it. "Unless . . . you want to practice with live sabers?"

Ram lit his, the yellow blade illuminating the wild smile that creased his face. "More fun?" he said with a shrug.

"Absolutely," Reath said, lighting his own green one and standing at the ready. "What were you going to ask me?"

Their sabers met with a jangly surge of power. Reath was careful to move slow, telegraphing his every move so Ram would see it coming and block. "Oh," Ram said, easily swiping away Reath's sizzling blade and then shoving him clean across the room with the Force. "Never mind."

Reath sat up with a huge grin plastered across his face. "It's like that, huh?" He stood, cracking his neck the way his master had. "Game on!"

SIX

STARLIGHT BEACON

Zeen Mrala and Lula Talisola sat across from each other in meditation position, like they had so many times before.

Zeen wasn't sure when they'd stopped sitting side by side during these sessions and started sitting face to face. She just knew that it felt more intimate this way, more right.

As always, an infinite skyscape seemed to open up between them, like the whole wild galaxy came to life in their connected minds, from its giant spinning planets to the tiniest drops of dew on each trembling leaf.

"Do you feel me?" Lula asked, and Zeen knew she was smiling. They both were.

"Always," she said. It was true. Even those rare times when they were far away from each other—like during the Republic Fair, when all hell was breaking loose and thousands of people cried out in fear and pain—Lula's presence still felt like a beacon amid the chaos. It wasn't that Zeen knew exactly where her friend was, just that she could feel her, her warmth, and it had calmed her, guided her through the carnage until their physical bodies actually found each other.

But Zeen felt something else, too—it had been growing inside her for months, and she had no idea what to do with it, even what to name it.

Fear maybe. Or perhaps love.

Whatever it was, she was pretty sure it was about to explode. *She* was about to explode.

Lula had been put in charge of the task force. For a Padawan, that was an incredible honor. It meant she'd probably be knighted soon. She didn't look happy about it, though. Lula was the most ambitious person Zeen had ever met, but it didn't seem to come from ego—she wasn't trying to get ahead of everyone else; she just loved learning, loved challenging herself, loved the thrill of forward motion. Zeen knew Lula had been trying to slow down, let each step of the journey be what it had to be, but this kind of honor would've lit her up a few weeks ago.

In the briefing room, she just looked sad. And Zeen's own first thought had been a selfish one: Lula would be knighted, and then what? What room would there be for a random girl from nowhere in the life of a Jedi Knight? The Jedi weren't supposed to form attachments; they didn't marry and settle down. They had more important things to do.

Zeen hated the bitter tone in her own thoughts; she should've been happy for her best friend in that moment. And what did it mean that Lula didn't seem happy, either? Only that Zeen was trouble, pure trouble, in her favorite person's life. A distraction.

That was when Zeen had decided to go to Corellia with Ram and Master Sy. She would get away for a bit, and maybe things would make sense when she got back.

She had instantly regretted the decision, but it was too late.

"Leaving will be good," Lula said a few minutes later, when they'd both opened their eyes. This was what they did, almost every day: They sat. They let the universe reveal its shimmering secrets around them through meditation, and then they spoke, quietly, gently, being as true as they knew how to be, about whatever was going on that day.

"I'm not sure," Zeen admitted. "I'm . . ." Was it fear she still felt? Not exactly. Just a discomfort. Uncertainty. But then . . . maybe that wasn't hers. "Are you?"

"I . . ." Lula didn't usually come up at a loss for words, but now she trailed off. "I don't want our hunt for Krix to become who you are."

Zeen flinched a little. She knew her friend was voicing a very real danger. Still, it hurt.

"What will you be when we catch him?"

"I . . ."

"Where will you go?"

"I figured I'd stay here," Zeen said, because the truth was, *After Krix* didn't seem like a real thing, and it wouldn't until he was caught. She hadn't given it much thought because it was possible they wouldn't catch him for years, and it was possible they'd catch him the next day. What point was there in planning when so much was uncertain?

Lula smiled in that way she had that made her look like a little kid. "That would be amazing."

Zeen returned the smile, but the sadness and uncertainty remained, and she still didn't know if it belonged to her or to Lula. "I don't know what it will be like, when the chase is over," Zeen admitted. "I don't know who I'll be."

"We can find out together," Lula said. "The galaxy's changing as fast as we are. I've been"—her face darkened—"trying to figure out who I'll be, too."

"You got put in charge of a task force, Lula. That's practically unheard of for a Padawan. What's wrong?"

An alert dinged over the speaker system, then Ram's voice came through, breathy with nervousness and restrained giggles. "Um, Zeen Mrala we're about to leave for Corellia without yo—"

Reath cut him off. "No, we're not! Don't listen to him, Zeen. He's still practicing his jokes. But we are packing up the shuttle, so hurry up, please!"

Lula and Zeen rolled their eyes at each other, and then simultaneously got serious again.

Zeen didn't want to go anywhere where Lula's face wasn't going to be across from her, ready with a thoughtful answer or calm silence. But Zeen was also desperate to get as far away from all this confusion and turmoil as possible.

"I don't know," Lula said. "To answer your question. It's been on me the past few weeks. You've seen it. I still don't have an answer." She met Zeen's eyes with that determined gaze, the one that meant victory was imminent. "But I will figure it out, I promise."

Zeen smiled. She believed her. What else could she do?

Lula smiled too, and it looked real. "Now let's get you sent off to Corellia."

SEVEN

STARLIGHT BEACON

Corellia?

Was that where Reath's path lay?

He shook his head, trying to keep his feet moving steadily in the same direction, trying to keep his thoughts from running off without him.

He had no idea how he was supposed to find answers to any deep questions, like how to be a Jedi, when every five minutes he had to pack his bags and run off to this planet or that station, getting attacked, barely surviving, then doing it all again.

He was tired. That was the thing. He was tired, and every

day seemed to take him further and further from the answers he needed.

Especially the days like this.

But at least now he knew he needed to go ahead and ask Master Cohmac for guidance.

He rounded the corner of the hallway and entered the meditation center, where his master could always be found before a mission.

"You are sure of your path," Cohmac had said to Reath on that same day when Reath had asked him to be his master. And he *had* felt so sure then, and that sureness had been a blessing after so much chaos and confusion. But it turned out paths only revealed themselves one step at a time, and Reath was ready for another step.

"Ah, Master?" Reath said, walking into the small dark room his master favored. But then he stopped.

A holo image hovered in the air in front of Cohmac: Orla Jareni. She and Cohmac had been friends as Padawans, and their friendship had endured ever since. Orla Jareni had been with them on the Amaxine station to fight the Drengir, and then she had taken off to become a Wayseeker, letting the Force guide her path, even if it meant going beyond the Jedi Order's sense of duty.

Sometimes Reath wondered what it must feel like, the freedom and openness that would come with following the Force like that. The idea terrified him. The Order could feel restrictive sometimes, like a too-tight uniform shirt, but there was a certain safety to those regulations, a sense of ease in allowing yourself to move within the same parameters Jedi had followed for thousands of years.

"Hello, Reath," Orla said. "It's okay, you may come in."

"I didn't mean to interrupt," Reath said.

"It's fine," Cohmac insisted, so Reath walked farther into the dimly lit room.

"I . . ." he started, then noticed the tear tracks on his master's face, the wet sheen of his eyes. "What's wrong?"

Cohmac shook his head. "Doesn't matter."

"Don't lie to the boy," Orla said sharply.

Cohmac shot her a look, then shook his head. "I am struggling, my Padawan. I do not know . . ." He glanced back at Orla, and she nodded at him to go on. "A great sadness has been welling up in me. It is bigger than any I have known. It seems to cover the whole galaxy. I cannot see clearly through it. I do not know if it is within me or something beyond, something that's coming. Orla has been helping me meditate with it, try to suss out a meaning, but . . ." His voice trailed off.

"But I feel it, too," Orla said solemnly. "And that makes it difficult to help."

Suddenly, everything Reath wanted to talk about seemed trivial, juvenile. He didn't know his path, big deal. Two of the most powerful Jedi he knew, one of them his own master, were besieged by their own emotions. It was beyond him, but he refused to be helpless. "What can I do?"

Orla smiled. "You cannot take on other people's problems, young Padawan. That is all."

"But—"

"No," Cohmac said sternly. "This is not something you can help with, Reath. I'm sorry. I know you want to." He closed his eyes. "I will sit with these feelings and work through them as I always have."

A moment passed, and with it, some silent understanding between Cohmac and Orla. Then Cohmac nodded and stood.

"Take care of yourself, old friend," the Wayseeker Jedi said.

"May the Force be with you, Orla."

Cohmac clicked off the holocaster and led Reath out of the room.

EIGHT

STARLIGHT BEACON

Kantam Sy could tell when something was troubling their Padawan, and they also knew her well enough to know she would talk about it when she was good and ready, and not a moment sooner. And it seemed like that moment was finally coming.

"Master?" Lula asked quietly as they stood in the hangar bay, checking the last few tech configurations on the *Talmadge*. Over by the ramp, Reath, Zeen, and Ram chatted excitedly about what might await them on Corellia.

"You ready to talk?" Kantam asked their Padawan.

Lula nodded, wearing that stern and determined expression Kantam had come to know so well over the years.

Kantam smiled. "That's the face you used to make when you didn't want to go to sleep. What's wrong?"

She finally relented with a sigh that turned into a laugh, then rubbed her face. "I don't know, Master. I don't feel fear. I don't feel hesitancy. I don't feel confusion even."

"That's good. So what's wrong?"

"I . . ." She looked away. "It meant so much to me, that you put me in charge of the mission along with Master Buck."

"But?"

She scrunched up her face. "I feel like the old me would've been even more excited? And I know that's not a bad thing, but . . ."

Kantam waited. Whatever the heart of the matter was, Lula was circling it like a drain. There was no need to push.

"You said something to me once." Her eyes met Kantam's, newly determined. "That I had taught you a lesson you were still trying to learn."

An urgent alert blared out of the comm system overhead. "All task force members to the briefing room!" someone called. "Farzala and Qort have found Krix's hideout! We're preparing for an assault."

Lula's focus was gone. Kantam watched their Padawan lock eyes with Zeen.

"I . . ." Zeen said, glancing at Kantam, then the doorway.

"It's okay," Kantam said. "Go along with them. But do not let your anger consume you. Remember what we taught you."

"I'll remember," Zeen promised.

Lula turned back to Kantam. "I'll talk to you about it when we all get back. I promise."

Kantam raised their eyebrows. "I'm proud of you, Lula Talisola. I always have been."

She smiled sadly, an ancient smile; it seemed to hold whole centuries. "I know. Thank you. For everything."

She hugged them hard. "I'll keep you up to date! I promise! And with Master Buckets and the others, I know we'll be safe!"

"And I swear I'll come find you all as soon as we follow up on this lead!" Zeen promised, squeezing Ram so tightly he looked like he might choke.

"It's okay," Ram assured her. "I understand! And anyway, we're going to Corellia. We'll be fine! You're the one going into almost certain battle against a vicious foe. Anyway"—he nudged Reath—"I have this master dueler to keep me safe, right?"

"Hey! I only lost to you twice and you keep changing the rules! Don't act like—"

"Wait!" Ram cut him off with a raised hand and a yelp. "I did it! I DID IT!"

"What's happening?" Cohmac asked, somewhere between amused and concerned.

"Ram finally made a joke." Kantam chuckled. "Nice work, Ram!"

"Did I miss a meeting?" Reath asked.

"Most of 'em!" Ram zinged. "OH! I am on *fire*! I *cannot* be stopped! Wizard!"

Reath shook his head. "Maybe I'll come along with you and Lula instead, Zeen."

"Let's do it again!" Ram insisted.

Zeen put her hand on Ram's shoulder and looked him in the eye. "I'm proud of you, kiddo. You're taking after the true master of disaster on this space station: me. Stay at it!" She headed off. "I expect great things from you!"

And then she was gone, side by side with Lula as always, off down the corridors and into whatever danger lay in wait.

"They're the most impossible puzzle, aren't they?" Cohmac chuckled when Kantam turned around.

"Padawans?"

Cohmac nodded, and the two Jedi Masters fell into stride together.

"They're the best teachers we'll ever have," Kantam said. "Besides Master Yoda, of course."

"Of course," Cohmac said. "Still no word, huh?"

Kantam shook their head. "I . . . I don't feel him, but . . . that doesn't mean . . . anything, really. I do think if he'd become one with the Force, we all would've felt it."

Master Yoda had simply vanished a few months back on the junk moon Quantxi. He'd left a message saying not to follow or look for him, and that had been that. What could they do? Everyone thought he would've come back by now, and his ongoing absence sent a low rumble of concern through Kantam.

They stood on either end of a large, flat cargo container and lifted it together, then headed onto the ship.

"I agree," Cohmac said. "But that doesn't make me any less worried about him being gone this long."

"I just know," Kantam said, "everything happening right now would be much easier to make sense of if Master Yoda were here."

"Any more cargo?" Cohmac called as Reath and Ram picked up their travel packs and headed up the ramp.

"No, we got the rest of them, but thanks for your help," Ram said, his face twitching on one side.

"What's wrong with your eye?" Cohmac asked.

Reath kept walking. "He's trying to wink because he thinks he just made a joke. Let's get this over with, please. This is clearly going to be a long journey!"

"Ah? Ah?" Ram tried, still squinching half his face.

"Who will stop this child?" Cohmac wondered out loud. "The child must be stopped."

Then Kantam slid into the pilot's seat beside Cohmac. They both put on their headsets as the small shuttle, the *Talmadge*, rumbled, lifted into the air, and blasted out into the gaping maw of space.

NINE

CORONET CITY

"Of *course* that was the plan!" Crash insisted, slapping her desk for added drama and upsetting the caf mug just enough to splatter some knickknacks. "What kind of shoddy operation do you think I run?"

"One that almost got me murdered." Svi'no Atchapat was unimpressed, but that was Svi'no's resting state. It was part of her charm, Crash figured, and made it all the more hilarious how vulnerable and desperate she managed to look onstage. An actress through and through.

Probably why they got along so well.

Except when they didn't.

"I would *never*"—Crash thunked her desk again—"ever"—and again—"put you in danger! You are my *friend*!"

"Um, hello?" A polite little voice came from the doorway, followed by the polite little head of Minister Chips Fendirfal. "Did someone say someone's in danger?"

"No!" Crash snapped. She softened. "Sorry—come in, please, Minister. My"—she gestured toward where Svi'no had just been standing, but the girl was gone—"office is yours, of course."

"Too kind, too kind," the minister tittered, taking a few steps closer and glancing around at the shadows as if one of them might be poised to take a shot at her. Which, to be fair, was probably a safe guess. "Reeeeeegarding your report, of course, with the holomessage from your Grindalid friend." The woman suddenly smiled way too brightly, then seemed to realize it wasn't the time for all that wattage and turned it down a few notches. Crash just stared at her.

"Unfortunately, the Republic offices are currently quite, ah, deluged, with various problems in the system, especially the union dispute on—"

"Gus Talon, I know."

"Which has also, regrettably, just about emptied out the Jedi temple, as the dispute seems to involve some complicated matter that only Jedi understand, of course. Over my head, you see."

"I see."

"Anyhoo, I did pass it along to some experts on the

matter of the supposed Nihil threat, and the good news is, they have elected to send a small contingent of Jedi from Starlight Beacon to look into the matter."

"Starlight? So they'll be here in a few weeks?"

"Ah, no, no, they should be arriving imminently, I believe!"

Crash sighed. "It was a joke. Because Starlight is so far away?"

"Ah, yes, yes, of course!"

Crash's mind was already spinning into action though. She still didn't have any leads on Prybolt and Ovarto's disappearances, just a hundred hunches to follow up on. She was about to be busy chasing down each one, or deploying other people to do so. How would a group of Starlight Jedi change the equation on the ground? Would they try to muscle in on everything and get in the way? Could they be useful, at least as a distraction? Everyone loved the Jedi, and they were probably excellent at parlor tricks—or they would be if they'd put those Force powers to actual use instead of just levitating and looking serene.

Then again, they were also great warriors. They'd been pivotal in fighting off the Nihil attack on Valo and elsewhere, of course. . . . There was much to consider.

"Ah, Miss Crash?" the minister said.

Crash realized she had steepled her fingers in front of her face and arched her eyebrows like a villainous mastermind, and she was probably terrifying Fendirfal. She popped up and ushered the woman to the door. "Erm . . . yes! Thank you, Minister, for passing the message along." There was a lot to do if she was going to take full advantage of this new quirk in the equation. "I'll be on the lookout for these Jedi flung from afar, heheh."

"Very well, Miss Crash, very well, haha." The minister dithered as Crash shoved her out of the office. "I do hope they find your employees."

"Me too," Crash said quietly after the door slid shut.

"Alys!"

Crash yelped with surprise, then softened. "Only my mom calls me that, Svi'no."

The sparkling starlet fluttered out from the shadows, her expression somewhere between aggrieved and pissed. "You didn't tell me Prybolt had gone missing!"

"I . . ." Crash slinked back to her desk, shoulders slumped. "I didn't, no."

"If I'd known I would've—"

"I didn't want to use something bad happening to get a favor out of you, okay?"

For a moment, they just looked at each other.

"Weren't we arguing or something?" Crash pointed out, because the moment seemed suddenly serious in a way she couldn't wrap her head around, so it needed to end, whatever it was.

"You would *never*"—Svi'no thunked the desk, affecting a

pretty solid Crash imitation—"ever"—and again—"put me in danger! I am your *friend*!"

Crash slammed the desk, too, and got up in Svi'no's face. "That's right!"

"And? You do realize you don't have total control over every, or even *any* situation, don't you, Crash?"

Crash scowled. "That's a matter of opinion, and I disagree."

Svi'no flashed a cruel smile. "Then why did I almost die today?"

Footsteps clomped up the stairs toward the office. Big heavy ones. Crash closed her eyes. Everything had finally gone right, more or less—she had wrangled it back to right against all efforts of the galaxy, in fact. And now here came the galaxy getting its revenge.

Svi'no retreated into the shadows again as the door slid open and Tamo the Savrip ducked in, those huge arms threatening to shatter everything in sight. He looked crestfallen, like he was terribly sorry about having failed at the one job he'd been given, which, of course, he had, which was exactly the point, but he was speaking Savripian or whatever that gargled roaring cacophony was called, so who could say, really?

"The mighty Tamo apologizes for not murdering the beautiful starlet like you asked him to," 10-K8 announced helpfully, popping up from behind a file cabinet.

Crash dragged a hand down her own face. "Kayt! Have you *no* ability to read the room?"

Svi'no swept forward out of the shadows, a grand entrance as always. "*Murder,* you say?"

"Hrraaaagh!" Tamo roared, and then immediately laid waste to about half of Crash's cluttered office with a single sweep of his arm.

Svi'no slipped easily out of the way. "Why, Crash, I do believe this beast thinks he's supposed to *murder* me!"

"Tamo! Down!" Crash yelled. Then she lunged to the ground as the huge creature's next swipe sent shards of a statue and several caf mugs exploding around her. "Stop!"

"It's fine," Svi'no said, once again slipping away from Tamo's grasp with a smile. "I got this." She pulled an elegant pistol out of her robes and, with a tiny *fwip,* sent one dart flying smack into the Savrip's neck.

Tamo stood up very straight, groaned, and then mumbled something that Crash didn't need translated and slammed to the ground with a wheeze.

"The mighty Tamo says, 'Not again, you—'"

"We get it!" Crash snapped, jumping to her feet. Then she glared at Svi'no, who made a big show of blowing nonexistent smoke from the tip of her dart gun.

"He's sort of cute when he sleeps like that," Svi'no said.

Tamo let out a horrific snore.

"Now do you honestly think that this guy would've been able to *pretend* to want to murder you?" Crash demanded.

"Well, that's hardly—"

"And anyway," Crash went on, trying desperately to hold some sense of the high ground, "you!"

Svi'no blinked with mock innocence. "Me what?"

"All that mess about me almost getting you killed and you could've handled him all by yourself!"

"But I didn't, did I?"

"You didn't," Crash said, sitting back down, deflated. "Why didn't you?"

"Because you needed my help, silly! What's the point of staging an elaborate drama to show what great bodyguards you all are if the person doesn't even need protecting?" The galactic superstar got right up in Crash's face, bringing a gentle and obviously way-too-expensive fruity perfume cloud with her. "And I actually trust you, even though you're intent on lying to everyone you care about."

Crash had long since given up any thought of anything happening between the two of them. It was a question of leagues: Svi'no was in one all her own. And anyway, they'd almost instantly become way better friends than Crash would've imagined possible, so what was the point in ruining that?

Still—when she got up close like that, Crash was never sure what to do with her body. "I . . ."

"But I'll tell you this," Svi'no said, whirling majestically away and heading for the door. "We'd all trust you a whole lot more if you would simply trust us back."

"But—"

She stopped at the doorway, glancing back with melodramatic flare. "Just *imagine* the power you would possess with actual friends instead of just people you manipulate into doing your bidding even though they love you and would do anything for you anyway!"

And then she was gone.

For a few moments, Crash just sat there, listening to the not-so-gentle Savrip snores as the twinkling lights of Coronet City and final rays of the setting sun illuminated the otherwise dim office. The gentle early evening glow sparkled over the bay, mingled with the brilliant golden haze of the buildings and streetlamps. It always brought Crash a sense of peace, the way the city itself seemed to defeat the darkness of night. Even with all its secrets and shadows, Coronet was made of light, and Crash loved it with all her heart.

"Is that true, Kayt? What she said?" Crash stood, stepped over Tamo's huge slumbering form, and stood in front of the massive window overlooking Sionaro Shallows and the brightly lit flyways stretching across it. It seemed like the whole city was ablaze at night, and this fleeting moment right between day and night was always Crash's favorite.

"Ah, in some ways, sure," 10-K8 said quietly. "But you are also in mourning, I'll remind you."

"He's not—"

"He's not dead—that we know—but he's also not here,"

the droid said sharply. "And we both know it's very unlikely he'll be—"

The window blinds suddenly slid shut with a whir. "Hey!" Crash yelled, then she gulped. A towering figure stood silhouetted in the doorway. Crash knew those robes and that hunched-over position.

"Ezvangolt? What's going on?"

He didn't answer, just stood there staring. Of Prybolt's however many hundreds of Grindalid siblings, Ezvangolt was the only one who had stayed close with him after he left the tunnels to become one of Crash's best bodyguards. He would even come by for dinner sometimes, and had turned out to be pretty good company once he relaxed and got some food in him.

But this was weird.

"You can't just come in here, closing my windows and not answering my questions, budzo!"

The Grindalid immediately proved her wrong by hitting the control panel again. The far window slid shut.

"I don't appreciate tha—" More boots clomped up the steps, shutting Crash up. Then more Grindalids appeared in her doorway. "This is not gonna be good," she muttered, "whatever this is."

"The Exalted Mother Fastidima," Ezvangolt announced as several other Grindalids walked in carrying a pallet with an even taller robed figure on top. She wore a dark cloak with various chained jewels dangling off it that jingled softly as she slinked off the pallet and then reared up to her full, terrifying height over Crash.

"My dear child," Mother Fastidima moaned regally. She pulled the front of her cowl away, revealing that shiny white flesh, some of those squirmy little arms, and the dripping folds of skin around her enormous glistening mouth. "I do so hate to be out and about in that thing. I'm sure you understand."

"Of course," Crash said, doing everything in her power not to flinch or act intimidated. "It's good to see you again."

"Please don't lie to me like I'm one of your little hoodlums," Mother Fastidima said. "Like . . . my son."

"Mother Fastidima, I promise we're searching everywhe—"

The Grindalid silenced Crash with a wave of her bejeweled claw. "I told him. I told him this would happen, you know."

"I didn't know, but I figured you probably had."

"Hm, he didn't talk about me much, did he?"

"All the time, actually," Crash said. Usually it was to complain, but that wasn't the point.

"Well, the matter remains what it is. If young Prybolt was killed, we are honor bound to devour his killer, of course."

"Of course."

"And if his killer isn't found, well, *someone* has to pay." She aimed her tiny squinting eyes pointedly at Crash. "Tradition says the one who is responsible for the murdered

Grindalid shall pay the price when the murderer is unknown or unavailable, hm? Did you know that, *Crash*?"

"Maybe he wasn't murdered?"

Mother Fastidima made a horrific raspy choking sound that Crash hoped was her actually choking. No dice. It was laughter. "Wouldn't that be something!" the towering worm chortled.

"It's possible," Crash said, pressing the point. "There was no—"

"*Of course there wasn't a body*," Mother Fastidima snapped. "We're Grindalids, you sunsoaker. We disintegrate. My poor, precious baby is probably dust. Because of *you*, Ongwa."

"I didn't—"

Mother Fastidima craned her long body all the way down so her snarling slimy face was right in Crash's. She didn't smell nearly as good as Svi'no. "Did Prybolt ever tell you how many worms the Garavult Clan counts among its family?"

"Nine hundred and seventy-six," Crash said smoothly.

"Mmm, that's a very out-of-date number, unfortunately, short by almost half. He must've told you quite a while ago."

"Just last month, actua—"

"*Exactly* my point," Mother Fastidima rasped. "We grow exponentially every day, my child. We are a terrible enemy to have at your back, because a good portion of the tunnel system of greater Coronet City belongs to us. Which means we can appear anywhere we want. You see?"

Crash nodded once, refusing to flinch or even wrinkle her nose against the rising stench of bile and sewer water.

Mother Fastidima reared back, those tiny probing eyes still locked with Crash's. She pulled her cowl back over her face and crawled smoothly back onto the pallet. There, she paused. "You have until three sunsets from now, my dear. After that, you belong to us."

"You're not even gonna clean up all this goo you dripped on my floor?" Crash demanded, but the worms had made their exit.

She slumped back into her chair and let out a long sigh. Now there was a sleeping Savrip *and* a puddle of sewer-worm muck on her floor.

"What are we going to do?" 10-K8 asked, reappearing glumly from the shadows.

"Find Prybolt," Crash said. "Or find who killed him."

TEN

THE *TALMADGE*

"Hey, Reath?"

"Hm?"

"Have you ever tried this before?"

"Uh-uh."

"So how do we know if it's working?"

"I think we'll just know, Ram."

"I guess. But—"

"You know how we're never gonna know if it's working?"

"How?"

"By not being able to do it because you keep talking instead of focusing."

"Oh, wow."

"Uh-huh."

"Wow, wow, wow. It's like that, huh?"

"Indeed."

Ram Jomaram and Reath Silas sat cross-legged a meter apart on the deck of the cargo hold. The idea was to try to link their minds via the Force, the way Master Avar Kriss had done during the Great Disaster—except she'd done it with hundreds of Jedi, and they were just trying to do it with two. Kantam and Buckets of Blood had done something similar recently, too—Ram and some of the others had walked in on them one day, both seated, facing each other, in deep meditation, preparing, they said, for the task ahead.

Ram and Reath had made it about ten minutes sitting that way in silence before Ram felt the need to pipe up. It wasn't that he didn't think it would work; it was that he had no idea *how* it was supposed to work, and without the *how*—well, how exactly was anyone supposed to do anything without the *how*?

"I think we should try it while levitating," Ram suggested.

"I'm awful at levitating," Reath said.

"Me too."

"Well, there goes that idea."

"What if I float you?"

"Huh?" Reath popped one eye open, which Ram was relieved by, because he'd had both his open for a good five minutes already.

"I'm saying," Ram explained, trying not to be too

frustrating, "we're both no good at floating ourselves, but I know how to float things really well—I do it all the time when I'm taking things apart and putting them back together. And I'm sure you're good at it—you're good at basically everything!"

"I am?" Reath looked genuinely stunned by that, like it was some big revelation.

"Obviously?" Ram scoffed. "You're both bookish and badass! How many people is that true of?"

"I never thought of it that way," Reath admitted.

"Besides Lula, of course, but she's the exception to just about everything."

"True," Reath allowed. Then: "Okay, float me."

"Really?" Ram gaped. "I didn't expect you to say yes!"

"Go ahead." The older Padawan closed his eyes and straightened his back, sliding back into meditation just like that. Ram resisted the urge to say, *See! Even good at meditating!* Instead he focused on lifting Reath.

Like every task, using the Force was a matter of steps. Each step had its place and led to the next one. If you could focus on the one you were doing—and not the fifteen others up ahead or whether you'd done the earlier ones right—amazing things tended to happen. That's what Ram had learned, over and over. The most important thing was the thing right in front of your face.

In a moment, that thing would be Reath, but he had to back up a step. There was something even more important, even more in front of Ram's face, that he had to concentrate on first: the Force.

Ram allowed that sense of flow to move through him like a slow tide. It almost tingled; it almost had a sound. But more than anything, it was a certainty. A sense of something huge being present within Ram, as part of Ram. Then all he had to do was follow it on its course through the galaxy and put his mind toward imagining where it would go, what it would do, aligning what he wanted to happen with the path of the Force. And then watch it happen.

It was less like pushing a button on a machine and more like having a best friend who was incredibly powerful. Kind of like Reath, in fact, which brought Ram's attention exactly where it needed to be, on the Force as it moved around Reath and then lifted him into the air, at first ever so slightly, as if testing how much effort it would take, then suddenly with ease.

Reath, eyes still closed, let a big grin stretch across his face. "Niiiice," he whispered.

Ram wiggled his eyebrows at himself. "Okay, your turn."

A huge gust of wind seemed to whoosh across Ram and then spin him upside down and whip him sideways into a pile of sleeping mats and cushions, knocking the breath out of him. "D'oof!"

Reath collapsed with laughter, opening his eyes just in time to see a pillow swinging directly at his face.

ELEVEN

THE *TALMADGE*

"Sounds like you lost your sparring partner," Kantam said as another crash came from the cargo hold, followed by more giggles and yells.

Cohmac shrugged. "Bah, he was getting too good for me anyway. Probably better that he gets a change of pace."

Space slid past, the whole churn of the galaxy reduced to a blur of smooth-lined stars. Kantam loved hyperspace, the way it felt like entering another reality, outside of the regular one. Everything seemed slightly different once a ship launched into that wild slipstream, and it was always a ferocious and beautiful reminder of how truly in motion every moment of space and time was. The normal world seemed so still after traveling through the perception-defying corridors of hyperspace, but Kantam tried to hold on to the lesson of constant motion, the fluidity of reality, every time they had the opportunity.

"You ever . . . ?" Cohmac said, but then he just looked out the viewport instead of finishing.

"You remind me of Lula," Kantam said warmly. "She finally found something she can't talk to me about, and what does she do? Come tell me exactly that." They threw their hands up. "What am I supposed to do with that?"

"Appreciate her openness and keep it moving," Cohmac said.

"That's my plan, yes."

Cohmac spat it out. "You ever think about doing a walk-about? Wayseeking?"

"Like your friend Orla, you mean?"

"Something like that," Cohmac said, his voice a low rumble.

"I did, actually." Kantam didn't talk about it often, but the memory was always there, a strange sparkling moment amid many others. "When I was a Padawan."

Cohmac sat up, stunned. "Master Yoda *let* you do that?"

"Heh. I think he knew if he didn't, it would've been the end of things between me and the Order."

"But . . . why?"

"Why does anyone do anything ludicrous and obviously dangerous?" Kantam said with a hoarse laugh. "Love."

"Go on," Cohmac said, getting comfortable.

THEN

He was eighteen and lithe, an acrobat in a circus passing through Endovar, and Kantam had never seen anyone like him. The boy seemed to hover between each swinging hoop, like time itself slowed around him. Then he'd grasp the next one and spin at impossible speeds around it, release, and launch himself so far into the air he'd seem to become a speck. Up there, yet another hoop awaited him, and he'd tangle around that one and continue his routine like some kind of muscly tights-wearing angel hopping easily from cloud to cloud.

The boy had to be Force-sensitive, Kantam thought at first, but no. Watching more carefully on the second night, they could tell it was all within the realm of a non-Force-user's abilities—just very, very difficult. And it wasn't just the exertion and skill at play; it was the grace of it all.

"Aytar," the boy said, walking through the stands and coming face to face with Kantam after Kantam had sat in the front row of the sweaty circus tent for the fourth performance in a row.

"Padawan Kantam Sy," Kantam said, and Aytar laughed, but not in an unfriendly way. "What?" Kantam asked, smiling without fully knowing why.

"No, it's just I've heard about you lot—the Jedi, right? And I *thought* you might be one, but I wasn't sure."

"The robes," Kantam said, still smiling much more than they wanted to be.

Aytar made a growling sound that Kantam wasn't sure what to make of, then said, "Can I be a Jedi?"

"You can be anything you want," Kantam said, too quickly to stop themself, realizing only afterward that what they were doing was, in fact, flirting. Flirting back, technically. But still.

"We both know that's not true." Suddenly they were very close together, and the flickering torches around them, or perhaps the hot Endovar night winds—*something*—was making Kantam sweat more than they usually did. "But I like how it sounds anyway."

"Well, everything is possible," Kantam said.

"You're dangerous, Padawan Sy," Aytar countered, suddenly serious. The moment had broken, but in doing so it became something else, something somehow much more intense.

Kantam adjusted their face accordingly, that huge grin finally gone. "I don't think I'm the dangerous one, actually."

That night, they walked. The wispy salios bushes that Endovar was so famous for seemed to lean extra low, grazing the tops of their heads as they strolled along winding dirt paths through forests and fields and finally out to the crashing waves of Santiv Ru Bay.

"What time is it?" Kantam asked, once one conversation that had been a random offshoot of about three others finally wound down.

"Who cares?" Aytar suggested. Kantam agreed, and they sat beside each other in the sand, just out of reach of the spraying foam.

An old Mon Calamari man hobbled past, nodded at them, and then wandered off. Somewhere nearby, the sounds of another wild carnival, drums and shouts, simmered through the night. Beyond that, the Jedi temple, with its dim hallways and reverent silence, awaited Kantam's return.

For the first time in their life, Kantam didn't want to go back. That silence didn't seem like the sweet solace it usually did. It seemed menacing, unforgiving. They sighed at the thought, how suddenly everything could change.

"What's wrong?" Aytar asked, and meant it.

Kantam shook their head. "Master Yoda knew this would happen."

"Who?"

"That's why he held off my knighting. Now I understand."

"What are you talking about?"

Kantam finally met Aytar's eyes. "I'm ahead of everyone else in my class. I'm higher ranked in combat and meditation and basically everything else than most of my elders. Even

Master Yoda has said I'm the most disciplined Padawan he's ever trained and one of the most connected to the Force."

"And yet?"

"And yet nothing. I'm fine with it. I'm not in a hurry to be knighted. It'll happen when it happens. But everyone around me keeps wondering when it's going to happen, why it hasn't happened yet, I'm so skilled, blah blah blah. And I know it's not about skill. It's deeper than that. And Yoda knows that, but still . . . there was something, I think, we were both waiting for to happen."

"And?"

"And I think it just did."

TWELVE

CORONET CITY

Crash stood under an awning as rain covered the empty streets of the Syllain District. She had the whole block memorized now. That fishmonger with its coppergrins and garsmelts hanging in the window, fresh ones every day. The two vacant storefronts, their entrances covered with competing political posters for various candidates Crash had helped protect. The way the cobblestones felt beneath her boots. The crumbling part of the curb, not far from where it sloped downward slightly toward the sewer grate.

The scurry of screerats had its own particular rhythm in each neighborhood, Crash had realized a while back. The

Syllain rats emerged around dusk and worked well together, passing scraps of food along some kind of assembly line system until one of them vanished underground with it, presumably to divide it up among their young.

None of this knowledge had revealed even a tiny hint about where Prybolt or Tralmat or Ovarto or the pups might be, though, so what damn good was it?

Crash sighed, then clenched her fists with irritation.

She'd gone there every night since Prybolt and the others had disappeared. She'd walked maybe hundreds of circles around that ridiculous stump of a building where that strange late-night rendezvous had been scheduled. It appeared to be like all the other ones in the area—just a big bright-orange storage unit of some kind. There seemed to be only one door, although somehow that didn't seem right to her, and no windows. It was listed as public property, and the city tended to use those things to keep random equipment near whatever project was happening. Nothing too abnormal there.

She'd pored over the data for the run. Prybolt and Ovarto had served as their own advance team. Earlier that day they'd taken the three hounds and swept the neighborhood within a five-block radius of the meeting site for unusual activity, sniper nests, or random irritating reporters like Malfac Orfk, who were known to sometimes pop up during secret meetings, microphones out, cam droids rolling. And . . . nothing. They even checked the sewers and tunnels running underneath the area—a danger point Crash had to remind most of the team about over and over. But Prybolt was a Grindalid, and the tunnels were his home. Also, he prided himself on being a good listener. Whether Crash was relaying info or, on the rare occasion she needed to, pouring out her heart about something, he knew how to sit with her words and take it all in, how to respond in a way that let her know he'd heard and reflected. And then, when it was time, he'd ask questions. And they wouldn't be those corny questions people asked when they already knew the answers or just to sound like they were paying attention. Prybolt would ask real questions that always made Crash have to think harder about whatever was going on.

Damn, she missed him.

She stepped into the street, let the rain cover her.

Nomar Tralmat, whom Prybolt and Ovarto had been protecting. That was a whole other part of this mess she had no idea what to do with. Secret late-night meetings among otherwise boring bureaucrats were also nothing unusual in Coronet City.

Tralmat was one of the four City Fathers, and while, yes, his purview included the Coronet municipal police, he was basically a bureaucrat—pure data pusher. And not one of those ones who loved the limelight, either. Sure, crime had spiked some in the past few months, but it was random thuggery, nothing organized, and there hadn't been any threats reported against him.

He had recently hired a slew of new officers to deal with

both the rising crime and those high-profile star cruisers being built over in the yards, and that had been a popular move overall, certainly nothing controversial enough to have anyone bother disappearing the guy.

But Tralmat was gone without a trace, and so were Prybolt and Ovarto. And the pups.

It just didn't make sense. And if there was one thing Crash hated, it was when things didn't make sense.

"It just doesn't make sense," she said aloud. Then she took a sip of caf.

"It really doesn't," Svi'no said, appearing apparently out of the ether beside her.

Crash splortched her caf into the rainy street. "You have absolutely *got* to stop doing that!"

Svi'no shrugged, forever unimpressed to death. "Maybe you should pay better attention to your surroundings."

"That's the thing," Crash groaned. "I *do*! Who do you know who pays better attention to their surroundings than me? It's literally my job! And I am great at it!"

"You're yelling."

"I am *not* yelling!" Crash yelled. "I'm sad!"

"I know, sweetie." Svi'no pulled her into a sparkly, aromatic hug, and they stood there like that for a few moments, letting the rain fall while Crash sobbed quietly into her friend's expensive blouse.

"It's just . . . one thing"—Crash whimpered like a daytime holo melodrama goober—"and then another, and I . . . can't seem to . . . *hrggggg* . . ." She sighed, then slumped. "Thanks for being here."

"It's what friends are for and all that," Svi'no said, floating back a little to give Crash room to snorfle more nastiness.

"Also," Crash said, already feeling more on the ball now that she'd had a good sob, "how exactly do you keep creeping up on me? No one else can do that except—"

"Caf?" 10-K8 asked right beside Crash.

"Gah!" Crash leapt back, then put her face in her hand. "Yes, please." She took the mug from 10-K8 and glumly sipped at it. "Mm, caf."

"You're welcome," 10-K8 said chipperly.

Crash reeled on both of them. "Now! What are you two doing here?"

"Who said it was just two?" a gruff voice demanded.

"*Reeeargh ragh*!" came a Shyriiwook agreement.

"Fezzonk? Tangor?" Crash gasped as the towering Dowutin and the silverback Wookiee walked out of an alleyway side by side. Smeemarm and Barchibar came just behind them, along with a whole crew of sniffing, keening Corellian hounds on chain leashes.

"Aw, shucks, the whole team is here?" Crash gushed. "I didn't . . . Why?"

"To help you out, silly," Svi'no chided. "I asked them to come. You don't have to—you *shouldn't* be doing this alone."

"I know, but . . . I guess."

"You didn't want to bother us since he's your best friend,"

Fezzonk said, rolling his eyes and stroking the massive horns jutting out of his chin. "Well, guess what? He's our friend, too, and so is Ovarto."

"And Beeta, Serenata, and Sibak!" Barchibar added, to howls of agreement from the hounds.

A roar came from behind them, and Tamo stepped out, smiling agreeably at everyone.

"You brought the Savrip, too?" Crash said. "Uh, did anyone tell him not to kill Svi'no?"

"Affirmative," 10-K8 chirped. "Turns out he's a fan, so he was quite relieved."

"Yeah, I haven't forgotten about that, Crash," Svi'no added. "Just so you know."

Crash turned to the team. "Well, since we're all here! Let's do what we do best." And without another word, everyone spread out across the small block.

Smeemarm slithered down the nearest sewer entrance, muttering something to herself about litter. 10-K8 released a crew of small cam droids that went sputtering and chirping through the air, instantly sending her more reams of digital information than any organic could fathom. Fezzonk found a ladder nearby that led to the rooftops, his favorite place to be besides in that little flier of his, and there he perched like some giant, murder-faced gargoyle, surveying the world below. Tamo and Tangor, now buddies, apparently, trolled the perimeter, searching the ground for clues. And Barchibar, with a single word of encouragement—"Find"—

simply released the hounds into the rainy Corellian night.

"It feels good to let people in sometimes, huh?" Svi'no said, seeing Crash with what felt like her first real smile in days.

Crash conceded the point with a nod and leaned her shoulder against Svi'no's.

"Ah, about me being good at disappearing," Svi'no said, an uncharacteristic flash of nervousness in her voice. "I thought, maybe . . ."

Crash whirled on her, eyes wide. "You want to join the team?" she yelped. "Oh, stars, Svisvi! I didn't think . . . But! Of course!" She wrapped her arms around Svi'no and squeezed with all her might.

"Haha," Svi'no giggled nervously. "I guess I didn't think, either, but . . . truth is I've always—Ow! Not so hard please!—I've always wanted to, and I need a break from this starlet crap, seriously. It's exhausting. And I *am* really good at blending into the background. . . ."

"We would be honored to have you! Want to be opposition reconnaissance chief?"

Svi'no grinned mischievously. "That's my middle name, in fact."

A howling commotion at the far end of the block yanked them both from the moment.

"What is it?" Crash yelled, running through the pouring rain. The hounds had gotten something; that much was clear. They'd all congregated around . . . Was that . . . ?

"Serenata!" Barchibar hollered, bolting past Crash and

shoving through the crowd of hounds to where Serenata sat, wagging her stumpy tail and shaking her face tendrils happily. "You're okay!"

"I gotta say," Crash said, walking up beside him and giving Serenata some scritches, "bringing the other pups was an ace move, Barchi. She must've smelled them and come looking. We're too far away from the base for her to know how to find her way back." She patted his shoulder, then squatted down to get a better look at Serenata. "Nice work, man. Now we just . . . Whoa."

Something was in the hound's huge back teeth. A scrap of something. Crash got closer. "Is that . . . ? Barchibar, can you hold her jaws open for me?"

To his credit, Barchibar didn't hesitate. He just pulled on those thick, bite-proof gloves of his and straddled the hound, then gently placed a hand on either side of her mouth and opened it.

Crash blinked through the haze of bad breath and slimy saliva.

Very, very carefully, she reached in and yanked out what turned out to be a single shred of fabric.

The same kind of fabric as Prybolt's robes.

Crash stood, blinking through all the possibilities this implied. None of them made much sense.

She shook her head. "Well, kark."

PART TWO

THIRTEEN

GUS TALON

The Er'Kit girl was pretty cute, Graim Torv had to admit. Cute in an awkward, uncertain kind of way, like she was still figuring out who she was, her bright red face and big eyes wide open to the world.

Was she cute enough to trust, though? That was the question.

She'd just shown up at the barricades earlier that day, but that wasn't unusual. The Gus Talon Student Syndicate had put out a general call two nights back for allies to come and join their picket lines with the union, and folks had been flooding in from all over the system ever since. Soon the picket line had sprouted barbwire like some vicious spiny plant sprung up overnight (not unlike those Drengir creatures that had gone berserk in the Outer Rim not long before, in fact!), and the CorSec unit holding them at bay kept showing up in heavier and heavier armor.

The strikers and their various allies, some of them armed, had responded by pelting the unit with fruits and the occasional bottle over the barricade, and then CorSec had made a quick raid, scooping up some students who'd been standing around, minding their business, enraging everybody even more.

So events were going about normal, Graim figured, for this type of thing.

Okay, "this type of thing" wasn't really something he could honestly say, since he was just a third-year bio major and had never even been to a protest before, let alone some giant barricaded run-in with CorSec cops that the whole system had eyes on. But it seemed about right, from the holos he'd watched and from what his older sisters, Brana and Fai, said. He couldn't wait to see their faces when he told them about this. They'd always been the more rebellious ones in the family, and Graim had watched starry-eyed when they staged a takeover of their college admissions office on Corellia and got wall-to-wall media coverage before winning a somewhat conciliatory watered-down version of their demands from the admin.

Anyway, the Er'Kit girl, who was tall for her species,

seemed to think all this was pretty cool. She had a million questions and looked at Graim with absolute awe.

It was endearing.

Sabata, her name was. She said she'd dropped out of Coronet U but was hoping to go back in the fall after seeing the galaxy some. She wore an oversize military jacket that she'd probably stolen from her dad. "Want to cause some trouble?" she'd said with a wicked and toothy grin just as the sun was setting.

Graim looked up from the sign he was painting. He let the corner of his mouth tilt up just slightly, eyes sleepy, head craned to one side. He knew she was taking him in, enjoying the sight of his bare shoulders and unkempt hair. He liked being looked at. "What kind of trouble?" he asked, getting to his feet and standing close enough to her to feel the tiny puffs of her breath on his face.

She raised one eyebrow, not backing away. "The kind that will make headlines."

"Go on." He wanted to kiss her, but there were a bunch of people around, so what was the point? Later. Later would be better. For now, there was adventure to be had. Yes, he could trust her. How could he not trust that easy smile and sweet mischievousness?

"That building." She pointed past the area between the barricades and the rows of CorSec officers, to where the campus library rose above it all, a stern, bright tower against the darkening sky. "It can be seen for kilometers around. CorSec has the media cordoned too far away to get any good footage of what we're doing, so the messaging is lost, you know?"

"I like how you think," Graim said smoothly. "Banner drop?"

She nodded, pleased that he was picking up what she was dropping. Then she patted her satchel. "Already got it painted and packed up and ready to go."

"Better yet," he said, "we go late at night, right? Then when they wake up, it'll just be there—pow!"

For the first time since she'd arrived and attached herself to Graim earlier that day, Sabata's smile fell. Even her big Er'Kit ears drooped, adorably. "It's just . . . I was so excited to go now. I figured we could catch the little bit of sunlight still out and everyone would see *tonight* how much power we have! How we're unstoppable! You know?"

Graim wanted to stand his ground, but he'd really just been making up stuff anyway. He had no idea whether the next day was better than that night. He squinted as if he were considering all the different possibilities, nodded slowly, then brightened. "You know what? I think you're right. Let's do it!"

It was worth it, giving in, just to see Sabata brighten like that. They set out immediately, working through surly crowds of organizers, students, and all the random riffraff who'd shown up.

Brana and Fai were going to go bonkers when they found

out he was behind this. The whole sector would see what he'd done. Holos would show the footage for days.

At the far edge of the barricades, the CorSec presence was thinner, and it wouldn't be hard to slip across, past their lines, into the library. Perfect. Clearly, Sabata had thought this out pretty well.

She motioned him to stay down while she stole over first. He would've objected, but she seemed to know what she was doing, and he wanted to see the best way to go.

She winked at him, then seemed to vanish into the shadows. A few moments later, Sabata reappeared at the library side entrance, her back flat against a wall that kept her out of sight from the five or six CorSec troopers in riot gear standing nearby, their backs turned.

Graim stood, his palms suddenly sweaty. This was it—how heroes were made. He waited a beat to make sure the cops were still looking the other way, then, with Sabata signaling him frantically, he burst into a run.

Up ahead, he saw Sabata raise a blaster. Where had she gotten that? She wasn't pointing it at him, of course, but she was aiming directly at the group of CorSec cops. "No!" Graim shouted just as Sabata let off five blasts, each of them slamming into a cop.

"Hey!" someone yelled as screams sounded and boots clomped nearby.

Graim skidded to a halt, his brain short-circuiting

between fear and confusion. It had all happened so fast, and five CorSec cops were laid out on the ground, some squirming, some eerily still. Smoke plumed upward from their wounds.

"Hurry up!" Sabata yelled. "They're coming!"

He stepped once toward her, still unsure what was happening, and then a blaster bolt thwacked into him from the side and sent him sprawling.

It burned! Stars, it burned!

More blaster fire smashed the pavement around him. He was going to die. Graim stumbled up and dashed with all the strength left in him toward the library.

Sabata grabbed his arm as he reached her and yanked him inside amid a hail of more blaster fire.

"Why did you . . . ? Why did you . . . ?" he mumbled, following her into the bright mezzanine at a desperate, lopsided run. Words didn't make much sense. His breath came short and ragged. Most of all, that burning, sizzling sensation kept expanding outward from the spot on his right flank where he'd been hit. His insides were probably toast, some of them anyway. Maybe, though, maybe Sabata could get him to a doctor somehow . . . something. *Anything.*

"This way." She led him to the right down a dark corridor, then hit a glowing button to call the turbolift.

He slammed his back against the wall, barely standing. "Why did . . . why did you do that?" he finally asked as a quiet ding sounded.

"Come, stand here," she said, holding him up right in

front of the turbolift doors. They slid open. She looked him in the eye and smiled. "Because I needed you to be seen."

"Me seen?" His brain kept transmitting frantic signals at him to run, find help, get away, get away. But there was nowhere to go, and he could barely stand. "For what?"

"So they know it was you that did this." She shoved him hard into the small compartment. He landed with a painful thud that he was pretty sure ruptured some already frizzle-fried part of his innards. When he looked up, gasping for air, Sabata was sliding off her jacket. She tossed it in after him. It was too heavy. The pockets must have been filled with something . . . several somethings, Graim realized, squirming to get up, all the alarms inside him clanging to life at once.

Whatever was in those pockets was heavy and round and beeping urgently.

The last thing Graim saw was the turbolift doors closing on Sabata's smiling red face.

FOURTEEN

CORONET CITY

Ram tossed the last duffel bag into his and Reath's bunk at the Coronet City Jedi quarters and brushed himself off. "Hey, can I ask you something?"

Reath pulled one arm across his chest and then the other, stretching. "Of course! What's up?"

Tip and Breebak had wandered off to explore the kitchen and were probably already busy setting mildly irksome booby traps or something. Kantam and Cohmac had headed off to find the administrators, and the whole place seemed basically empty.

Even though the two boys hadn't hung out much before this and had spent the entire flight to Corellia demolishing each other in an epic battle that ranged across the entirety of the *Talmadge* and almost made even Kantam lose their patience—Ram felt like he could tell Reath literally anything. He was pretty sure he could say, "Reath, I am actually several Bonbraks wearing a human suit," and Reath would raise his eyebrows genially and say, "Hmm . . . let's discuss." And then go find an ancient Jedi text about it.

Fortunately, this was slightly less weird, but still hard to explain. Ram sat on one of the beds and pulled his goggles down over his eyes, which he figured everybody knew meant he was about to say something serious. "It's like . . . I've lost track of how many months have passed since the attack on the Republic Fair. And I've been with you all fighting the Nihil, yeah?"

"And the Drengir," Reath added. He'd been part of the crew that first faced the evil plants, and he'd gone toe to—root?—with them a number of times already.

"Right. And like . . . me? I grew up never really thinking I'd even have to draw my lightsaber, you know?"

"Same!" Reath said brightly. "I was a library kid, through and through."

"Heh, *was*." Ram chuckled. "Okay, right. Anyway! Liiiiike . . . it was scary at first, right? Really scary. Back on Valo, during the attack? Basically every second, I thought I was going to die. I still kinda can't believe I didn't. Plus, so many others did. But that feeling was also only during the first couple hours."

"Right," Reath said. "Because the mind and body can't sustain that much constant strain. It's like running laps over and over, thinking you're going to die. At some point, you have to, you know . . . stop. But you can't just pause and take a nap in the middle of a huge galactic conflict, right?"

"Exactly!" Ram said, hopping up because he felt a joke coming and he wanted to mark the moment. "Unless you're Master Obratuk! Ahhh?" The legendary Parwan Jedi had famously gone into a temporary state of hibernation on a mission recently, leaving Farzala to negotiate with the Hutts. He had woken up just in time to chop an enemy droid into little pieces and help save the day, though.

Reath tilted his head, eyebrows raised. "That wasn't bad, but you have to do it deadpan, Ram. If I can't tell you're about to tell a joke, it's funnier, because then it catches me off guard. But if you keep winking like that, I see it coming a kilometer away. Get it?"

Ram nodded, determined to get it right. "Deadpan, no winking. Got it, got it, thanks."

"Anytime. But what I'm saying is, I get it. Ever since, I don't know, the past three or four times I almost died—I feel like I can't figure out everyday life because I'm constantly thinking about being attacked by more Drengir or getting shot at. And so it's like I'm lost all the time. I don't know what the path forward looks like because it seems to keep blowing up."

Ram blinked at him. He hadn't been expecting Reath to

share his fears, and he definitely hadn't expected them to be exactly the opposite of his own.

"What's wrong?" Reath asked. He looked down. "I'm sorry, maybe I shouldn't have said all that. I know you're figuring your own stuff out and I just dumped all of mine onto you."

"No," Ram said quickly. "Reath, it's okay." It felt like the whole conversation was spinning away from him. He was *glad* Reath had been honest with him, even if it was a totally different experience. "I'm glad you said something. Just hearing that another Padawan is struggling to make sense of things makes me feel less alone."

"Oh." Reath looked genuinely surprised, then relieved. "Good."

"For me, it's totally different," Ram said. Reath had been so honest with him; he wanted to do the same. "With battle, I feel like I should still have a lot of, I dunno—dread? A lot of emotions about it."

Reath put out both hands like he was weighing two small objects. "I mean . . . isn't that sort of what we're supposed to be aiming for? A little bit?

Ram scrunched up his face. "I hope not. I don't think this is anything to strive for. We're supposed to be balanced. This doesn't feel like balance. It just feels empty."

"Okay, I can see how that's unnerving, yeah. On the other hand, you're not ruled by your fear, though. That's good."

"What if it's my fear that's keeping me from feeling fear?"

They both looked at each other for a moment.

"Are you scanning the Starlight archive catalog you memorized for an answer?" Ram asked.

Reath guffawed and then looked somber. "Okay, yes. Haven't found anything yet, but I will!"

"Fellas!" a girl with bright pink hair said, barging into the room, wily smile first, and startling both of them.

"Whoa!" Reath said.

"It's a girl!" Ram yelled, jumping up.

She looked at them with puzzled amusement. "They really don't let you guys out much, huh?"

"Uh, can we help you?" Reath asked, standing beside Ram.

She looked about Reath's age, a couple of years older than Ram, and wore baggy green overalls and a sleeveless purple shirt with a hood. Utility belts were slung over both shoulders, clearly filled with a ton of interesting doodads and thingamabobs. "You guys are the Jedi from Starlight, right?"

The old Ram, back on Valo, would've quietly deferred to Reath to explain that they were just humble Padawan apprentices and the Jedi Masters were off politicking with the local Jedi.

The new Ram just extended his hand amiably and said, "Yes!"

FIFTEEN

CORONET CITY

It wasn't *technically* a lie but definitely wasn't the whole truth, either, Reath thought as the momentum of Ram's not-quite-lie carried them out the door and onto the bright, busy streets of Coronet City.

"Excellent!" the girl had said without a second thought—almost *too* quickly, Reath realized in retrospect. Then she'd explained that she'd sent the holorecording to the Republic officials.

"Crash!" Ram and Reath had both yelled excitedly, and she'd looked, for the first time since she'd popped up, a little thrown.

That was definitely the moment when they should've let

Cohmac and Kantam know what was going on. Reath knew that. Ram probably did, too. But they'd already committed to being *the* Jedi from Starlight, and calling in their adult supervisors would mean admitting they hadn't really been up-front about that.

And anyway, Reath had to admit he was curious about this fast-talking girl and what she had planned.

"Uh, yeah," she'd said, already walking toward the door, the boys on either side, following along easily as if it were the most natural thing to do. And it had seemed natural, Reath thought, trying to put all the pieces together as they strolled down a large boulevard, chatting like old friends.

"Anyway, I'm trying really hard to stop not telling people my plans," Crash said. "It's . . . a struggle, I admit it. But see? Even admitting that is, like, a big deal, frankly. So, look, we have a few hours before the meeting, and what I'm asking of you is a big favor, so I figured I could return the favor in advance by taking you somewhere in Coronet City you've always wanted to go! Because let's be honest, you two don't look like you've ever been here before."

"Wait, wait, wait, slow down," Reath said, stopping in the middle of the part of the sidewalk where apparently speeder bikes were allowed, because Crash immediately yanked him out of the way as one whizzed past. "Oof!" He whirled on her, trying to regain some sense of authority. "First of all, I'm from Coruscant, okay? We didn't grow up on Starlight.

Doesn't make you more metropolitan than us just because you Corellians let people run over pedestrians like barbarians!"

"Wow, touchy," Crash said, but she was still smiling.

"Was that what you meant by deadpan?" Ram asked.

Reath exhaled and realized he was having fun. Sure, it was all weird and happening way too fast, but still . . . he liked Crash and how brazen she was. And it was clear she didn't mean any harm with her gentle jibes. In fact, it was probably how she made friends. He let his scowl slide into a smirk and nodded at Ram. "Yes, indeed it was. Take notes."

"Ooh, are we practicing joke delivery?" Crash piped up. "I have some tips!"

"Wait," Reath said before she had a chance to zing him again. "What's the meeting you're talking about?"

"Well, that goes back to me being up-front," she said, "which in my defense I was *trying* to do before you threw yourself in front of a speeder bike!"

"I was on the—" Reath started.

Crash cut him off. "Which is absolutely your right and extremely cosmopolitan!" She winked at him. He didn't *think* it was in a flirtatious way, but he'd long since given up trying to figure out how flirting worked. Not well, that was how. At least not when he was involved in any way. And that was probably for the best.

"You still haven't answered us," he pointed out, one eyebrow raised. Was that flirting? He hoped not.

"Right. The meeting is of various city leaders and important people, as well as me and my constantly humiliated and deeply bitter rival, Dizcaro!"

"Rival *what*?" Ram asked.

"Oh, yeah, I thought I'd told you," Crash said, slapping her forehead. "I run a diplomat protection company. And I need—rrrrr—*want* you to work for me! With me, rather! Temporarily!"

"What?" Reath asked.

"Can we go back to the part about doing *us* a favor?" Ram requested.

"Wait," Reath said, stepping forward a little as another speeder bike zoomed past, along with a stream of colorful Ithorian curses.

"The shipyards," Ram said. "Where they're building the fleet of MPO-1400 *Purgill*-class star cruisers? Like the one that towed Starlight! Oh, man! They did this one thing—"

"Yes, those shipyards," Crash interrupted, with a knowing smile and a wiggle of her eyebrows. "The ones that are basically impossible to get into even for fancy Jedi like yourselves."

"Yes, those," Ram said.

"Thought you'd never ask. Right this way!"

And off they went.

"Wait!" Reath called, hurrying to catch up.

SIXTEEN

CORONET CITY

"Okay, hold up." Crash raised her hand as they approached the turnoff that led to where two burly municipal officers guarded the shipyard entrance. The boys stopped in their tracks and glanced around warily. At least they knew enough to keep an eye out for trouble; that was something. And they seemed overall to be sensible lads with good hearts. Whether or not they were any use in a jam was another question, but time would tell. She eyed them. "We have a deal?"

Ram grinned. "Abso—"

"Ram," Reath said. "Hold on. We don't agree to deals we don't fully understand."

"That's wise," Crash allowed.

"The deal is this: you take us to the famous, impossible-to-get-into shipyard that Ram is dying to see, and we . . ." Reath made *go on* circles with his hands.

"Pretend to be my minions so we can solve the disappearance of my frie—employees."

"And whether the Nihil are responsible," Ram added. "Our interests actually align, basically."

"If we're helping you," Reath said, "it means you're being up-front with us. We're sharing information. Remember, we just met you."

"And yet you find me strangely charming and reliable?" Crash suggested.

"I do," Ram admitted.

"That's beside the point," Reath said. "But yes."

"Yes, we have a deal, or yes, you find me charming and reliable?"

Ram and Reath traded glances. Then the older boy narrowed his eyes. "Yes, I find you charming. Reliable remains to be seen." He stuck out his hand. "And yes, we have a deal."

"Wizard!" Ram yelled, pumping his fist one time.

Crash blinked at him. "I'm going to understand that to be a good thing." She placed a single credit in Reath's hand and another in Ram's. "So here. Let's do it!"

Ram squinted at it like it might jump up and bite him. "What's this?"

"Money," Crash said. "For to purchase things."

"I *know* that!" Ram growled. "But I mean—"

"You can't pay us," Reath said, offering the credit back to her. "We're Jedi. That would be . . . weird."

Crash was already heading toward the corner. "It's *one* credit. Give it away, for all I care. But if you're working for me, even just *pretend* working for me, you gotta be on payroll. For clarity's sake, if nothing else." She pulled out her comlink. "Ten-Kayt?"

"Here, Master Crash."

"Make a note in the files that we have two new employees, please. Just put"—she eyed them—"Starlight A and Starlight B. Fee: one credit each."

"Done."

She rounded the corner and immediately let out a low groan.

"What is it?" Ram asked as he and Reath fell into step beside her.

The two guards, a Gamorrean and a bored-looking burly human, were in municipal police uniforms, but they weren't any of the ones she knew. Of course they weren't. Most of the recent hires were brought specifically to protect the Santhe Shipyards, and from what Crash had heard, they were a bunch of randoms that nobody, not even the assorted low-lifes and street thugs of the Bottoms, knew anything about.

"Things are just never as simple as they could be," she said. She had hoped maybe one thing could be easy one time. But no. "Doesn't matter. C'mon."

"Greetings, excellent pig!" Crash snorted in Gamorrean as the first guard strutted up to them, already looking for a fight.

He released a string of swears that they definitely didn't teach in Intro to Gamorrean. Fortunately, she had learned on the mean streets of the shipyards, so she replied in kind, with an even more colorful epic saga of horrific things about the guy's grandma, forefathers, how he had sprung from a pile of rancor poodoo and looked it, and how all his nieces and nephews were regurgitated fetal worrts. A lovely language, truly.

For a brief moment, the guard just blinked at her with his piggy little eyes.

"Uh," Reath said quietly. The kid was probably reaching for his lightsaber, just in case.

Then the guard let out an enormous, fatuous guffaw and ran over to embrace Crash. It was one of the least pleasant hugs she'd ever gotten, but it was better than having her face split in two by his sizable bayonet. He threw a sweaty arm over her shoulder and proceeded to escort her and the others toward the gate, demanding to know how she had come to speak Gamorrean so colorfully and how she knew so much about his family, and on and on.

"Hold it," the human guard demanded, putting up one hand and still looking like he could barely be bothered to even stand at all. "Borgar, what are you doing making friends? Nobody gets in. Period. Not even Jedi."

The guy had a large blaster rifle slung over his shoulder, which was . . . unusual for a muni. Crash made a tiny mental note about it and then got to work. "My friends are visiting from out of town, sir, to get medicine, you see—they're from a very small planet with no resources, and I promised their dear dying mother that I would show them the famous shipyards of Coronet City before they returned to her bedside!"

"It's true," Ram piped up awkwardly. It was a good effort though; at least he was willing to play along.

"Not my problem," the guard said. "Their problem."

Borgar released Crash and got in the other guard's personal space, snorting and squealing.

"I don't speak pig!" the guy yelled, right before getting his jaw broken by a solid left hook. He dropped fast, and Borgar got to work lugging him into the guard house.

"Thanks, excellent pig!" Crash yelled in Gamorrean, gesturing elaborately at the boys to follow her into the yards. "Your grandfather is an absolute bag of festering garbage!"

Borgar waved and snorted a cheerful curse-out in reply and then went about his business.

"When you said you could get us into anywhere in Corellia we wanted to go," Reath said, glaring down at her once they'd made it a little ways in and ducked behind a warehouse, "I thought you meant you had behind-the-scenes passes or something! Not that you were going to con some helpless Gamorrean into assaulting his work buddy."

Crash got on her tiptoes to almost reach Reath's chin

and held up one finger. "He was *hardly* helpless." Then another. "That was *clearly not* his buddy." Then a third. "And I never said how we'd get in, in part because I didn't know. It depended where you guys wanted to go and also who happened to be at the door that day. Okay?"

"I thought it was pretty wizard," Ram said, standing between them but a safe distance away. "Personally."

"What happened to you being up-front with us about your plans?" Reath demanded.

"It's called improvising. I can't be up-front with you about plans I don't know about until they happen. Next time I'll ask the huge war hog to hold on a moment while I explain to my partners how we're going to confuse him. Cool?"

"I—"

"And anyway, who's the one being deceitful, mighty Jedi Knights?"

That stopped Reath like a smack in the face, just like it was supposed to. Crash kept her smile inside—there was no point rubbing it in.

"Oh, yeah, that one was my bad," Ram said.

Reath pivoted, but it was too late for that. "We are *technically* Jedi of Starlight Beacon, which is what you asked."

"Uh-huh. A lie by omission is still a lie, last I heard," Crash countered.

"How did you know?" Reath asked, deflated.

Crash cocked her head to one side, eyes wide. "How did I know that the Jedi Council, in their infinite wisdom, didn't send two goofy kids to investigate a potential incursion of Nihil raiders deeper into the galactic Core than they've ever been, *all by themselves*?"

"Goofy?" Ram complained.

"Okay, I take that part back," Crash allowed. "The point remains. Also, I saw the other two Jedi leaving before I came in, and they were clearly older than you two. And they didn't have those cute little plaits you fellas wear."

Ram pulled his Padawan braid out from where he'd tucked it into his bun and held it in front of his face. "You think they're cute?"

"You mean you were staking out the place," Reath said, "waiting for us to be on our own before you came over and conned us."

"It's not a con!" Crash insisted. "I've told you exactly what I'm doing this whole time!" She shook her head. "I gotta tell Svi'no this being up-front with people thing is not all it's cracked up to be."

"Who'no?" Ram asked.

"She's a big-deal singer," Reath informed him, not looking particularly impressed. "And Crash here is clearly name-dropping."

"She's the greatest music artist the galaxy has ever known," Crash said. "And I can't help it if my friends are a big deal. She's also a royal pain in my ass. Point is—we're even, okay? Yes, I waited till the adults were gone, because I deal with enough already at work, and all they do is underestimate you until you prove yourself smarter than them and then act surprised that what you've been saying all along is true. It's exhausting. I keep a very small, select group of 'em in my inner circle, and all of them are on payroll. And anyway: adults come with too many rules. Can you honestly imagine Master Surly Ponytail and Master Muttonchops rolling with us on that last little stunt?"

"Master Muttonchops!" Ram squealed, covering his mouth to mute the giggles.

Reath looked like he was doing everything in his power not to crack up. Crash decided she liked him all right, even if he was a little stuck in his ways. And Ram was obviously the greatest kid in the galaxy; he just needed to work on his acting skills a bit.

All things considered, she'd ended up with a pretty good set of potential partners, she had to admit. "So," she said, folding her arms across her chest. "We're even. Truce?"

Reath smiled out of the corner of his mouth, still trying not to laugh. Nodded. "Truce."

"Now let's go see these starshiiiiips!" Ram yelled, already running off.

SEVENTEEN

DOL'HAR HYDE

Zeen had imagined it many times—victory, finally catching up to Krix and stopping him for good.

She'd tossed it around her mind over many sleepless nights, almost as many times as she'd wondered what death would feel like, especially if it came at his hands.

A hundred different scenarios had tumbled through her thoughts, then pursued her into dreams.

And now . . . now the possibility of victory was so close, she could feel it thickening into reality like a physical thing.

She could almost taste it.

Up above, the heavy booms of starfighter cannons

sounded as the task force ships smashed through what remained of the Nihil's forces.

But Krix was somewhere down there in the tunnels. Zeen was sure of it. She'd seen him leap out of the gunner tower he'd blasted her ship from. She'd watched him run, debris exploding around him. And then he'd vanished.

Krix had killed so many, but like all the Nihil, he was a coward at heart. His squad was known for attacking civilian targets with a small advance team and then returning full force to rampage the aid workers who'd come to help those in need.

He'd once taken care of Zeen when she was afraid, sworn to keep her safe no matter what. Then he'd become a monster.

A monster she would finally, finally stop.

It had been Lula, Farzala, and Qort alongside her as they went into the tunnels. The team! The Padawans who had first found her on Trymant IV, the people she trusted most in the world. She had seen them as heroes, and they'd turned out to be amazing friends, too, accepting her as one of them even though she couldn't become a full Jedi.

And now they were closing in on their enemy together. They'd split up at the juncture of tunnels, and now Qort—reliable, caring Qort—trekked along through the darkness beside her, lightsaber ready.

They were so close. It wasn't Krix himself that Zeen could feel, just the certainty that one way or another, the end of this chapter of her life loomed, swung toward her, unstoppable now. She hoped it was just the end of a chapter and not her whole life. Or anyone else's.

She glanced at Qort as they headed deeper into the dingy tunnel. An Aloxian, he was smaller than the other Padawans, with light blue skin and a kind face. But all that could be deceiving. Zeen had never seen someone fight the way Qort had back on Takodana when the Jedi temple had exploded and Nihil fighters were closing in.

The skull mask he'd worn his whole life had shattered, and in breaking, it had unchained a warrior spirit deep within him. And somehow he'd still been that sweet lovable boy when the fighting was all over.

She doubted he'd need her help in a jam, but with someone as underhanded and tricky as Krix around, there was no telling what could happen.

And Lula. Lula was heading down the other tunnel with Farzala. If anything happened to either of them . . .

No.

She would not let her own wrath consume her like it had back on Quantxi. There, she'd come face to face with Krix after he shot her down, and she'd used the Force to choke him—would've killed him if it hadn't been for Lula stepping in, her calming presence, her hand on Zeen's, lowering it.

"That isn't our way," she'd said. And Zeen had felt the truth of it move through her. She'd been with the Padawans only a few weeks at that point, and still she knew. . . . She knew that their power and presence in her life, especially

Lula's, was more important than any sense of fulfillment she'd get from feeling Krix's life snuffed out in her hands.

She took in a deep breath of stale tunnel air. Released.

The Force was with her. She was one with it.

Up ahead an iron door sealed off their path farther into the tunnel.

He was here. This was the safe room. The knowledge of it thrummed through Zeen. The inevitable ending flashed toward her in crude, vague bursts. Lula was near, too.

Lula.

Zeen raised her blasters, the sweat of her palms slick against the grips. Ready.

Not ready. Not at all.

Her breath came faster and faster.

Everything about this seemed like a trap. Where were Lula and Farzala? She glanced at Qort. He blinked back, face determined, inscrutable.

A wrong move would kill them all. Zeen felt that truth in the pit of her stomach. Or was it fear? Waiting too long was a move, too, and could be just as fatal. The comms didn't work this deep in the tunnels.

Usually she could feel Lula. Usually she knew instinctively what her friend would do next.

Now everything was muddled.

Fear rippled through her, dragging a hundred different tragedies across her mind.

No.

She had to trust the Force. It was all she could do. Trust the Force. Trust love. Trust Lula.

Zeen closed her eyes, reached out.

She felt the familiar surge of the Force rising in her; she felt Lula, her warmth suddenly near and gigantic, a gentle, unstoppable sun.

Lula, whose face she had opened her eyes to after a long meditation so many times now.

Lula, who was reaching out, too, trusting the Force. Trusting love. Trusting Zeen.

Are you ready, Zeen? Her voice was as clear as if she were standing right there.

"Always," Zeen whispered.

Zeen's eyes flew open, and for a flickering moment she saw Lula across from her, face calm, eyes opening, too. "Now!"

She grabbed the handle of the door, nodding at Qort to ready himself, then pulled it open.

There, huddled in the small hideaway room, was Krix, already leaping up, reaching for his blaster rifle. Beyond him, Lula had flung open another door, and the first thing Zeen thought was that it was strange they weren't locked.

But it didn't matter. She had the drop on Krix, and there was no way he would reach his own weapon before—"Zeen! No!" Lula yelled, and then with a clang, the door closest to Zeen slammed shut in her face.

There was a yelp from within, then the shriek of a blaster bolt, followed almost instantly by another door clattering shut. Then a horrific snarl of flame sounded.

Qort sniffed once, frowned. "Rhydonium," he said in his scratchy little voice. "Would have made fire of all of us."

Lula had saved them. She had saved them all. But were she and Farzala okay?

"Come on!" Zeen yelled, already charging back through the tunnel. Qort was beside her, running, mumbling his concerns in Aloxian.

"I don't know, either," Zeen said. They rounded back past the divide, then dashed to where the sounds of struggle grew louder.

"We . . . we got him!" Lula yelled as Zeen and Qort came around the corner. Krix was on the ground, squirming beneath Farzala's foot.

"And stay down," Farzala menaced with a grim smile. Qort ran over to join him as Krix yelped gutless threats.

Zeen felt like she could collapse into Lula's soft gaze and never rise from it again.

For a few blissful seconds in that dark tunnel, they just took each other in, relishing the small and gigantic victory. There was still so much to do, Krix's plans to unravel, a million impossible questions to answer.

But for just that moment, Zeen felt the galaxy slide into a tiny, perfect kind of balance around them.

And that, right then, was enough.

EIGHTEEN

THEN

"I don't know how you do it," Kantam said as Aytar ran the brush in a long arc down his own face, completing the bright silver wave.

In the mirror, their eyes met. Aytar flashed that smile of his, the disarming one that made Kantam feel an unfamiliar surge of . . . something, something hot and fierce, deep inside. "Put on my own makeup? It's easy, really. Takes some practice, but you get the hang of it. Dondar Volt taught me. She's incredible."

"That's fascinating," Kantam said, throwing some silky robes to the side and leaning back on the antique couch in Aytar's cluttered dressing room. "But I meant perform. Every night. I don't know how you can get up there again and again, and . . . be someone else, and smile and feel all those eyes on you, and . . ." They shook their head, rustling a hand through their short hair. "I admire it, I guess I'm saying."

Aytar rinsed out the brush in a jar of murky water and then dipped it in the gold paint. "Does it bother you?"

"I . . ." It hadn't occurred to Kantam to be bothered by it. Should they be? The two had known each other for only five days. Four days and eight hours, really. They had been the most truly wild days and nights of Kantam's life, easily, and neither of them had known what to call this . . . whatever it was. Thing. It had no name and so no rules, and no clear beginning or obvious end. And that's what made it so perfect.

Everything back at the temple was regimented, clear, delineated, put in a box and labeled until it became something else, and then it got a new box, a new label. Okay, that wasn't entirely true. The Jedi Order certainly had an understanding of the endless complexities of the universe, those definition-defying parts of life, especially the Force—always the Force and only the Force. Kantam hadn't realized how sick of it all they had grown until they'd spent some time away.

"Padawan Sy?" Aytar said piously.

Kantam grinned, shaking away the rambling thoughts. "I can't decide whether I love or hate that you call me that with such obvious mockery in your voice," they said.

"Mockery?" Aytar gasped, fake offended. "Only a little."

Then he got serious. "Truth is, I admire that about you, Kantam. What you are. Your dedication. Sure I perform over and over, and yes, it is exhausting, but I love it. It's who I am, and I couldn't really do anything else, so . . . I see what you do, the respect you walk with for the galaxy, for your elders, and . . . it's beautiful to me."

Kantam looked away, unsure what to do with their body, what to say. "It hasn't felt so simple since . . ." They looked back, caught Aytar's gaze, locked eyes with him. "Since you, Aytar."

"Mm," Aytar said. That neither-here-nor-there kind of grunt Kantam had already gotten so used to that it had started popping up in their own speech patterns, unbidden.

They hadn't even made love, but Kantam was pretty sure that when they did—and there was no question that they would—a star or two might explode somewhere. They'd talked about it plenty, enjoyed taking each other right to the edge and then pulling back—a thrilling exercise in trust and temptation. It hadn't been a conscious decision, to wait. It was just clear: that was the right thing to do at the moment. When the time came, they would do it. The understanding seemed—in a weird, impossible way—easy. They didn't have to speak; it was simply true.

"I don't want to make things complicated for you," Aytar said.

Kantam scoffed. "That's nice but . . . too late. I'm talking to Master Yoda tomorrow."

Aytar spun around. "About what?"

Kantam sighed, sat up. "I—I don't know, actually. I don't know."

"You're not thinking of leaving the Order, are you, Kantam?"

"Do you not want me to?"

Everything was happening so fast. Kantam felt the speed of it around them, like the sudden burst of stars stretching into hyperspace. There was no stopping it, whatever it was. It was bigger than both of them.

"I don't know," Aytar said, and Kantam wanted to curl up inside the brutal, gentle honesty of his words and sob.

CORONET CITY

"As much as I'd rather hear the rest of this story than deal with some Republic bureaucratic silliness," Cohmac said, "and I really would—haven't we been sitting here an awfully long time?"

Kantam disentangled themself from all those vibrating images and feelings that seemed to spring to life in their mind just in the telling, and then released them all into the stale air of the waiting room and nodded. "Indeed we have. What do you make of it?"

Cohmac stroked his goatee and arched an eyebrow. "I

would say typical official-type nonsense, but things being what they are . . . I'm suspicious it might be more than that."

They both glanced around the dull room that they'd been sitting in for . . . had it already been almost an hour? An ancient Twi'lek woman had greeted them warmly, offered some watery caf, and then escorted them down a brightly lit corridor and asked them to have a seat, explaining that the minister would be with them shortly.

She wasn't.

Then Kantam had gotten back to reminiscing, mostly because Cohmac prodded them—the story had been cut short during the flight over by some turbulence and an asteroid belt, and then too much had been going on to pick it up again.

Now . . . they'd been waiting long enough for it to indicate either an intentional insult or something more afoot. Both Jedi stood, hands at their sabers. "I'm listening," Kantam said.

"What do you say we bypass the secretary and pay a visit to the minister directly?" Cohmac proposed.

"I say a minor diplomatic incident is better than another hour sitting in this room," Kantam replied.

"Excellent logic." They headed back into the corridor, each glancing to either side before proceeding toward the far end, where a fancy doorway took up the entire wall.

Kantam and Cohmac traded glances, then nods, then Cohmac tapped the control pad.

The minister's large, extravagant office had been converted into a kind of war room—a large holotable in the center projected spinning images of a crumbling building, a moon, and what appeared to be troop movements along a city map.

A handful of uniformed officers leaned over the table, checking numbers, consulting with each other in urgent whispers. Messenger droids zipped around the floor and out through small hatchways that probably led to a whole other command center somewhere in the complex.

"Ah, Masters Sy and Vitus, I presume!" Minister Fendirfal exclaimed, walking around the holotable and spreading her arms majestically. The windows behind her opened up to a breathtaking view of the Port District; just beyond that, the midday sun danced across the churning waves. "I'm so sorry to have kept you waiting!"

"Quite all right," Cohmac assured her. "Seems you were otherwise occupied. Anything we can be of assistance with?"

"Minister," an aide said, fast-walking to Fendirfal's side and muttering something in her ear. She nodded, all pretense of formalities gone, whispered something back, and then dialed her smile back to ten and directed it at the two Jedi.

"I doubt it, my friends, but thank you."

"Might we inquire about what has occurred?" Kantam said, trying to stem the irritation at even having to ask in the first place. Seemed like they should just go ahead and tell them, but politics and the Republic being what they were,

Kantam tried not to make assumptions. There were probably security clearances that needed to be authorized and so on.

"A bombing at Gus Talon University, I'm afraid."

"Was it the Nihil?" Kantam asked, and then immediately wished they hadn't.

The minister's face crinkled into a kind of pained smile. "You do realize, my dear Jedi, that not *everything* that goes wrong in the galaxy has to do with those marauders, don't you?"

Kantam felt a flicker of emotion from Cohmac, then was relieved to sense it passing like an errant gust of wind. "Of course," they said, "we just—"

"We have been quite effective at making sure the Nihil raiders have no hope whatsoever of making their way this deep into the core of the galaxy," the minister continued. "They are *not welcome* here on Corellia, you know."

"They're not welcome in the Outer Rim, either." Cohmac managed to keep his voice at a steady, cool drone, but Kantam knew those words held pure fire waiting to be unleashed. "And yet we've been fighting them off for the past year. They certainly weren't welcome in hyperspace, and yet Hetzal was nearly obliterated. Surely you're not suggesting that any of the planets these raiders have victimized have welcomed them, Minister."

"What I'm *suggesting*," Fendirfal nearly spat, "is that we have no Nihil here, nor do we plan on having them. If we did, they would be dealt with and dismissed. Now, you two on the other hand"—she shifted suddenly back into her eerie million-credit smile—"are our welcome guests, of course, and are free to pursue whatever avenues of investigation you need to get the answers you need."

Kantam bowed slightly, more than ready to be done with this conversation. "Tha—"

"I must warn you, though, we have our hands quite full at the moment, as you can see, and won't be able to help you."

"How many of the Jedi from the Coronet City temple have been deployed to Gus Talon?" Cohmac asked.

"Oh, all of them, of course." Fendirfal chuckled whimsically. Then she tensed. "It appears that the union strike has exploded quite viciously into an all-out insurrection."

"Ah," Cohmac said. "That explains why there was no one to greet us at the lodgings."

"Thank you, Minister," Kantam said, backing toward the door. "Please let us know if we can be of any assistance whatsoever."

She bowed, smile tight. "Of course. I would offer the same, but it wouldn't be accurate, alas."

Kantam blinked at the slight. "I . . ."

"I will, however, be attending to some matters later tonight that may relate to your *investigation*. You may join me, if you'd like."

"I suppose—" Cohmac began.

Fendirfal cut him off. "Very well. I will stop by your quarters on my way out."

Both Jedi let out long exhales as the door slid closed behind them, blocking out the anxious clatter of the war room.

"Well, I was wrong," Kantam said. "Another hour sitting in that awful waiting area would've been better than that any day."

NINETEEN

CORONET CITY

"This," Ram said breathlessly, to himself more than anyone else, "is the greatest place IN THE ENTIRE GALAXY!"

He stood at the far end of the grandest ship he'd ever seen: an MPO-1400 *Purgill*-class star cruiser. It seemed to stretch all the way to the horizon, and all along it various beings tinkered and hammered and chattered to one another. Cranes and great big walkers maneuvered across the bulky cruiser, and droids hovered around, rolled out of ventilation ducts, maneuvered through wing channels and wiring casings.

The best part: Beside it, there was another MPO just like it! And another beside that!

He had run all the way there once he'd realized they were close, but that wasn't why he was panting. He was panting because he'd never been so happy in all his life. And apparently, neither had the Bonbraks.

"Breekpatz!" yelped Tip, crawling out of Ram's robes and perching on one shoulder.

"Prakapraka," agreed Breebak, climbing up on the other.

"I know, right?" Ram sighed. "Heaven."

"Um," Crash said, walking up on one side of Ram as Reath appeared on the other. "Reath, your friend has a rat on each of his shoulders."

"Fika fika prap!" Tip snarled, all his fur getting pointy.

"Yeah, you get used to it," Reath sighed. "They're Bonbraks. And they understand Basic."

"I figured that," Crash said, "because it sounded like one of them just cursed me out." She pulled a handful of pellets out of one of those pouches on her utility belt and held some out to each Bonbrak. "Gork gork treats?"

"They're probably mad you called them rats," Reath pointed out as Tip and Breebak gobbled up the pellets happily. "Oh, look, they love you already just like everyone else."

"Well . . ." Crash shrugged, already digging more treats out of the pouch, "I keep these around for the hounds, and more recently I've found they work on Tamo, too. But rats do love gork gork treats." The Bonbraks started cursing again while noshing on more treats and then just gave up and blazed through the next two handfuls Crash gave them.

Ram only halfway noticed. He was too busy imagining what the specs of those gigantic cruisers must be, how they balanced lift/mass ratio considerations with slick commercial design, how it all came together.

Some people talked with awe about the wonders of nature, how the Force itself must have been the great master designer behind such a complex and beautiful galaxy. And sure, that made sense, and Ram loved the Force, of course.

But mostly because it helped him better understand and play with all the cool mechanical gadgets and machines of the galaxy! And this . . . What had gone through the mind of Shug Drabor, the great master designer behind these magnificent giants?

Also—Ram took a few stumbling steps down the main walkway, narrowing his eyes at something up ahead—a display of some kind. It looked like a single-pilot ship.

"This kid is something else." Crash chuckled.

"There's no one like him," Reath confirmed.

Was that . . . ? He got closer, ignoring the quips from either side, then broke into a run.

"Fellas," he said to the Bonbraks, both of whom had finally finished all their snacks and were also staring with wide eyes at the miracle before them, "is that what I think it is?"

The small, all-black starfighter looked like someone had taken one of Ram's arc-drill bits, made it about a hundred times larger, and welded sleek wings on either side and cannons all around it. Strafing scars covered the ship's heavy carapace—this thing had seen serious action and made it out in one piece somehow. Then again, it didn't look like much of anything could get through that metal.

There wasn't even a viewport anywhere! The pilot probably had to use whatever primitive sensor system and . . . "The Force," Ram said in a reverent whisper.

"Verrry agood, small Jedi boy," someone with a tiny voice croaked behind and above Ram. He spun around, then looked up, up, up along the metal exoskeleton of an enormous loadlifter workframe that was proportioned something like a gigantic turbo-powered Anzellan—short stubby legs and huge four-fingered pincer hands at the ends of extra-long metal arms.

"Ah, thanks!" Ram said, blocking out the sun with his palm so he could get a better look at the . . . tiny Anzellan in the driver's seat at the top of the workframe. "Wait, did you just call me small?"

"I see you've met the great Shug Drabor himself," Crash said, catching up with Reath by her side.

"Wait," Ram gasped. "This is . . ."

"Hey, Doc!" Crash waved up at the Anzellan as if she were just talking to some buddy of hers, not the greatest starship engineer of literally ALL TIME. Then Ram realized that was because she *was* talking to some buddy of hers, who also just happened to be the greatest starship engineer of literally all time.

"Abacrash!" Shug did a jaunty little dance—which the workframe mimicked, almost stepping on Ram—and then gave a small bow. "Always agood to see!"

"You *know* him?" Ram said, trying to contain himself. "You two are, like . . . friends?"

"Dr. Drabor," Crash said, ignoring him, "this is Ram Jomaram and Reath Silas, Jedi apprentices of Starlight Beacon. Ram adores you, in case you hadn't noticed."

"Jedi-no bá!" the little engineer exclaimed, pushing a button and hopping down from his control seat onto the top of the ancient starfighter.

Ram didn't speak Anzellan, but he figured it was a good thing, from the Anzellan's tiny whimsical smile as he removed his goggles and blinked at Ram.

"Eh-vi ya Bonabaraka?" he shrieked happily, spreading his arms.

Tip and Breebak, who had been watching in awed silence, finally yipped and scampered off Ram's shoulders and onto the starfighter, where they proceeded to engage in some kind of elaborate group hug with Shug.

"Well, the doctor loves your rats," Crash said, already scrounging up more gork gork treats.

"Can you . . . ? I don't speak Anzellan," Ram said. "Can you ask him about this ship?"

Crash nodded and turned to Shug, who had an arm around each of the Bonbraks like they had all just had a wild night barhopping together. *"Vizi vizi starfih ho-ka?"*

"Just how many languages do you speak, Crash?" Reath demanded with unchecked admiration in his voice.

Crash shimmied and then winked. "A lot. I protect people for a living and manage a big team. It helps to be able to speak to folks in their own language. Plus it catches everyone off guard. And it's a great way to learn secrets, because no one expects me to know what they're saying when they switch out of Basic."

"I am . . . impressed," Reath said.

Ram shushed them both because Dr. Drabor had launched into an elaborate extended monologue.

"He says it's about two hundred years old," Crash explained when the engineer had finished talking and went back to cuddling his new friends. "Shug didn't build it, but he keeps it around as a source of inspiration. It's the only one left of its kind, but these babies, as the good doctor here calls them, were in service all the way up through the Eiram and E'ronoh War. This one served in the Battle of Jedha, right before the Republic petitioned to shut down production entirely and got them banned. It's a *Spiral*-class Viz-Core Eviscerator with twin-canister omega cannons, VIX-force metallic blast-proof shielding, and a modulated navicomputer for seek-and-destroy missions."

"Unreal," Ram whispered.

"That drill part on the front was used to puncture the hulls of large enemy ships and then burrow through to their reactor cores. I guess," Crash added, clearly editorializing on top of her translation, "that's why it's the only one left."

"I would like . . . to have . . . one of these . . . please," Ram said under his breath. Crash did him the favor of not translating that for Shug, who immediately launched into another monologue about something. "What's he saying?"

Crash smiled. "He wants to know if you'd like a tour of the rest of the shipyard."

"WIZAAAARD!"

TWENTY

CORONET CITY

Reath had to admit, he was having fun. A lot of fun.

He was doing his best to keep his guard up, stay cautious, but he hadn't realized how badly he'd needed to just be a teenager hanging out with other teenagers for a little bit, after all that fighting and escaping and getting knocked out. And he was glad that, in Ram, he'd found someone to talk with about the more hard-to-describe parts of being a Padawan.

He'd been resistant to leaving Starlight at first, but maybe on Corellia an answer awaited him about what direction he was supposed to point himself, how to move forward.

They made their way along the vast corridors of the *Wanderlight*, a sister ship to the famed *Halcyon* that had helped tow Starlight on its rescue mission to Dalna. Turned out Bonbreez had some linguistic ancestors in common with Anzellan, so Tip and Breebak took over translating duties between Shug and Ram, leaving Crash and Reath free to stroll behind at a leisurely pace and take in the immensity and lushness of the gorgeous starship.

Crash was a tricky one, Reath thought as they walked along a near-invisible catwalk that took them over what looked like a tiny ecosystem—flower-covered trees reached up toward them through the artificial mist.

Could she be trusted? Just because she'd acted like she was being up-front about including them in her plans, that didn't mean it was true. Or not all of it anyway. His instinct said she was all right, and he was pretty sure that wasn't just because she was good-looking. He hoped it wasn't, anyway. He'd been fooled by good looks and an easy smile before, duped into telling a Nihil operative way too much about the Jedi Order, and the memory of it still made him cringe inside.

And then there was Vernestra—an entirely different kind of beautiful and an entirely different kind of crush. She seemed like the kind of person who would understand things about Reath before he even had a chance to explain them. He imagined them exploring the galaxy together—hand in hand sometimes, even though that was kind of corny—and discovering entire new ways to use the Force.

Reath had given up trying not to have crushes, opting instead to neutralize the whole situation by having *all* the crushes. Surely there was an old Jedi saying about that, or maybe that *was* an old Jedi saying. If not, he'd make it one.

Crash was different from the others. (Although she did look a little like Nan. Reath wondered if that was what people meant when they said someone had a *type*.) At least, she seemed different. He'd never met anyone quite like her, and if she was working for the Nihil somehow, why would she turn the holo of her friend over to the authorities and thus draw more attention to whatever was going on? That would have to be a very elaborate ruse, even by Nihil standards.

"Trying to figure me out?" Crash asked with a sly wiggle of her eyebrows. They'd paused on the catwalk to take in the fresh soil smell and the chirping song of whatever creatures had been imported to live in the biosystem below.

Reath had to smile. "Something like that."

"Did you consult with your old buddy, *the Force*?"

"How do you do that?" he asked, narrowing his eyes at her.

"What, read people's minds?"

"No—that thing where you're clearly making fun of everyone in existence and all they do is like you more instead of hate you for it."

"Oh, that ol' thing!" She waved away the notion like it was no big deal, then immediately looked puzzled. "Wait—I'm not sure. It's not actually on purpose. I only do it to people I like though." She pulled her mouth to one side. "Except that Gamorrean guy, but that doesn't count—he was a mark."

"Are we not marks?"

She rolled her eyes and kept walking. "I already told you you're not." Then she stopped, looked at him seriously. "Do you believe me?"

Reath nodded, meeting her eyes so she knew he meant it. "I do. And yes, I've been tumbling it over in my head. I trust you, Crash. I'm not one hundred percent sure why, but I do."

"Because the Force told you to, obviously!"

They fell back into stride. Up ahead, Ram squealed something unintelligible and the Bonbraks gibbered away as Shug chuckled.

"So, about tonight," Crash said, sounding a little uncharacteristically nervous. Then she paused and pressed an earpiece that Reath hadn't noticed she was wearing until just then. "Advance Team Seven, go." He blinked at her, and she held up one finger and smiled apologetically. "Okay, check. Confirmed, yeah. Sounds good. Check in with Air-Eleven about that."

Air-Eleven? Reath mouthed incredulously.

Crash shrugged.

"Are there really ten other air support units?" he whispered.

She shook her head. "We just thought it sounded cool.

Sorry, not you, Barchibar. What were you saying?" Crash scrunched up her face. "*Powlo is there, too?*" she practically spat. "That's . . . that's Dizcaro's guy."

Reath could practically see the meticulous, terrific gears of her mind spin into overdrive.

Crash strode toward the far platform. "Find out what detail he's on, Barchi. But don't be obvious about it, you hear me? Do *not* just ask him. And . . . matter of fact, don't do anything. I mean it. I'm sending Kayt your way. Yeah. Okay, we'll be over there soon." She stopped. "Yes, *we*." She glanced at Reath. "We have some new team members. Don't worry, you'll like them."

Then she clicked off the call and broke into a run.

"What's going on?" Reath asked, catching up with a few long steps and falling into stride with her.

"That meeting tonight," Crash said huffily, "which *I* called, by the way—"

"The one with all the diplomats and fancy city leaders and whatnot?"

"Exactly. Normally, since I called it and run protection for all the attendees, I would be responsible for the security of the whole meet."

"But?"

"Correct, there is a but. There's always a but!" They rounded a corner and crossed a long fancy room full of various gambling devices. "My main competitor, Dizcaro, has an advance team on site, too."

"Which means . . ."

"Which means he's trying to use the disappearance the other night to nudge in on my turf—nothing new there—but now he's apparently made some headway with one of the city leaders. And that means things are going on behind the scenes that I don't know about."

"It must be exhausting to be you," Reath marveled.

Crash scoff-laughed. "You have no idea. Ram! Ram and the ra—Bonbraks!" she called across the hall. Ram and the others looked up.

"We gotta run! Sorry to tear your new friends away, Dr. Drabor, but we gotta get them outfitted in their disguises!"

"Disguises?" Reath gaped, turning suddenly toward the exit along with Crash as Ram sighed and said his goodbyes.

Crash flashed that grin. "Disguises!"

TWENTY-ONE

CORONET CITY

"I feel ridiculous," Ram complained.

Svi'no grabbed him by the shoulders and squinted into his eyes. "If you don't hold still, you'll look a whole lot more ridiculous. Believe me."

He grumbled, and she leaned in and got back to work, sliding her brush along his cheeks and then up across his forehead. It wasn't the most unpleasant feeling; in fact it was kind of nice, and Svi'no was a big-deal diva, apparently. She had a slim turquoise face and eyes that seemed to sparkle with starlight. Ram didn't know what species she was—she had a bunch of arms and somehow managed to float, but her face looked like a human's.

"Aren't you a big star or something?" Ram asked, settling back into the gentle rhythm of the girl's breathing and the cool feeling of paint on his face.

She chortled conspiratorially. "Something like that. But don't tell anyone."

Around Ram, the strange after-hours lounge seemed to be in constant motion, with various members of Crash's team setting up tables and checking under furniture—probably for bombs or secret recording devices. The place was pretty sweet, Ram had to admit. All the seats were made out of some kind of extremely soft exotic leather. The wood the walls and shelves had been made from was a rich, warm umber color that added to the coziness. And a giant fish skeleton at one end turned out to be the bar!

Reath had walked in beside Ram and gasped. Shelves lined the walls, and on them sat a collection of ancient-looking tubes—the kind some civilizations used to house their archival documents. He'd run up to one and tried to pull it down, but the thing was stuck fast. "What the—" Reath grunted, pulling even harder. Then he got up close, eyeballing it with that archive-expert glare of his. "This isn't even real! It's plasti-flex! What kind of rank subterfuge is this?"

Crash had rolled her eyes with a chuckle and escorted them to a corner of the room someone had set up for makeup, and that was where they now sat, complaining.

TWENTY-ONE

"What are we even supposed to be?" Reath asked, in the seat next to Ram, where he was getting his own extreme makeover from a cheerful Ithorian named Ansh, who kept humming and muttering to herself.

Crash appeared between the two of them and burst out laughing. "Perfection! You've outdone yourselves, ladies!"

Svi'no floated back a little and took in Ram with an admiring nod. "Okay, yeah. That's working. Fellas, you may have a look."

Ram and Reath spun around in their chairs to the mirror behind them.

"Whoa," Reath gasped.

"Awesome!" Ram yelped. "I take it all back."

"Why do we have bright red skulls painted over our faces?" Reath asked.

"Because," Crash said, putting her arms around their shoulders and grinning back at them in the mirror, "you're members of the Scarlet Skull Cult, the most feared assassin squad in the sector, made up entirely of children and teenagers."

"That's horrible," Ram said. "But also kind of wizard."

Reath made a face, which was all the more alarming with his morbid makeup. "I wonder how the members of that cult would feel about people dressing up like them. . . ."

"Well," Crash said brightly, "we'll never know, because they've all been dead for about a century."

"Oh!" Ram got closer to the mirror to inspect the intricate lines Svi'no had rendered along his jawline. "Well then why are we—"

"Because even though they're long dead, people on Corellia are still terrified of them. And this way people will think they came back and joined my squad."

"Aren't assassins, like . . . the opposite of bodyguards?" Reath pointed out.

Crash was unimpressed. "As the ancient Jedi saying goes—sometimes to save a life, you gotta end a life, right?"

"I am absolutely one hundred percent positive," Reath insisted, "that is *not* an ancient Jedi sa—"

"It's all in the balance," Crash rattled on. "Anyway, the other good thing is everyone knows the Scarlet Skulls took a lifelong vow of silence by chopping off their own tongues—"

"That seems . . . overly effective," Reath said.

Crash ignored him. "So you guys don't have to worry about saying anything goofy and giving yourselves away—rrrrrrr, not that I was worried about that happening!"

"Hey!" Reath said.

"Oops, gotta go give a speech." Crash made herself scarce.

"She might have a point," Ram admitted.

Svi'no raised a wide-brimmed black hat over Ram's head. "And for the finishing touch!"

Ansh did the same for Reath, and they both ceremoniously lowered them.

"Perfecto!" Crash called from across the room, where she was standing on a table, gathering everyone around her.

Reath and Ram exchanged glances and then both shrugged. They'd already changed out of their Jedi robes and stashed them in a back room and now wore mysterious all-black bodysuits adorned with about a dozen gold buttons and tassels. "How did those kids manage to kill anybody with all these stupid things hanging off their sleeves?" Ram muttered. "That's what I'd like to know."

"People will probably wonder that about Jedi robes one day," Reath said as they crossed the room.

"Master Crash," a short mushroom-headed droid called from the doorway, "most of the guests have arrived and are extremely eager to come in."

"Good," Crash said. "Let 'em squirm. Gather 'round, everyone. I'll make this quick."

Ram and Reath found themselves shoulder to shoulder with a motley crowd of ruffians and weirdos, all of whom had become extremely pleasant and welcoming once Crash had let them know the Padawans were new members of their team.

"You all know the drill," Crash said, "but I'll go over it again because we got some newbies on board. Everyone wave at the first newly initiated Scarlet Skulls in about a century!"

The whole room chuckled, and several burly arms patted Ram on the back.

"But seriously," Crash continued, swinging somber,

"tonight is more than just a regular protection gig, as you are all aware. We've lost two of our own, and we all need to be on high alert for any—and I do mean any—information that may lead to the culprit. On top of that, Dizcaro has already managed to elbow his way in on some of our clients." Various boos and curses erupted around Ram. "And who knows what else he has planned." She looked indefinably sad for a moment, like the truth of all that was going on had suddenly fallen out of the sky and onto her shoulders. Then she seemed to shake it off, and her gaze tightened. "So remember: stay sharp. Whatever happens, we're still bodyguards, and bodyguards don't get emotionally involved. We're not here to get revenge for our fallen brothers tonight—we're here to find out the truth so we can get a proper revenge later. Tonight, the game is reconnaissance. You with me?"

Enthusiastic yelps and growls rang out, and then Crash signaled the droid, and the doors slid open.

Several middle-aged human men in robes entered, looking somewhat stuffy and self-important, then a few other folks, and everyone started chatting and mingling.

"Who are those guys?" Ram asked when Crash hopped off the table and made her way over to them.

"That's a whole lot of words for a guy without a tongue, kiddo," Crash informed him. "No more chatting. You're here to listen, and find out whatever you can, and then tell me. Use your woo-woo Jedi powers if you have to."

"That's not how—" Reath started.

Crash silenced him with a glare. “These guys call themselves the City Fathers. It’s old Corellian money, industry, and tradition crap mostly, but the power they wield is very real. That guy over there”—she nodded toward a tall broad-shouldered man with a poof of gray hair perched on top of his otherwise shiny head—“Ovus Buckell, Father of Finances. That one”—a short burly fellow with a bright red beard—“Finmos Tagge, Father of Chemicals. That’s Deklar Graf, Father of Metals.” The last one, Deklar, had an elaborate mustache and a shimmery tall hat that screamed for people to pay attention to its wearer.

“Aren’t there any foremothers of the city?” Ram asked.

“Yes,” Crash said, “but she’s a giant worm who probably wants me dead and is allergic to sunlight, so you won’t be meeting her tonight. But she manages the waterworks. Now, hush.”

The big broad guy made a joke that everyone pretended to laugh at.

Crash rolled her eyes. “Buckell is the one who just recently took over for Nomar Tralmat—that’s who disappeared along with my two bodyguards. He’s in charge of the municipal police, by some weird overcomplicated arrangement—don’t ask. So he had something to gain by what happened, in a way, but don’t be fooled by that overconfident swagger—the man has no idea what he’s doing and is in way over his head. Trust me on that.”

Ram and Reath nodded, finally managing to stay quiet.

"Oh, look, here comes our final guest," Crash marveled, already heading toward the door to greet the tall sallow-cheeked woman walking in ahead of a small entourage. "Minister Fendirfal—the Republic liaison officer."

Ram grabbed Reath's arm. "Did she say—"

There was no point in finishing his sentence, because then the next two guests walked in, looking almost as uncomfortable as Ram and Reath felt: Masters Cohmac Vitus and Kantam Sy.

TWENTY-TWO

CORONET CITY

Well, that's probably extremely awkward, Crash thought as the Jedi with the rambunctious sideburns—Kantam, the boys had said—discreetly nudged the other one—Cohmac, that would be—and nodded toward where Ram and Reath stood trying to disappear into the wall. Of course, that was especially impossible considering they were decked out like ancient child assassins.

Ah, well. It was truly none of Crash's business. And anyway, Cohmac and Kantam seemed like reasonable types. They'd all work it out. She had bigger problems to deal with.

She climbed up on a table again, ignoring several gasps

and tut-tuts from the assorted diplomats, and held up her hand for their attention. Several dozen eyes—some on stalks, some gazing out from beneath folds of slime-crusted flesh, some behind goggles—turned her way.

"I've asked you all here because both our communities have lost one or more of our own recently," Crash said, her gaze finding and locking briefly with different eyes in the crowd. The City Fathers had brought their various spouses and attendants, of course, and a slew of Dizcaro's bodyguards milled about, mean-mugging Crash's people like the rank amateurs they surely were. Somewhere, Svi'no lurked through the shadows, a thought that brought Crash a warm swirl of comfort. "And I know we are all anxious to get to the bottom of what happened, and also to share in our common sorrow."

Inwardly, Crash scoffed. These old fuddy-duds almost certainly had no such emotions, but they were invested in performing that doddering ritual of vague grief, even behind closed doors, possibly even to themselves, so Crash was more than happy to play along. They would drink and carry on, and someone, almost certainly, would mess up.

"Tomorrow night, we will mingle with a wider circle of our great city's elite—the entertainers and tastemakers, the wealthy and powerful corporate magnates and shipyard barons at the Finance Ball. But tonight, it's just those of us who share this common loss, and you, the Fathers, know me well, as I know you. So let us toast to our lost ones together."

It wasn't bad, Crash thought, raising her glass. "To Nomar Tralmat!"

"Nomar Tralmat!" the room yelled back, and drank.

Crash threw back a shot of pure water, then raised another glass of the same. "To Ovarto Bitolo-Bash!"

They mostly butchered the name, but an effort was made, and the crowd was that much sloppier.

Crash raised the final glass. "To—" She had to stop. A sob, unannounced, unbidden, had slipped quietly up from the depths of her and cut off the next word. Dammit. She wasn't even drinking, and here she was showing too much to a room full of enemies with their knives out. She laughed, turning the moment, she hoped, into a simple joke, nothing more, and forced away the sadness. "Prybolt Garavult!"

The crowd echoed her, drank again, and began chatting among themselves. She wished he was there beside her, waiting as she stepped down from the table, patting her on the back with a smug laugh and some little parable of encouragement.

Damn she missed him.

Instead of her best friend, though, the absolute last person Crash wanted to see made his way through the crowd toward her.

"Dizcaro," she said smugly as the slim, well-coiffed man strolled up nonchalantly and cracked a curt smile.

"Ongwa."

She nodded at Ovus Buckell, who was climbing onto a table himself, a little unsteadily, to address the room. "I see you've wrangled yourself a new client."

"Yes, you can imagine how they had reservations about you, considering . . ." Dizcaro let his vague hand motions finish the thought.

Crash dampened a surge of wrath. This wasn't the time for that. This was the time for information gathering. That was it.

"I don't know if the rumors about those horrific Nihil raiders being involved in this are true," Ovus declaimed with gusto, "but mark my words: Corellia is for Corellians! We don't need outsiders coming in here telling us how to live our lives—just look at that mess on Gus Talon!" Various boos and hisses sounded, but that was no surprise. The City Fathers hated unions, and of course they'd be quick to jump on board a completely nonexistent tie between union agitators and the Nihil. "And we especially don't need those Nihil *thugs*! Am I right?"

Some cheers went up; others grumbled. The longstanding debate about how open Corellia should be to non-Corellian shipbuilding companies rattled on. Ovus soaked it all in and managed to climb down without braining himself. Crash, for her part, managed not to groan.

"Oh, also," Dizcaro added as if it were an afterthought, "Varb Tenart arranged new talent for the gala tomorrow night."

Crash's eyes darted to the bar, where a dapper, gregarious Dug sat hobnobbing with some diplomat's wife. Varb Tenart organized all the celebrity appearances at fancy state shindigs. He was not particularly bright or nice, but he had a talent for networking and Crash got on with him all right, usually.

"He said Svi'no should probably take some time to recuperate," Dizcaro went on, "given the assassination attempt yesterday and all."

Crash had to wrestle with her own face to keep it from showing the explosion of irritation she felt. She hated when people pretended to care as a pretense for smarmy maneuvering. And the gala was a big deal. Crash had been counting on it both for the sheer amount of money it would bring her and the opportunity to gather more info about who knew what. "No one told me."

"Of course they didn't. The new guest of honor is Crufeela, the legendary Shani sing—"

"I *know* who Crufeela is," Crash snapped, getting closer every second to losing the battle to remain in control of her emotions. "And *legendary* is a stretch." She didn't like where any of this was going.

"Then you know she's one of my clients."

"Well, then hopefully you can steer her away from those endangered animals the gossip holos keep catching her eating."

"Which is—"

"I heard," Crash said, cheerful again now that Dizcaro had

presented her with such an easy target, "there were already some warrants out for her from environmental authorities in several systems."

Dizcaro plowed on, undeterred by Crash's jibe. "Which is why—"

"Good thing it's just a meet and greet, right? What if someone tried to make a song request while she was performing? She'd have to figure out how to lip-synch on the fly."

"*Which is why*," Dizcaro growled, "my team and I will be handling security for the gala now. You won't be needed. You're welcome to come, of course, to protect any of your own clients. If . . ." He let his voice trail off, mouth creasing into a cruel smile. A sleazeball, through and through. "If you have any left tomorrow night, of course."

Unbelievable.

Crash felt the urge to deck him but managed to hold off. Then Ovus Buckell's big grinning face popped up beside Dizcaro. "Ah, Crash, Crash," the Father of Finances cheesed. "It's so terrible what happened. Truly, I'm sorry for this terrible tragedy."

Crash just nodded; if she spoke it wouldn't go well, that much was clear.

Ovus squinted down at her like she was a lost child, face creased with mock concern. "I heard you found a scrap of Hyehole—"

"Prybolt," Crash corrected, knowing her voice sounded like pure fire, not caring even though she knew she should.

"Right—his fabric in one of your hound's teeth? Is that right? Goodness!"

Even Dizcaro looked visibly uncomfortable. There was just something off about the way this guy was going on, especially considering his own predecessor had likely died in the same incident.

"But you know what they say about Corellian hounds." Ovus chuckled, and that was when Crash knew, whatever he said next, she was going to hit him. She should've walked away right then, in that exact moment. Just walked away and taken a breather and come back refreshed. Instead, she stood there quietly while Ovus said, "They'll eat just about anything, heh, even wo—" And then she knocked him the kark out.

PART THREE

TWENTY-THREE

THE *STAR HOPPER*

Once, when Zeen was little, a glass storm had swept through one of the modest encampments where her people had settled. First a shrill wind howled across the sandy embankment where they'd set up their shacks. The spot had seemed too good to be true when they'd found it after a full day of getting kicked out of various residential areas. It was wide open, with tufts of grass popping up amid the dunes and a huge open sky above. Turned out, of course, there was indeed a reason the locals steered clear.

Just beyond the dunes, a small canyon led down to an underground basin. There, the interior temperature of the planet would rise very suddenly, liquefying all the sand that had blown in, and then drop again just as quickly. The result was a billion tiny shards of quartz, which would then get burped back out into the atmosphere by a series of tiny groundquakes, picked up by the whipping gusts coming in from a nearby coastline, and weaponized into vicious, pointy shards that could blast through the air fast enough to shred through clothing, flesh, tendon, bone.

Zeen had stood on a dune just outside camp and felt it coming. The world around her made it clear enough that something big was happening—the way the air changed so suddenly it made her ears pop, the icky thick smell of something burning, the violent bursts of wind that seemed to come out of nowhere. And even if she didn't understand what each change meant, the heaviness welling up inside left her no doubt about what they added up to: certain tragedy.

But there was something else she knew even more clearly: the feeling she had, that dread, that certainty that seemed to gift her with an awareness of things she knew to be beyond her . . . that was the Force. That dense, shimmering energy within her that would sometimes bubble up like a geyser from the depths. It was her one and only secret from the Elders, from her best friend, Krix, to whom she told absolutely everything . . . except this. The Elders forbade the use of the Force. It was too sacred to be encompassed or manipulated by living beings, and anyone who dared allow it to manifest within them was a heretic. A demon, even, according to some of the most ancient understandings.

Zeen didn't feel like a demon, but the Elders said all it took was using the Force once, and she didn't know if what she felt inside counted as using it or not. The worst part was, she could never ask, because what if it was? Then she'd be expelled from the only family she'd ever known, and she'd never see Krix again. Plus he and all the others would probably hate her. And maybe they'd be right to. Who wouldn't hate a demon?

So she had clenched her jaw against the restless, nervous feeling that crackled through her like lightning, tried to push it away, ignore it, wished it to become a void and vanish.

It didn't, though, and then she watched in horror as a maelstrom of tiny, sparkling shards exploded out of the ground just by the horizon and whipped through the air toward them.

Zeen turned and ran. Alarms bleated across the sky, and that deathlike rattle and tinkle grew louder.

Most of the community managed to make it into an abandoned underground shelter before the worst of the glass storm hit, but a few people refused and were never seen again. Zeen huddled close to Krix in the darkness as the wind howled over shrieks of terror and then anguish. And then all she heard was the wind.

She'd felt something similar on Trymant IV, the day

the Emergence from the hyperspace disaster had sent fiery chunks of debris careening down on Bralanak City. The day her life had changed forever.

And she felt it again now, sitting on the *Star Hopper* across from Lula Talisola, both of them still raw and joyous and nervous from the chaotic thrill of finally having ended Krix Kamarat's deadly rampage across the Outer Rim.

But this time . . . the feeling was different. It wasn't about the world outside. This feeling, the Force moving through her in sudden bright waves, spoke to the turmoil of her own heart. She didn't fully understand it, couldn't exactly name it; she just knew all the microscopic parts of her body felt like they were full of a strange, impossible light, something like fear, something—maybe—like love.

Was it just the sudden intoxication of victory? No. She'd finally learned to stop second-guessing the Force and trust it for what it was. But she still didn't know what it was trying to tell her. Everything seemed muddled, impossible.

Lula leaned forward across the small space between them and put her smiling face near Zeen's. "Spit it out."

Lula was always three steps ahead of everything, always seemed to have the world figured out, even at its most impossible and chaotic. But Zeen could feel turmoil in her, too. She just didn't know what to name it, or how to say it.

"I . . . feel . . . a lot of things . . . at the same time," she finally said, trying the technique Master Kantam had taught her a few months back of just saying each word slowly and making sure it was true, rather than spitting out whole sentences half-formed.

Lula sat back, nodded, her mouth still crescented into that gentle smile of hers that was like a song. "Me too." Then she put on her serious face. "Do you want to try to both say what we're feeling and maybe we can make sense of it together?"

Zeen couldn't meet her friend's eyes. She didn't know why. Everything felt like it was falling apart somehow, and they'd just finally, finally started putting it back together. "I . . . I don't know," she admitted, and it felt like a betrayal, but she didn't know why.

"Uh, Zeen," Farzala said, poking his head into the meditation room. "Krix said he'll only speak to you."

Zeen shook her head, standing. "Of course he did." She held out her hand to Lula, relief and disappointment warring inexplicably within her. Lula took it, not meeting Zeen's eyes, and rose. They walked side by side down the corridor toward the brig, an entire ocean of unsaid, impossible things floating in the silence between them.

Zeen didn't have the words. Even if she'd tried Kantam's each true word technique, nothing would've come out. She simply didn't understand whatever it was she felt.

Turmoil.

They stopped outside the quarters Master Yoda had lived in before he'd vanished on Quantxi. Zeen missed him in a way she'd only thought possible to feel about someone you'd known your whole life. But then, the Jedi seemed to have that effect—she'd only known any of them for a handful of months, and she trusted them all with her life and would've done anything to protect them.

A lot of Jedi had been lost in the past year, but Yoda's absence left a void in their small crew in a way that seemed deeper, irreparable. The tiny green sage had a way of welcoming everyone around him just by his very presence, that gentle laugh, the tiny wrinkles that reached away from his eyes.

And now he was who knew where, and even though they'd caught Krix, Zeen was pretty sure they needed Master Yoda more than ever to prepare for whatever was about to happen.

"Do you think he's coming back?" Zeen asked after they'd both taken a moment to silently reflect on Master Yoda.

Lula put on the face she had for when she was trying to look brave. "Definitely." Then her shoulders sagged, and her whole body seemed to deflate. "I just don't know when. But I do know he wouldn't want us to be standing here worrying about him."

Zeen nodded.

Lula tilted her chin at the door. "You want me to go with you?"

Zeen did and didn't at the same time. The answer to whether she wanted Lula to go with her was always yes. Period. But she knew Krix would either clam up with Lula there or try to play them off each other. It wouldn't work, but his flailing efforts at it would probably make Zeen want to hurt him even more than she already did.

She'd been planning on this meeting for a long time, and she didn't want anything to throw off her focus. She needed to know whatever the remnants of his Nihil cell were up to. A planet, a sector . . . just some scrap of a hint; they could figure the rest out from that, she was sure. But the galaxy was huge, and Nihil plans trended chaotic. There was no guessing from scratch.

"I do," she said. "But we both know what'll happen if you do."

Lula nodded. "I'll be right here." She took Zeen's hand, squeezed it once, and then stepped back as the door slid open.

Zeen wished she could just stand there, feeling Lula's fingers around hers, and then let their hands pull their bodies into a hug and take a long breath and sob out all the confusion. Instead she walked into the makeshift brig and stood in front of the boy she once would've given her life for, then had almost murdered, and now just wanted never to have to think about again.

"Well, here I am," Krix said from the shadows. His head was drooped, hands bound. "Ready to be sacrificed."

He was so hurt and predictable. That was a blessing, she supposed. "Is that what you'd like me to do, Krix?"

He looked up with a grim smile. "It doesn't matter. Everything is already in motion. There's nothing you can do to stop it. Killing me will only hurt you."

She pulled up a tiny stool and sat across from him, managing not to look too ridiculous on the Yoda-sized furniture. "That doesn't mean I wouldn't enjoy it, though."

That wiped his smile off, if only for a moment. "You've really fallen so far, haven't you? This is what they've done to you."

That was rich, coming from someone who'd blown up innocent bystanders and first responders by the dozens. But she kept the quips to herself. There was no point in a tit for tat. It was time to get what she came for. She held out her hand, raising one eyebrow, and wiggled her fingers at Krix's forehead, straining with concentration.

"Wha—what are you doing?" Krix demanded.

"Shh."

"What are you trying to do?" he raged. "Stop that!"

"It's going to happen one way or another, so you might as well stop yelling."

"What's going to happen?"

"I'm using the Force to extract all your secrets. Here, let me help you understand." She pointed at her outstretched hand. "Imagine this is one of those sanitation sweep-crawlers we used to see, and the Force is its tractor beam, right? And all your plans and hopes and dreams are, well"—she smiled—"trash."

"You can't do that! That's not the Jedi way!"

Zeen shrugged. "Do you see any Jedi here?"

She was doing no such thing, of course. The Force didn't let people read minds, not like that anyway, and even if it did she probably wasn't skilled enough to use it that way. But Krix didn't need to know that. They'd both grown up hearing the same horror stories about Force users. To hear the Elders tell it, people like her could commit all kinds of twisted magic, from turning people into brain-dead warriors to raising the dead. Mind reading wouldn't be a big stretch for Krix to believe.

"Wow," she said after a few moments of enjoying watching him squirm. "You all really have something terrible in store, huh."

Krix scowled. "You're bluffing."

Zeen nodded sagely. "Sure I am."

"I know you, Zeen Mrala. I know when you're bluffing."

"Okay, Krix. I'm just sorry you pinned so many of your hopes on that Er'Kit girl, considering . . ."

"Wait, how do you . . . ? What do you mean? Considering what?"

"How do you think we found you, Krix? Did you think it was luck? Or the Force?" She shook her head with mock sadness. "It's too bad. Seemed like you two had a really nice partnership going there."

"She had potential, and I was showing her the ropes, taking her under my wing, like . . . Doesn't matter. What did she do?"

"She's been feeding us information all along," Zeen said smugly. An absolute lie, but a credible one. "You think she just blew up the Takodana temple to impress you and be welcomed back a hero? I mean—she did, but only after we told her to, knowing that would get her the right kind of attention and move her up in the ranks fast."

"Stop lying!" Krix spat. "The Jedi would never blow up their own temple just to—"

"It was scheduled for demolition anyway," Zeen said. "The Republic has been upgrading temples all over the Outer Rim as part of the Great Works program. Also to upgrade their defenses because of people like you." She sent him a sneer made from pure disdain. Then she softened. "Anyway, she played you, Krix, and all the Nihil, and now it seems your whole little plan rests on her shoulders, which is a shame because—"

"You're lying!" Krix shouted, and Zeen knew she had him. "She may have betrayed me, sure, but it was to take over, not help the Republic! There's no way she was feeding you info all along! That's not! Possible! And you know why? Because I taught her everything she knows! I introduced her to my contacts, and I sent her to Gus T—" He caught himself one word too late. There were two moons of Corellia that started with *Gus*, and only one had a *T* in the next word.

Zeen stood. Nodded. She hoped she'd never see Krix again, but she knew no matter what, this was how she'd remember him. Pathetic, out of breath, defeated and outwitted and powerless and enraged. The world refused to fit into the simplistic little box he'd tried to squeeze it into, no matter how much he screamed and blew things up.

"You said something to me once," Zeen said as he caught his breath, still shaken from his own admission. "When you were trying to get me to run away with you. You said I could just stop using the Force and it would go away. And we could be normal." She shook her head, suddenly calmer than she'd felt in weeks, if not months. "But that's what I'd been doing my whole life. Hoping the power inside me would go away. Lessening myself for others. For *you*." The word came out like a curse. "Wishing I was *normal*. I'm so, so glad I found people who love me for who I am and not for some version of myself that had to be lesser to make them comfortable."

"I always lo—" Krix panted.

"Keep it," Zeen said, already at the doorway. "That moment? That's when I knew you had to be stopped. That you would become a curse on this galaxy now that you'd linked up with people who brought out the worst in you. I just thought—I thought I had to do it myself, because I thought you were my responsibility. But you're not. You're not my problem. You're just some kid I knew. You and I have nothing to do with each other."

She let the door slide closed on his screams. Then she fell into Lula's arms with what felt like the longest sigh of her life. She realized she was laughing. And crying some, too. And for a few moments, all she knew was Lula—the gentle, familiar smell of her, her shoulder rising and falling with each breath, the beating of her heart, and the comforting swirl of the Force as it flowed through both of them.

She finally released the hug, wiped some tears from her eyes, and said, "I'm okay. We have to . . ."

"I know," Lula said, already back in go mode. They headed down the corridor together, the moment already morphed into a new one—their partnership easily sliding from delicate intimacy to strategic badassery without a beat missed. "Gus Talon. There are reports of escalating unrest there after a union dispute and a bombing. CorSec has deployed there from Corellia, since the moon doesn't have much security of its own."

"The others . . ." Zeen said, still finding it hard to make full sentences.

Lula looked crestfallen. "I tried to raise them on the comms, and no one's answering."

"What?" Zeen gaped. "*None* of them?"

Lula flailed for an explanation, her eyes sad. "They could be somewhere there isn't a good comm system, or hiding or something. Who knows?"

"What's the last we've heard from them?" The road ahead suddenly felt like it was unfolding before Zeen in a straight line. It did that sometimes; whether it was the Force or simply the sheer momentum of knowing what had to be done, Zeen wasn't sure. In a way, *everything* was the Force, so what did it matter? She was already pivoting toward the hangar.

Lula stayed on pace with her, scanning through a datapad

as they walked. "Masters Kantam and Cohmac checked in upon arrival a while back, and everything seemed fine. We haven't heard anything from Ram or Reath, but that's not unusual. With everything going on, though . . ."

"There are no units available to reinforce them," Zeen finished, already hitting the release button on one of the lock-down mechanisms of a small shuttle. "And the *Star Hopper* needs to bring Krix back to Starlight."

Lula's face fell. "You're going."

"We don't know what's happening, but it's definitely bad. Sabata Krill is out there, planning something, and our friends are about to walk into it, if they haven't already." It felt good to be in motion, to be about to leave. It felt . . . clear. Zeen could get some distance from everything that had just happened with Krix, and from Lula and all she meant, whatever that was. And hopefully save her friends, too.

"I'll make sure Krix gets delivered to Starlight," Lula said. "Zeen, wait, just . . ."

Zeen froze, a duffel bag halfway closed in her hands. She didn't have any more emotions left in her. It was easier just to run away.

"Be careful," Lula said to Zeen's back. "I know I'm not supposed to, but . . . I need you."

Zeen nodded. Whispered, "I need you, too."

"I feel like you're not coming back."

"I am," Zeen said, even though she wasn't sure if it was true. She turned around, found she couldn't meet Lula's eyes.

"Cham-Cham is in my room." Lula knew better than anyone that Zeen would never leave her pet cru behind for long. "Take care of him for me while I'm gone?"

Lula nodded. "Of course, but . . ." Her words trailed off—probably there were none that could describe how she felt. Zeen knew that was true for herself, anyway. So instead of responding, she stepped forward and put her forehead to Lula's. They stood there for a moment, eyes closed, amid the rumbling engines and smell of ship fuel.

Then Zeen stepped back, wiped something out of her eye, and climbed up the ladder to the cockpit.

"May the Force be with you," they both said as the engines rumbled to life and Lula took a step back. She was smiling, Zeen realized. Zeen had been expecting Lula to look grief-stricken or desperate, to display almost anything besides the calm, clear-eyed serenity that radiated from her now. But of course—the girl was unstoppable, Zeen thought, and that was why she loved her.

The truth of it, the sudden certainty, hit her like a punch in the gut. It was undeniable. But she managed to shove away all the complications and possibilities and tragedies that love might entail and instead just match her friend's smile, that glow.

Stay alive for me, Lula mouthed. *Please.*

Zeen blew one kiss through the viewport as the deck fell away, and then pointed her shuttle toward the stars and blasted off.

TWENTY-FOUR

CORONET CITY

It had been ages since Kantam Sy had been in a good bar brawl.

Sure, this was technically more of an after-hours lounge of some kind, and the vibe leaned more toward art gallery than backwater dive. But still—that particular explosive violence that erupted when too many bodies ingested too much alcohol while holding too many secrets, that was the same from slums to ballrooms, Nar Shaddaa to Coruscant.

And Kantam had to admit, as a plush stool whizzed by and clobbered a muscular Quarren, there was a part of them that still relished the chaos of it all.

As with all these drunken skirmishes, everything had

been pretty calm until very suddenly it wasn't. Clearly, plenty of attendants had something—several somethings—to hide from one another and most were doing a halfway decent job of keeping their cards close while trying to draw others out. And then within seconds it went from cheerful guffaws and pointed jibes to broken teeth and probable concussions.

Kantam ducked another stool—who was throwing those?—and took a step back so they were shoulder to shoulder with Cohmac, who was taking it all in with a sharp eye. "Did you see what happened?" Kantam asked. "I was busy keeping my eye on our extravagantly outfitted Padawans."

"The girl in the middle there," Cohmac said, tipping his chin to where a flash of bright pink hair could be seen bouncing up and down amid the fray. "The one who called the meeting. The famous Crash, if I'm not mistaken."

"Ah, yes." Kantam watched Crash drop-kick a hulking Crolute and then leap out of the way as a silverback Wookiee followed up with a one-two punch, effectively ending the Crolute for the foreseeable future. "She seems to be holding her own. How are the boys?"

Cohmac angled his head to a far corner, where Reath and Ram lurked in the shadows, eyes darting around the room.

"Good lads," Kantam said. "But also what the stars are they doing here? And dressed like Scarlet Skulls, no less!"

Cohmac shrugged. "I look forward to finding out."

The Quarren stumbled up, swinging those giant muscly

arms indiscriminately as she charged back into the fray. A tiny, squawking Aleena in an upscale dinner suit tried to talk sense to her and immediately got laid out.

"Can you make heads or tails of it?" Cohmac asked.

Kantam narrowed their eyes at the center of the room, where Crash was reeling from an uppercut that some kind of four-armed furry creature had delivered before scampering off. "I do believe they managed to set that one off, probably with an off-color remark about her Grindalid friend from the holo, and with two opposing teams of bodyguards on the loose, plus a couple of tipsy politicos and their spouses, well . . . it was a blast chamber."

"Sounds about right," Cohmac said, walking carefully into the melee. "Shall we take the opportunity to have a word with our wards?"

"Indeed," Kantam said, falling into stride with him. "They do have explaining to do."

They let the Force guide them through the smashing bottles and colliding bodies. Kantam only once had to pause and slide two fingers through the air, tossing a Gran to the side who had been careening toward them.

"A word?" Cohmac said as he and Kantam appeared on either side of the Padawans. "But not here," he added with a tight grin. "Unless I'm mistaken, you've both taken a gruesome and lifelong vow of silence."

Reath and Ram nodded, eyes wide, and all four of them

slipped through a nearby passageway into a side room clearly meant for clandestine meetings.

"We can explain," Ram blurted as soon as the door slid closed.

"Oh, I'm very much looking forward to this," Cohmac said with a wily grin.

"Crash asked us for a favor," Reath said, stepping in front of Ram.

"And she showed us the shipyards where they're building the MPO cruisers!" Ram said.

"Was it quite wizard?" Kantam asked.

"Extremely!" Ram yelled before clamming up at a nudge from Reath.

"She said she's been investigating the disappearance and asked for our help," Reath said. "And she's quite connected to Coronet City politics, so . . ." His voice trailed off.

"So you dressed up like long-dead child assassins and infiltrated a secret meeting," Cohmac finished helpfully.

"Exactly!" Ram said. "The shipyards were *really* cool!"

"You didn't want to let us know where you were, perhaps?" Kantam suggested. "In case you needed backup?"

"I did. *We* did," Reath said. "Want to, that is. We did want to. But we didn't actually do it. But anyway, here you are! The Force provided."

Cohmac narrowed his eyes at the Padawan, but both Masters were a little too amused to bother reprimanding them much. "Uh-huh. Did you at least find out anything useful amidst all this sightseeing and dressing up?"

"We may have, actually," Reath said. "Crash is pretty convinced one of these City Father guys had some involvement."

"Do we trust Crash?" Kantam asked.

Reath and Ram traded glances. They'd become so close in such a short amount of time, Kantam marveled, already sharing those quiet, unspoken understandings that were the hallmark of Jedi teamwork.

"We do," Reath said. "And not just because she was nice to us. I really do believe she's both on the level and an extremely resourceful ally."

"And she's good in a fight," Ram added. "Plus she knows, like, *everybody* and about a billion languages."

Cohmac unleashed a large, generous smile, the kind that made anyone studying under him feel like they'd really done something special. "Sounds like they've done much better than we have, Kantam."

Kantam nodded. "All we did was sit in a waiting room for several hours and find out a little more about the escalating conflict on Gus Talon, where apparently just about *all* of Corellia's Jedi and planetary security forces have been deployed, and then we were kicked out by an ornery Republic minister and then unceremoniously summoned out of meditation by the same minister to come here."

"Wow," Ram said. "That's an ordeal."

"Can we go make sure Crash is all right then?" Reath asked, a slightly charming anxiousness in his unsteady voice.

"It seemed like she has quite a team doing that already," Cohmac said, "but I don't see why we shouldn't give them a hand."

TWENTY-FIVE

CORONET CITY

Ram's comlink buzzed with an incoming call just as he was heading out the door behind the others. "Uh, be right with you!" he called, and dipped back into the side room.

A tiny holo of Zeen Mrala appeared before him. "Oh, thank the stars!" she gasped. "You're okay!"

"Of course we're okay, Zeen. What's going—"

"Wait, is that a skull painted on your face?" she demanded, older sister mode fully activated. "What's going on? *Are* you okay?"

Ram rolled his eyes. "Long story, and yes! We are okay!

Just in a bit of a bar-fight-type situation is all, but it's fine. The others are handling it."

"A *bar fight*?" Zeen boggled. "What in the—"

"Zeen!" Ram insisted. "Talk to me! Did you catch Krix or what? Where's Lula?"

"Yes!" Zeen said. "And Lula's okay. She's taking him to Starlight." Then she looked at something ahead of her and adjusted her hands.

She was piloting something, Ram realized. "Yay!" he said. "Congrats! Where are you?"

Zeen turned back to face him. "Coming to where you are. Well, now that I know you're okay, I'm going to stop by a moon nearby first. Krix's second-in-command is launching a plot of some kind on Gus Talon. I'm going to—"

"Wait," Ram said. "Come to us." He glanced around. "We *are* okay, but something's going on here and I think it's big. Anyway, there are a bunch of Jedi on or heading to Gus Talon right now, so I think they can handle whatever's happening without you. Here, on the other hand, we might need all the help we can get."

"I . . ." Zeen thought it over. She looked like she had a hundred hopes and fears running through her head at once—like half of her wanted to turn around and the other wanted to just keep flying and flying and never look back, and the two halves were so strong they were threatening to tear her apart.

"Plus," he added, hoping it would help, "we miss you!"

Zeen let out a long breath, her eyes closed. "Okay," she finally said. "I'll let you know when I'm close."

"Woo-hoo!" Ram yipped. "I'll tell the others we caught Krix and you're on your way!"

He headed down the hall back into the lounge area, where the brawl had finally dwindled—a few drunken, bruised-up heavies still stumbled around trying to regain their shattered pride, but Crash's people were quickly collecting them and sending them on their way.

Crash sat on a table near the door, nursing a black eye and sulking.

"Don't say it," she warned.

"Say what?" Ram asked.

"Bodyguards don't get emotionally involved," Crash spat out in a cruel imitation of her own voice.

"We're not here to get revenge tonight," Svi'no added helpfully, emerging from the shadows nearby. "Tonight! The game is . . ."

The whole room turned to them and yelled, as one: "RECONAISSANCE!"

Crash, to her credit, burst out laughing with everyone else. She could take a joke, even at her own expense, Ram thought warmly as he and Svi'no helped her stand on top of the table again.

TWENTY-SIX

CORONET CITY

"Look, everyone," Crash announced, "I know I messed up. . . ."

Assorted nos and nahs arose from the gathering group of bodyguards. Crash waited a beat, and then everyone burst out laughing again with a chorus of, "Okay, yeah you messed up," and "Yeah, that was a bad." She continued: "Also, we lost the Finance Ball contract for tomorrow night." Several groans and dramatic sighs. "Which is important both for our company to stay afloat *and* because after tonight's events, I still suspect that *someone* who was here had *something* to do with whatever happened to Prybolt and Ovarto. My droid, Ten-Kayt, will be collecting and collating whatever info you may have gathered, so please let her know what you got when you have a moment. But either way, it's clear there are more than the usual foul dealings abounding in Coronet City."

"There was a lot of chatter about the ball!" someone yelled.

Fezzonk raised a hand. "I heard it, too. No one seems to know what's going to happen, but nervous consensus is, *something*."

Theories and curses rose up as various debates broke out.

"All right! All right!" Crash yelled, calming them down some. "That makes it even more important that we get inside tomorrow, and this game is far from over, my friends! In fact—"

The main entrance across the room slid open, and the place got very, very quiet suddenly as Dizcaro walked in, both hands raised.

"Hey, hey," he said, face bruised and grave. "I come in peace. Empty-handed, see? And alone."

"Uh-huh," Crash said. "Say what you gotta say and be off, Diz."

He approached, glancing side to side warily, and stood before her. "I just wanted to say that I know we have our disagreements, but that doesn't change that what Ovus said tonight was wrong. It was out of line. And I can't apologize on his behalf, but I can say that I, personally, was disgusted."

"Yeah, this shiner on my eye says differently," Crash grunted.

"Crash, you know better than anyone that regardless of my opinion about who he is or what he said, our job—both of our jobs—is to protect the client. That's all that matters."

"Is it?" Crash said, her face suddenly open, the question a real one, not a quick clapback. And then, when Dizcaro just stared at her, she glanced away. "I wonder. . . ."

"Well, anyway, I'm sorry it had to get like . . ." He gestured to the wrecked lounge around them. "Like this. It shouldn't have."

"Not sorry enough to stop trying to profit off our vanished team members, though, are you?" Crash jibed.

Dizcaro turned, scowling. "All right, look, you know what? I just came to . . . Never mind."

"Dizcaro," Crash called, her face making it clear she was serious. "I accept your apology."

He turned around, bowed elaborately, and then saw himself out.

"All right," Crash said once the door had slid closed behind him, "we're still in this."

"How?" someone demanded gruffly. "The gala is tomorrow night!"

Crash scanned the room for who had spoken. It was Barchibar, of course. "That's why we're still in this," she yelled. "If it was tonight, we might be in trouble!"

"I heard Crufeela has the guest of honor spot now," 10-K8 said. "How are we going to take over protection for her?"

Crash's grin got wider. "Oh, we're not. We're going to give her something more exciting to do that night."

Smeemarm lowered herself upside down from one of the ironwork chandeliers. "How are we going to even get in to—"

"We'll reach out from a contact she's sure to trust," Crash said, holding up a comlink.

"Is that Dizcaro's?" Fezzonk gaped approvingly.

Crash beamed. "Nabbed it while we were tussling. Mama always said don't ever let getting your ass beat go to waste." A cheer went up.

"So I'm back on the roster?" Svi'no asked, sounding, Crash noticed, a little disappointed.

"No, my dear. That would be too obvious a play, and even if Varb Tenart is insincere with his concern for your well-being, I'm guessing you'd rather work the party from this end of things."

Svi'no smiled her appreciation, then asked: "Who's gonna do it?"

Crash turned to the crowd. "That's where I need your help. Making a star overnight is no problem, really. Not for us. We have the media, and more importantly, we have the street. Plus we have the reigning queen of pop on our side!" She nodded at Svi'no, who gave a loving wave. "So we make a star. Then Varb will come prowling for them when he finds out Crufeela's gonna be a no-show. Question is, who? We need someone totally anonymous to Corellian societies both high and low, who also knows how to work a room."

"Ooh!" Ram yelled from the back, his hand shooting up. "Ooh!"

Crash pointed at him, unable to contain her smile. This kid was too great. "You're my favorite, Ram, but I'm not sure if you're right for the part!"

He looked horrified for a moment, then realized she was kidding. "No, but I have the *perfect* person!"

TWENTY-SEVEN

CORONET CITY

After hours *at the after-hours lounge,* Reath Silas thought. Once the meeting had ended and most of the bodyguards had spread out into the Corellian night—on various complex missions assigned by Crash—he and Ram had finally gotten a chance to wash off all that red face paint. Refreshed and feeling pretty good, he strolled out of the bathroom to find what looked more like a quiet, relaxed gathering of old friends than an urgent propaganda-war strategy session.

Crash had somehow found a comfortable position with her shins pointing upward along the back of one of those big leather chairs, her chin cradled in her palms, elbows pressing into the cushion, eyes level with the central table. On it, they'd positioned some holoprojectors showing various data points, including a big map of Coronet City and another of its underground tunnel system. Svi'no, the famous singer, was splayed out on the same chair, partially over Crash, partially draped across the armrest, also remarkably comfortable-looking. Cohmac and Kantam shared a couch on the other side of the table. They had apparently made themselves right at home, conversing animatedly about some finer tactical point or another with Ram, who sat perched on a footstool, fiddling with some kind of tiny machine, as always. Crash's droid, 10-K8, was zipping around, checking various coordinates against whatever info she had on her datapad and singing a little ditty to herself.

"Hey, Ram," Reath began, pulling up a barstool and plopping onto it, "did Zeen say anything about the Er'Kit Nihil girl?"

Crash nearly fell out of her chair trying to hurl herself upright. "Did you say *Er'Kit*?"

"Yeah," Ram said. "Two Nihil sisters defected when they attacked Takodana. Well, just one of them defected. The other—Sabata Krill—it turned out was just fake defecting to flush out her own sister. Then she destroyed the Jedi temple before escaping back to her group."

"Red skin?" Crash demanded, finally standing, both her fists clenched at her sides. "Tall and gangly?"

"How did you—" Reath started.

"Crash!" Svi'no yelled, floating up in the air and rounding on the girl. "What have you been hiding?"

Crash put both hands up, suddenly on the defense. "Look, everyone. I'm *trying* to do better, okay? I am a work in progress. I really am trying, though."

"Well," Reath pressed, "what have you got?"

TWENTY-EIGHT

CORONET CITY

Crash pulled out yet another holoprojector. "You talk, I'll get this cued up. Tell me everything you know."

"It's not much more than what I said," Ram admitted. "From what we can gather, all that maneuvering and destruction earned her a second-in-command position to Krix."

"Who's Krix?" Crash asked.

"He's another one who managed to vault ahead into an upper-echelon rank among the Nihil through sheer violence," Reath said. "Our forces just captured him tonight, ending a brutal rampage throughout the Outer Rim."

Crash placed the holoprojector on the central table. "And you're telling me he's been working closely with . . ." A flickering image appeared—the same one Ram had shown Reath on their way to Corellia to catch him up on the mission: a Grindalid in a coverall suit, stumbling through the streets of Coronet City, terrified.

Crash hit a button and the holo froze. "Her," Crash said, pointing at a long figure just visible over the Grindalid's shoulder. She was tall and gangly all right, especially for an Er'kit, and Reath could see her red ears sticking out on either side of what looked like a Nihil breather mask.

Ram jumped up. "That's her! That's Sabata Krill! But this is from an earlier moment in the recording. We didn't see this!" Then he turned to Crash, realizing what that meant. "You . . ."

"Yes," Crash said solemnly. "I cut this part out before I sent it to the authorities."

"You didn't even tell *us* about it," Svi'no complained, her eyes sharp on Crash. "What if we had . . . what if we had run into this person while we were looking into all this?"

"I *had* to keep it close," Crash insisted, "because I had to see who knew there was an Er'Kit involved without seeing the footage! That's how this works!" Information was power, sometimes the only power Crash had. And when things got as tangled and vicious as they were now, well . . . one had to grasp for whatever power they could get. But this was all going so, so wrong, so, so quickly, and she had no idea how to make it better.

"But *me*, Crash?" Svi'no growled. "You thought I might've known?"

"No!" Crash said. "That's not it! When was I going to tell just you, Svi'no? We haven't had time!"

"Maybe if you weren't always busy with ten thousand other things and people that you have to protect, you'd have noticed that I'm right here, ready to be confided in!"

The room seemed suddenly very, very quiet. Was Svi'no saying she wanted Crash to pay more attention to her? That was certainly a better problem to have than Crash being an untrustworthy secretmonger who couldn't let anyone she cared about get too close!

Svi'no looked more shocked than anyone else by what she'd just said.

"Uh . . ." Ram said, nudging between the two women, who were just staring at each other. "I know this is, like, a *moment* of some kind? But we have to . . . you know, figure this situation out? Quickly!"

Crash snapped out of it and turned to address the Jedi, who were all turning their wide eyes her way. "I'm sorry I didn't share this earlier. I do have trust issues, but in this case, no offense, I only just met you."

"That's understandable," Kantam said. They had kind eyes and a smile that seemed to understand deeper secrets of the universe than Crash would ever fathom. She liked them.

And appreciated the lifeline. "Especially given our interaction with Minister Fendirfal earlier. She's the one you turned the holo over to, correct?"

"Yep," said Crash. Svi'no's still shocked glare burned into the side of her face. She thought if she turned to look at the girl, she might get slapped or she might get kissed, and she had no idea which. Part of her was dying to find out; the more reasonable part concentrated on the task at hand. "I'm glad you see my predicament. The Republic as a whole, I have no problem with. But some of our liaison ministers and local politicos, well . . . you've already had your first experience. So you can see why I've kept my cards a little close."

Cohmac rose. "Indeed. No need to explain further." He glanced warily at Svi'no. "To us, anyway. I can only speak for us, of course." Then he turned to Ram. "Padawan Jomaram, what else did Zeen say?"

"Gus Talon," Ram said. "She was heading to Gus Talon to stop Sabata. I convinced her we needed her here more."

"Good move," Crash said. "Gus Talon has all the help it needs right now."

"That's my concern, too," Cohmac said, massaging his goatee gallantly. "Particularly with the shipyards being here."

"I've been thinking that, too," Kantam added. "They must be impossible to fully protect on a regular day. But with the majority of Coronet City's larger defense forces offworld . . ."

"We didn't have much trouble getting in today," Reath

pointed out. "Just two guards at a checkpoint, and they weren't at their best."

Crash started pacing. "Those were muni cops. Nomar Tralmat—the guy who disappeared the other night—had just hired a bunch of new ones specifically to keep the shipyards safe, what with all the excitement around the Anzellan working on those cruisers."

"Which are extremely wizard, by the way," Ram said. "If you get a chance, you should definitely—"

"The thing is," Crash went on, "the guy who replaced him, Ovus—"

"The guy you sucker punched earlier?" Cohmac asked.

"That one, yeah. If he'd been plotting with some Nihil to take out Tralmat and take over the munis, wouldn't he immediately, I don't know, fire all the new hires? Or have all the munis disarmed or something? Why go through the trouble of a political assassination just to keep things the way they were?"

"And he was railing against the Nihil in his speech," Reath said. "Not that that really means much."

Crash shook her head. "The promise of a politician is trash, as the old Corellian saying goes." She stopped pacing, scratched the back of her neck, and scowled. "All right, everyone. It's almost midnight. We have a plan to put into place and a random Mikkian girl to make famous by the morning. Let's get started!"

TWENTY-NINE

CORONET CITY

"This seems like an incredibly reckless plan," Reath said as they headed out into the dark streets of Coronet City.

Ram wiggled his eyebrows. "I know! I love it!"

Reath grinned in spite of himself. "Of course you do. I kinda do, too, to be honest. I'm just surprised the Masters let us handle it without them."

"They're big into learning by doing these days," Ram said, "in case you hadn't noticed. They probably never got to do anything as Padawans, and they want us to have an easier go of it."

Reath ran a hand absently through his hair. "I don't know. Kantam's master was Yoda. He seemed like he'd be pretty fun."

"Yoda . . ." Ram said in an awed whisper. "You met him?"

Up ahead, Smeemarm, the gangly Arcona with a triangular head who ran the underground tunnel ops for Crash's team, darted back and forth through the dark alley, checking for traps or attackers. Her bulbous eyes glittered green in the shadows.

"Just briefly," Reath said. "And I was at some events with him. But with Master Yoda, you could just feel his wisdom from a kilometer away, his power. I wish . . ." He paused. The sudden swell of emotion had caught him off guard. He'd barely known Yoda, and now the Jedi Master was gone without a trace and no one knew where. And he might never come back. Everyone said they'd know if he had died, they would feel it, but . . . would they really? Or what if he hadn't died but was unconscious somewhere, in a ditch or something, just waiting to die? Or being kept alive medically while his body rotted? Reath shuddered, trying to swallow back all the horror stories he was telling himself.

"You okay?" Ram asked. They were approaching the end of the alley; a mellow golden light seemed to radiate from the street up ahead.

"Yeah." Reath shook it off. "Just worried about Master Yoda, you know? Even though, like I said, I barely met him."

"Oh, I know," Ram said. "I literally never met him and I

spend at least an hour a day trying to stop making up nightmare scenarios of what happened to him!"

Reath had to smile. Leave it to Ram to be right there with him, even when it came to doubts and fears.

"Not very Jedi, I know," Ram admitted.

Reath patted his shoulder. "We're doing our best. Being a Jedi doesn't mean not having a heart. If Master Yoda were here, he'd probably say, 'Forgive himself, a Jedi must, mm? Not being ruled by fear does not mean not feeling any fear at all, mm!' "

Ram chuckled. "Sounds about right."

They rounded the corner and stopped, mouths open wide. They'd stepped onto a large boulevard. It had been cordoned off from vehicle traffic, so people could stroll leisurely along the cobblestones beneath the gentle glow of gas lanterns. On either side, cafes and saloons had set up outdoor dining tables, and flashing signs announced various entertainment venues with neon excitement.

"Isn't it, like, after midnight?" Ram asked, his eyes lit up by the spectacle ahead.

"On Coruscant," Reath said with wonder, "there are spots open late, sure, but most of the ones I've seen . . . you wouldn't want to be in without a protective suit."

"Boys?" Smeemarm called from up ahead. "You okay?"

"Yeah," Reath assured her. "Just . . . impressed."

She whirled around to appreciate the shops and restaurants. "Ah, yes! We locals forget how lovely the city can be until an offworlder comes through and is taken by the thrill of it! That's why they call us the Golden City, you know?"

"It's perfect," Ram said.

"This is the Kalamu District. Most of the hotels are here, so when we get in touch with Crufeela, she'll probably be staying somewhere nearby. Plus, there's an all-night market, so all our needs will be met! You ready?" She held out the comlink Crash had nicked from Dizcaro. "Who's doing it?"

Reath and Ram traded glances.

"I got it," Reath said, taking the comlink.

"You sure?" Ram asked, a skeptical eyebrow raised.

"Absolutely! I'm the more even-keeled one."

"*What?* You are chaos incarnate!"

"Yeah, yeah, give me the script. This means you get to rustle up the goods."

Ram passed him a datapad, and Reath pulled up the script Crash had written out for them. " 'Yes, this is Borgo Val. I work for Dizcaro,' " Reath practiced.

"Maybe don't try to change your voice so much," Smeemarm suggested. "Especially since Crufeela doesn't know you, so you don't have to disguise who you are. Just be someone different."

Reath nodded. "Just be someone different, got it."

Ram rubbed his eyes. "Hoo boy."

"Quiet, you," Reath snapped. "I got this."

"Acting isn't about pretending to be someone else," Smeemarm went on. "It's about finding someone else inside you and using that little shard to *become* someone else, hm?"

"That sounds confusing," Ram said.

"Well, good thing you don't have to worry about it," Reath said. He pushed the button to contact Crufeela.

"Dizcaro, my love," a high-pitched voice sang out. "I have been waiting for you!"

For a moment, all any of them could do was stare back and forth among one another in horror.

"Diz? Are you there?"

"Ah, yes," Reath finally said through his cringe. Then he changed voices unintentionally. "Well, no, rather." Then cringed even deeper. Why had he done that? "That is," he said going back to his normal voice. "It's me, ah . . ." Ram snatched the forgotten datapad and held it up in front of Reath's face, pointing urgently at the script. "Borgo Val!"

"Oh," Crufeela said with obvious disappointment. "Did something happen to my Diz?"

"Ah, no, ma'am," Reath assured her. "Quite the opposite in fact! Nothing at all happened to him!"

"That's good, but then why are you calling me at this late hour?"

"Yes, well, exactly that." Reath tried to ignore Ram's squinting and Smeemarm's blank stare. "Hrrrrrg, see the thing is, ah! Ahhhhh, that Mister Dizcaro actually in fact has would like you, rather, to join him for a one dinner."

Ram bit his fist and walked away.

"Oh!" Crufeela said brightly. "Of course!"

"It's a special dinner," Reath went on, back on script. "One with a very special main course!"

"Is that main course . . . Dizcaro?" the singer suggested.

"No!" Reath yelled. "Absolutely not!"

"Oh."

"It's something better!" His voice had gone high-pitched. Why? What was happening? Everything was sweaty. Smeemarm was still staring at him. "Way, uh, way better! Something"—he checked the script—"rare and incredibly intelligent. Hint, hint."

"Oh?" He thought maybe he heard the moment when whatever had to click finally clicked for Crufeela. "Oh! Oh, Diz . . . He's such a thoughtful man! Just give me a moment to get myself ready! Is he picking me up here at the hotel?"

"Ah, no, ma'am." This would be the hard part, Reath knew. He spat it out. "He sent me to, but he didn't tell me which hotel you're at. . . ."

"Oh, that's odd. I'm at the Feather, of course. I always stay here."

"Yes, yes, of course," Reath said. "I'll be right there, ma'am. Take your time getting ready, no hurry!"

"Why, yes I—"

Reath ended the call and let out a loud sigh. "Sheeeeeesh!"

Smeemarm blinked at him. "That was an attempt."

"I did it though!" Reath argued. "We got what we needed!"

"Is it over?" Ram called from halfway up the block. "I just couldn't listen anymore. I couldn't."

"I can't wait till it's your turn," Reath sniped. "You'll see."

Ram walked back over, shaking his head. "All I have to do is go get the thingymadoo. I'm good."

"I was going to go with you," Smeemarm said to Ram. "But I think I'll be accompanying the nervous one to pick up the singer. He may need someone who can speak Basic. You will go with Tangor to retrieve the item."

Ram looked up as a huge furry shape emerged from a nearby alley. "We've had a Wookiee trailing us this whole time? And now I get to hang out with her? Perfection!"

THIRTY

CORONET CITY

Ram didn't speak Shyriiwook, so they walked in silence through the crowds of tourists and revelers along Kalamu Boulevard. Still, Ram felt like Tangor probably would've shredded an entire battalion of attackers to keep him safe, and not just because it was her job, either. Tangor seemed like the type who, once she knew someone was on her team for real, was ready to do anything for them. He had to constantly suppress the urge to hug her, except he only came up to her waist, and since she was walking ahead of him it would basically mean getting a mouthful of Wookiee butt hair.

So he kept his hug to himself for the moment, and

anyway, the whole glowing golden city seemed to present itself to him in a marvelous panorama of sights, sounds, and smells. They turned off the main avenue and wound through quiet side streets lit by globes of incandescent gas, in what Ram imagined had to be the old-city part of town. Little bakeries churned away through the night, sending a warm smell of fresh-baked dough into the misty air. A few Twi'lek kids ran past, obviously up way past their bedtime, with an old man who must've been their grandpa waddling along in their wake. Somewhere nearby—a rooftop, Ram thought—a band was going absolutely berserk to the screams of a small crowd.

Then the thick blubber-and-salt smell of fish took over everything, and they turned into a dark plaza beneath a cathedral, where several stands had been set up and groups of vendors in long bibs hawked their freshly caught specialties in about ten different languages.

Tangor led Ram along the edge of the market to a bundar tree at the foot of the cathedral, where a long-snouted Kubaz stood, looking every possible flavor of shady. Kubaz didn't speak Basic, and neither did Wookiees. None of this was going to be easy, Ram thought, steeling himself. But he'd figure it out.

He pulled up the datapad and scrolled to the name of the animal he was supposed to acquire.

"Vo'vrrrr grangrrrak?" the merchant asked, which Ram hoped meant, "What can I do for you?"

"Barat-karabak," he pronounced carefully. "One, please."

He'd never heard of barat-karabaks, probably because they were apparently endangered or something, but he hoped they were small and easy to carry.

The reaction was immediate and very bad. The Kubaz waved his hands in the air, rocking back and forth and warbling some kind of prayer or curse; Ram wasn't sure which. Then he started backing away.

"No, I just . . . wait!" Ram called.

But the Kubaz kept shaking his head and retreating until finally he was gone and the market seemed eerily quiet.

"Uh . . ." Ram said. "That was bad. Are we about to get arrested or something?"

Tangor's huge warm hand landed on his shoulder, and that meant that, one way or another, everything was okay. Nothing could be *too* bad when there was a Wookiee hand on you, keeping you steady. She made a soft barking noise and Ram agreed silently to be patient.

"Fzooo brrrrrrrzzak ak!" the Kubaz hissed, gesturing impatiently from the side of the cathedral. *"Fzzrrak ak!"*

"I guess we should follow him," Ram said, readying himself. They might get mugged, they might get arrested, or they might get what they'd come for. But either way, Ram had a Wookiee on his team, so that was what mattered.

"Den'tizbar brrrra," the Kubaz muttered, plucking a small crate off a rickety cart that was attached to some kind of snorting six-legged creature.

Ram tried to see through the little breathing holes but couldn't make out anything.

The Kubaz snatched away the box with a grumbled retort and held out his hand.

"Okay, okay," Ram said, sounding, he hoped, like a grumpy underworld dweller and not some random Jedi kid. "I got the credits, calm down."

Crash had given Ram a bunch of chips and ingots—more than he'd ever seen before—so he handed over the pile, realizing a moment too late that he was probably supposed to use only some of it, or at the very least try to bargain.

"Fazoooo!" exclaimed the Kubaz, pocketing the cash. He handed Ram the box.

Tangor dragged a big hairy hand down her big hairy face and grumbled.

"Ah, thank you for doing business!" Ram said. The Kubaz garbled something—probably "Come back anytime, you tiny clown!"—then hopped onto his beast and sent it loping off into the night.

"That went well, I think," Ram said.

Tangor just shook her head and started walking.

THIRTY-ONE

THEN

Kantam already had tears welling up in their eyes when they stepped up to the door of the meditation room. A million scenarios pounded through their head, each more elaborate and ridiculous than the last. A million ways to try to explain. None made any sense—because *this* didn't make sense. That was all there was to it. Some things were beyond logic and reason. The Force, for instance. And love.

Was that what this was? Kantam had read about it, watched those goofy holos about people falling in love, sometimes even Jedi. It had always seemed like a big joke—something other people did. Not that Kantam judged love, or people who fell in love. It just wasn't for them.

Until, very suddenly, it seemed to consume Kantam's every movement and breath.

Didn't matter. This was the moment they existed in, the reality they had to face. No amount of logic, or even poetry about the lack of logic, would change that.

The door slid open.

Master Yoda stood inside, back straight, facing the far wall.

For a flickering moment, Kantam wondered absurdly if Yoda was going to challenge him to a duel, as punishment for tarnishing the image of the Jedi Order and throwing all that training out the window.

Then Yoda extended his lightsaber.

Kantam let out an audible gasp.

Yoda chuckled in that Yoda way: raspy, high-pitched, relentlessly endearing. "Many times, have we dueled in this very room, Padawan Sy. No?"

"I . . ."

"One last session," Yoda said solemnly, then turned and looked up, meeting Kantam's gaze. "Perhaps?"

Kantam extended their saber. You didn't say no to a duel with Master Yoda. Even in these fraught circumstances. It just wasn't done. "Of course, Master. But . . . you know?"

Yoda whipped up into the air in a swirling cartwheel,

that bright green blade flashing in fierce spirals around him. He landed in a crouch, one hand out, lightsaber poised above his head.

From any other Master, that may have been intimidating. Paired with the implicit understanding that something very real was up, Kantam would've normally understood this to be a veiled threat of some kind.

But this was exactly how Kantam and Master Yoda had always found understanding, ever since Kantam was just a tiny Youngling. They would spar, and spar, and spar some more, and somehow in that grapple of stick against stick—then later, saber against saber—whatever was troubling Kantam would start to untangle itself; the world would slip back into harmony. Even if the problem wasn't resolved, Kantam would leave sweat-soaked and invigorated and feeling like somehow there was an answer out there, and if there was an answer, Kantam would find it.

They had no such expectations of this duel, but it didn't matter. Sparring with Yoda was the answer, in this moment, the only moment that truly mattered. So they leapt forward, unleashing a controlled downward slice that Yoda easily parried, then followed up with a straight sweep across their shoulders. Yoda ducked, then sprang straight up, lightsaber needling directly at Kantam, who swatted each stab away while backstepping gracefully.

"Come, the time has," Yoda said, "to make a choice, hm."

"Yes, but . . ." Kantam leapt sideways, avoiding an upswing

from Yoda, and backflipped away, gaining enough distance to catch their breath. "How can I make a choice for the rest of my life when I barely understand what the choice is?"

Yoda lowered his head, sighed. It was a loving sigh, not exasperation. But there was a sadness there, too; Kantam felt it. "Not that choice, my Padawan. Every day, hm? The Force chooses Kantam Sy. The Force chose you to be its conduit, its living embodiment, as it does all Jedi, when you were born, yes?"

"Of course," Kantam said, holding very still to preserve energy. Yoda's counterattack would come at any moment, whenever Kantam least expected it.

"But when does Kantam choose the Force, hm?"

"Every day!" Kantam yelled, a surge of anger moving through them. They released it, as Yoda had taught them to do, and then released it again because it hadn't gone anywhere. "Every day," they said again, quieter. "I wake up here, a Padawan. I train, I meditate, I study. I—" They were getting worked up, shoulders rising and falling with fury, confusion, so of course that's when Yoda chose to attack again.

Kantam never understood how such a tiny body could move with so much explosiveness. Yoda seemed to simply burst sideways with barely even a muscle twitch of anticipation. He went running along the wall, flipped upward off the ceiling, and came down swinging at Kantam.

Kantam raised their own saber to block Yoda's and was rewarded with a sharp green foot landing on their shoulder.

Yoda flipped forward, landed in a squat behind Kantam, then sprang into a curved sweep past Kantam's feet, which they barely had time to hurl out of the way of. They landed in a heap on the floor and rolled onto their back.

"Hm," Yoda said gravely, "is it a choice we make when we don't truly believe other options there are?" He extinguished his saber.

Kantam propped themself up on their elbows. "I don't understand."

"A reason there is, why I have not knighted you yet, even though immensely qualified in almost every way, you are."

"I know, Master, and I'm not in a hurry. I've never been."

Yoda nodded, offering his tiny green hand to help Kantam up, just as he had done so many years before, when Kantam was the tiny one, and so many times since. "Mm."

Without another word, they sat facing each other and let the silence speak a while.

Kantam tried every meditation trick they knew to calm all those raging thoughts, doubts, fears, hopes.

Desires.

There was a reason Yoda hadn't knighted them. This had never bothered Kantam before. The time would come; there was no question. Now it seemed foolish to ever think there wasn't a question. "Are you saying I should leave the Order, Master Yoda?"

Yoda let out a small chuckle, eyes closed. "There is no *should*, young Kantam. *The right thing to do* very often is an idea we invent, hm? To make ourselves feel better. What *I* know, my Padawan, is that stopped listening, you have."

Even as Yoda spoke, Kantam knew it was true. They could barely hang on to a single sentence, let alone concentrate on the Force. Too many thoughts danced through them.

"Very like the wind, our feelings are," Yoda said. It was something he'd repeated many times over the years Kantam had been training with him, and Kantam had never totally known what to do with it.

"The wind touches us. We experience it," Kantam said, finishing the teaching. "It is real. But it passes. So, too, do our feelings."

Yoda nodded. "But sometimes, there is a hurricane. The winds are so strong, they lift us. Carried away, we can be. Everything we know and trust, gone, hm? Then easy it becomes to give in to anger, aggression, hm? Fear."

"So I should stay?" Kantam knew that wasn't the right answer, that there wasn't one. But all these poems and metaphors just seemed a million light-years away, even as they hit home to what Kantam felt.

Yoda opened his eyes, met Kantam's worried gaze. "You must choose the Force. One does not fall into being a Jedi Knight by mistake, hm? Or because it is convenient! You must choose the Force, with your whole heart. To do this, you must learn, again, to listen. To hear the world, the world outside of your own emotions. Even when they are very, very loud, heh, a hurricane."

"I—"

"Patient, Yoda is, hm? The only one in a hurry is Kantam."

A strange peace finally fell over Kantam. The emotions still surged, the nightmares and fantasies. But the path ahead was clear. Or as clear as it could be in that moment. The next step, which was the only step Kantam needed to understand.

Slowly, they unsheathed their lightsaber and placed it on the mat in front of Master Yoda.

Master Yoda nodded, ever so slightly.

And then Kantam walked away.

CORONET CITY

Cohmac stopped walking, eyebrows raised. "You absolute *rogue*!"

Kantam couldn't help smiling. It was nice, in a strange sort of way, digging through all these tormented memories. And it seemed to take the other Jedi's mind off whatever was troubling him. It had all been so heavy at the time, each moment a riddle with no right answer. And that was the point, Kantam supposed, what Yoda meant by "There is no *should*." Still . . . all these years later, and Kantam could still taste the shuddering sense of barely having made it out of all that alive.

In the street ahead, excited cheers and rhythmic clapping rose into the night along with the clanking, grinding, thumping sounds of the Atchapat Family Galan-Kalank Orchestra.

It was an appropriately named music style, Kantam mused. All six brothers and their mom and dad laid down a rhythmic wall of hard-driving industrial clatter. And it sounded exactly like the shipyard factories it had been born in, except probably much more danceable. The audience responded with knowing yells and coordinated dances. It was as Corellian a sound as one could imagine, and the capital city had claimed it with love that bordered on obsession.

At the thundering height of the song, Svi'no's gentle, hypnotic voice rang out over everything, and it sounded like a ray of sunlight breaking through the surface of a dark ocean. She hit a note that Kantam had trouble even fathoming—her family hammering away at those greasy instruments all the while—and then somehow mingled it with another note, the two sounds harmonizing through the night air like shimmering crystals.

Kantam glanced sideways at Cohmac, who was still reveling in the whole of it. "You just . . . put your saber down in front of *Master Yoda*, of all Jedi, and walked away," Cohmac said. "I can hardly imagine it."

"He was my master," Kantam said. "Is. Who else would I have done it for? Who else would've had the foresight and grace to know that the only way in for me was out?"

"Mmm," Cohmac said, nodding sagely. "I keep wondering what Master Yoda would make of all this."

Kantam paused and gave grace to the surge of sorrow that rose every time their master's name was mentioned. It felt like a hole—just emptiness, unfathomable emptiness. It opened wider and wider. Kantam breathed into it, accepted it, and released it, knowing it would return, and return again. They nodded. "Indeed."

The song finished with a triumphant climax. Cheers exploded all around, and Svi'no floated among a crowd of fans, confiding in them excitedly about an underground pop sensation no one had heard of yet. There didn't seem to be any trouble lurking about, although it was clear the shadows of Coronet City could harbor all manner of mysterious threats.

And then that tiny fluttering within alerted Kantam that something was up. They glanced around, eyes sharp, until a movement in the shadows ahead pulled their gaze. "There," they said, lightly tapping Cohmac.

The figure launched out of the alleyway he'd been hiding in and broke toward Svi'no. But Kantam already had one hand out, and the Force was ready within them, as always. It surged through them, seemed to dance like invisible lightning along the empty air, and then shoved the attacker aside. He yelped, suddenly airborne, then went smashing into a pile of trash cans.

"You've really taken to this bodyguard thing," Cohmac pointed out as the two Jedi walked over to the toppled attacker.

Kantam smiled with one corner of their mouth. "I had many jobs in my time away from the Order."

Cohmac let out a hearty laugh and grabbed up the man, pulling him to his feet. "Don't think I'm going to let you get away without finishing that story, Kantam."

"Wouldn't dream of it," Kantam said, then turned to the attacker, a scrawny, ponytailed young man in a designer poncho. "Now, you. What's this about, hm?"

"I just . . . I just . . ." he stammered.

"Oh, Tivbak . . ." Svi'no's melodious voice came from behind them.

Kantam and Cohmac turned. The singer had slipped away from the crowds and was hovering just within the shadows nearby, her glow dimmed to blend with the haze from the street lanterns.

"My love!" Tivbak cried, and started squirming. Cohmac stilled him with a glance.

Svi'no rolled her eyes. "We dated at uni for, like . . . ten minutes. Obviously that's all it took to completely ruin his life. Please stop doing this, Tiv. It's extra creepy."

"My . . . my love!" he whimpered.

"We'll handle it," Kantam assured her. They yanked him off to a side alley as Svi'no returned to her other adoring fans.

"How did you know she was here?" Cohmac demanded with that quiet Cohmac intensity that set his enemies on edge more than any yelling ever could.

"It's—it's all over the gossip holos," Tivbak moaned.

"I swear, I stopped using the tracker when the court mandated it!"

Kantam and Cohmac traded looks. "What are the holos saying?" Cohmac asked.

"Just the usual lies!" Tivbak growled, suddenly incensed. " 'Wounded starlet hits the streets on farewell tour as she names next big thing in superstardom!' "

Kantam raised their eyebrows. "Oh?"

"Some Mikkian girl everybody's been talking about all night on the gossips. Doesn't hold a candle to my Svi'no, I'm sure!"

Kantam raised two fingers in front of Tivbak's eyes and slid them to the side. "Perhaps it's time to head home and consider the societal factors that led you to this moment."

Tivbak nodded. "Makes sense, yeah."

"Maybe you could work to undo them."

"Mmm! Maybe!"

"And you don't need to think any more about Svi'no."

Tivbak scrunched up his face, confused. "Who?"

Kantam nodded. "Very good. Run along now."

Tivbak scampered off, looking longingly at the night sky.

"Thanks," Svi'no said, sliding back over with a confiding wink. "If my brothers had seen him here they'd have put him in the hospital again for sure. Last thing I need right now, to be honest."

"Who would we have put in the hospital?" someone with

a gruff voice said, and then Barg'no Atchapat, the oldest of the brothers, slid up alongside his sister.

Kantam would never have thought that a being capable of floating could also be burly, but Barg'no and several other of the Atchapats, including their mom, were exactly that.

"No one, big brother," Svi'no assured him. "These are my new friends, by the way, the ones I told you about."

Barg'no sent an intense glare over Cohmac and Kantam, then nodded. "Heard we may be looking at some kind of Nihil situation here on Corellia," he said. Three of the other brothers floated up nearby, their many arms crossed over their wide chests.

"We don't know for sure yet," Kantam said. "But it certainly seems likely."

"Corellians don't like raider scum trying to use our beautiful planet for their foul scheming ways."

Kantam nodded. "Agreed. Neither do Jedi."

"If there is a fight," Barg'no declared, "the Atchapats fight with you." The rest of the family had gathered, along with a sizable crowd of their fans. They all raised fists. "Corellia will stand up to the Nihil!" Barg'no yelled. "We are all the Republic!"

"We are all the Republic!" the crowd echoed.

Kantam felt a surprise surge of emotion. Even the Republic's own politicos hadn't taken the Nihil threat seriously, but the streets, at least, were on the Jedi's side. And maybe that was what mattered most of all. "We thank you," Kantam said. "For light and life."

"For light and life!" the crowd repeated, and then everyone fell into a frenzy of conversations about fighting the Nihil and when they'd get to meet the famous Mz. Z.

"It sounds," Cohmac said, "like Crash's plan is in full effect."

Kantam took out their comlink. "I'll let her know."

THIRTY-TWO

CORONET CITY

"Excellent," Crash said into her comlink. "Stay with her. I'll make the call."

Fezzonk glanced at her, then turned his attention back to the sparkling East Coronet rooftops their small flier skimmed above.

It was a good thing Crash was short and slim, otherwise there was no way she would've fit in the tiny side seat Fezzonk had rigged up for Betzo, a Lurmen who'd gone off to become a bounty hunter a few years back. As it was, Crash had barely squeezed herself in, but she was used to it—the Dowutin often gave her a ride home after long nights. The truth was, there weren't many ways to get to the Green after a certain hour, and Crash's little hover platform was good for maneuvering and overseeing ops, but took forever to work up any speed.

Down below, apartment complexes became smaller units, which gradually dwindled to shantytowns and shacks. Finally, the thick darkness surrounded them, with just a sprinkling of lights here and there marking the encampments of various swamp dwellers.

"What'sa matter?" Fezzonk asked.

Crash scowled. She hated how transparent she could be sometimes but also appreciated that he'd bothered to ask. "Do you think I withhold too much?"

Fezzonk rasped out a gargly guffaw.

Crash rolled her eyes. "Thanks, man."

"No, no," Fezzonk said, waving his huge hands (and almost hitting Crash in that cramped cockpit). "It's that . . . withholding is part of this business. It's hard to know who to trust. Plus there are some things we simply don't need to know, and sometimes that info can only complicate the job."

"That's right!" Crash said, pleased to finally have someone on her side of the issue.

"On the other hand," Fezzonk went on.

Crash put her head in her hands.

"We *are* a team, and we do function better overall when we have more info. Because intelligence, as you often tell us, is the whole game, really. In fact, I believe it was your mom who told us that first."

"Ah, yes," Crash grumbled. "Sounds like Mom." She softened. "She's got a point, though. It's that . . . with Prybolt disappearing, and Ovarto . . . I just . . ." She glanced at Fezzonk and finally spat it out, throwing both hands up, almost swatting one of her friend's giant chin horns. "I'm scared. That's all."

Fezzonk nodded at her to go on, eyes still on the dark sky.

"I'm scared for me, and I'm scared for you all. I don't want anyone else to get hurt on my watch."

"It was hardly *your* watch," Fezzonk pointed out. "I'm not just trying to make you feel better. That's not how this works. Yes, you're running things. But in the field, we all make our decisions and we live and die by those decisions. Literally. That wasn't a job that needed more than two operatives—"

"Except apparently it was," Crash interrupted.

Fezzonk wasn't having it. "But we didn't know that. There was no way to know that. Clearly, it was an ambush of some kind, a setup on Tralmat, if I had to guess. And so it was a regular to-and-from run until it wasn't. We can't send the whole team out every time a City Father needs to go see his mistress after midnight or whatever. It's not tactically smart and we don't have the resources."

Crash nodded. He was right, and she knew it. She just . . . Wallowing felt better than grieving, was really the thing.

"So we make decisions. And they're smart decisions." He took them low over the treetops, then swung left and swooped into a gradual incline toward the twinkling lights of a runway. "They're not wrong just because a freak incident occurred. And if something needs to be fixed, we put our heads together and fix it, Crash. Like always."

"I know," she said, feeling the ongoing tightness of guilt, self-doubt, second-guessing seep out of her tired body. "I just . . ." There it was. She shook her head, and the tears made slow tracks down her cheeks. "I'm sad."

Fezzonk carefully maneuvered his humongous arm behind Crash and pulled her close so her wet face was squished into his massive shoulder. "I know." He wiped his eyes with his other hand. "Me too."

THE GREEN

"Crash!" Baynoo Ongwa yelled, hurrying down the steps of her stilted house and running toward the flier.

"Hey, Mom!" Crash met her halfway, and they wrapped each other in a long hug.

"I didn't think you were coming home tonight!" Baynoo smelled like some kind of flowery perfume—of course she would be just lounging around the house wearing perfume!—and was wearing flowy pajama pants and a matching blouse that made Crash's clothes look like full combat gear. "There's caf on the stove if you want it. And I made dinner for the Green elders, so there's plenty left."

"No caf," Crash said, walking arm in arm with Baynoo

toward the house. "I have one call to make, then I gotta sleep."

"You staying for a bite, Fezzonk?" Baynoo called over her shoulder.

"Can't say no to my old boss, can I, Mrs. Ongwa?" he yelled back.

"He's such a gentleman." Baynoo snickered. "I do hope he settles down one day."

"Mom," Crash warned as they mounted the rickety but well-painted wooden staircase. "Retirement also means keeping your nose out of everyone's personal life, you know."

"Nonsense! The opposite, in fact! I finally have time to meddle. Leave an old lady to her mischief, please!"

They walked inside, and Crash immediately knew she shouldn't have waited so long to make her final work call of the evening. An iron cauldron dangled from the ceiling; inside, flames danced around crackling firestones and sent warmth and serene shadows stretching across the cozy cottage. The whole place smelled like Veevherb and sweetwater, and Crash knew a bed covered in fur blankets awaited just beyond that small doorway in the far corner.

"Let me do this outside real quick," she said, making an about-face and almost bumping into Fezzonk on her way out.

Baynoo's small hand caught her daughter's forearm. The older woman certainly looked like a kindly retired swamp dweller, but that grip said otherwise. Crash had to smile.

"Anything on Prybolt?" Baynoo asked.

Crash's smile vanished faster than it had appeared. She shook her head. "Nothing good."

Baynoo's whole bubbly demeanor seemed to sag. She nodded, released Crash, and was already perking back up by the time she turned to the Dowutin taking up most of her living room. "Sit! Dinner and caf! Coming right up!"

Crash sighed, pulling out her holocaster as she strolled along the wraparound porch toward the back of the house. The swampy darkness seethed with the growls of creedoks—amphibious reptiles that would hunt themselves literally into a coma—and high-pitched chirps of ten thousand snomats getting ready to find their life partners, mate exactly one time, and then immediately die. She tried not to relate to either of them too much.

"Crash!" Malfac Orfk appeared in holo form in front of her. "Finally! I've been trying to reach you for hours! You're too important to return a call to an old friend now?"

Crash had to chuckle. They'd been buddies growing up, sure, but *friend* was a stretch. Still, Malfac was known to be capable of much more extravagant reaches than that, if it meant ingratiating himself to a potential source. He'd also been known to conveniently forget that they had anything to do with each other when necessary. So his playing up their buddyhood meant that everything was working exactly as it should be. "Oh, Malfac. You really are mildly amusing, vaguely grating, and entirely untrustworthy."

"That's what the ladies tell me, yes!"

"I presume you're interested in knowing whether one of my *actual* old friends can give you any info on the mysterious and elusive Mz. Z?"

"I mean . . ." Malfac made a big show of playing coy, then immediately gave it up. "Literally anything would help! No one has uncovered a single recording, a gossip posting, a home address, anything on this girl! She is a *complete enigma*! But the streets are dying to know more, Crash! We don't even know where she's from, for void's sake! I just need a scrap of something, a description, anything!"

Crash winked, summoning the last of her ability to be pleasant. "I can do you one better."

Malfac got uncomfortably close to his own holocam. "I'm listening."

"I'm sending over a holo of the one and only Mz. Z."

"Crash! *What?*"

"It's from fairly recently, before stardom hit, of course. Before she caught the attention of the one and only Svi'no."

"I cannot believe this!"

"And she's . . . wait for it . . . singing and dancing around her room, hoping she becomes a star one day."

"SHUT UP AND GET OUT OF MY FACE, ALYS ONGWA!"

"Okay, talk to you later!" Crash made a show of being about to end the call.

"No! No! No! Kidding, of course!" Malfac screeched. "Send it! Stars, send it now!"

The image of a Mikkian girl about Crash's age swirled into existence as it transferred over to Malfac's receiver. She was beautiful, with sleepy eyes and a direct, no-nonsense half smile that would shatter a hundred hearts. She reached an arm off to one side and swung her whole body after it, slipping through the air like water. All those head tendrils swayed as if dancing amid an invisible breeze. The image got jangly for a moment—Ram must've been adjusting to follow her around the room—and then resolved on her again as she started laughing at something.

"I've always thought maybe in another lifetime, I would've been a famous star!" One pink shoulder poked out of her loose robe. The girl smiled shyly at the camera, then looked away. "But that's not for me, not really. . . ."

"Incredible!" Malfac yelled, probably loud enough to disturb the delicate swamp mating rituals happening all around. "Perfection!"

"It is pretty good," Crash marveled. *Like we planned it,* she thought. She'd only caught a glimpse of the footage when Ram had transferred it to her holocaster earlier—there'd been too much going on to really pay attention then. But wow . . . she truly couldn't have asked for a better clip.

"I owe you one!" Malfac yelped, already clacking away on two datapads at once, beaming messages out into the holosphere, no doubt, to get everyone excited about an imminent exclusive content drop. "No! I owe you a hundred! Seriously, Crash, thank you!"

"The pleasure is quite literally mine," Crash said, and snapped off the call.

The wild swamp life swarmed and simmered all through the night around her. It was a thousand times more cutthroat and complex than the teeming city she worked in; there were a million more ways to die. But to Crash, it was the sound of peace. She loved her work, sure, and the Coronet office was home in its own right. She just loved to have somewhere that was the exact opposite to escape to, to quiet her mind.

"A success," Baynoo said from the couch when Crash strolled back inside. Fezzonk was snoring loudly on the floor, and the older woman had her feet resting comfortably on his chest and a glass of Corellian wine in hand. "I can tell from that smug smile you inherited from me, eh."

"Unqualified success," Crash said, making a direct line for the bedroom.

"Crash."

Crash froze. She knew that tone. Should've known better than to say anything—her mom always could read straight past the words she said into what she really felt.

Baynoo had already crossed the room and wrapped her arms around Crash before she could escape to the quiet bedroom. "What's wrong, babyloo?"

Crash shook her head, then buried it in her mom's soft shirt. "I've been trying to do what you taught me—keep them all at arm's length. Especially since what happened with Prybolt and Ovarto, but . . . it keeps backfiring on me. I keep not telling people things I should, and everything is falling apart."

"Ah, Crash, love. The clients, I meant, not your team. Your team is your family. You can't keep them that far away."

Crash slumped even farther, trying to burrow deeper into her mom's soft embrace. She knew that it hadn't meant everyone, but . . . Prybolt had vanished, and as the gradual truth of his death settled into her subconscious—sooner even than she had been willing to admit—it seemed to poison everything around her, every friendship, every business deal.

The only way to survive in the industry, or hell, at all really, was to keep everyone an arm's length away.

It didn't really make sense—Crash knew that, deep down—but it was easier than feeling all the pain of losing someone again and again. Or potentially having to work for the very person who had taken your friend away.

"I'll do better, Mom. I promise."

Baynoo kissed her on the forehead and squeezed her tight one more time before letting go. "I know, babygirl. If not, I'll take the business right back from you and leave you to be the old swamp witch! Heh."

Crash shuffled off to the bedroom.

Now all that was left was for those Jedi kids to execute a very straightforward tempt-and-grab, and then the real work would begin.

What could go wrong? Crash had to snicker a little at the

ridiculousness of that thought. *Literally everything* was the only answer.

Ah, well.

She was asleep before she'd even pulled the covers all the way up.

THIRTY-THREE

CORONET CITY

Reath had only ever seen Crufeela wearing an elegant gown of blue and gold, so he wondered, as he sat on an extremely puffy and uncomfortable lounge chair in the lobby of the Hotel Feather, whether he'd even recognize her in whatever her normal going-about-life outfit was. Blue and gold were the official planetary colors of Corellia, and Crufeela was nothing if not all about Corellia. The one time Reath had seen her, in fact, it had been on the holos when she performed at some corny galactic talent show—some high-pitched, unfortunate jingo called "Corellia for Corellians," if he remembered right. Yes! She'd made a big deal about how she wrote it for the victims of some natural disaster that had happened there, but then it turned out the song was actually forty years old and written by an Alderaanian as a joke. To make matters worse, it also turned out that it hadn't been Crufeela singing at all—it was some teenager from Naboo who'd gotten scammed trying to make it big on the holos and had her voice recording delivered to an already big name for use in the competition.

And all that was *after* the whole endangered papdoo scandal. In fact, that talent show bit was supposed to be her big comeback from the papdoo thing. Reath looked around anxiously. He was still dressed in the black outfit of the Scarlet Skulls, and even with the face paint washed off, he felt ridiculous. The Jedi robes were home; nothing could compare. He took a drink of water. He was annoyed at himself for even knowing that much about pop-culture silliness, but some of the other Padawans were more tuned in than he was, and he couldn't help overhearing their idle chatter while he tried to study.

"Ah, you are . . . Dizcaro's man?" a timid voice said, shoving Reath out of his rambling thoughts. He looked up and then almost spat out the water he'd forgotten he was sipping.

"Ah, yes!" he said, standing quickly. "Are you ready to go?"

Turned out, he needn't have worried whether or not he'd be able to recognize Crufeela in her regular outfit, because Crufeela apparently didn't own a regular outfit. She stood before him in the glittering blue-and-gold gown she'd worn at the talent show. The only difference was, now she had a tiny blue-and-gold purse to go along with it. Maybe she didn't *have* any other outfits, Reath thought. Crufeela had light green skin, with slight silver lines running over it that Reath hadn't noticed in the holos. A plume of colorful feathers rose from the top of her otherwise bald head.

"Of course," she said, with a nervous glance around. She couldn't be worried about being recognized, not wearing that thing. They headed through the lobby, Reath ignoring all the curious gazes.

"Make a right out the door," Smeemarm ordered through the earpiece she'd given Reath before vanishing down a utility hole. ("There's an off chance Crufeela will recognize me," the Arcona had explained, her head poking out of the ground. "I used to work for Dizcaro before Crash found me. I doubt Crufeela paid much attention to anyone but Dizcaro, but better to be safe.")

Reath stepped out onto the bustling illuminated boulevard with Crufeela at his side. He gazed around slyly, the way he imagined a bodyguard would, and then waved his hand for Crufeela to follow him and headed off to the right.

"Walk behind her," Smeemarm said, not unkindly. "A bodyguard never stands in front of the client unless it's to take a blaster shot."

"Right," Reath whispered, slowing his steps.

Crufeela slowed hers, too, looking worriedly at him. "Something the matter?"

"Ah, no, no," Reath assured her, waving like ground control in a hangar bay. "Carry on! Just . . . keeping an eye out."

"Very well," she said, clearly unconvinced and unimpressed.

"Cross the street and hook a left at the corner," Smeemarm advised. "You're doing all right."

Reath headed into the street at an angle that would bring him almost alongside Crufeela so she'd notice where he was heading. Face-painted street performers twirled and squawked through some kind of maniacal reenactment of a murder. One of them had on a bird mask and wore only feathers. It was a lot.

"Eyes sharp," Smeemarm chirped. "Lots of attack points here. I know we're not technically her protection unit, but it wouldn't do to have a famous singer get attacked on our watch. Even if she is a vapid extinction-monger."

"Copy," Reath said under his breath. Crufeela crossed the open area just ahead of him, and no one got too close. Then he directed her off to the left and they headed down a quieter block.

"The hotel entrance is coming up on your right," Smeemarm said. "Open the door for her, and check for anyone on the other side when you do."

It all felt like a very delicate dance, Reath thought, trying not to trip over himself getting around and just ahead of Crufeela enough to reach the keypad. A dance at which he was absolutely terrible.

The glass hotel door slid open, and Reath didn't see

anyone at all inside the elegant lobby, not even at the front desk. That probably wasn't good. But Crufeela had already stomped past him and was making for the turbolift.

"Get ahead of her," Smeemarm said. "Hit the button. Everything is set upstairs for you. All we need is for her to be plausibly about to take a bite of the item."

How can that woman see everything? Reath wondered idly. *She's underground!* He moved quickly to the turbolift doors and called it down, trying not to look out of breath or like the complete disaster he felt like.

"Rooftop suite," Smeemarm said when the door slid open. Reath hit the button.

"Ooh, rrrrrooftop!" Crufeela squealed, rolling the *r* with unnecessary flair.

Reath's entire soul was uncomfortable.

The doors opened to a lovely open-air garden with twinkling lights strung overhead and an elegant table in the center. There were two place settings on the sheer fabric covering, complete with wine glasses, candles, and dessert plates.

"Nice, right?" Smeemarm said proudly in Reath's ear.

Crufeela took one step in, then spun around and reached into her purse.

"Uh," Reath said.

"Down!" Smeemarm yelled. "It's a—"

But the singer had already pulled out a tiny blaster and pointed it directly at Reath.

THIRTY-FOUR

CORONET CITY

"All we need is for her to be plausibly about to eat the item," they'd told Ram. "If not, the whole thing is out the window."

The words circled round and round through his mind as he stood in the underbrush, holding the box. Every once in a while, the creature would shuffle, or let out a little cooing noise, and Ram would cringe and shush it. Each time, it got harder not to just free it, whatever it was.

Ram wasn't even a cute-cuddly-creatures type. Pets and beasts of burden in general, they were wizard and all, but they could be wizard somewhere else, preferably a ways away, where Ram wouldn't have to interact with or smell them. Machines, baby. That was all Ram needed.

And yes, he *had* been realizing recently that friends were pretty great to have, too. Friends who weren't tiny, hairy ornery creatures, even.

Focus, Ram.

He'd been standing there in the fragrant darkness in that elegant rooftop garden for . . . longer than he'd imagined he would be. He was getting antsy.

Also, he had no idea how he was supposed to get this diva to eat this little creature. Would she try to fry it first? Ram didn't see any cooking equipment around. The Arcona woman, Smeemarm, had said Crufeela would be excited right away when she saw it, and wouldn't pay attention to much else, so all he had to do was offer it. But she'd still have to cook it! And what if she killed it before whoever was supposed to come stop her arrived?

Ram figured folks like this usually had a plan B, but given how quickly they'd had to throw this together, that seemed unlikely.

And how was he supposed to do any of this without knowing what he'd actually bought?

They hadn't told him not to open the box. That would be something you'd tell someone if it was important, probably.

Couldn't hurt to look.

Very, very carefully, Ram slid open the box.

"Akapropak?" a tiny voice chirped from the darkness inside.

Was that . . . ? *It couldn't be. . . .*

His heart thundering in his ears, Ram reached in, wrapped his hands around a small furry body, and pulled out a very young, very scared Bonbrak.

"Daka-daka!" she chirped, apparently happy to see him.

"Ah!" Ram gasped. "I . . . I . . ."

This was horrible! This wasn't the plan! It was supposed to be an animal of some kind, not something *sentient*! Not something Ram would be friends with! He would've saved it one way or the other, but this . . . And anyway, there were Bonbraks all over Valo; they certainly weren't endangered there.

He had to . . . he had to . . .

The turbolift dinged, the doors slid open, and Crufeela stepped out, looking absurd in a bright gold-and-blue gown. She whirled around, pulling a tiny blaster out of her purse and pointing it at Reath just as the turbolift doors closed behind him.

Crap.

All we need is for her to be plausibly about to eat the item, Ram reminded himself. Except now "the item" wasn't an item at all; it was a Bonbrak. And much as he needed to make sure she made it out of this alive, he also had to make absolutely sure this woman wouldn't get a chance to eat any other innocent little creatures. So he couldn't just go out there swinging his lightsaber and save Reath. Reath, for his part, was almost definitely thinking the same thing. But what if she just shot him? Then what? Reath was Ram's best friend, Ram realized as he stood there, sweating. Ram had never had a best friend before. He'd never really had any friends who weren't Bonbraks. And now he had a whole bunch, and his favorite one was about to get murdered right in front of his face by some maniac singer who hated cute animals.

"Ata Teetak!" the Bonbrak chirped proudly. *Ata* meant "can call" in Bonbreez, so she was probably announcing that her name was Teetak.

"Shhh!" Ram said, putting her back in the box. "Teetak shhh!"

"Teetak shhh!" she mimicked with a giggle.

"*Ata Ram*. But you gotta be quiet, okay, Teetak?"

She nodded. *"Teetak shh!"*

Ram closed the lid, cringing.

"You really thought I was a fool, didn't you?" Crufeela seethed.

Reath stared at her, hands raised. "I . . . what do you mean?"

"Why would my darling Dizcaro send someone to pick me up and not tell them what hotel I'm in? Hm?"

"I—"

"How does that make sense? I'd call him, but clearly *you've* commandeered his comlink, so . . . What did you do to my Diz?" she snarled, putting the blaster in Reath's face.

"Nothing!" Reath insisted. "I swear it! I don't even know that guy!"

"Well, explain!"

"Wait," Reath pleaded. "Both of you, stop yelling!"

Both? Ram thought, just as Crufeela screeched, *"Both?"*

"No, I . . . Wait . . . too much happening."

The Arcona had to have given him a comlink for his ear, like the ones bodyguards wore in the holos. She was probably freaking out while Crufeela was yelling, and Reath couldn't hear either of them.

"Who are you talking to?" Crufeela demanded. Then she whirled around, blaster pointing every which way, including at Ram. "Is it that floating turquoise hussy? She's always disappearing and slinking around through the shadows! That's how she stole my crown, you know! Slinking around behind my back, that slippery—"

"Aha!" Ram said cheerfully, stepping out of the underbrush. "Zer you are! Your meal is arready-oh!"

Reath gaped at him, probably wondering what accent he was butchering and why. Ram wished he knew. It had just come out that way.

Fortunately, Crufeela either didn't notice or didn't care. For once, something went the way it was supposed to. From the second Ram appeared, the diva's eyes were only for the box he carried. "Is that . . . ?" she gasped. "Is that . . . what I think it is?"

Ram, resisting the urge to vomit, raised one eyebrow instead. "Ahaha, of course, my deeeearah! Ze very especial-ah dish-oh!"

"Let me see," she whined. "Please, let me just . . . let me see my delicacy."

"Ah ah ah," Ram chided, waving her away. "Please-ah step-oh backa!" He placed the box on the ground, willed his fingers to stop shaking, and opened it.

The little adorable ball of puff and cuteness peered up, blinking against the sudden brightness, saw Ram again, and seemed to . . . Was that a smile? Ram wanted to curl up and explode.

Crufeela gasped. "It's *real!*" She reached her long-fingered hands into the box and caged them around the tiny Bonbrak. "And it's *mine*!"

Ram resisted the urge to go for his lightsaber. Behind Crufeela, Reath stood at the ready. But ready to do what? They were at the whim of a whole whirling set of machinations that neither understood or controlled. Ram hoped Smeemarm was saying something useful in that earpiece.

"The Republic classified these creatures as protected," Crufeela said sadly, "because on their home planet of Bartokan V, the giant Svor Clan worship them as gods and call them barat-karabak: fierce teeth. They demanded the special designation, and the pathetic whimpering sods on Coruscant complied. But I personally know of planets on which they are an *infestation*! Still . . . that doesn't make them any less *delicious.*"

"Erm," Ram said.

"Do you know the correct way to eat a barat-karabak?" Crufeela's sly reptilian eyes stayed glued on her prey.

"Uh . . . ah . . ." Ram stuttered.

"I've heard of people roasting them or even deep-frying, like absolute *barbarians*!" she went on, revving up into an ecstasy of culinary villainy. She shook her head, barely able to withstand the tragedy of it all. "No, no!" she moaned. "They must be eaten . . ." For a moment, all Ram heard were the whirrs and fizzes of after-hours traffic, the swirl of the Corellian night wind, the beating of his own heart.

Then Crufeela yelled, "*ALIVE!*" and her mouth opened to an inhumanly huge gape.

The Bonbrak squealed as those gigantic jaws and jagged teeth rushed down to clamp around it. Ram reached out with the Force and yanked the Bonbrak from Crufeela's grasp just as a dozen million-watt spotlights burst to life all around them.

"No!" Crufeela shrieked. Four armored soldiers rushed in, blasters drawn, followed by a portly Twi'lek looking very pleased with herself.

"Crukibolt Nart Adeen," the Twi'lek pronounced loftily, "aka Crufeela, I am Chief Inspector Deemus Abrus of the Coronet City Chapter of the Galactic Society of Creature

Enthusiasts! We work with local authorities to make sure various critters like this one aren't sold on the black market."

The Bonbrak shuddered in Ram's grasp, cooing softly and trying to nuzzle her way into his armpit.

"You vile dotards," Crufeela raged in a desperate whisper.

"Yeah, yeah," Deemus sighed. "Save it for the behind-the-scenes special about your—what is this—third fall from grace?"

Crufeela glanced around, the reality of the situation closing in. "I . . . I was just playing with it!"

Deemus nodded agreeably. "And I'm a world-class podracer. Fellas." She shot a cheerful nod at the soldiers. "Take her away."

"What? You can't!" Crufeela screeched, already halfway to the turbolift.

"I quite literally just did, my dear." Deemus chuckled. "It's all right, they'll probably just give you community service picking up happabore dung at the city zoo." She waved amiably as the soldiers dragged Crufeela into the turbolift. "Don't eat the happabores!" The detective turned to Ram, who still had the Bonbrak cuddled up in his arms. "Ah, hello, young man! You've done a great service for the wildlife of the galaxy."

"I have?" He gave the Bonbrak one more squeeze and then passed it over to Deemus's open hands.

"Of course! Every being is sacred! Why, this single Bonbrak may go on to help repopulate the Blue Peaks of the southern hemisphere, which haven't had a stable Bonbrak population in more than a century, thanks to illicit trade and fiends like Crufeela!"

"Wow."

The turbolift door slid open again. Smeemarm beckoned Ram and Reath from inside. She made pointed eye contact with Deemus Abrus, and both women nodded at each other as the two Padawans headed off the roof.

PART FOUR

THIRTY-FIVE

CORONET CITY

"Understood, yes." Varb Tenart pressed his two handlike feet together over the desk and blinked about a thousand times. "Well, that is . . . mmm."

Crash recognized this move. It meant the event organizer Dug was stressed, irritated, backed into a corner, and would rather be almost anywhere else. She could hear someone rattling on and on through Varb's headset, delivering the bad news. Crash sipped her caf and managed not to smile.

"The thing is . . ." Varb muttered. "Right, right. No, of course I understand."

The midmorning sun poured through the office windows,

dancing along the various holos of Varb's littermates and his approximately four dozen pups. Crash picked up one of the images and made gooey faces at it. Baby Dugs were exceptionally cute, she had to admit. If she ignored the thought of all of them growing up into fully formed Varb Tenarts, they really weren't so bad.

"Right, well, that's a shame, yeah," Varb went on, apologizing elaborately to Crash with one foot and an eye roll.

It's fine, Crash mouthed, waving him off. Because it was, it really was. And it was about to be even finer.

"All right then, we'll speak soon. Give her my best if you manage to talk to her before . . . yeah, well, you know." He clicked off the call and rubbed a foot across his eyes with a long exhale. "Sweet Suspirala! What a morning."

"I won't ask," Crash said warmly. "Just popped by to pick up some forms for a few of my clients."

Varb blinked, snapping himself out of it and managing a smile. "It's fine! It will be. Somehow. Just . . . this business, you know?"

"Do I!" Crash *almost* felt bad for him. She did know, and she deeply related to that Dug determination. He *would* find a new performer to make an appearance at the gala that night, he was probably telling himself with that warm grit of self-assurance. He *would.*

Indeed, she thought wryly.

"Well, if you need to talk it out, I'm right here." She slid her datapad across the desk, Zeen's picture gazing thoughtfully out from the screen. "Just need your signature on a few of these forms for an—"

"Is that—" Varb snatched his glasses off the desk with one foot and then used both to shove them over his snout. "Is that the Z lady no one will shut up about?"

"Hm?" Crash said, pretending to be super interested in one of the litter holos. "Oh, Mz. Z? Yep. Just signed her this morning, in fact. All the rave, you know." She pointed at the image. "Cute kids."

"Yeah, yeah, yeah, they're a mess. But wait . . . wait wait wait." Varb leaned all the way forward across his desk. "You *represent* her?"

"Who?"

"This Z girl! The one everyone's—"

"Oh! Yeah. Stars know she'll need a detail at this rate. She's barely hit the scene and already the demand is through the roof. You can imagine what the security situation must be like."

Varb just stared for a moment, eyes glassy. His breath smelled like milk.

"It is ridiculous," Crash said. "The security situation."

"Ah! Of course it is! She's a star! A bona fide star! All the morning shows were yammering about her! All the kids are getting those creepy fake tendril attachments for their heads and painting themselves pink! Ridiculous!"

"Indeed," Crash said, shaking her head.

"Say . . ." Varb looked up at her over his glasses and pouted. "You don't suppose she's available tonight, by any chance, do you?"

THIRTY-SIX

HYPERSPACE

"So," the flickering image of Lula Talisola said shyly, "look . . ."

Zeen hit pause. She didn't want to watch the rest. Every part of her was dying to watch the rest. This was agony. Suddenly, the cockpit felt very, very small and the galaxy very big.

She put a hand on the control console, trying to find something real to keep her grounded. All around her, the stars streamed past; the galaxy seemed peaceful. It was not.

Everything was war, inside and out. She couldn't tell one sense of doom from another and had no idea which were the gentle nudges of the Force telling her that something was very wrong, and which were just panic. All of it was blotted out by a knotted feeling that reached from the core of who she was and wrestled through her insides straight to the dome of her head.

If this was love, love was the absolute worst.

"I don't know how to say any of this. I've never been afraid to speak my mind or say my truth. I'm not even afraid of the Nihil or the Drengir, not anymore. I don't fear death, Zeen, but I have no idea how to talk to you about my own feelings." She stopped, wiped her eyes. Took a breath. "Make *that* make sense."

It doesn't make sense, Zeen wanted to yell.

Every inner alarm bell was going off at the same time. *Run!* her mind urged. Or was it the Force saying that? It probably was, because everything happening right now was almost definitely an abomination in the eyes of the Order! Jedi weren't supposed to form attachments, and what was this if not exactly that? And Lula wanted to be the best Jedi of all time. That's all she'd ever wanted to be. And then Zeen had shown up and ruined Lula's whole life just by existing, just like she'd ruined—no.

Suddenly everything inside her stopped shivering. Krix had made his own choices. She knew that. And Zeen had made hers. And Lula would have to make hers.

But one thing Zeen did know was that she wouldn't let herself become an obstacle in anyone else's path to becoming what they'd always wanted to be.

And that meant Zeen had to get away. Far, far away.

Away from all of it. The idea felt like a relief and a nightmare at the same time. Starlight Beacon had become her home. More important, she had found a home inside herself while on Starlight. She had found her true self—not the one that kept trying to be smaller, lesser, quieter, weaker, for people who pretended to love her but only as long as she played the role they imagined her in.

That wasn't love, Zeen thought. Love was what she had with the Padawans.

Love was . . .

Entering the Corellian system, the navicomputer readout advised with a ping. *Prepare to exit hyperspace.*

Very well. Zeen clicked off the paused holo, grateful for the distraction.

She would help her friends in Coronet City, make sure they were okay. She'd keep a low profile. Just do what she had to do, and that was it. She would take out Sabata Krill, all by herself if need be.

She would hug them all and say goodbye. And then she'd get in her ship and fly away and never look back.

THIRTY-SEVEN

CORONET CITY

Kantam and Cohmac both looked up from their meal as the door to their living quarters slid open. "Good day, Jedi," Minister Fendirfal said. "I trust you enjoyed the festivities and chaos of last night."

"Without question," Cohmac said gamely.

Kantam just smiled.

A curt smile shoved its way across the minister's face. "A very Corellian welcome, I'd say. Anyway, there's been some reports of trouble at the municipal police barracks across town."

The Jedi looked at each other across the table, then back at Fendirfal.

"What kind of trouble?" Kantam asked.

"It's not clear." She frowned. "Seems a fistfight has escalated. There may be casualties. Or a possible"—she looked away—"low-level hostage situation, but probably nothing, I'm sure."

Both Jedi were already standing.

"I was planning on heading over once I finished some datawork and meetings. You could ride along with me if you like."

"We'll just head over now," Cohmac assured her, moving quickly past the minister and shooting a wild-eyed glare over her head at Kantam.

"Ah, very well," Fendirfal said, flustered. "There's an extra speeder bike you can borrow in the garage, I suppose."

"Perhaps we'll see you there," Kantam said, hurrying to catch up with Cohmac. "If your work allows."

"Do we wake the boys?" Cohmac asked with a nod at the other bunk.

Kantam shook their head. "They'll just want to come, and they're probably better off seeing what they can find out at the ball tonight. There's bound to be people there involved in whatever's happening. And who knows how long this mess will have us tied up. Anyway, I'm sure they need their sleep."

"I know the Republic can have its bureaucratic . . . issues," Cohmac said delicately as the wind off the harbor whipped his long black hair into a fierce cascade behind him. "But that minister seems a tad too enthusiastic about wallowing in useless gridlock and abject mediocrity."

Kantam veered around a slow-moving hauler and then took them up, up, up, toward the higher, more open lanes, which were largely free of midmorning traffic. They'd crossed Whyren Boulevard and were heading north past the civic center, the water glistening brightly below, the city a majestic conflagration of skyscrapers on one side and shipyards on the other. "I don't think there's anything nefarious about it," Kantam said. "If that's what you're asking."

"Not intentionally, no," Cohmac agreed. "Just . . . jarring, knowing how much the Republic has done in recent years to avoid that type of behavior."

"My sense is that her sentiments and movements are less in tune with the Republic and more with Corellia. Or Coronet City, more to the point. Their whole political system is a giant old-fashioned disaster zone, as I'm sure you noticed last night. Less corruption and more simple, straightforward gratuitous fatuousness with a sprinkling of greed."

"Imagine making Coruscant look efficient," Cohmac marveled. "Anyway, you left me at what the holo dramas call a cliffhanger in your story, I do believe. And we have some time."

"Ah, yes," Kantam said, veering off the seaside highway and taking them between the towering monuments of industry and largess toward the Teeno Village sector. They smiled, remembering.

THEN

Kantam watched from the wings as Aytar launched himself through the air, spun once, twice, and then grabbed the swinging bar and hoisted himself up onto it. He stuck out his chest, balancing on the bar, and threw his arms to either side in an elaborate bow as applause thundered around him.

That slight smile, the one Kantam had no idea what to do with, slid across Aytar's face. And then the boy dropped, catching his midsection against the bar. He kicked his legs back, swinging all the way around it twice, then released. Kantam took it all in as if it were happening in slow motion. Aytar's tensed body shot straight up, and he twirled, flipped, spun, and then tumbled gracefully toward the net below. The whole world seemed to erupt with screams of excitement. He sank all the way down in the net and then went zipping back up into the air, a bright smile on his face. The routine was done; all he had left to do was soak in the love from the crowd.

As Aytar reached the height of his bounce and started to descend again, Kantam held up one hand, allowing the Force to cushion Aytar into a gentle pause, and there, in midair, for just a moment, he hovered.

Everyone gasped, including Aytar.

Kantam felt a rude, wily smile cross their face. It wasn't a smile they were used to. A new smile for a new era. A new Kantam.

They let Aytar down slowly, wild yelps of amusement and confusion ringing out all around, and finally the boy's eyes found Kantam's and widened. He stood, his face a wild mix of confusion, fury, and . . . something else, something Kantam couldn't name but hoped was love.

They would find out soon enough.

The backstage area was a sweaty, stinky mess of half-naked torsos and overly costumed creatures. Kantam ducked around an Ithorian in the full royal regalia of some faraway system, then had to hop out of the way of a group of chuckling Narquois, faces painted in extravagant clown makeup, as they paraded to the performance arena.

The circus had stopped at a town center on Elphrona this time, and the layout was a little different than it had been on Endovar. Still, Kantam found the acrobats' dressing room and knocked politely, heart pounding a reckless, desperate staccato in their ears.

"You," Aytar said, appearing in the doorway. It was half accusation, half love song.

Kantam wasn't sure which half to believe. Both were true.

They stared each other down for a moment, then Aytar

sighed and stepped to the side, making a theatrical hand gesture for Kantam to enter.

"You . . ." Aytar perched on the makeup table, elbows resting on his bent knees, and steepled his fingers against his face. "You."

"Me," Kantam said, standing perfectly still, back straight, facing Aytar head-on. "Live and in the flesh."

"I told you . . . not to leave the Order for me," Aytar said quietly.

"I didn't," Kantam said, realizing the truth of it as the words came out. "I left it for me."

In some ways, it was just that simple. In other ways, it could never be simple. Both were true, and a million other things, too.

Aytar shook his head. "I can't be responsible for you . . . for you throwing away everything you have worked your whole life for. That's too big a burden to put on me."

"I'm not asking that of you."

Aytar lifted his eyes. "You're not?"

"Nor is it your decision to make for me, whether or not I can throw something away." This strange calmness—Kantam had not expected it to last. They'd imagined a tearful, desperate kind of reunion. Fighting, lovemaking, both probably. Something snatched from bad dramas and half-read storybooks.

Kantam thought that sudden gust of emotion they'd felt all the past week was simply what life would be like from there on out. A storm. But Master Yoda had been correct, as always. Change was the one reliable thing. Emotions were wind. Kantam knew what they wanted right then, in that moment, and it was to be exactly where they were—and in a way, nothing else mattered.

"The only decision you have to make right now," Kantam said, "is whether you want me to stay or go. The rest is up to me."

Aytar put his head in his hands and just breathed for a few very long moments. When he looked up, he was smiling.

CORONET CITY

"There's more, isn't there?" Cohmac demanded over the whipping wind. "I know that story's not over."

Kantam smiled. "There's always more."

"How long were you out there?"

"A while," Kantam said. "I lost track, to be honest. Anyway, we're getting close."

They zipped up a wide boulevard between warehouses, then curved around a corner into a crowded commercial district. Grocers, tech shops, and fishmongers lined the streets, and everyone went about their business. It seemed eerily calm, somehow. Kantam couldn't put their finger on why. People were out and about, but they glanced shiftily at one another and seemed ready to run at any given moment.

"What do you suppose it is?" Cohmac asked.

Kantam slowed the speeder bike and glanced at a group of old men watching an empty spot of sky in the distance, muttering to one another. "They're trying to figure out if whatever happened at the police barracks is about to spread to them." They sped back up, cresting a hill and then descending toward an open area of mostly parking lots and industrial sites spread around one central building several stories high, with receiver dishes and antennas adorning the roof. "There it is," Kantam said. A single plume of black smoke rose from the far end of the building. It easily could've been confused for any of the ones coming from smokestacks in factories all around the city, except this one, Kantam realized as they looked closer, came from a yellowish chemical cloud encompassing the whole building. The war sign of the Nihil.

THIRTY-EIGHT

CORONET CITY

"I can't believe they left without us!" Ram complained, shoving stale crackers into his mouth and chewing aggressively.

"Did you really want to go tour a police barracks?" Reath asked across the table.

"That's not the point. We're supposed to be a team, and we've barely gotten to do Jedi stuff together because one or the other of us is always running off."

"Or, more often than not, both of us," Reath pointed out.

"Yeah, yeah, yeah, true," Ram admitted. "Still."

"Have some caf." Reath slid a cup in front of Ram. "It's not as bad as you might think."

Ram shook his head. "I don't drink caf." Then he thought better of it. "Actually, I'll bring some to the Bonbraks. They love the stuff."

"Of course they do," Reath snorted. "Any word from—"

Crash's very self-congratulatory face appeared from Ram's holoprojector before Reath could say her name. "It is I! A girl!"

"I'm never gonna live down announcing that when you first showed up here, am I?" Ram asked.

"Absolutely not," Crash said. "Nor should you. It was an iconic moment of boyhood. I salute you."

"What's the word?" Reath asked.

"The word, my friends, is that you are both extremely effective operatives and are always welcome to be part of Supreme Protection as long as I'm running things."

"It worked!" Reath said, reaching through the holo to high-five Ram.

"That Dug guy offered you the gig for tonight's gala?" Ram asked

"Offered Mz. Z the gig," Crash said, "and as her representative, that gives me the overall contract for the event, so yes. Now all we have to do is tell the mysterious new starlet that she's a mysterious new starlet! Any update?"

Ram shook his head. "I tried her a few times, but comms can be funny in hyperspace. She should be here anytime now."

"Well, bring her over to the office when she shows up so we can give her the rundown and get her dressed all pretty.

I gotta go set up the spot and see what else I can find out!" Crash gave some kind of elaborate hand signal that Ram took to be Corellian visual slang and tried to do back, but she'd already ended the call.

"Well, I guess . . ." The rumble of a ship entering the docking bay sounded. Ram and Reath ran out of the living quarters into the wide-open landing area. It reeked of rubber, fuel, and the sharp tang of burnt metallics. A shuttle slowed overhead and then gently lowered onto the landing pad.

"Zeen!" Ram yelled as a pink face appeared in the viewport. The cockpit swung open with a whoosh and a gasp, and Zeen Mrala climbed out looking surprised and confused. "Hey, I . . ." Zeen said. Then she just grabbed Ram and hugged him.

"What's wrong?" Ram asked. Reath stood nearby, trying to figure out if he should join the hug or just mind his business.

Zeen stepped back, shook her head. She wasn't crying, but she looked empty somehow, more lost than Ram had ever seen her. "I don't . . . know how to explain it."

"Did you run into trouble on the way here?" Reath asked. "We couldn't reach you for a while."

"No, it was a smooth trip. Let me . . . I'm sorry, you two. I'm just overthinking everything and . . . I thought I was going to show up here and save the day or something, but now I feel like I'll just end up causing more problems."

"Did something happen with Krix?" Ram tried.

Zeen rolled her eyes. "That fool is in custody. No . . . I'll be okay. I mean it."

Ram picked up her go bag and started leading her out of the docking bay. "Come on," he said. "Let's get some food in you and all that. You have a, uh, long day ahead. . . ."

"Huh?"

"Padawan Silas, come in," chirped the comlink on Reath's belt. It was Cohmac, and he sounded pressed.

"Yes, Master, I'm here," Reath said.

"Is Ram with you?"

"He's here, Master, and Zeen just got in."

"Ah, thank the Force," Cohmac sighed. "Where are you?"

"We're still at the living quarters. What's going on?"

"Listen, all of you. The Nihil are on Corellia. There's no question of that anymore. We don't know how many or what their goal is, but they're definitely here, and in some force, I'd say."

Zeen's wide eyes met Ram's. If there really was Nihil infiltration on Corellia, Ram had always imagined it would be a politician or two, someone working things from the inside. But not any kind of military force. The Nihil were ambitious, sure, but they were mostly cowards, from what Ram had seen. They'd attack soft targets, civilian sites, where they knew they could wreak maximum havoc and destruction and get away with it. Head-on confrontations with bigger armies than theirs wasn't their style.

Then again—Ram felt his heartbeat zip into double

time—the planet-wide defense force, CorSec, was concentrated on the nearby moon Gus Talon, along with most of Coronet City's Jedi. So who was really there to stop the Nihil?

He glanced at his friends, standing alone in the mostly empty hangar.

It was a trap. The whole thing. And there they were in the middle of it, still with no idea what plan they were trying to stop. With no backup and no way out, not if they planned on keeping the Nihil at bay. They'd have to reach out to Coruscant for reinforcements, but what would they even say was happening? It was all too vague still, and no one would be able to show up right away. By the time they did send help, it would probably be too late.

All they had was each other.

Ram leaned over to talk into Reath's comlink. "We'll come to you. Are you at the barracks still?"

"No," Cohmac said firmly. "We don't know if this is just another diversion, or the real attack, or some accident. If we gather here and then find out they've already launched an assault all the way downtown, we'll have lost precious moments averting it. For now, we have to stay separated and alert."

"Yes, Master," Reath said.

"And this is a direct order, Padawans: from here on out, no more running off on missions without telling the others. And, yes, that goes for Kantam and myself, as well. We *must* stay coordinated, stay disciplined, and be in touch with each other about everything. Clear?"

"Clear," Ram, Zeen, and Reath said.

"You're to act like everything is fine. The Nihil don't know we know they're here yet, and that may be the only bit of advantage we have left. Head over to the gala site. Tell Crash—I believe we can trust her—and then proceed with everything as planned. Anyway"—a touch of warmth tinged the edges of Cohmac's otherwise tense voice—"this is a big night for Zeen. She shouldn't miss it! Cohmac out."

Zeen blinked at Ram and Reath. "Um?"

"Come on," Ram said. "We have a lot to catch you up on!"

THIRTY-NINE

CORONET CITY

"Still nothing happening," Kantam said, sweeping the macronocs across the haze-covered police barracks one last time. "Just smoke and gas."

They'd headed up a nearby hill that overlooked the site, found some rusted-out speeders to hide behind, and set up a little surveillance outpost to keep an eye on things.

Starlight hadn't responded to any of their messages yet, and the rumbling sense of something being very wrong that Kantam had felt all day was rising to a roar.

Cohmac, standing with his arms crossed and tensed face lowered, eyes closed, clearly felt it, too.

It wasn't a question anymore: something *was* very wrong.

Whether it was on Corellia or somewhere else entirely or just . . . everywhere, Kantam wasn't sure. For a moment, they closed their eyes, as well, letting the faraway churn of machinery, the chirping mocricks, the faint smell of Nihil war gas all slip into the background as the elemental song of the Force swept over everything, became the world.

Stillness.

The Force sang of stillness. Not the gentle stillness of an untouched snowfield. This was much more sinister, a gaping emptiness where once so much life had thrived, thousands of stories entwined. And now there was nothing.

Kantam let it move through them, felt even the notion of it weaken them somehow—it seemed to come alive, pulse through each organ and vessel.

They could not get lost in it.

But that wasn't how meditation worked, wasn't how the Force worked. So what did it mean?

Sorrow. Grief. Regret. Uncertainty.

It wasn't the dark side itself, just the emotions that led to it, rising, rising, among so many beings. So many . . . loved ones.

Kantam's eyes shot open. Nothing had happened, not where they stood anyway. The thick yellow haze was starting to dissipate from the building, but the smoke still rose, the mocricks still chirped. Beside them, Cohmac still stood in solemn meditation, but his face had twisted into an agonized scowl.

He felt it, too, whatever it was. They were safe for the moment, and Kantam needed to know more.

They closed their eyes once again and reached out with the Force.

A song of pure devastation trilled out so suddenly it almost knocked Kantam over. It rose to a sharp keening and then burst, an explosion that rocked the very stars, and then emptiness once again devoured the entirety of a space once filled with laughter, concern, thoughtfulness, love.

Kantam was more prepared for it this time. They nodded inwardly, the slow creep of understanding spreading through them.

Whatever it was, many would die.

Most probably, many of those Kantam loved and cherished the most were the ones in danger. That was why the connection was so strong to this . . . *thing.* It felt like an apocalypse, and maybe it was.

Starlight.

They hadn't responded to any of their messages.

And Torban Buck . . . he and Kantam had forged a Force-based connection with each other through intensive meditation. They both knew there were many battles ahead, and especially with so many young people in their care, they needed any degree of preparedness they could get. Even so far away, their link hadn't been severed. But it was murky, cut through with sharp spikes of pain, fear.

Torban wasn't dead—Kantam would've sensed that. But

something terrible was happening all around him, to him.

Kantam struggled to calm their frantic thoughts, all the possibilities, the options for action.

There were no options for action.

Returning to Starlight now wouldn't save it. That was folly. If anything, it would give free rein to whatever devastation was about to happen right there on Corellia.

No.

Kantam knew without a single doubt that whatever had to happen next, their role in it did not involve doing the one thing their entire body longed to do. Racing headlong into certain destruction would help nobody.

The path was in Coronet City, and Kantam knew it would not be an easy one.

The Masters taught non-attachment—it was part of the Jedi vow. And many Jedi twisted that notion into the opposite of what Kantam understood it to mean. They spoke of suppressing emotions, of forsaking love, burying any discomfort until it was a mere whisper.

But emotions couldn't be mastered, Kantam knew. The very idea of mastering something like a feeling seemed so ego-driven and reckless. Neither could emotions become the masters of a Jedi. But there were more than those two simple options.

For Kantam, the principle and practice of non-attachment was made for moments exactly like this.

Master Yoda was already gone, and the only person

Kantam loved as much as their master was their Padawan, Lula Talisola. She was, almost certainly, in mortal danger—that truth echoed over and over through Kantam's entire being. But to best serve the Force, to best serve Lula, even, and certainly to survive the battle ahead, Kantam could truly be present only to that which was immediately in front of them. That was the only truth. Lula may well die, and Kantam would mourn her. But losing themself entirely in a swirl of worry in a different corner of the galaxy would not save her.

It wasn't just Lula. Farzala, Qort—all the Padawans had been under Kantam's care in some way or another over the past few months. They would face untold horrors, and Kantam couldn't be there with them.

A shudder ran through Kantam. It felt like a hundred sets of teeth closing around their arms, legs, heart.

So much life, so much death.

Kantam would trust the Force—not to ensure everything would be all right, or victory, or even survival. No. Kantam would trust the Force to keep them grounded, present, awake to each moment and all the colliding details of the spinning galaxy that they would need to fulfill their journey in this life.

That was all they could ask.

"Someone's making a run," Cohmac said, his voice a choked sob.

Kantam opened their eyes. Cohmac looked ashen, face stricken; tears teased the edges of his eyes. Up by the barracks, a single figure dashed from the building toward a speeder.

"I'll go," Kantam said, already regaining their center. "You need—"

"I'm fine," Cohmac insisted. "You drive, I'll shoot."

Kantam wasn't wild about the slight hunger that tinged Cohmac's voice when he said *shoot*, but there wasn't time to argue. They raced down the hill to the waiting speeder bike. Kantam leapt over the front, grabbing the handlebars and swinging onto the seat, then landed with each foot on a pedal.

"I see you never really left the circus behind after all," Cohmac said, climbing on the back and patting Kantam's arm to say he was ready.

"You know what they say. . . ." Kantam was just glad to hear Cohmac make a play at being normal, even as sorrow and fear rippled through him in incessant waves.

They swung along a winding dirt path to the open lot around the barracks, then cut a hard left to follow where the escaping speeder had gone.

"That way," Cohmac called over the wind. He pointed over Kantam's shoulder to a ramp leading up to an ancient overpass. Ivy-covered stone made up most of it—seemed like it had been around for at least a thousand years. The speeder could just be seen zipping up the ramp and out of sight.

Kantam floored it, racing past one-story shacks and a weigh station, then taking them up onto the speedway, where wide sargolo trees provided a gentle canopy against the blazing sun. The long stone road seemed to stretch on forever.

"Faster, my friend," Cohmac urged. "He's getting away."

Kantam felt the wrath radiating off Cohmac, and the urgent efforts he was making to dampen it. He had already been struggling—for a while now, from what Kantam understood—with his own faith and understanding his path. This emerging disaster they both felt could send Cohmac spinning into a dangerous cycle. Or it could strengthen his resolve. Either way, there was a perilous journey ahead for both of them.

With the engine beneath Kantam pushed to its limit and clanking irritably, they were closing on the speeder.

Cohmac reached an arm over Kantam's shoulder from behind, blaster in hand. "Steady . . ."

"I didn't know you carried one of those," Kantam said.

"Came with our ride, handily," Cohmac said. He let off one shot, then another, reducing the rear thrusters of the speeder ahead to smoldering shrapnel.

The driver—he looked to be in a muni uniform, but that didn't mean much—glanced back and shrieked. He tried to shove the speeder into overdrive, milking any last gasps of power from it, but without the thrusters, it sputtered into a clumsy glide. "No!" he yelled, jumping out and running toward the edge of the speedway.

"Stop!" Cohmac commanded.

Kantam veered to the side, narrowly missing the stopped speeder, then leapt from the bike just as the driver hurled himself over the side with a yelp.

"No!" Cohmac yelled behind Kantam.

Kantam had him though. He'd reached out with the Force just before the man jumped and managed to stop his fall, though only barely. "Go," he said to Cohmac, his hands still out and open. "Careful he doesn't have a blaster, too."

Cohmac pulled his lightsaber out, extended it with a flourish, and leapt onto the edge of the speedway, gazing down. "Let me help you," he said, and together he and Kantam hoisted the man up onto the stone ground, where he lay panting and screaming.

"Enough," Cohmac said. That edge was creeping back into his voice. Kantam wished they could sit and talk quietly about the visions they'd seen, compare notes and help each other understand it, help each other make it through.

But there was no time, and too many plots seemed to be unfolding all around them.

"Speak," Kantam said calmly. "We're not trying to hurt you. We just want answers."

"I . . . I . . . Who are you?" the man gasped, finally calming down enough to make words. His holster was empty, and he didn't seem to have any hidden weapons, so that was something.

"We're Jedi," Kantam said. "From Starlight Beacon. Tell us what happened. Start with your name, please."

He glanced around, confused, then seemed to deflate—all the fight and desperation leaving him in a sigh. "I . . . I'm Sanke Paro. I'm a muni officer. Two years on the force." Sanke looked to be in his mid-twenties, with the first wisps of an orange beard and curly hair.

"Very well," Cohmac said. "Now tell us why your barracks are smoking."

"There was a girl, a fight. . . . It all happened so fast, I barely understood it."

"This girl," Kantam said. "Was she a human?"

Sanke shook his head. "Red skin . . . long floppy ears. Maybe eighteen, nineteen?"

Kantam and Cohmac looked at each other, then back down at Sanke. "She came in with one of the new guys," he went on. "There are so many new guys."

"How many?" Cohmac demanded, then seemed to catch himself, softened some. "More or less?"

"Ah, a hundred and fifty, maybe? A whole bunch of them are Mimbanese. But a lot of humans, too. And other species. They've been hiring them all month, boosting up the force to—"

"Protect the shipyards during the high-profile construction project," Cohmac said. "We've heard."

"Yeah, and they don't . . . No one knows who they are, really. Which is normal, I guess? It's a big city, and some of them were probably shipped in from Kol Vella or Tyrena, but still . . . all of them? For no one to know any of them is weird."

"That is odd." Kantam stroked their chin, then offered Sanke a hand.

He took it, struggled to his feet. "Thanks. So anyway,

there'd been tensions, little comments, an occasional fistfight even. And it seemed like it was getting worse. All between the new guys and us veterans of the force. Then this guy shows up today with the bright red girl, and you know you're not supposed to have guests at the barracks. It was really obvious something was gonna go wrong. I just don't think anyone knew *how* wrong. At least, we didn't. . . ." He shook his head, eyes getting teary. "Captain Orban said something, told him to get her out of there, and the guy took it as disrespect—the girl egging him on the whole time—and it turned into a shoving match. Everyone gathered around like they do, then someone showed up with a bat and they just . . . they just beat Orban . . . just . . . He's done. It was the most horrible thing I've ever seen."

Kantam nodded, extending a friendly hand to the man's trembling shoulder. "You've been through a lot, Sanke."

"It got worse after that. Others came to his defense and they got beaten, too, then blasters were drawn and each side—the new and the old—started overturning tables in the mess room, firing back and forth. Then someone, I don't know who, released some kind of gas. An explosion went off. Everyone started running, hiding, screaming. Blaster fire cut through the mist. I . . . I don't know." He snorted, wiping away tears. "I hid inside a cruiser cockpit that sealed me off from the chemical, then waited. All around me, screams. I don't know whose, but I can guess. I waited for it to quiet down, then I made a run for it . . . and here I am."

"The girl," Cohmac said, heading for the bike. "Is she still at the station?"

"No, she's in the wind. The new guys got her out of there quick, as soon as things started to get nasty."

Cohmac let out a low growl that only Kantam could hear. "Any idea where she might be?"

"None," Sanke moaned, then his eyes got wide. "And . . . I think I'm gonna . . . I'm gonna go!" He turned and ran off down the speedway.

Cohmac and Kantam already had their lightsabers extended when they whirled around.

FORTY

CORONET CITY

"They said *what?*" Crash gaped. Then, almost immediately, the pieces started to fall together.

She'd been sitting in her office, feet on the desk, trying to enjoy a moment of peace before the storm of the gala. And then Ram had barged in, arm in arm with their brand-new starlet, Zeen, who looked completely shell-shocked, and Reath in tow.

The Padawans had then proceeded to tell her some wild story about the older Jedi running off to investigate a situation at the muni barracks. The holos had mentioned it in an off-hand sort of way that morning—there were reports of an explosion of some kind, smoke rising, but an official police spokesman had given a statement saying that everything was absolutely fine and normal, nothing to be concerned about, so that was the story all the holos went with. Never mind that the spokesman was clearly nursing a black eye while giving the statement—he was wearing a uniform, so that was all that mattered.

Crash had rolled her eyes and tried to put it out of her mind at the time; she had to focus.

But now the Padawans were telling her that the Nihil were definitely on Corellia, may have infiltrated the muni police, and could potentially have some significant numbers with them, to boot.

Crash took her feet off the desk and leaned across it, like she was about to say something important. The Padawans and Zeen stared at her, waiting.

Truth was: if she was going to attack Coronet City, the first thing she would do was create some kind of distraction that would thin any planet security forces. She stood up, vaguely aware that the others were still waiting for whatever she was about to say—not caring. Gus Talon had a security pact with CorSec, and they *didn't* have a Jedi temple, crucially.

That meant that any crisis on Gus Talon would almost immediately pull significant numbers from both entities away from Coronet City. The worse the crisis, the greater the pull.

And of course, these were details that only someone as

enmeshed in local politics as Crash or an actual member of the political establishment would know.

Then of course, Coronet City defenses would be left up to the munis and, in case of a major incident, potentially any of the other units that could be pulled from nearby cities. But that would all take a while, especially given all the political piss-marking and territorialism that would ensue.

Crash stood at the window, three pairs of anxious eyes glued to the back of her head.

Below, the afternoon sun was just starting its long descent toward the harbor.

"This whole . . . dirty . . . filthy . . . situation," she finally said, very, very slowly, "has been an inside job from the very beginning."

She'd known that, or suspected it anyway, since the night Prybolt, Tralmat, and Ovarto went missing. But she'd figured it was just some messy local tit-for-tat type deal. City Fathers were constantly snipping and snapping at each other like a pack of gundarks. Occasionally, all that pettiness would erupt into an all-out dispute and then various assassination attempts or successes. It's what kept Crash with steady work, quite frankly, and it was part of why she'd sworn off ever picking sides. They were all corrupt, power-hungry clowns, so the best thing to do was just collect credits and keep it moving. That was lesson one from Baynoo's book of bodyguarding, a lesson she had made sure Crash learned on day one.

But this . . . this was something different altogether. The Nihil had been brutalizing the frontier for years. They'd caused the Great Disaster, nearly wiping out Hetzal and several other planets. They'd massacred innocent people at the Republic Fair; they'd probably murdered tens of thousands, all told, if not more.

And now they were on Corellia. And almost definitely connected to someone Crash either had been or was still protecting.

The thought made her sick to her stomach.

She coughed, realized she was leaning against the window sill, and suddenly it was the only thing keeping her up.

"Crash?" someone said—Ram, probably. "You okay?"

Had she . . . helped this happen somehow? She coughed again, blinking away tears. Bile tickled the back of her throat, threatening to rush up and out. "I . . . *hrk*."

A hand touched her back, then another, and a third.

Crash took in a deep breath, then let out a long, shaky sigh. She wasn't okay. But there was work to do, even if, for the first time, she wasn't totally sure it was work she should be doing. If it would make her mama proud. Would Baynoo protect someone who was helping the Nihil get a foothold in their city? There was no way. She'd left the business over a dustup with a now-dead City Father who'd been caught planting surveillance equipment in his workers' dressing rooms but kept his office. Baynoo had refused to protect him, leaving him to one of the lesser agencies, which was why he was a now-dead City Father. Crash had loved her for that, and knew that more than anything, Baynoo didn't want the agency to fall apart, putting dozens out of work, all because of her.

Crash had grown up in the business. She was universally regarded as the company's best operative. When she was twelve, Baynoo had tried half-heartedly to get her excited about another career—one that didn't involve getting shot at—but it was no use. Crash wanted to be just like her mom, and just like her mom, when Crash wanted something, there was no stopping her from getting it.

So she took over the agency, running the ops and business side of things, and she was damn good at it. And it worked out, because even though she detested politics and most politicians, she loved her city. And protecting them felt somehow like she was protecting Coronet.

But now Coronet was under attack, and it may well be that the attack was coming in part from the inside.

The problem was: *who*?

She turned to Zeen and the Padawans, wiping her eyes and tensing her face, then trying to relax it. "Not many people have seen me get upset and lived," she said. "And all of them are either close, close friends or my mom."

"So . . ." Ram made like he was going for his lightsaber, then cracked a winning smile. "Just trying to lighten the mood!"

"Ha," Crash said, rolling her eyes with a grin. "You're

getting better at that straight-faced thing. Point is—Zeen, I don't know you at all, but Ram adores you and Reath seems to like you all right, too, and even though I only met them, like, yesterday and I don't make a habit of complimenting strangers, they're two of the most genuine people I've ever met."

"Aw, shoot," Ram said.

"And I've met a lot of people," Crash added. "Although, to be fair most of them are politicians and criminals. Anyway, point is, the galaxy being what it is, I have no choice but to trust you, and ask you to trust me. Because whatever happens next, we're gonna need a whole lot of trust."

Zeen's worried face had eased into a gentle, calm gaze, and now she met Crash's eyes with a slight smile, one that made her look every bit as enigmatic and luminous as the holo footage had suggested she was. "I trust you, too," Zeen said. "I don't totally know why—maybe it's the Force telling me you're okay—but I do. Plus, if these boys say you're all right, then you're all right."

"I agree," Ram said.

"You agree that if we say someone's all right then they're all right?" Reath chided.

Ram beamed. "Without a doubt! We have impeccable taste in people."

Crash made her way back to the desk, trying to shake off the dizziness of not knowing who was secretly working with whom. It was a routine part of the job she'd gotten used to, but that was under normal, intergovernmental-backstabbing circumstances, not galactic warmongers invading the Core Worlds circumstances.

"Nice job on the setup last night, by the way," she said, nodding her approval at Ram and Reath. They both shrugged and made awkward pleased-with-themselves gestures. "Smeemarm said it went off pretty smooth, and Smeemarm is another who does not give praise lightly."

"Just doing our job, ma'am," Ram said with a smug wink.

"Where's the change from that creature delicacy buy, speaking of which? I have to return it to the expense drawer."

His eyes widened. "Uh . . ."

"Kidding," Crash said. "I know you blew it all. It's fine. You're learning. But on a serious note, do you two still have those credits I gave you yesterday when I hired you?"

"You mean when you"—Reath made little Lepi-ear quotes with his fingers—"*hired* us?" He pulled out the credit. "Yes." Ram pulled his out, too.

Crash narrowed her eyes at him. "I know Jedi are too cool to worry about things like contracts and agreements, but it matters to *me*, okay? Now hand 'em over."

"What?" Ram yelped. "Did we get fired? I'm sorry I overpaid for the Bonbrak! I don't understand money that well!"

Crash snorted, taking the credits from them. "No, silly. You're hiring me."

"Huh?" Reath said.

"Things are about to get even uglier, and there's going to be a lot going on. You being my clients, under my—the company's—direct protection, means . . ."

"I kinda thought you might just look out for us because we're your friends," Ram said, seeming more than a little hurt. "Not because we paid you."

Crash suppressed a scowl. She hated being misunderstood, but she also knew that people who weren't in her line of work couldn't really understand. "It's not about the money," she said, holding up the measly two credits. "*Clearly.* If it was, you wouldn't be able to afford me. It's about clarity. I . . . everyone on my team—we have a split second to make life-and-death decisions. Decisions that someone could easily agonize for days over, but if we hesitate, the decision is made for us. And there are multiple threats, multiple clients to protect, not to mention our fellow team members, ourselves. And the client comes first, no matter what. That's the job, and we do it. So . . . I know one thing I need to happen tonight is for you three to come out alive. And that's a lot more likely to happen if you're logged in as under my care. Period."

Reath and Ram had been listening intently, thoughtfully, and they both nodded.

"Kayt," Crash said. "I know you're lurking in one of these dark corners."

"I have already deleted their employee records," the droid said, popping out of a nearby crate, "and entered them in as clients, Master Crash."

"Good," Crash said. "Add Zeen Mrala as an attached client under one of their entries."

"Done."

"Does this mean we don't get to dress up as child assassins again?" Ram complained.

Crash released a wry smile. "Oh, not at all," she said. "It just means I'm asking you to do it for free this time."

FORTY-ONE

CORONET CITY

A muni gunship barreled down the ancient stone speedway toward Kantam and Cohmac. It looked like a relic—all rusted and boxy, with steam pouring out the back, but those engines had a roaring kick to them, and there was a guy on top manning some kind of built-in antiaircraft cannon.

"Based on what we just heard," Kantam said, "any chance these are actual muni police?"

Cohmac didn't bother answering; he ran forward to meet the first burst of cannon fire head-on, smashing away one shot, then another with his saber. That had to be some heavy artillery—each deflected hit knocked Cohmac back a half meter.

"That's what I thought," Kantam said. They raced ahead to smack back the next few shots, taking care to adjust their balance for the weight of each one. With the gunship bearing down on them, Kantam sent the final laser blast zinging directly into it, taking out the cannon and gunner in a sparkling explosion.

Kantam sidestepped and held out their lightsaber as the gunship hurtled past, shredding a vicious gash into its metal armor.

Cohmac had already leapt on top when Kantam looked up. A hatch popped open on the roof of the gunship, and a Weequay with a thermal detonator in one hand tried to leap out. Cohmac lopped off the hand holding the detonator with one swing of his lightsaber, then kicked the Weequay in the face, sending him flailing back into the gunship after his hand. Cohmac slammed the door and leapt just as a sharp pop erupted inside.

The gunship careened to the left, smashing into the stone guardrail and bursting into flames. Cohmac landed in a crouch, then rose facing Kantam, who regarded him with a blank face. Cohmac had moved with unhesitant precision. He had wiped out the lot of them—however many had been in that thing—with barely half a dozen moves. It was impressive and unsettling at the same time, and Kantam was at a loss for words.

For most of Kantam's life, a lightsaber extended for the kill had been a rare sight. A generation earlier, during the Republic's expansion into the Outer Rim, things had been thornier, sure, but most of those conflicts had simmered by the time Kantam was born.

But the Outer Rim Jedi had been mired in a near constant battle for more than a year, and their enemy had proved ruthless, unbound by any sense of honor or code, and almost unstoppable in its destructive urges. More Jedi had been killed in the past few months than in all the other years of Kantam's life combined.

And Kantam knew they were not alone in having trouble adjusting to this new war-torn frontier. The Jedi were supposed to be messengers of peace, but that seemed more and more like methodology for defeat.

"What?" Cohmac asked, powering down his lightsaber.

"I am"—Kantam blinked, searching for the words—"adjusting still, to constant warfare. Even after all we've been through. And you, Cohmac, of all people—"

Cohmac waved a hand, stopping them. "I know what I've said in the past." His voice became a broken gravelly whisper. "But these past months . . . and especially everything that's happening right now—it's changed me, Kantam. The galaxy is not . . . it's not the one we grew up in. It's not the one the Order we know was built for. I don't know where we go from here, but I know if we don't face the new reality head-on, it will devour us whole." He took a shaking deep breath. "We don't have a choice. Now, more than ever. Flinching means losing everything."

"I don't—"

"They were trying to kill us," Cohmac insisted. "There is nothing in our code about letting ourselves be murdered on some Force-forsaken aqueduct on the outskirts of Coronet."

"I—"

"And sometimes, we must strike first, Kantam. We all celebrated after Quantxi when we heard about how your Padawan restrained Zeen's hand, stopped her from killing Krix. But given all that's happened since—can we really say that was the right thing? How many lives—"

"We both know," Kantam said, struggling to keep their voice cool, even, "if it hadn't been Krix attacking those planets, it would've been Sabata, or Nan, or who knows who else."

"All the more reason we have to take out who we can when we have the chance."

"You're losing sight of Zeen in this scenario," Kantam warned. "She should've murdered her former friend as he was pleading for his life? Are we to pretend that would've been just fine for the girl, not traumatized her? Not sent her into a spiral she may well not have returned from? That she would've just forgotten it and gone on with her life?"

"We all must make sacrifices," Cohmac said in a hoarse whisper. He turned and started walking down the speedway.

"Cohmac," Kantam said, catching up with him. "What did you see?"

Cohmac kept walking, his face a cemetery.

"Cohmac? Starlight. What did you see?"

He stopped. Faced Kantam. The whole infinity of space seemed to widen within his sad eyes; concern crisscrossed his forehead. "It doesn't matter what I saw. We have to go there. *Now.* Come on."

Kantam caught Cohmac's arm before he could turn away. "No."

"Excuse me?"

"I don't know what you saw, but right now, here is where we're needed. Clearly the Nihil are trying to get a foothold on Corellia, and whatever they're up to may well have to do with whatever's happening on Starlight."

"Kantam." His voice was so low, Kantam could barely hear him. "We have to. It's . . . it's our home." He started off again.

"There's nothing we can do there that the Jedi already on the station can't."

Cohmac whirled, one finger already pointing, eyes sharp. "Is that what you know, Kantam, or is that what you're telling yourself so the weight of regret doesn't crush you from the inside?"

"I know it," Kantam said calmly.

"Well *I* don't."

"We need you, Cohmac. We need you here."

"She needs me on—" Cohmac froze, eyes wide, mouth hanging open. He shook his head. "They need us."

Kantam waited a beat. "Orla."

Cohmac seemed to crumple into himself, all that wrath suddenly swept away like a layer of dust in the Corellian wind. Kantam knew Cohmac was close with the Wayseeker Jedi. They'd been Padawans together and had gone through some hard experiences, both back then and more than a few times since. It wasn't anything sordid or dramatic, what they had, just the genuine care of two inexorably bonded friends who had seen and shared things few others could understand.

"She is . . . The danger . . ." Cohmac rasped. "Whatever it is, it's . . . it's so horrible. Something . . . much worse than the Drengir."

"I know," Kantam said, stepping closer, extending an arm as Cohmac lowered his head into his hands and sobbed. "I felt it, too."

"It took Loden. Infected the twins . . ."

Kantam nodded. That unfathomable horror had been stalking through everyone's nightmares since Loden Greatstorm had been turned to dust by some unknown entity on Grizal. And then the twin Jedi Terec and Ceret had been partially calcified, probably by the same thing, and barely survived.

Whatever the Nihil had, they were sure to be hoarding it, perfecting it for an assault on the heart of the Jedi. And perhaps that moment had finally come.

"We need you here," Kantam said again, now that Cohmac's anger had passed. "All of us, but especially Reath."

Cohmac looked up, eyes suddenly clear. Then he blinked at Kantam, as if seeing them for the first time. "Stars . . . Lula! I'm . . . I wasn't thinking. Of course you're . . ."

Kantam shook their head. "We can't . . . give in to fear." It kept rising and rising, the fear, even as Kantam moved through each new wave of it. They knew it would keep coming, that it would not stop. But neither would Kantam. They would face it and release it, every single time, again and again. "Even with the ones we care for the most in danger and out of our reach. There's much we don't understand still, but I do know that right now, our place is here. The Padawans here need us, and it may very well be that those on Starlight need us, if nothing else, to stay alive, to keep this fight against the Nihil alive, to stop them in their tracks. I feel the pull to fly into uncertain disaster and leave this much more palpable danger behind. But I know that's fear pulling me, pulling both of us. And we must face that fear, discard it as we were trained, and do what we have to do."

Cohmac stepped back, met Kantam's eyes. "Very well. But if we stay, we stay and *fight.* We don't sit on our hands and hope someone gives us cause to strike back. We don't engage in the same folly that's had us on our heels all year, barely ready for each new wave of attacks, lashing out reactively instead of taking the initiative. Yes?"

Kantam nodded. "For light and life."

"For light and li—" A rumbling from farther down the speedway interrupted them. Both Jedi looked up. An entire convoy of tanks, transports, construction walkers—Kantam couldn't make out how many or what else—lumbered toward them from the direction of the barracks. The Nihil were on the move.

"We may be a bit over our heads here, numbers-wise," Cohmac said, collecting himself.

"Oh, we are," Kantam said. "But that's all right—I have a better idea."

FORTY-TWO

CORONET CITY

Crash stood on a balcony overlooking the event hall—a brightly lit penthouse suite at the Mangrove Hotel in the trendy Financial District. Floor-to-ceiling windows revealed the long golden patterns of shadow and light that the afternoon sun sent across the city all around them; farther off, the bay sparkled, preparing for another glorious twilight hour.

Somewhere, the Nihil were probably preparing whatever attack they had in the works.

And soon Mother Fastidima would come calling, or send one of her henchworms, more likely.

Everything, without a doubt, was terrible and falling apart.

Crash's attention was on the floor below though. Tangor and Barchibar moved in slow, methodical circles through the room, Tangor with a weapons scanner, Barchi with the hounds. Between the two of them, Crash could rest assured there were no hidden devices. Smeemarm was searching the hotel basement and the tunnels beneath it. Some of her slimmer, slimier tunnel team slid through the pipes and vent ducts throughout the penthouse level, sniffing, tasting, watching. Somewhere up above, Fezzonk circled in his flier, making sure the only snipers on any nearby rooftops were either theirs or Dizcaro's. 10-K8's droids buzzed in small circles through the wide-open room, their little whirring systems tracking and checking each detail and draft for an aberration.

And at various points out in the city, her operatives were opening doors in advance of a client, double-checking corners and backstreets, sliding under vehicles with an eye for explosives or recording devices, scouting intersections for sniper posts and ways to beat a hasty retreat. Soon they would converge, and they would be safe, because Crash had willed it to be so, and Crash got what Crash wanted, it was known.

She smiled. It was all like a beautiful, vast symphony—each individual played their part, then all those parts flowed together into something greater than the sum. And Crash was the conductor, watching it all, taking in each element, each surprise or twist or possibility as it arose, turning it, adjusting it, fitting it into the larger whole. It was delicious, really.

And it managed, if only momentarily, to take her mind off the growing unease she'd been feeling ever since the Padawans confirmed that the Nihil were indeed on Corellia.

Down below, Varb Tenart wandered around the room in that ambling Dug gait, conducting his own wild symphony with polylingual yells as different-sized creatures in matching formalwear set up tablecloths, sound equipment, and decorations.

Crash didn't envy him his job. She knew he loved it, but doing all this work just to make a party go off right for people she didn't care much about seemed like actual hell.

This, though—she turned her attention back to the bustling bodyguards, each checking off various boxes to ensure no one would get hurt. Of course, that didn't mean no one actually *would* get hurt—there was always an element of chaos at play, a missing piece, a chink in the armor. That's what made it all a challenge, and the challenge made it worthwhile.

If only Prybolt were there to revel with her in all of it coming together.

Anyway, Tangor and Barchi were finishing up their device sweeps, and Tamo the Savrip, who was working the downstairs, had just pinged Crash with a message. "Go with it," Crash said.

He gargled something to the effect of "Talent on lock," one of the Basic phrases they'd taught him. The Padawans and Zeen had arrived, and were passing Tamo on their way into the hotel lobby.

"I just wanted to say," someone whispered behind Crash.

"Gah!" Crash yelled, almost toppling over the balcony railing. She whirled around to face Svi'no. "You have *got* to stop doing that!"

"Oops," the singer said without much effort to sound like she meant it.

Crash grimaced. "Did you come to berate me again in front of my team?"

Svi'no looked genuinely regretful. "No. I came to say I was a little out of line with that."

Crash raised both eyebrows and stuck out her chin. "Oh, just a little, huh?"

Svi'no looked away, then back. "You have to be so stubborn, don't you? I wasn't entirely wrong, you know. I just needn't have popped off so . . . publicly about it, is all."

Crash crossed her arms over her chest. Of course Svi'no knew the way to chip away at Crash's armor was with a good, thoughtful explanation of something that was neither here nor there. "I see."

Svi'no swatted her but gently, and she left her hand on Crash's bare wrist, like she didn't want to let her go. Crash looked at her friend's hand, then looked in her eyes.

"You do have a right to keep things from your team," Svi'no said. She rolled her eyes. "I think most things work out better when you don't, but that's beside the point."

"What's the point?" Crash asked, very softly.

"The point is I—most of us, really, but especially me—we're not *just* on your team. It's more than a team."

Crash blinked. She was sure if she said something, it would be the wrong thing. If she moved, it would be the wrong move. It would end whatever was happening. All this—this tenderness—would turn to dust.

"We are friends. *Your* friends. And that's why this works. That's why it's different. And that matters. And you're going to throw all that away if you're not careful with it."

"I . . ." Crash opened her mouth like she was still speaking, but it turned out she wasn't. She probably looked like the goofiest fish. Finally, she said, "Do you . . . mean maybe also . . . *more* than friends?"

A slight smile creased Svi'no's mouth, then vanished. "Maybe," she allowed solemnly. Then she narrowed her eyes, like they could burrow into Crash's. "I mean, yes, I hope so. Down the road. But for me, right now, nothing can be anything if it's not based in friendship first."

Crash nodded, trying to ignore the way her heart wouldn't shut up with all that pounding away in her ears. "I can do that."

The smile came back, and it was wide this time; it stayed. "Good."

And then Svi'no was gone, evaporating back into the shadows.

"Ahhaha!" Varb suddenly gargled with gusto. "The talent has-a arrived!"

There was no need for an announcement. The whole room, all that frantic preparing, stopped cold when Zeen walked in wearing a shimmering silver bodysuit beneath a translucent ball gown of seafoam that perfectly offset her magenta skin. Ansh, the Ithorian fashionista, had done an incredible job on the girl's makeup, too—a sparkling half sun filled one side of her face, then seemed to simmer into a series of bright gems that led up the bridge of her nose and across her forehead. Purple lipstick with gold highlights completed the picture. Around a diamond tiara, her head tendrils waved as if underwater.

All that, and Crash could think only of what Svi'no had just said. They would have her back. All of them. Crash just had to let them.

But that was fine. It was exactly as things should be. The rest of the room was lost in Zeen, so Zeen's mission was already accomplished. Soon the guests would arrive, and they, too, would lose themselves beholding this stunning superstar who had risen, quite literally overnight, from nobody to galactic phenomenon with nary a word sang on the holos. Let them chatter, and wonder, and show off. In their excitement, one of them would slip up. And Crash would be there, ready, when they did. She would find out who was working with the Nihil, and she'd handle whoever it was.

"Truly a sight to behold," Varb sighed, making his way up the stairs to Crash. "I must thank you for helping me make this happen."

Crash brushed off the notion, making room for him at the bannister. "Eh, we helped each other."

The boys had taken up their positions on either side of Zeen, and a few of Varb's workers were gathering around to get a glimpse of this strange trinity—two Scarlet Skull assassins, long thought extinct, and a pop sensation whom no one had heard sing.

"The guests will probably end up taking off their masks to get a better view of her," Varb said.

Crash pulled her attention from the floor and directed the full strength of her glare at the Dug. "Did you just say *masks*?"

Varb shrugged, irritated at the clear accusation in her tone. "Of course! That's been in the works for a few months."

Masks brought a whole new layer of danger into any given situation. Automatic anonymity, plenty of new places to conceal a weapon, the near impossibility of keeping track of anyone. Crash's mind reeled at all the ways this changed things.

"It was Tralmat's idea, actually," Varb rambled. "And we figured we'd stick with it, considering *everything*. . . . You know, just seemed like the right thing, to honor his wishes. Although, I admit I thought it was strange when he suggested it." Varb shook his head. "A *Nihil*-themed party. Just weird."

"A *what*?" Crash demanded.

"It was basically his way of mocking the notion that the Nihil could ever come to Corellia, like 'Haha, what a joke, we'll all wear gas masks because that could never happen, haha.'" Varb looked at Crash. "Haha?"

Down below, the first guests were already arriving. They wore fancy ball gowns and tailored suits beneath greasy breather masks with goggles and helmets.

Crash pushed past Varb and headed down the stairs. "What did you *do*?"

FORTY-THREE

CORONET CITY

What was happening? Ram didn't know whether to go for the lightsaber he'd concealed in his assassin suit or . . . just stand there looking ridiculous while his sworn enemies milled about, enjoying sparkly beverages and chuckling amiably.

It wasn't the Nihil, was it? It couldn't be. At least, not all of them.

He knew this was someone's horrific idea of a joke—he could tell by how they were carrying on, and obviously Nihil didn't wear formal attire. Or, if they did, they didn't do it for the same occasions they'd wear their battle masks to. Right?

It was all just nauseatingly weird and unbalancing. Even

if none of them were actually Nihil—why would anyone think it was funny or cute to dress up as the very people who had been terrorizing the galaxy, who'd attacked Ram's home planet, slaughtered innocent people in droves, all while laughing and promising more destruction to come? *What is so funny about that?* Ram wanted to scream. *How is this a joke to you?* None of those people the Nihil had killed were around to endure this disrespect, but Ram was, and it shuddered through him like groundquake after groundquake.

It's because the Nihil aren't terrorizing the galaxy, a quiet voice inside Ram reminded him. *They're terrorizing the Outer Rim.* And he knew that even if the Nihil were to get a foothold this deep in the Core planets, it wouldn't be these dithering bejeweled socialites who'd feel their wrath. It would be regular people, cut down in the streets, in their own homes, just like always. And then the rich and powerful would throw a soiree to commemorate them and dress up like their murderers again.

To make things worse, Ram had felt off since . . . just about all day. It rose within him in sudden waves, that feeling, like a pool of dirty water was climbing higher and higher up his chest and soon it would cover his heart, his lungs, and he would drown from the inside.

Suddenly, the room seemed to spin and Ram wasn't sure if he could breathe.

How dare all these people make light of so much death and suffering? Ram screamed inside.

They just stood there chortling and carrying on, checking their little comm devices for more gossip and chitter-chatter. Meanwhile, people had fought and died to protect the galaxy from the Nihil. Not just people—Ram's friends.

What would they do if they had to face the Nihil? If they had been on Valo, on Takodana, anywhere amid the war and ruin that had been reaped? He imagined all those comlinks and holoprojectors shattering at once, exploding in everyone's faces as they screamed and ducked for cover.

And then someone did scream, and a spark lanced upward somewhere nearby.

Ram gulped, glancing around. Another little pop sounded from the other side of the room; everyone was muttering, concerned. *What was happening?*

A hand landed on Ram's shoulder, and he almost smacked it off.

Then he was glad he didn't—it was Reath.

The room slowed. Most folks looked back and forth and went about their business. Then Ram took a breath. Reath squeezed his shoulder, looked him in the eyes. *Be cool,* the look said. *I'm here.*

The couple of people whose comlinks had mysteriously shorted out scowled at their broken devices, then shrugged and pocketed them.

"Was that . . . you?" Reath whispered as they holed up in an out-of-the-way corner, out of sight.

Ram blinked. Had it been? He had been so, so angry, and

he'd imagined those devices exploding. . . . It might've been. He met his friend's eyes. "I think . . . so?"

"You felt nothing," Reath said. "And now you feel everything."

Ram nodded. That was it exactly. How did Reath show up out of nowhere with the answers? It wasn't magic really, Ram realized. His friend had simply listened to him, observed him, and paid attention.

Still, sadness rippled through Ram, for everyone he knew, for the Republic. . . . It tempered out the rage, but it was almost as overwhelming. "What do I do?" Ram whispered. "It hurts."

Reath nodded sagely. "It's okay. Literally, it is. Even when it's not. It's okay to feel everything you feel—"

"But," Ram started.

Reath stopped him with a raised hand. "I wasn't finished. It's okay to feel everything you feel, *but* you gotta find balance."

Ram cocked his head to the side. He knew this. This was not a newsflash. So why did it feel like such a simple shortcut to the whole problem in that moment? "Balance," he repeated.

"That's it. You can't stop it, the rage, the sorrow. So you have to balance it."

"But . . . how?"

"Well, the way I see it—now that you feel so many things, *including* nothing at all, it's like you have a very full palette to paint with. Or, in your case, I guess, a . . . tray with doohickies on it?"

Ram brightened. "Oh! Like my utility cart?"

"Right. Each emotion is a tool, and once you've felt it, now it's on your utility cart. You know how to recognize them, so you can use one to balance the other, maybe. You can't be all empty and unfeeling all the time—that's not balance. You'd be a droid. But you can't run around blowing up everybody's comlinks, either."

Ram let out a laugh that startled even himself. Then he shook his head. "So many emotions! But . . . balance. I think . . . I think I can do that."

"Good. Because we have a job to do."

Ram nodded, determined, as they headed back into the crowd.

Balance. It seemed so simple and so impossible at the same time, but it was more pragmatic and attainable than trying to wish away anger.

He'd felt nothing, then he'd felt everything. And now he had to balance the two.

He could do that.

And Reath was right about something else, too: they did have a job to do. Tasteless, disgusting, compassionless excuse for a joke or not, there was a good chance some real Nihil could be there, intermingled with the goofy fatuous pretenders.

And anyway, the Padawans had to keep Zeen safe.

Ram watched her move like a living beam of light through the crowd of well-dressed socialites in marauder headgear. They fawned over her, gasped and gawked through goggles and blast shields. Some stared, others pretended not to be wowed, trying to make casual small talk. Others kept their distance. But all eyes were on Zeen.

Ram kept his own gaze moving, checking the hands of everyone who approached, the way Crash had taught him. He couldn't make out many faces, which Crash said was often the first place you could see an attack coming—that intense determination of a hired killer, for example, or the wild-eyed glare of a fanatic. But the next place to look was the hands. People with something to hide would often conceal theirs. Nerves might make them shake. A blaster pistol, a dagger could be retrieved by one.

By that logic, these partygoers had plenty to hide. Hands, sometimes as many as a half dozen, hid beneath fur muffs or in the long pockets of silk trousers. Hands clasped each other behind backs or rustled endlessly within purses and pouches. Fingers trembled around the long stems of champagne glasses, cigarra holders, other fingers.

"I hate all of this," Ram muttered, moving close enough to Reath to speak into his ear. "But anyway, *balance*!"

"Balance," Reath whispered back.

"Wizard," Ram hissed.

"Well, well!" an elderly woman in a lime green gown and elaborately tubed helmet said triumphantly. Then she chuckled, because apparently everything was a funny party joke. "I always thought that initiation into the Scarlet Skull Cult required members to remove their own tongues!"

Ram leaned uncomfortably close and made his voice a harsh whisper. "What makes you think this is *my* tongue?"

She gasped and teetered off, probably already figuring out how to turn the incident into a hilarious anecdote.

"Did you just imply—" Reath whispered. "Never mind. You're getting a little *too* good at that straight-faced delivery thing."

Ram shrugged. "It worked." He hoped Crash hadn't seen that; effective or not, she wouldn't be pleased. Ram glanced around and spotted her in a far corner having a heated conversation with that guy Dizcaro, her well-coiffed rival. She was getting in his face (on tiptoes), and he looked downright regretful. Crash called her droid over, gave her some instructions, and then ushered Dizcaro behind a curtain.

What is going on? Ram wondered.

FORTY-FOUR

CORONET CITY

Reath Silas felt like his whole world was sinking into a pit of trash.

That was the only way to describe it.

Sure, no one was shooting at him at the moment, but he had a feeling that wouldn't be the case for much longer. And anyway, they didn't have to be actively trying to kill him; their little dress-up party let him know his life didn't matter to them at all.

He tried to clear his mind. Waves of anger and heartbreak kept rising as he thought of the people who'd died, how many times he'd nearly died.

He released them.

They returned.

He released them.

Worst part was: he wasn't even sure if this feeling was just from the sick masquerade going on all around him or something else . . . something worse. Deep down, he sensed a profound disturbance in the galaxy, but he couldn't sense it clearly from the middle of all these other emotions.

If only he could just go somewhere and close his eyes and tune into the Force.

If only he were back on Starlight, happily scanning the Jedi archives for some new thread of logic and lore to unspool.

If only . . . something caught his eye, a flickering of movement that didn't fit in. He scanned the room, and his gaze landed on someone walking a little too quickly through the crowd.

Were they heading toward Zeen? He squinted, already nudging Ram. It looked like a woman in a red bodysuit and a horned breathing mask.

She was definitely heading for Zeen.

And red . . . was that a bodysuit, or was it Sabata Krill?

Reath shoved through the crowd, ignoring the indignant gasps and grunts. Ram was right behind him.

"How dare you?" someone yelped just as Reath pushed them into another party patron. He heard the clatter of broken glass, angry mutters. Didn't matter. Nothing mattered but getting to Zeen before Sabata, or whoever that was.

But he was too late, he could already tell—the person had broken into a run while Reath was tangled up amid the partiers and she was closing in on Zeen, and Zeen was turning, face open wide with surprise and . . .

"Can I have your autograph?" Her voice came out muffled through the breathing mask. Reath stumbled to a halt just short of barreling into the two of them.

"Of course," Zeen said, doing an admirable job of hiding the horror she had to be feeling about being surrounded by Nihil masks.

It wasn't Sabata Krill—this woman was shorter and had green skin; the red was indeed a bodysuit. But that didn't mean she wasn't Nihil. Ram came up beside Reath, panting, and heaved a sigh of relief.

"You guys okay?" Zeen asked when the green woman disappeared back into the crowd.

"Absolutely not," Reath muttered. He had gotten lost in his thoughts, which was fine back at home, on Starlight, when people weren't trying to kill him. But in Coronet City, in this viper's nest full of killers and people pretending to be killers . . . Reath couldn't afford to get so caught up again.

A murmur moved through the crowd. Worry, surprise, fear . . . a hundred anxious emotions seemed to rise at once from all around. Reath and Ram and Zeen traded wary looks and then turned their attention to the center of the room, where someone had turned on the holo news.

Reath couldn't make out what it said at first, but he heard gasps. Hands reached for comlinks to find out more information from local gossips or to alert loved ones.

Alert them about what though? Reath peered over the heads around him and finally saw a slowly turning holo image that caught his breath in his throat: smoke pouring out of Starlight Beacon.

FORTY-FIVE

CORONET CITY

"What the *kark* were you thinking, Dizcaro?" Crash spat when the door slid closed behind them.

The elegant meeting room had the chic vibe of a place where high-end people snuck off to snort high-end powders that would result in their high-end funerals in a few years. A short, stylish table sat between two absurdly tall leather lounge chairs—it all seemed like some twisted caricature of the world, and Crash hated it. Everything was black and shiny, with sharp edges—even, somehow, the thick curtains that dangled in front of the gigantic windows, letting only a sliver of light in. The curtains danced slightly in the air from the vents just below, and that was the only movement in this otherwise stale, fashionable, and dead place.

"I didn't know about the Nihil costumes," Dizcaro insisted. "Varb said it was in the original contract though, so really the question is—what were *you* thinking, Crash?"

"I didn't see it there," Crash said. It would've jumped out at her if she had; there was no way . . . "Point is"—she rounded on him—"something really messed up is going on and it's not just the same old City Fathers crap."

"I've been getting that sense, too," Dizcaro said. "But what am I supposed to do about it?"

"Same thing I'm doing," Crash said. "Figure out what it is."

"And?"

"And stop it."

They glared at each other. Both of them knew the chances were, whoever was involved with the Nihil was under one of their protective contracts or the other. Whichever it was was about to be in the middle of a moral/financial/protocol quandary that few outsiders could understand.

Dizcaro's face fell. "I don't know—"

"Ah, this is Principal One Protector," a voice said over Dizcaro's comlink.

Crash raised her eyebrows. "Oh, you got a new comlink? Congrats."

Dizcaro shot her a glare. "I'm sending you the bill for the one you took, by the way. And for Crufeela's bail money."

"I'll be sure to forward it to the Bonbrak Protection Society," Crash zinged.

"Principal One Protector to Team Leader One," the voice on the comm said.

Crash scowled at him. "*Team Leader One?* Is that the best you could come up with?"

"Go for Lead One," he said. Then, holding the comlink away from his face, "What do your people call you?"

"Crash," Crash said. "When you have a cool nickname, you don't have to come up with goofy code names."

"Principal One needs the private meeting room," the bodyguard said. "He's heading there in two."

Dizcaro made a wide-eyed face at Crash. "Ah, ten-four Pee-Onepee, I am already there. Standing by."

"Oh, very well then."

"Hide," Dizcaro hissed. *"Now!"*

"Hide?" Crash growled. "I *hate* hi—"

Approaching footsteps cut her off. And anyway, Dizcaro was right. There was no better way to get to the bottom of something than to listen to what people said when they thought they were alone. She slipped behind the heavy black curtains just as the door slid open, her back pressed against the window, the breeze of the air vents shooting uncomfortably up her pant leg.

"What were you doing in here?" Ovus asked, walking in briskly.

"Oh, just had to handle a personal matter," Dizcaro said. A terrible liar, Crash thought. That was handy to know.

"Ah, well, hope everything is all right. My meeting should be showing up momenta—"

Something whirred from the far wall. A door, Crash realized. A hidden door! How were there hidden doors in this place that *she* didn't know about? What better way for an assassin to get in and out with no one being the wiser? She'd have to ream Varb over this—it was probably his fault somehow.

She peeked through the curtain. A hunched-over figure stepped out of the passageway. He was wearing a velvety robe and had on some kind of mask that looked like it was designed to fit a creature with an extra-long proboscis—a Kubaz maybe, or an unusually tall and bulky Culisetto. "You're late," the robed man said, his voice garbled slightly by a vocalizer.

"Now, listen here, Respriler," Ovus said, towering over the hunched figure, "or whatever your *real* name is—"

"I will not be spoken to this way," Respriler croaked.

Crash heard Dizcaro shift his weight from one foot to the other, probably trying to figure out if he should intervene.

"Won't you?" Ovus demanded. "You have strung me along for months now, with barely anything to show for it. And now I'm hearing reports that the muni barracks have been overrun and a Nihil convoy is heading downtown! Is that true?"

"I owe you precisely zero answers, *Finance Minister* Ovus." Clearly, this Respriler character felt the need to remind Ovus of his title.

"We agreed on a *few small* Nihil attacks here and there! Scattered and easily fought off. Just enough to get people rallied around closing down Corellia to outsiders. That was it! Not a whole army marching on downtown Coronet!"

Crash had to bite her hand to keep from screaming. Ovus was working with the Nihil! And he was clearly in way over his head. Could there really be a convoy headed into the city?

"We agreed to no such thing," Respriler said haughtily. "That was a request you made during our negotiation. That is all. And anyway, to what authority would you bring a dispute about our agreement, hm? Should we take it up with the trade commission? The city magistrate?"

"You know that's not—"

Respriler cut off the minister sharply. "What I know, Ovus, is that I have held up my end of the agreement thus far. I said CorSec and the Jedi would be removed from your path, giving the muni forces supremacy in Coronet, and it has happened. I said I would make you Father of Finance. That is the current title you possess, is it not? It is."

"Murdering Nomar Tralmat was certainly not part of our deal, either," Ovus insisted.

"Would you have pulled out if it was?" Respriler asked. "Didn't think so. I said I would make you ruler of Coronet City and then Corellia, and I shall, oh, impatient one, I shall.

But to achieve this lofty goal, I need to do things my way, and that's exactly what I am doing and what I will continue to do."

"You can't just—"

Respriler brushed off Ovus, heading for the door as it slid open. "I can, I have, and I will continue to do so. Now, if you'll excuse me, I have a victory party to attend."

Victory party? Crash thought. Could the whole galaxy be falling apart all around them?

"You're working with . . . the Nihil," Dizcaro said, his voice a steel blade.

Ovus whirled around, immediately closing the gap between them. "Are you a bodyguard or are you a pundit for the local news?" he demanded.

"It doesn't take a pundit to realize the Nihil are bent on destroying everything we care about!"

Crash had never heard Dizcaro so upset, and she'd certainly never seen him raise his voice to a client.

"When I want policy advice from the muscle," Ovus spat, "I'll ask for it. Until then, just do your job." Dizcaro took a step back like he'd been slapped.

Ovus hurried out of the room.

"I . . ." Dizcaro said when Crash slipped out of the curtains and stood next to him. "I don't know what just happened."

"Whatever it is," Crash said, already halfway out the door. "It's still happening."

In the main party hall, people were taking off their

masks and helmets—not because they'd finally discovered good taste, but so they could see better. The whole room was focused on a single holo image floating in a slow circle as frantic updates spun around it. Starlight Beacon had been attacked. It hung at an off angle, leaning too far over—not at the jaunty tilt they were all used to seeing. Smoke poured from an upper area of the station.

Not everyone had taken off their Nihil gear though, Crash realized, moving through the crowd. And not everyone was astonished. Some were snickering, whispering gleefully to one another, nodding. Were they Nihil or just heinous?

"Welcome to a new era!" Respriler yelled through his vocalizer as he hauled himself up on a table triumphantly. A woman screamed, and someone shouted, "Hey!" uselessly.

Where was Svi'no? Probably lurking somewhere nearby, Crash hoped out of sight. And the rest of Crash's crew—she saw the top of Tangor's shaggy head on the far end of the room—were probably moving into position to do whatever needed to be done. Zeen and the boys stood off to one side, their horrified expressions glued to the shimmering image of their home being destroyed.

Respriler stood to his full height and tore off his mask. Nomar Tralmat's tired, clenched face looked out at the crowd defiantly. "It is a new era of Corellian history! Of galactic history! The age of the Republic is over! Today it falls, just like its mighty beacon falls, right before your eyes!"

Screams and gasps sounded, but . . . no one did anything.

They just stared at him. It all seemed like some weird joke.

"I was lost like so many of you for so long. But a young woman showed me the light, the way . . . the path!" Tralmat rambled.

"This is madness!" It was Ovus, climbing onto a chair and pointing across the room. "You can't bring the Nihil to Corellia! We will fight them and win! Corellia will *always* stand strong!"

Nomar shook his head, smiling like a benevolent grandfather. "Oh, my dear Ovus." His eyes crinkled with wrath as he reached into his robes. And that was when Crash knew what was about to happen. She looked across the room, hoping, even against her worst instincts, that Dizcaro hadn't seen what she had. He was a sloppy, sometimes unprofessional bodyguard, but not sloppy enough. Already, he was leaping into action, one foot planted on a chair, then launching up and across the short distance between himself and Ovus.

Tralmat, very much not a soldier, started letting off shots as soon as his blaster was out. One singed past Crash, barely missing her. Another hit an elderly woman's arm, and her screams mixed with the rest of the room's. Then Tralmat found his mark and shot once, twice, and then again, just as Dizcaro's body went crashing into Ovus's, taking all three hits across his neck and head.

"Damn you, Dizcaro," Crash whispered, the room bursting into motion around her. "You fool."

FORTY-SIX

CORONET CITY

Kantam and Cohmac crouched in the darkness of a storage area in the underbelly of an ancient construction walker. Around them, the convoy of muni transport speeders rumbled and clanked on, a constant grind of rusty engines and clomping stabilizer pads.

"I would've thought the industrial hub of the galaxy would be able to update its own police fleet a little better," Kantam said dryly. "These things are falling apart."

"Probably for the best, all things considered," Cohmac pointed out. "We might have to dismantle them piece by piece before the end of the day."

Sneaking on board had been easy. They'd simply hidden in a nearby bush till the parade stopped at their abandoned speeder bike to investigate. Then Kantam had rolled a detonator under the nearest gunship and directly into the speeder. "You're going to have to reimburse Minister Fendirfal for that," Cohmac had said with a smirk. In the ensuing chaos, the two Jedi climbed the walker and slipped inside.

And now they sat in the darkness and waited. "Should we try Coruscant again?" Cohmac asked.

"Mm. I'll do it." Kantam pulled out their comlink, tried once more to raise the Jedi Temple, the main Republic communication nexus, *anyone* at all—once more to no avail. They'd gotten through once or twice but each time had been placed on a wait tone by a frantic and irritated operator. And then the calls just stopped going through.

They clicked on a general channel and sent out a recording. "This is Jedi Master Kantam Sy of Starlight Beacon, with an urgent message for the Republic. The Nihil have infiltrated the municipal police force in Coronet City, Corellia. We believe they have a significant presence and possibly contacts in the higher-up political circles. We don't know their final aim, but we know they are a destructive, murderous force that butchers civilians at will and will stop at nothing to bring down the Republic. Most Jedi and Corellian Security forces are on Gus Talon and unable to assist. This is an urgent call for any forces available to join our struggle against this Nihil foothold in the Core."

Cohmac frowned. "It does sound dire, when you put it like that."

"Just stating what we know and suspect."

"You never know what you're going to get when you ask for any available forces," Cohmac said. "That's how we ended up fighting side by side with the Hutts."

Kantam shrugged. "It worked."

"Coded Republic Channel Five-Zero-Five," the comlink chirped, "for Master Sy. Come in please."

"Kantam here. Did you receive my general call just now?"

"Ah, no," the operator said, sounding harried. "I got a message you'd reached out about the Nihil."

"Yes, we're on Corellia and—"

"You're on Corellia?" the guy sounded disgusted.

"Yes, and—"

"You're not on one of the ships sent to Starlight?"

"No, we—"

Static erupted, cutting off Kantam, and then a new voice came on. "We're on Corellia, too, Jedi scum. And we're coming for you."

The call went dead.

"The Nihil have taken over some of the comms," Kantam said.

THEN

The galaxy was so much more gigantic than Kantam had ever imagined.

There came a day when Aytar appeared at the doorway of the small room they shared; the tiny dangling lanterns cast a warm light over his solemn face. Kantam knew with a single look that he was leaving, and was surprised to find that it was okay. It seemed right, somehow. Whatever they'd had, it was magnificent. Kantam had never expected it to last forever, or even very long. They stood, before Aytar could turn himself inside out trying to explain and justify, and kissed the boy on his forehead. "I'll miss you, is all. But I'm also happy. For both of us. Because it's right."

Aytar nodded, holding back tears, and then smiled instead. "I'll miss you, too."

Kantam had stayed. It turned out being in the circus was a pretty good gig for a Force user. They traveled to systems they never would have otherwise, met tons of strange beings, some of them so beautiful they took Kantam's breath away. And there were the many good and wild folks to perform alongside, each with a hundred different stories from their long, winding lives.

And then one day, Kantam was done, too, and they moved on, setting out into the stars in a clunky little starship with just a handful of credits and a heart that longed for more adventure.

They worked as a messenger, a mechanic, a smuggler, a waiter, and a bodyguard, along with various other odd jobs to make ends meet. They fell in love with the way the planets danced toward you when you slowed out of hyperspace, and how the stars stretched, the gentle glow of the galaxy and the sense that all those billions of secrets in the great beyond would stay just that: secrets, right up until the end of time.

They were on Naboo, standing at the railing of one of those majestic palisade parks that overlooked tumbling waterfalls and soaring peaks, when everything changed once again for Kantam Sy.

It was a simple drop-off, but a high-priority one. Kantam had been running covert messages back and forth between diplomats for a high-end communication company. The two parties were closing out the last few details of a complicated land usage policy, and the information was too sensitive to be sent via transmission, at least according to the aging manager of one of the largest real estate conglomerates in the galaxy. He wanted everything done person-to-person as much as possible, even if that meant paying Kantam Sy a fortune to travel between Alderaan and Naboo several times a month for a simple signature or adjustment memo.

Kantam didn't mind. The money was great, but all that travel was wearing them out, and the sudden beauty of Naboo's lush wildlife always helped refresh them. A local orphanage had brought their wards out to enjoy the beautiful summer day; squeals and giggles filled the air over a fast-moving afternoon breeze and some chirping birds.

Kantam took in a deep breath, letting the warm sun work its revitalizing magic against their eyelids, and then they felt it: a stirring within, the gentle nudge of the Force. Something was about to happen. Kantam spun, took in the towering polar trees, the burbling fountain not far away, the playing kids. There. Perched on the cupola atop a nearby gazebo, a rustle of gray feathers. Kantam stepped forward, unsure where to move, or how. A shrill caw shred through the beautiful afternoon, and in a flash the creature hurled forward, a dark blur against the pale blue sky. It was a kolvor, Kantam realized, lunging out into the park, trying to gauge where the bird would strike. The kolvor were known for snatching children and dashing them against rocks; the villagers up in the mountains called them *vangartraks*—vanishers—and always kept blasters nearby in case one attacked.

Kantam didn't have a blaster handy though—this was a diplomatic mission, nothing more—and was about to be too late getting to the far side of the park, where the kolvor was careening at a speed beyond comprehension.

"No!" one of the orphanage matrons yelped, breaking into a run.

Before Kantam could even pause to reach out with the Force, the bird had snatched up two kids, a girl and a boy—one in each claw. It simply plucked them from where they sat playing in the grass, and then flapped off into the air.

"A speeder!" Kantam yelled at the gaping strangers all around them. "A blaster! Something! Get me something!" Kantam cast out desperately with the Force, grasping for some purchase, anything that would let them bring that bird down, or even knock the children free somehow. But it was no use; the kolvor had already flown too far up.

"Someone!" the matron yelled. "Someone do something!"

Kantam had tried, had done everything they could. Still, the thing had gotten away with two children. It could still be seen, flapping toward a beachside mountain.

Kantam tensed their body. The message was supposed to be delivered in exactly seventeen minutes, and it was, of course, equipped with a small device that would make note of its exact time of arrival, etc., etc.

No matter.

If the kolvor was visible, it could be found, and the kids with it.

If there was a chance they would live, and Kantam was that chance, then so be it.

Without a word, they ran at the railing, leapt onto it with one foot, and then hurtled off into the wide-open sky and dove straight down, down, down into the waiting waters below.

The brutal current yanked at Kantam, shoved them

sideways, forward, nearly dashed them against a rock, then pushed them off to the side again.

Far up above, a tiny dark shape marked the kolvor's flight toward the mountain.

"Blast," Kantam grunted, dashing out of the river, then through the underbrush along the banks that sloped steeply upward.

Halfway up the mountain, Kantam caught sight of the bird again. The thing must've been circling. It seemed like their eyes met, and the creature probably would've smiled, if birds could, as it released both kids at the same time.

Kantam nearly leapt from the mountain, but it wouldn't have done any good. They had to run.

Maybe, just maybe, if they pushed harder than they ever had before, they could get close enough to catch the plummeting children with the Force. Way up ahead, one let out a shrill scream.

Kantam wasn't going to make it. Their lungs felt like they'd caught fire. The two tiny shapes zoomed closer and closer to the rocky embankment below.

With just a few meters to go before the children smashed to their deaths, Kantam leapt into the air, covering as much of the distance between them as possible, and reached out with one hand, tuning into the Force.

One child—the girl—slowed to a stop; the boy kept falling, disappearing behind the tree line up ahead. Kantam had failed, but they still had to make sure they kept the one in the air alive. Kantam landed with a bound, heart pounding away in their chest, and willed the Force to bring the girl slowly toward the ground.

She was tiny, in a little blue orphanage dress, and clenching her face tightly, with one hand stretched out, just like Kantam's had been.

Wait.

When the girl was close enough to be reached, Kantam leapt again, grabbing her out of the sky and holding her close as they landed at the far edge of the embankment, just by the trees the little boy had disappeared behind.

The girl in their arms still had her hand outstretched.

Kantam looked down and nearly burst into tears. The boy hung in the air just over the ledge as if dangling from an invisible string in the sky.

"Did you—" Kantam gasped, putting the girl down and reeling the boy in with a quick tug. "Did you . . . ?" Both kids seemed uninjured except for a few scratches from the kolvor's talons. The boy was sobbing, but that was to be expected.

Kantam turned his attention to the little girl, crouching to be closer to her eye level. She had dark brown skin, and her hair was done up in two neat little buns. "Did you do that?" Kantam asked, looking her right in the eyes. "Did you stop your friend from falling?"

She nodded, eyes wide like she wasn't sure if she'd done something wrong. Kantam wanted to hug her, tell her everything was going to be okay, but they also needed answers.

"*How* did you do that?"

She lifted her tiny shoulders all the way up to her ears. "Is what *you* did," she said, almost accusingly. "So I did."

Kantam nodded, blinking back tears. She'd used the Force on instinct, performing a maneuver that took concentration, will, and training to master. She'd done it simply by observing.

"I did a bad?" the girl asked, starting to cry, too.

"No," Kantam said, shaking their head. "No, you did a very, very good."

The world seemed so alive, even more than it had moments before. Kantam felt the Force quickening around them, like a rush of wind. Nothing had made sense, not since Aytar had shown up like a sudden storm in Kantam's life. And finally, without warning, that was okay. Nothing needed to make sense. Kantam had allowed the galaxy to be what it was, and now the galaxy seemed to be curving around Kantam, reminding them, allowing them to be what they were.

And that, very simply and without complication or doubt, was a Jedi.

The little girl grabbed Kantam's sleeve. "Then why are you crying?"

"Because I can finally listen again," Kantam said, smiling.

Then Kantam rose and took both those tiny hands in theirs, and all three started the long walk back.

Stubborn creature, the happabore.

This one in particular—Monsalmo, Yoda liked to call her—had always taken any opportunity to make things as complicated as possible, ever since she was a pup. She'd escape from her pen, leave a trail of trampled bushes and mud leading right into the Younglings' bunks. There Yoda would find her happily curled up on the ground with a small bed on top of her, probably thinking she was hiding beneath it, even though she was three times as large. Usually there would be a very startled kid on top, either laughing or sobbing.

Yoda had awakened from his late-afternoon nap to a horrible squealing and snorting. It was definitely Monsalmo. Everyone else had headed into town for yet another of Andovar's seemingly endless seasonal festivals, so it was up to Yoda to find out what the commotion was.

Very well. He'd hurried out into the golden light of the dwindling day, then down the small dirt path to the happabore pen, and there he stopped, blinking to take in the scene.

Somehow . . . somehow . . . Monsalmo had found her way onto the wooden roof of the pen. Yoda glanced to the far side of it, where a few stacks of large feed crates had been left a little too close to the fence. Just close enough to be crawled on top of and then nudged into an almost staircase-like incline. Most beings would need a loadlifter workframe to move those things, but a happabore could probably manage it without much effort. Then it would only be a matter of climbing the rest of the way and plopping down onto the rooftop. Yoda would have to talk to the Padawans about making sure they stored the feed crates farther from the pen.

But in the meantime, there was a more immediate problem to deal with: Monsalmo was still squealing and writhing like she was in pain. And all four wooden beams holding up that roof had already splintered from the added weight; they probably wouldn't hold up much longer. Also, it was starting to rain.

Just a drizzle, sure, but it didn't help.

Yoda took a breath and quieted his churning mind, reaching out with the Force. Immediately, the world around him snapped into crisp clarity. The Force brought Yoda a precise vision of each drop of rain and trembling leaf, all the urgent physics of the problem before him.

The roof had already cratered inward some, which meant the rain would soon pool there, adding even more weight to the already dangerously besieged rooftop.

Moving the gigantic creature wouldn't be a problem, but there was the more complicated question of what was troubling her and *why* she was on the roof.

Monsalmo's pain arced outward to Yoda in sharp bursts, and immediately he understood.

"Congratulations are in order, hm?" he said, leaping quickly up the crates so he was on the same level with the roof. "But why . . . ?" A sheen down below caught his eye, the dying sunlight shimmering back up at him from some sleek substance. Of course. He hadn't been able to see it from where he stood on the ground, but now it was clear. His eyes followed a darkened trail along the ground back to its source: an overturned fuel barrel in a storage bin a little ways away.

Monsalmo wasn't just being her usual playful self when she climbed up on the roof—she was protecting the litter of pups she was about to give birth to! "Clever mama," Yoda muttered, reaching out with the Force to lift her just as one of the beams splintered, then snapped.

Monsalmo squealed, the rooftop suddenly becoming a crumbled ramp beneath her. She didn't fall though, even as the sudden weight shift of the collapsing roof caused another beam to topple.

Yoda, one hand outstretched, kept her hovering in mid-air. The happabore bucked and gave a snorted yelp, panicked and riled with birthing pains.

"Easy," Yoda urged gently, but then, with a sudden squelching burst, there was another happabore in the world, and then, just as Yoda reached out to keep the first pup from splashing into the oil below, a second popped out.

"Accelerated, this labor is," Yoda muttered, trying to remember how many pups came in an average happabore litter. He had just managed to keep Monsalmo and her two babies balanced in a gentle hover when the third and fourth popped out simultaneously.

"Hrm," Yoda grunted softly. He blinked through the rain, trying to figure out a safe place to ease the whole litter down. The strain of it all was like a gentle nudge on his razor-sharp focus, but it was getting less gentle by the second. "Very well."

A fifth, then a sixth appeared before Yoda could figure out a good landing spot, and then, very suddenly, the intense pressure of keeping all the babies and the mama hovering at once eased.

Monsalmo was hovering all by herself, along with one of her pups. Or rather, Yoda realized, glancing around, someone else was doing it for her.

"I did a good," a tiny voice proclaimed. Yoda looked down, into the bright brown eyes of a little girl with both hands outstretched. Behind her, Kantam Sy stood, their own arm extended to take the weight of Monsalmo.

Yoda chuckled, already swinging the litter off toward safety. "Aheh! Left a Padawan, you did, hm? Returned, you have, a Knight."

Kantam couldn't stop the smile from spreading across their face. "Master Yoda, this is Lula Talisola."

Hours later, after the modest knighting ceremony, Kantam and Yoda sat beside a small fire near the cleaned-up happabore enclosure. Lula snored mightily in Kantam's lap as Yoda wrapped up his enthusiastic recap of the afternoon's excitement. Nearby, all fifteen happapups guzzled milk from their worn-out and very proud mama.

A deep sense of calm settled over Kantam. Tiny seedpods

popped and snapped amid the burning logs, releasing puffs of fragrant smoke into the dark sky.

"I don't really understand what happened, Master Yoda."

Yoda nodded with a wry smile. "Become used to that, we must."

"I know, but . . . it was so sudden."

"Sudden?" Yoda was laughing, a full-throated raspy cackle that seemed to cut through the evening stillness. "Gone for more than a year, you were. All this time, all your life, hm, led up to that moment. Opposite of sudden, it was. Long time in coming, really."

"But what changed? I felt the shift like a clap of thunder: one moment I was moving along like I had been, just gliding along the surface of my own life, and then this tiny person came along and . . ."

Yoda let out an amused snort and poked the fire. "The young are our greatest teachers, it is said. But why? Not for the things they say, hehe—still several years it will be before this one has wisdom to impart in that way, hm."

"She did a good," Kantam said with a grin. "Or she did a bad."

"Mm, exactly. No, it is in who they are to us that their wisdom lives. Do the work, we must. The lesson of Younglings we take on is one of the hardest ones for most Jedi to learn. Indeed, some never do."

"Detachment," Kantam said.

Yoda nodded, serious now. "To let go. Elusive it is, but also, always available to us, always there. And then, when we grasp, gone again. Takes practice, it does. Repetition. To have to do it again does not mean we have failed, only that we must do it again. And again."

"Hm." Kantam knew the truth of those words in their bones. How many times had they managed to let go of doubt, fear, arrogance, jealousy . . . only to have each tumble back in like nothing had ever happened? Yoda was right though—those weren't failures. The struggle, the lesson, really, was simply ongoing.

"Who but the young can offer us this lesson, hm?" Yoda snapped a small cracker in half and scooped some sweetpuff jam onto one piece and topped it with the other. He handed the tiny delicious sandwich to Kantam, who put it alongside their own on a metal tray. "Over and over and over, we must learn to let go."

Kantam sent the tray hovering over the bonfire.

"To love is to let go," Yoda said, watching the flames. "To be Jedi is to let go." His eyes seemed unfathomably sad suddenly, but then he smiled, and the smile was a real one.

"I taught you this lesson," Kantam said, realizing it was true as the words came out.

"Easy, you think it was, to send you into the galaxy that day?"

It hadn't even occurred to Kantam that Yoda had struggled with that moment. He had seemed so poised, so level about it all. "I . . . Yes, I thought it was easy. You made it look easy. I assumed you knew I would return one day."

Yoda chortled softly, without much humor. "Elusive, the future is. Stubborn. Much like detachment. And happabores!" He laughed for real then, and Kantam felt the heavy air around them loosen, ease. Yoda was demonstrating letting go in real time, allowing his own sadness to be seen, allowing it to be carried away like the fragrant plumes of smoke from their bonfire.

"A little too crispy, the sweetpuff jam is about to be," Yoda pointed out, and Kantam quickly pulled the tray from the flames.

"And now for the second most important lesson having a Youngling around will teach you," Yoda announced, nudging Lula gently so she woke up to the warmth of the fire and the tangy smell of toasted sweetpuff jamwiches. He snapped Kantam's in half and handed one part to her, the other to Kantam with a chuckle. "How to share."

FORTY-SEVEN

CORONET CITY

Everything had happened so fast, so suddenly. Reath felt like thunder kept clapping inside him, spinning him around.

The world had seemed to stop as the news about Starlight flashed across the holo images in the middle of the room.

Part of Reath couldn't breathe; the other part felt a cruel understanding click into place. This was what he'd felt, that sliding, sinking sense of loss, like the sudden evacuation of air from his lungs, again and again and again throughout the past hour, worse every time.

In the middle of it all, that strange robed man had jumped on a table and pulled off his mask, revealing himself to be—some old guy. But he was talking like he was one of the Nihil, ranting maniacally. Reath hadn't been totally sure it wasn't just another part of the elaborate party tricks until the guy had reached into his robes and sprayed the room with blaster fire.

That was when everything went from way too fast to very, very slow. Bolts lanced through a man's arm a few meters away. Reath was diving toward the ground, along with everyone else, and explosions seemed to be pounding out from every corner, but it was just his own heartbeat, and the bolts left smoking charred holes in the man's silky shirt sleeve, and Reath could see his burnt flesh beneath it, and the man was screaming, and Reath was on the floor then, and everyone was screaming, and the room seemed to be collapsing in on Reath, but it wasn't, it wasn't.

The Force was with him.

He didn't know the path forward, nor would he anytime soon. But he couldn't get lost in his head. He'd let himself get distracted too many times that night. He would find his own path later; now he had to survive.

And survival meant standing up and fighting.

Reath Silas rose.

People were screaming and running around, and some seemed terrified, while others definitely knew exactly what was going on. And those, Reath figured, picking up a chair and smashing it across one of them as he tried to run past, those were the Nihil.

"Reath!" Zeen yelled nearby. "Over there!" A group of masked partiers had formed a tight circle around the old man, and together they made their way toward the far end of the room. Reath started after them, shoving his way through the panicking people. Zeen was soon alongside him, and he glimpsed Ram through the crowd, heading that way, too.

A bright light took over the darkening sky just outside the window they were heading toward, and then the window itself exploded inward with a single concussion blast. More people screamed and ran the opposite way. Reath had to use the Force to toss a couple of them out of his way and clear a path. Already, the Nihil—because without a doubt, that crew protecting the raving old guy *had* to be Nihil—were making their way through the window onto a drawbridge of some kind.

"This is Air-Eleven," a gruff voice said in Reath's ear. "I have eyes on a metal bridge being laid across the building tops to the eastern window."

"That's the Nihil!" Reath yelled, still trying to get through the bustling crowd. "That's the Nihil!"

"On it," Fezzonk growled.

"This is Crash," said another voice on the comms. "Be careful, Fezzonk. They'll be heavily armed, and we don't know if they have any of the clients we're protecting with them. You *can't* just take out the bridge. Copy?"

She was right, Reath realized. They weren't even completely

sure if it was the real Nihil or just some local pretenders. Or if there was really much of a difference anyway.

This would not be easy to untangle.

Reath heard blaster fire and then a loud bang up ahead.

"Ah . . . That's a copy," Fezzonk said, sounding suddenly out of breath. "Oh, yeah . . . taking fire now. The antiaircraft kind."

"Pull back!" Reath yelled. "We're almost there."

Reath reached the shattered window first and extended his lightsaber just in time to swat away the flashes of red laser fire blitzing toward him.

Up ahead, a bunch of figures were scurrying toward the far end of the bridge.

With one swipe of his hand, Reath could probably send that makeshift contraption tumbling to the streets below, along with everyone on it. But Crash was right—they didn't know who the Nihil had with them, or much at all, for that matter. And they wouldn't find out by killing a bunch of people. And anyway—Reath took a deep breath, deflected another shot, and centered himself—yes, Starlight was under attack and would, perhaps, fall into enemy hands, or even be destroyed. But Reath Silas was a Jedi. And he wouldn't let this fight, or any fight, tear the core of what that meant away from him. Even if it cost him his life. He had a code, and he was part of a lineage of great Jedi, including Jora Malli, who had lived and died by that code, too. And he would honor it.

The fighters on the far end of that bridge did not have a code, though, and Reath was pretty sure they would be destroying it once they'd made it across. Reath glanced at Ram and Zeen, by his side, and saw they were thinking the same thing.

All together, they broke into a run.

FORTY-EIGHT

CORONET CITY

The makeshift iron bridge creaked and squealed beneath Ram's pounding feet.

In a couple of seconds, probably, the group of Nihil would be on the other side, and then it would be a very simple thing for them to just blow up the whole bridge, and Ram, Reath, and Zeen along with it.

Master Sy had taught that battle strategy was more about what you knew and didn't know, and what your enemy knew and didn't know than it was about who had more fighters or better equipment. And right then, Ram and the others seemed to know barely anything, and the Nihil probably knew just about *everything*. They stayed one step ahead of everyone, always, and they were more ruthless, more bloodthirsty, and more than ready to let a whole slew of their own get blasted to hell if it meant causing whatever damage they could and the rest getting away.

Red blaster bolts flew through the dark blue sky toward Ram. He swung his lightsaber as he ran—once up, then across, then in a wide arc around himself—smashing the laser fire away with each slash.

There were about a dozen figures up ahead, gathered on a rooftop, their bodies dark against the setting sun. The last three to make it across the bridge were backing toward their comrades, firing on Ram, Reath, and Zeen. Another group was trying to set up a second bridge at the far end of the building.

Reath and Ram deflected the last few laser shots, and then both lunged with one foot, side by side, and thrust their left hands forward, palms out. The three Nihil at the end of the bridge were flung backward in a clatter of weapons and armor.

More turned, raising blaster rifles and something bigger, probably that antiaircraft artillery Fezzonk had mentioned.

Ram had something for them, though. "Cover me," he said, passing his lightsaber to Zeen while Reath held off the first few shots. He'd been trusting Zeen with his most important object in the world since they'd first met back on Valo. It happened only out of necessity, and she always treated it with the respect it deserved. And kept Ram alive. This was no exception. She stood beside Reath and knocked away each laser bolt.

Ram reached out with the Force.

The Nihil were also cowardly, Ram had learned, and didn't bother pausing to think things through. They didn't have much organization during a fight, which meant it took them longer to evolve their strategy along with a changing situation, and everything was always changing in battle—it was the only constant. Master Sy had taught Ram that, too. And the Nihil were arrogant; for all their big plans to wreck the Republic, they didn't have enough imagination to conceive of the many ways even a young Jedi apprentice like Ram could unravel whatever they had in mind.

Like by causing the ventilation fans near where they had gathered to overheat and . . . Ram strained, his mind fussing through various wiring configurations and airflow ducts. *There.* He twisted his wrist, willing the Force to shove aside a small regulator dial that let hot air pour into the one place it shouldn't. And then the whole thing went up with a fiery *KA-POW!* And Nihil leapt for cover, screaming.

There was a fuel line right beside the duct. It would take only one more twist to turn a mostly harmless blast into something much, much worse.

Ram thought about the smoke pouring out of Starlight, the way some people were still laughing, hidden safely behind their masks as Ram's home once again burned, as his friends fought for their lives.

Rage rose in him, a pure fire, and suddenly Ram was a volcano, that wrath poised to explode and cover the whole city around him. A trembling reached from his core all the way to his fingertips—*How dare they?* a voice inside him thundered, sending the sky overhead into a dizzying spin. *His* voice, he realized. His rage. He knew it, recognized it. It had been hiding beneath all those layers of coldness he'd built. But now he knew its name, could sense its presence.

And Reath had given him the antidote. "Balance," Ram whispered. He had a utility cart full of other emotions. Sadness. Love. And the eerie calm of that emptiness he'd been feeling for some time. He would need all of them if he was going to make it through this. They would keep each other in check. The sky slowed its spin, clicked back into place. *Balance.*

He refused to cause needless death. Not now. They still had no idea who was there, who was Nihil and who wasn't. They barely knew anything. He held off, blinking back to the world around him.

"Nice," Reath said, admiring Ram's handiwork, probably totally oblivious to the fact that he'd once again come to the rescue. Then all three of them burst onto the rooftop, where the scattered raiders were already regrouping and making a break for the far bridge. A few people lay cowering still—hostages, Ram thought, but he kept his lightsaber extended. You could never be sure, not these days.

Crash's bodyguards had kept a steady stream of chatter throughout the whole thing—checking on one another, reporting back about which clients were where. Ram had tuned most of it out, but now the big guy in the flier came on the comms with a gruff, "Listen up, Jedi."

"We're here," Reath said.

"They're heading toward the Finance Tower—it's a little bit ahead of where you are now," he reported. "There's a covering of some kind on that rooftop, so I can't make it all out, but it looks like there are more of them gathered there."

Ram scanned the city around him, looking past where the Nihil were scurrying off on their new bridge.

One building had a makeshift tent erected on top and . . . yep, Ram could see the shifting of bodies in the shadows up there. He saw Reath notice the same thing. The sun dipped beneath a cloud bank, painting the sky with majestic crimson streaks as the last bits of day faded.

"We could chase these clowns on their own bridges," Zeen said, looking off in a different direction. "Or we could go our own way."

The boys followed her pointing finger. A hotel complex led up to the Finance Tower. The rooftops were just close enough together to be jumpable with some help from the Force, but definitely too far for most regular beings.

Ram nodded. "Let's go."

FORTY-NINE

CORONET CITY

Laser blasts zinged against the small permacrete wall as Reath leapt behind it.

Another close one.

He wondered how long he'd manage *not* to get shot that day. From the look of things, he'd be providing plenty of opportunities for Nihil target practice in the hours ahead. Whatever was going on, they'd been planning it for a while, and it was probably connected to the attack on Starlight.

Or maybe there were attacks happening all over the galaxy. For all Reath knew, the Jedi of the Coruscant temple could be fighting for their lives, too.

He had to stay focused though. The most important

thing was right in front him, as Master Sy often said. And right now, that was a wall that was keeping him from getting fried by another barrage from the Nihil.

"How we lookin'?" Ram asked, landing with a grunt in the gravel beside Reath.

"About the same as we've been looking since we landed on this planet," Reath grumbled. "Completely in the dark and barely afloat. Where's Zeen?"

"Oh, she kept going. I thought you saw."

Reath poked his head up, then dipped back down as more blaster fire sang out from the nearby rooftop. The Nihil had figured out they were being outflanked pretty quickly and dispatched a few shooters to keep the Jedi busy.

Reath clicked on his comlink. "Reath to Air-Eleven."

Fezzonk's grizzled voice clicked through almost immediately. "Already on it."

Something whooshed past them in the night sky—Reath barely caught a glimpse of it, the thing was so fast, and then a sudden splatter of laser fire sounded. A heavy boom rang out, echoing across the skyscraper canyons all around them.

"All clear," Fezzonk reported. "Got a little scratched up but all good. Not sure how much more of this I can take though."

"Let's go," Reath said. Then, into the comlink, "Thanks, Air-Eleven! Stay safe up there."

They dashed across the open gravel area toward the far end of the roof.

Zeen crouched on the next building over, waiting out another Nihil attack squad.

The Nihil had taken up position on a rooftop adjacent to Zeen's, and they were lighting up her spot with some kind of rotary cannon. Reath and Ram leapt to the Nihil's building instead of Zeen's. They landed with a thud and rolled out of the way as cannon fire shredded the permacrete they'd just been standing on. A scream rang out, and the cannon fell silent as both boys stood and dusted themselves off. Zeen had blasted the three Nihil away as soon as they'd turned their attention elsewhere.

She waved the Padawans over to her.

Reath and Ram stepped past the sprawled bodies and leapt across the gap to where Zeen stood waiting.

"I think we gotta go dark from here out," Zeen said, leaning in. She'd gotten rid of the sheer gown—it had to be hell trying to fight in that thing—so she looked like some silver killer angel out of the holos in her bodysuit and tiara. Ram and Reath still had on their makeup and black bodysuits—the three of them together must've been quite a sight to behold. And hopefully, no one would. Zeen was right. The Finance Tower was one building over. It didn't seem like anyone was paying attention to them, from what Reath could tell. Something worth all their focus had to be happening on that rooftop, and whatever it was, Reath and the others needed to know about it.

They ran to a smokestack, ducked behind it, then dashed

to an electrical box with various antennas poking out. Finally, they skidded to a stop at the shoulder-high wall around the roof. Up ahead, a woman's voice sounded, amplified by a speaker. Reath couldn't quite make out what she was saying, but she sounded pleased with herself.

"There," Zeen said, pointing to a balcony on the floor just below the rooftop where the Nihil were gathered. Then she hoisted herself onto the wall and leapt. Ram went next. Reath glanced around, then lifted himself up, found his balance, and sprang out into the night between the two buildings. He aimed it so he came down just in front of the balcony railing, caught it, and flung himself over the top, landing beside his friends in a squat.

". . . the galaxy forever!" the woman yelled. It was Sabata, Reath realized. No question. He'd heard enough holo-recordings of her in intelligence reports to know that voice. "Tonight, there is no stopping us!"

The furious growl of an engine ripped suddenly out into the night. The whole Finance Tower shook. That's what was going on up there, Reath realized—what they were concealing. It was a launchpad. What did they have? Whatever it was, it was taking off any moment. He climbed onto the railing and leapt straight upward, clutching the edge of the rooftop and then pulling himself up just enough to see what was happening.

The tent was being pulled away, and a massive troop transport vehicle began lifting up from the landing pad. It was shaped like an X—four huge sections pointing off at diagonals. Turbines on top of each side thwacked heavily against the air, speeding up to full power. Gun turrets covered the thing, each wheeling around as if hungry for something to blast out of the sky. Bulky and ungainly, this ship was clearly built to move large groups of people from one part of the city to another, and smash away anything that tried to stop it. That was about all it could manage; speed and distance were not part of its equation.

And Sabata Krill stood on top of the transport ship, arms stretched out, grinning wildly at the city she was about to bring to heel.

The Nihil really were everywhere, Reath realized. They were trying to take out Starlight, and they were there, too, a galaxy away, launching a full-fledged attack on a Core World.

And up until then, everyone had thought they were in retreat.

They would never stop until the Jedi stopped them. There was no sitting around hoping this would pass.

There was no waiting for a moment to pause and think. The Nihil had made sure of that. There would be no figuring out a path ahead for Reath, because the only path ahead led straight through the Nihil.

"Where you think they're going?" Ram called from below.

"Only one way to find out!" Reath yelled. He pulled himself all the way up and ran.

FIFTY

CORONET CITY

Chaos.

And not the good kind.

Every job had a certain amount of it. That was a given. Crash knew it, both from Baynoo's expert advice and her own experience. Storm patterns shifted; traffic snarled. A child stopping to play with a small morkat could cause a parade to bottleneck, trapping a client in an intersection with a hundred angles from which to take a shot and none open to a quick getaway. And just like that, perfectly laid plans got blown to hell, and all you had to show for it was a dead body and a sullied street rep.

Unless you were Crash and you moved with the chaos, became one with it.

That was what Baynoo had taught her, and at first they had just been words that sounded pretty, and badass in theory. But what did they mean in practice?

Improvise.

Plan ahead and improvise. Those were the two tent poles of things going smoothly. Every possible option had to be in the plan, even the unimaginable ones. It took thinking like a ruthless assassin to stop one, so that was what Crash did. That meant each intersection would be scanned, each tunnel cleared, and each balcony locked. As much as could be accounted for was, and everything else went into the realm of chaos.

Crash had learned to relish it—that challenge, the sudden need to spring into action and pull a hundred different threads. It would probably kill her one day, but she would die with a smile.

That was the good chaos.

This, though . . . this unfolding disaster and growing sense of doom—this was something else entirely.

Dizcaro lay in a pool of his own blood. Little plumes of smoke still curled up from the charred wounds on the back of his head and neck. No one had touched him—there was no point. He was clearly gone. Meanwhile, the room was still rocked by the sudden burst of violence, the revelation of the Starlight attack, the appearance of a City Father everyone had presumed dead, his rants about the Nihil, the shattered window. So much had happened in so little time.

Medics were bandaging up the people who'd been grazed by Tralmat's blaster fire. They'd taken one look at Dizcaro and just shaken their heads.

Crash had never cared much for Dizcaro—he was messy and hungry in all the wrong ways, and he didn't treat his operatives well, which was why they were so easy to poach from him. But he was decent in other ways, and for someone she was constantly going head to head with (and winning against), she didn't despise him as much as she might've. And he had just been beginning to show signs of a moral core somewhere beneath all that sludge and ambition. But he knew what his job was, and when the moment every bodyguard wonders about came, Dizcaro did exactly what he was supposed to do, what the code said to do, what the job required, *demanded*, really.

And he'd done it for someone he clearly absolutely abhorred.

And that made it even more what the job demanded.

Would Crash do the same?

Dizcaro's mouth was open, his eyes glassy. The bolt had torn through his scalp, shattered a portion of his skull, and left what could be seen of his brain sizzling scar tissue.

Was he proud when he died? Did it matter?

"Ah, Crash," 10-K8 said. "We . . . you with us?"

Crash tuned back into the ongoing throb of panic in the

room. How long had she been just standing there, staring at a corpse? "Yeah. Uh, yeah. I'm here."

The blood was coming from his mouth. So much blood.

"The hotel security has asked that we keep everyone on scene for the moment while they secure the area."

"Yeah, of course," Crash said absently.

"Well, those who haven't left already, of course."

The holo news still spun in the center of the room, ongoing coverage of the attack on Starlight, but it was just talking heads repeating the same thing over and over from the safety of the Core: "No one knows anything yet. Stay tuned." Stay tuned for hours of speculation and punditry with zero actual info, was what they meant.

Crash wanted to scream.

So much blood. Was no one going to come put a sheet over the guy? Life could be snuffed out so quickly. She'd seen her share of dead bodies, had even caused a few of them to get that way. But this felt different. Minutes before, he'd been talking to her, arguing with her. She'd . . . Svi'no! What if she'd been hurt somehow? What if that moment, which felt like the truest, purest thing that had happened in Crash's life in a long, long time, was all they had?

Crash set her comlink to a private channel and pinged Svi'no.

"Here," that sweet voice came back, speaking just for Crash. She wanted to unravel herself inside that voice and sleep for years.

"You okay?"

"Yeah." Svi'no sounded surprised. "You?"

"Uh-huh. Just a little shook up."

"I was laying low off to the side, you know. Just . . . whoa."

"Whoa," Crash agreed.

"I'm gonna keep an eye on everything from here. Stay okay for me, please. Okay?"

"I will," Crash promised, and she meant it. "You too, please."

"Ah, Crash?" Ram's voice came over the general comms channel. "Small update for ya."

She wrenched her gaze away from Dizcaro's open mouth and dead, dead eyes and switched back over. "Go with it."

"There's a huge transport leaving from the roof of the Money Tower, or whatever it's called. And Sabata Krill is on it."

"The Er'Kit girl?" Crash almost yelled. Had no one thought to put a lightsaber through her as soon she showed her face? She hoped that was what the Padawans were in the midst of doing. "Air-Eleven?" she said, taking a step back.

"I was about to say just that," Fezzonk said. "Most of the Nihil boarded."

"Also, uh, Reath," Ram put in.

"*What?* All by himself?"

"He just went running over there without telling anyone what he was planning, and by the time we realized it, the thing was up in the air!"

"That might be a good thing," Fezzonk said. "That the others aren't with him, I mean. Some of the Nihil didn't board, either, and they're peeling off. I won't be able to keep eyes on them and track that transport."

"Ram?" Crash said.

"We can follow 'em. Stand by."

Nothing made sense.

Chaos was one part of the job that took experience to understand, to learn how to move with. But the other element, the one that most people avoided talking about, was death. And because folks kept quiet about it, the very notion of death seemed to lurk everywhere, in the negative spaces, the pauses of a conversation.

And now it was there in the room, a presence built from absence, an invisible form, yet undeniable in its weight and authority—nowhere and thus everywhere.

Crash glanced around the room. Those were real Nihil, the ones who had surrounded Tralmat like they were his bodyguard detail and charged for the window with him. Maybe a few people had decided right then and there that marauding around the galaxy was a good idea, actually, and what better time to join up than during the attack on a bastion of the Republic. But the real question was: Had any of the actual Nihil stayed behind to cause more problems or murder someone else?

"Where's Orvus?" Crash asked.

10-K8 made a tiny head tilt, checking her memory

banks. "He was escorted out by one of Dizcaro's men—the big Lasat guy."

"Powlo," Crash said. She liked Powlo. He didn't say much, but that was about right. He'd been next on her list of operatives to poach.

Technically, everyone who was a registered guest at the event was under Crash's protection, but she wasn't sure if she wanted to choke Ovus or keep him safe. Of course, it didn't matter what Crash wanted. Ovus was probably a target for the Nihil now that one of their local leaders had tried and failed to take him out.

Then again, he'd apparently had some part to play in the Nihil being on Corellia in the first place. If they were going to get to the bottom of that—and they were—they needed him alive enough to answer questions.

Crash made a mental note to track down Powlo and Ovus when things calmed down.

If things calmed down.

With CorSec and the Jedi gone, that might not be for a while.

"Weapons scan, please," Crash said.

"On it," 10-K8 chirped. The room was full of people Crash was supposed to keep safe. Suddenly, she felt very small, and the burden of their protection loomed over her, an impossible weight to carry. Any one of them could be involved in what had just happened. Should she protect the very people who would harm her and the others? Should she jump in front of the fire as Dizcaro had if the person being shot at wanted her dead?

There was a technical, professional answer to that question, and it was designed for simplicity of decision-making on the fly: yes.

And up until this moment, Crash would've said the same thing. But everything was different now. It had started when the Jedi showed up.

No.

It had started when Prybolt disappeared and Crash realized there was a very real possibility someone responsible for her friend's death was one of the people she was sworn to keep safe.

That didn't seem right.

Stay out of politics—rule number one.

But . . . politics didn't stay out of her life. There wasn't any way to opt out of politics, not really. It was all just make-believe.

Crash felt like she was going to throw up. The truth was, when the Jedi had leapt into action, following the Nihil out the window, lightsabers extended, Crash had had to dampen the impulse to go with them. That was wrong. Her place was at the event, doing her job, but . . .

"There's a group of Nihil on a small platform craft," Fezzonk reported over the comms. "They're heading down the western side of the Finance Tower, heading for the Eighty-Fourth Corridor. Jedi, you see them?"

"Negative, Air-Eleven," Ram said, out of breath. "We're in pursuit of another group heading down by foot along some kind of crude outdoor stairway."

"Also known as a fire escape," Fezzonk said with a slight chuckle.

"Right, that."

"Ah, Miss Crash?" came a deep, raspy voice almost directly over her.

Crash looked up into the eyes of a towering Lasat. "Powlo. You secured Ovus?"

He nodded, face inscrutable. "Secured with other team. I come to see if you need anything?"

Crash smiled. "Thanks. I . . ." The answer seemed more complicated than she was ready for, though. What did she need? So much, starting with needing all this to make sense.

"No weapons besides our own," 10-K8 reported. "And all clients are accounted for. Except, of course, uh . . ."

"Who?"

"Nomar Tralmat."

Crash blinked, then shot a sharp glare at 10-K8. "Excuse me?"

"Ah, yes, well, since he was never officially declared dead and he disappeared while under our protection, we technically still have him on the books as a client."

"Tralmat is with them on the platform craft," Fezzonk said. "My guess: they're heading for Tunnel Entrance Seven. It lines up with their trajectory and it'd make sense." He paused. "You want me to take the shot on Tralmat, Crash? That transport is about to be too far for me to track."

"Ah, you won't need to track it," a new voice said over the comms. Was that—"This is Jedi Master Kantam Sy. And we know where they're going."

"How?" Crash asked, her head reeling.

"Because we're already there. It's the shipyards. The Nihil are preparing an attack on Coronet's shipyards. A huge convoy of them just arrived."

"And we're in the trunk," Cohmac added.

"We'll do what we can to hold off the attack, but we're gonna need some help," Kantam said.

War. War had come to Corellia. It was already a brutal one, and it was about to get much, much worse. There was no such thing as not taking sides. It was sheer theater in peacetime and an absolute joke during war. Neutrality, the performance of it, was something powerful people demanded of everyone else so they could stay protected. In Crash's case, she was literally the one doing the protecting. The performing. It was all a lie.

And not one she had the luxury of being able to participate in anymore.

She glanced once more at Dizcaro's body. "Actually there is something you can do for me, Powlo."

"Hm?"

"Take over," she said, already walking toward the door.

"What—this event?" he asked behind her.

"Everything," she called. "Kayt!"

"Yes, Master Crash?" The droid fell into step with her as always, and she sounded . . . she sounded excited.

"Delete Tralmat's name from our files."

"Yes, Master Cra—"

"In fact, just delete our files."

"Yes, Master Crash!"

"Crash?" Fezzonk said in her ear. "Take the shot?"

"No," she said into the comms, out the door and heading to the turbolift. "We don't know who else is on that platform, and we don't know where they're headed. Follow the transport, but stay out of sight. Link with the Jedi at the shipyards."

Tralmat had been on the rooftop with the Er'Kit girl. They'd been plotting together all along, which meant that Tralmat was part of Prybolt and Ovarto's deaths. Sabata may have done the deed, but Crash had no doubt whatsoever that Tralmat had assured it would happen and stood by while the people sworn to protect him were cut down.

"On it," Fezzonk said.

"And anyway, I want to handle this one myself."

PART FIVE

FIFTY-ONE

CORONET CITY

Lula Talisola.

Zeen couldn't stop thinking of her name, her face, the certain rhythm of her laugh and silence, her calm face in meditation.

Was she dead? Would Zeen feel it if she died? Was she desperately fighting for her life? Hiding?

What about Farzala and Qort? They'd all taken Zeen in, treated her like one of their own even though she very much wasn't. They'd taught her what home was, and now the one place they all called home . . .

Zeen tried to shake off the thoughts. She and Ram had split up, agreeing it'd be best to spread the Force users amid the various fighting groups. Ram hopped in the flier with the huge Dowutin. Zeen had watched them zip off. Goodbyes felt so much more fraught now; any one of them might be the last. Then she'd leapt from building to building, making her way down to the street level. She'd kept a wary eye on the slowly descending platform craft as she went, tracked its gradual descent between the skyscrapers.

When the small crew of Nihil had made their way into the tunnel entrance, just as Fezzonk had predicted, Zeen had been watching from the shadows.

And now she waited. Crash was on her way. Soon they'd head into the tunnels together. But waiting was harder than fighting. Waiting meant there was time to think, and all Zeen's thoughts were bad ones.

She glanced up and down the deserted Financial District street to make sure she was alone, then pulled out her holoprojector.

"Lula," she said, recording herself. Then all the words left her. The next thing to come out was a sob. She had to get it together. There was a war breaking out all around her, and pining wasn't going to help her stay alive. She had to stay alive. She would live, and so would Lula. She willed it to be so. So it would be.

"Okay," she said out loud, laughing a little and wiping away a few tears. "Let's try that again. Lula." The name tasted like tears on her lips, but it also felt like light; the way she felt about Lula was a physical presence in her body, like the Force.

It was gigantic, bigger than Zeen herself. Zeen wasn't sure how she could encompass such a feeling. "Lula Talisola. I . . ." She shook her head. Her tendrils were probably revealing how she felt anyway—Lula always knew how to read them, sometimes even better than Zeen did.

She took a deep breath, deleted all that, and started over. For a few moments, she just collected herself, blinking away tears, taking breaths. Better for Lula to see all this—how hard it was to express herself, how uncertain everything felt. It was the truth. And that's what Lula deserved. Of course, there was no guarantee Lula ever would see it. Zeen couldn't think like that, though. She had to stop thinking like that. "I miss you. I . . . I love you. I'm sorry I . . . I ran away? I don't know. I thought maybe I would run away, because I don't want to make things complicated for you. I don't want you to have to stop being the thing you love being the most. But I also don't want to make that decision for you. Because the thing I love being the most is with you." She blinked away tears. "That's all. Please . . . please don't die. And I won't, either. Let's start there. And the rest . . . the rest we can figure out. Just stay alive." Then she just said, "Love," and ended the recording. And sent it.

"Zeen!" Crash called just as Zeen was shoving the holoprojector into one of her pouches. "I brought your clothes." She tossed Zeen a bundle, already heading into the tunnels. "But you gotta change on the way—we've got some catching up to do."

"Yeah, they went in a few minutes ago. And you have no idea how much this means to me," Zeen said, already pulling her jacket on as she hurried after Crash. "I feel naked in just this silvery thing! I think my pop star days are over."

"Too bad," Crash said. "You were great at it. But I understand, trust. My bodyguard days just came to a swashbuckling end, so we make a good team."

Zeen smiled. "That makes sense for you, somehow. Even though I barely know you. Swashbuckling ends are the best kind, right? And here we are, an ex-pop star and an ex-bodyguard, charging headfirst into a literal tunnel of death."

"Whose death, is the question," Crash said. "'Cause it won't be mine."

"Not mine either," a crinkly voice said above.

Zeen had a blaster trained on it before she took another step.

"Whoa whoa whoa!" Crash yelled. "It's Smeemarm!"

"What's a Smeemarm?" Zeen asked, not lowering the blaster.

A long gangly form seemed to unfold itself from the pipes above. "I am."

"Zeen, this is—was, rather—the head of my tunnel team, Smeemarm."

The woman landed and then rose—she had the wrinkled triangular head and glittering green eyes of an Arcona, and a bunch of pockets on her jumpsuit. "The galactic superstar!" she said with a playful wink. "Pleasure to meet you." She turned to Crash. "And you—just because the agency is done doesn't mean we are."

Crash looked dubious. "I . . . it doesn't?"

"We're at war, aren't we? Who better to lead us than someone who already does?"

"Hm," Crash said, falling back into her fast walk through the tunnels with Smeemarm. "Hmm."

Zeen pulled out her other blaster, glanced around in the darkness, and followed quickly behind.

FIFTY-TWO

CORONET CITY

Smeemarm had a point.

The Arcona was usually pretty on the money about stuff, Crash had to admit. And this was . . . this was no exception.

They were probably getting close to Tralmat and his squad of Nihil. And that meant that if Crash was going to do what she'd been pondering—if she was honest, for a little while now; Smeemarm had just brought the issue to a head—then she had to do it soon.

"Smeems, what's the status of your crew?"

The tunnel they were in stretched ahead into the darkness. Occasional flickering lanterns spread small pools of light throughout the whole underground system, but they were inconsistent. And putting a headlamp on in these circumstances was like begging to get shot.

"They're scattered throughout and ready to make any move you tell them," Smeemarm said. "You gonna raise them on the comlink?"

"No," Crash said, motioning everyone to stop and stay against the tunnel wall in case they were attacked. "I'm gonna raise everyone." She took out her comlink.

"The whole company?" Smeemarm asked.

"No, literally every contact in my list. *Everyone.*" She pressed a few keys and held the device to her lips. "Hello, Coronet City!"

"Yowza," Smeemarm whispered.

"This is Crash. If you're getting this message, it's because I have your contact info saved, so you may know me as Alys Ongwa. Anyway, bad news, folks: we're under attack. Like, no joke, very literally, the Nihil are attacking Coronet City. The main focus of their push is on the shipyards. Some Jedi from Starlight are trying to stop them, but as you may have heard, Starlight is also under attack, and most of our own Jedi and defense forces are dealing with the situation on Gus Talon, which was probably all a setup so the Nihil could move into our city without a fight."

She took a breath, glanced at Smeemarm and Zeen, who were both nodding and egging her on.

"Well, unfortunately for the Nihil, this is Corellia, and

we don't give things up without a fight, especially not our favorite city. Sorry, Tyrena, you know it's true! In all seriousness, though, we need your help. The Jedi and the Republic need your help. Corellia needs your help, and I, Crash, need your help. Many of you owe me a favor for one reason or another, and you know it. Looking at you, Baktor, Pavs, Mogark, Vinvin . . . among others. This is me collecting. Help us stop the Nihil. Help us save Corellia. If this planet falls to the Nihil, who knows what planet will be next, and you may have your gripes with the Republic, but that's nothing compared to the brutality and horror that life will become under the Nihil. Come to the shipyard! Come now! Fight for Corellia! Fight for the galaxy! Fight"—she couldn't believe she was going to say this, but it felt true—"for light and life!"

She closed out the message and clicked off the comlink. Things were about to get hairy, and there was no point in having a bunch of missed calls while she was fighting for her life.

"That was . . ." Smeemarm nodded approvingly. "That was a speech!"

"Where'd you learn to do that?" Zeen asked as they started back on their way.

"My mo—" A blaster bolt smacked with a fizzle into the wall next to Crash, cutting her words short. "There they are!"

More and more shots rained down as Crash, Zeen, and Smeemarm lunged for cover in a small inlet. Crash pulled out her own blaster. Zeen was already returning fire with a double-fisted laser barrage. Smeemarm slid into a crawl space between the pipes and vanished, eyes glinting as each blast sparkled around them.

"It seems like," Crash started, letting off a few shots into the darkness. She waited for the flash of return fire, then got low and aimed at that.

"Ayeee!" someone yelled, and a body hit the ground up ahead.

"It seems like there are more of them shooting at us than I imagined when Fezzonk said a small group on a platform craft."

Zeen let off a couple more shots and ducked behind the wall. "Yeah, I can't see kark, but this is definitely more than I saw go in."

"It's about thirty," Smeemarm reported over the comlink. Blaster fire sounded, then some screams of surprise and pain. Then more blaster fire. Much more.

"Make that twenty-seven," Smeemarm updated. "They're . . . dammit!"

"What's wrong?" Crash asked. "Are you okay?"

"The Tunnel Rail," Smeemarm said. "They're heading for it."

Crash dragged a hand over her face and started down the path deeper into the tunnel. "Grr."

"What is it?" Zeen asked, falling into step beside her.

"*That's* why they're down here. Probably a whole convoy heading to the shipyard." Their footsteps clanged against a metal catwalk. The sound of water swished in the darkness below.

"So we follow them," Zeen said.

"If they're moving this many raiders through the tunnels," Crash said, "it means they have safe passage. And the only way to get safe passage through the tunnels—"

"Is through us!" a raspy voice announced as four glistening white forms emerged from the water below.

FIFTY-THREE

CORONET CITY

"Are you ready?" Cohmac asked in the darkness of the walker's storage area.

Kantam listened to the same murmurs and growls they'd been hearing since the convoy finally pulled to a halt. "Hold on." Something was off. Kantam couldn't put their finger on what.

Cohmac exhaled slowly, probably trying to stem his impatience.

"I'm not stalling," Kantam said. "And I'm not hesitating. Something's not adding up."

"I'm listening."

"We've been here for a while. We're working under the assumption that their plan is to attack the shipyards, right?"

"Correct." Cohmac's frustration had spikes; it roiled through the empty air between them in thick, fierce waves. Kantam was glad the man's ire wasn't directed at him, knew better than to take it personally. Still, it was like sitting in a dark room with a glitchy thermal detonator.

"So why haven't they attacked yet? The ships are right across the yard from us." When they'd first pulled to a stop, both Jedi had ever so carefully slid open a wall panel to get a glimpse of where they were. Across a long airstrip bathed in floodlights, they could see the massive starships sprawled amid warehouses and shipping crates like sleeping giants.

"Probably waiting for the others to show," Cohmac said. "Which is all the more—"

"But why wait? There's no resistance. They've taken care of that already."

Cohmac stood, clicking his gear into place. "Out of an abundance of caution, Kantam, I don't know."

Kantam stood, too. "Have the Nihil in your experience ever once shown caution? It's not their way. You know this, Cohmac."

They glared at each other in the dim storage area. "What are you saying?"

"They're not coming to blow up the ships," Kantam said, realizing the truth of it as the words left their lips. "They're coming to take them."

Cohmac didn't move.

"And they haven't done it yet because they're waiting for everyone to get here. Not because they're worried about resistance—they're not expecting any—but because they want everyone with them to go along for the ride."

Cohmac's face tensed. "To Starlight."

"Imagine Starlight reeling from whatever just happened—is still happening—and here comes a fleet of Republic Longbeams and MPO star cruisers."

"The comms are down, so there'll be no way to confirm who's on board."

"It'll look like they're there to provide aid," Kantam said. "And then they'll strike."

"Even if Starlight falls before this wave arrives—there will be rescue missions, frontline workers, wounded . . . plenty of victims for them to prey on. Not to mention the symbolic victory it'll provide: the Nihil claiming a whole fleet of Republic ships from a Core World for their own and using them to terrorize the galaxy."

Something flared in Cohmac, and for a moment Kantam was worried they'd pushed him too far. On top of everything else, the very notion of this attack was . . . something beyond diabolical. But Kantam had no doubt that this was what they faced, what the whole Republic faced. And they had to deal with what it was head-on.

Cohmac breathed in deeply, steadied himself. Nodded. "What's the move?"

Kantam took out their comlink. "You heard Crash's call to help," they said, pulling up the general frequency of Crash's organization. "Attention all Corellian defenders helping to defeat the Nihil. This is Jedi Master Kantam Sy. The Nihil will be looking to commandeer any of the larger MPO star cruisers or Republic Longbeams in this yard. They must not be allowed to board a single ship until we have time to disable them. Any responding defenders, form a blockade between the Nihil forces and the cruisers. Relay this message to any who join our struggle. End transmission."

"Why don't we just destroy them?" Cohmac growled.

"What, with this walker? From here? We might get off a little damage on one before all the tanks around us simply turn their fire this way."

"Then when we get over there. We board one and use it on the others."

Kantam nodded. "If that's what we have to do, so be it. But we'll still have these Nihil to fight, and we may not want to destroy our best hope of a quick getaway." They keyed up Ram on the comlink.

"I'm in the air with Fezzonk," Ram reported. "Got your message."

"Did you happen to trade contact info with those Anzellans you met yesterday?" Kantam asked.

"No," Ram said. "I don't speak Anzellan well enough."

"Ah," Kantam sighed. That would've been too straightforward a solution, apparently.

"But the Bonbraks did!" Ram said brightly. "Want me to have them pass along a message?"

"Yes," Kantam said, finally smiling for the first time in what seemed like days. "But they're not going to like it."

FIFTY-FOUR

CORONET CITY

"Fizpatz-ma!" Tip insisted. *"Fitzpatz-ma!"*

Ram cringed, pulling on his Jedi robes and wiping the last bits of red skull makeup off as a slew of what were definitely Anzellan curses rattled from the other end of the comlink.

Even Fezzonk looked uncomfortable. "That doesn't sound good."

"Tell him to look out his window," Ram said. "The Nihil are *right* there on his front steps."

"Bobanchbo," Tip said in the most diplomatic voice Ram had ever heard him—or any Bonbrak, for that matter—speak in. *"Asa vi Nihil bo char."*

There was a pause. Outside, the night sky surrounded them, the lights of downtown Coronet slipped past. The darkness of the bay loomed up ahead, and Ram could make out the orange floodlights of the shipyard beyond.

They'd pulled away from the transport ship once Kantam sent out the directive. Clearly priorities were in flux, and there was little doubt where all those Nihil were headed. Fezzonk's ship was sleek and made up for its rudimentary weapons system with speed and stealth. Ram just hoped it had some decent shields, too.

"Ahh, Nihil kabacha," a subdued voice chirped over the comlink.

Tip nodded. *"Epa."*

"Barakoobasa," came the reply, and then the call clicked off.

Fezzonk and Ram both glared their question at Tip. *"Baka baka!"* he announced triumphantly. Ram exhaled. It was done then, that part anyway. Shug's crew would begin dismantling the flight controls on their MPOs immediately. Ram would help them when he got there, learn whatever he could, and then they'd deal with the Longbeams. He took a breath, reaching out for the Force to help balance him and prepare for whatever was ahead.

"You okay, kid?" Fezzonk asked.

Ram nodded. "Just getting myself ready. You?"

Fezzonk swiveled his head. "I live for this mess, so yes."

They shot out over the emptiness of the bay. Ram traced the dancing lights of the bridges, wondered what kinds of creatures lurked beneath the waves. And then the bright permacrete of the shipyards zoomed past below, and it was time.

"What's happening?" Ram asked, trying to make sense of the sprawling cruisers and gathering forces up ahead.

Fezzonk narrowed his eyes and swung them lower. "Let's find out."

Ram felt that familiar whoosh in his gut as they swooped into a dive, and he had to admit, he loved it. Flying had become one of his favorite skills since getting to Starlight—there hadn't been much chance or reason to back on Valo—and it was the perfect union of his passion for everything mechanized and the simple thrill of speeding through space.

And right now—with everything falling apart and the galaxy in the most fragile state he'd seen and everyone he knew in mortal danger—he would take whatever small joys he could get.

"Those are probably folks showing up to answer Crash's call to arms," Fezzonk said, pointing to where small groups of five and ten armed defenders were making their way stealthily from ship to ship toward the open airstrip ahead. It wasn't enough, not nearly. But maybe more would come. Maybe this was just the drip before the massive flood of armies that would sweep in from downtown, crushing the Nihil and bringing peace to Coronet City.

Seemed unlikely, Ram thought, but who knew? The lay of the land out in the Core was unlike anything he'd ever experienced. It seemed like it would take a lifetime to understand it as well as Crash clearly did.

"And that's what we're up against," Fezzonk said, swinging them up and around in a wide arc so the masses of Nihil foot soldiers stretched out beneath them.

"Stars," Ram gasped, "there's hundreds of them."

Fezzonk grunted. "Let me see if I can do something about that." He leveled out the flier, veered into a steep climb toward the stars, and then flipped over, sickeningly, and dove straight down, letting loose with all his firepower at once.

Ram thought he might puke. Straight ahead of them, bodies were flung to either side as laser fire exploded through the Nihil ranks, all of it rushing up toward his face faster than he could grasp.

"And away!" Fezzonk yelled, skimming into an even glide just above their heads and pulling up just as blaster fire exploded all around.

The small flier rocked, and a dozen warning alarms shrieked to life on the console. "Ah, we okay?" Ram asked.

"Uh-uh," Fezzonk said. "Gonna drop you off and take it down in that field over there."

More laser fire splattered against the ship, shaking them dangerously.

"Just fly over those MPO star cruisers," Ram said, squeezing whatever he could to stabilize as the flier bucked and vibrated through another barrage. "I'll hop out with the fellas."

"You got it," Fezzonk said, gritting his teeth.

"You gonna be all right?"

The Dowutin chuckled grimly. "Hoo yeah." He pulled open his dress shirt with one hand, revealing a splattering of scar tissue on his chest. "See all this? This is very, very hard to pierce. Most bodyguards wear blaster-proof vests. Me? I am one." He let out a long, self-satisfied rumble of a laugh.

"You're *blaster*-proof?" Ram gaped.

"I mean . . . practically! Hey, this is your stop. Do you want me to fly lower?"

They slowed to a hover over the first star cruiser in the row. "Nah," Ram said, patting the two furry lumps in his shirt. "We got this. Right, boys?"

"Ehhhh," one of the Bonbraks wheezed, but it was too late; Ram had already popped open the cockpit canopy and leapt into the night sky.

FIFTY-FIVE

CORONET CITY

Reath's heart sank as the transport ship swung slowly over the shipyards.

He'd found a comfortable-enough perch on one of the wheel turrets, changed back into his Jedi tunic, and managed to stay still and out of sight there for what felt like a horrific slow-motion tour of downtown Coronet City.

He had barely been able to hear Master Kantam over the thundering thrusters and engine roar, but he'd grasped enough of the message to understand what they were up against.

The Nihil would commandeer Republic ships or those fancy star cruisers the Anzellan was building. They would show up at Starlight, posing as reinforcements. And then they would attack. If there was any hope of saving Reath's friends and all the Jedi on board, it would be in stopping this second wave of attacks.

Reath tried to collect himself inwardly. The Force was with him. A hundred terrible thoughts came and went. The Force was with him. That night, he may well become one with it, join his master Jora Malli to become part of the living Force. And if that happened, so be it. He would die fighting to save his friends, for the Republic. The one thing left to him to do was fight.

Nihil forces below seemed to go on and on to all sides—there had to be at least five hundred gathered before an array of tanks and commandeered industrial walkers. And there, in front of the Republic shipyard, a small line of defenders gathered behind their makeshift barricade of shipping crates, scrap metal, and fencing. Reath thought he recognized some of Crash's crew: the floaty famous girl, Svi'no, definitely, and both the Wookiee and Savrip could easily be distinguished, loading more junk on top of their defensive wall.

Across the airstrip, the Nihil were already organizing into attack squads, glancing over at the newly arrived obstacles between themselves and the shipyards.

It would be a massacre.

Reath took a breath. They weren't directly over the battlefield yet, and he wasn't sure if he'd survive a fall from this height, even with the Force helping him. What good would he be to anyone if he was a stain on the permacrete?

But he couldn't just watch these people who had shown up to help the Republic get run down.

Finally, grudgingly, the transport began descending.

Below, the Nihil army turned as one to the Corellian defenders and charged.

There was no path that didn't lead through the Nihil. They had made sure of that.

But really, there was no path at all. Not now, not ever. Searching for one had always been folly. The only path was the one Reath was on, wherever he was, wherever he went.

And right now, his path was taking him right into the heart of yet another unfolding disaster.

This was what it meant to put *us* first.

Reath readied himself to jump. He was one with the Force, and the Force was with him.

The first few blaster shots zinged back and forth between the two sides as the Nihil closed within range.

In seconds, they'd simply crush and overrun the barricades.

And then screaming erupted from the Nihil rear guard.

Two flashes of pure light, one green, one blue, emerged swinging from the darkness. Kantam and Cohmac. Each slashed a vicious swath deep into the Nihil army from either side. All around them, bodies collapsed, raiders screamed and charged only to be cut down. The two Jedi cleaved toward each other; waves of blaster fire ricocheted through the surrounded forces as more and more Nihil turned to deal with this sudden assault.

There was no path. Which meant that the only way forward was to make one.

Reath leapt.

The wind shrieked in his ears. The raging battle below grew louder, a roar. He called on the Force, willing his plummet to slow, and landed, teeth clenched, with a thud on the permacrete, smack in the middle of the front line of Nihil raiders. His lightsaber extended as a hundred eyes turned to him at once. Reath took a breath, and swung.

FIFTY-SIX

CORONET CITY

There was a terrible arithmetic to all this, Kantam thought, swiping away another blaster shot, then another, and finally the hand that had fired them. It was an endurance game, really. Eventually, both Jedi would tire, falter. The hand dropped to the ground. The man whose hand it was shrieked and ran. How many Nihil would be left to kill them when that happened?

From the look of things: plenty.

Kantam and Cohmac had carved their way through the main body of the Nihil force, one from each side. They'd met in the middle, as planned, and now they stood back to back, chopping, hacking, blocking, stabbing. They were both bloody from various grazes, both covered in sweat and panting. Kantam wasn't sure how much longer they'd last.

At some point, Reath had dropped out of the sky, landing somewhere up ahead of them. It had been a small triumph amid so much death and desperation, seeing the Padawan appear out of nowhere. Kantam caught glimpses of the boy's lightsaber flashing through the ranks. But there was no time to see any more than that—the most important thing was the thing right in front of Kantam, and for the foreseeable future that thing would continue to be blaster bolts flinging at their head.

The plan might've been a little ambitious.

If they were going to survive, they needed to head for the small band of allies who'd shown up to block the Nihil assault. Their own two-pronged attack had done good work splitting the enemy and sending them into disarray, and now there were ships to protect.

"We have to make our way to the front!" Kantam yelled over the screams of pain and blaster shrieks. But Cohmac wasn't there. They whirled. "Cohmac?"

A hulking Nihil charged out of the crowd, swinging some kind of bladed staff over his head. Kantam lunged to the side, then dodged again as the Nihil stabbed out suddenly with a hidden blade in his other hand. The blade shredded cloth, skin, and muscle from Kantam's left arm. They pivoted to the side, letting the sudden burst of pain simmer to a throb, and brought their lightsaber down across the creature's arm, lopping it off. Then they stepped back, winding up the saber, and burst forward, shearing off his head.

Where was Cohmac?

All around, Nihil ran, sending off wild shots that slammed into one another as often as not. They would rally in small groups and charge, then scatter back into their chaotic ranks, regroup, and try again.

"Cohmac!" Kantam yelled. Had he fallen?

"What's going on?" Reath panted, running up beside Kantam. A Quarren rushed him from behind, yelling nonsensically, and Reath whirled and cut him down with a single smooth motion, then turned back to Kantam. "Where's my—"

"There!" Kantam yelled, spotting a sudden cluster of Nihil crowding around something. They both burst into a desperate run, slashing ahead to clear a path.

"Master!" Reath yelled, his voice cracking with fear.

Kantam slashed across the legs of the Nihil directly in front of them, then stepped forward and shoved both hands out, sending most of the others stumbling away with the Force. Cohmac rose unsteadily, covered in dirt and with several new gashes. "Thanks," he said, trying to smile. "I must've dropped my—"

A Gamorrean Nihil ran at him, screaming and raising a club, but a lightsaber hilt flew past, landing securely in Cohmac's hand. "This," Cohmac said, extending it through the attacking Gamorrean. The blade emerged from the raider's back. He dropped to his knees, then collapsed.

"Master, are you okay?" Reath asked, beating back another wave of blaster fire.

Cohmac shook his head. "We have to get to the front lines. We're not going to last much longer out here." Already, the Nihil around them were regrouping and closing in on all sides.

Kantam squinted at some commotion up ahead. "It seems like . . ." Several Nihil screamed and fell. Others whirled around to see what was happening behind them, then charged. "The front line has come to us."

Svi'no led the small group. She had a blaster in each of her four hands and was letting off shot after shot, pushing forward against each attack as it came. Behind her, Tamo and Tangor were lashing out to either side, smashing heads and sweeping away spears. Fezzonk, armed with a huge cannon, served as rear guard, making sure no one got too close.

They'd broken away from the barricades and pushed through the Nihil lines to the Jedi.

"This way," Svi'no said. "We made a path for you."

"After you," Kantam said, gesturing for Cohmac to go ahead. They took up a position on the far side of the group and batted away the incoming fire as everyone worked their way back to the barricades.

"They'll be making a move for the ships any moment now," Cohmac said, limping behind a crate and throwing his back against it, breathless. "We have to . . . We have to . . ."

"Easy," Kantam said. "Take it easy." Cohmac didn't have

any obvious mortal injuries, but he wasn't in good shape. Kantam had taken their share of hits, too, and Reath sported a gash down his face that looked like it wouldn't heal any time soon.

"I'm okay," Cohmac assured him. Then, eyebrows raised. "We did some damage."

"Indeed we did," Kantam said.

"Not enough."

Kantam shook their head. "Not yet, no. The night's still young."

"They're coming," Svi'no called from atop the barricades. Blaster fire careened overhead. "Full force."

FIFTY-SEVEN

CORONET CITY

"Ezvangolt," Crash said. His being there was *probably* better than if it had been Fastidima. Still. None of this was good. She took a step back on the catwalk, felt the cool metal railing press against her.

"Mm, yes," the Grindalid said. Water dripped from the tendrils of his chin and splashed in the darkness below. "You have some nerve, entering our realm while Mother Fastidima holds you responsible for the death of one of her own."

"The time isn't up," Crash reminded him, trying not to sound as desperate as she felt. "I have some left." True as that was, the Nihil were slipping out of her grasp, and Tralmat with them, that underground rail system whisking them off through the darkness so they could reinforce their buddies at the shipyards, surely.

Beside Crash, Zeen adjusted her grip on the blasters, waiting for a signal.

"I like humans with nerve," Ezvangolt hissed in a menacing whisper.

Crash held out a hand to let her know that shooting wasn't the move. Not yet, anyway.

"If you came here to kill me, I'd be dead," Crash said.

"Aheh, that is correct."

"Then . . . what do you want?"

"Several weeks ago, the human Tralmat made a deal with Mother Fastidima. It was for safe passage through our realm using the Tunnel Rail. The man disappeared along with Prybolt, and now he is back and calling in this part of the bargain."

"Go on," Crash said.

"We do not trust this man," Ezvangolt spat. That was practically a curse among the Garavult Clan. Trust was the highest form of respect, and it was either there or it wasn't. If it wasn't, you were an enemy. Crash had been teetering on the thin line in between, probably one of the few who ever had, and she knew it wouldn't last long. "And now he has brought the Nihil into our home."

"You're right not to trust him," Crash said. "I believe he is one of the people responsible for Prybolt's disappearance."

All four Grindalids hissed and conferred angrily with one another.

"We suspected as much!" Ezvangolt growled. "But Mother Fastidima does not have proof, and so she will not go back on her word. It is not our way."

"But?" Crash said, sensing the opening.

"But Ezvangolt made no such deal."

"Nor did Vanizma!" crowed another of the worms.

"Nor Zazima!" cried the third.

"Nor Proxima!" shrieked the smallest.

"Well . . . where does that leave us?" Crash asked.

"The rail is not faster than the worms," Ezvangolt declared proudly. "But we must leave at once."

Crash clung tightly to the gilded chain metal covering Ezvangolt's slimy upper back.

Her feet were soaked in tunnel water, and when all this was over, she'd probably have to set them on fire to get rid of whatever nasty fungus had taken up residence there. But it was all worth it when they saw the glint of the rickety old maglev train rattling along in the darkness ahead.

"Pull up alongside them," she called; Ezvangolt and the others had already sped up, their growls and snorts rising in the thick tunnel air. Frothy waves emanated from either side of them as they zoomed along the surface of the water.

"Here we go," Crash called to Zeen.

That girl lived her whole life ready, though. She was already raised up into a crouch on the Grindalid she was riding. She had both blasters trained on the last car as the worms reared suddenly out of the water, bringing both girls eye to eye with the handful of Nihil within. "Surprise," Crash said, and opened fire. All four of them collapsed, their bodies smoking. The worms had already splashed across the water when the other Nihil turned back to see what had happened.

Screams rang out up ahead, and Crash saw two shining flashes surge in majestic arcs toward the speeding train. Zazima and Proxima, she thought. They each snatched one raider in their jaws and then slipped smoothly back below the surface as the screams became gurgles and then nothing.

The Nihil started shooting. Of course. That was all they knew how to do—break things and shoot things. Ezvangolt swerved in and out of the pillars holding up the train tracks as laser fire danced across the dark water around them.

"Smeemarm," Crash said into her comlink. "You there?"

The Arcona responded immediately. "Up top."

Crash smiled at how effective her team was even though she'd disbanded it. "How big is this train? I can't get a read on it."

"It's big," Smeemarm reported. "About eighteen cars. And . . . you're not going to like this."

Crash growled preemptively.

"Tralmat's making a break for it. He was in the front car with a group of Nihil, and when the shooting started, they detached at the next turnoff and headed down a separate tunnel. It's coming up, not far from your position."

"Coward," Crash snarled. "Thanks, Smeemarm. Stay with the main rail."

She leaned to the side as more blaster fire fizzled into the water nearby. Then she sent a few bolts back their way just to keep them busy. "Zeen!"

Zeen pulled up alongside, and both slowed a little to stay out of range as the train rumbled on up ahead. "We're splitting up."

"What do you need me to do?"

Crash was glad that Zeen didn't get all sappy or make a thing about it. Right now, she just needed people around who could do what needed to be done. She needed to survive this, and she needed Svi'no to survive it, too. And ideally everyone else. "Stay on these guys. Make their lives miserable all the way to the battleground. Then link with our folks at the shipyards. Also, please stay alive and keep Svi'no alive if you can."

Zeen smiled. "I'll do my best. What are you gonna do?"

"Also stay alive, hopefully," Crash said, already pulling off toward the tunnel stretching to the right. "And make sure someone else doesn't."

FIFTY-EIGHT

CORONET CITY

"You can't do everything," Reath said out loud to himself. "You can only do one thing."

It sounded simple, but in the midst of so much fighting, so much death, so many explosions of noxious gas . . . and with the thought of Starlight under attack a constant clanging in the back of his mind—just doing one thing seemed like the more impossible task.

But Reath could do only one thing, and that one thing was protect the MPO star cruiser at the far end of the yard. Kantam had divvied up their forces, sending small groups to each ship. Ram had reported that the Anzellan and his crew had temporarily disabled most of the star cruisers, so most of the Corellian defenders had been sent to protect the Longbeams, one lot over. The Nihil would waste precious time and resources trying to take off on the cruisers before concentrating their forces on the Republic ships. That was the theory anyway.

But there was still one MPO that Ram and the Anzellan hadn't gotten to yet, and Reath already saw a crew of red-skinned, bug-eyed Mimbanese Nihil approaching it just as he was. The two Corellians at his side ran headlong into the group of Nihil, firing and screaming, before he could stop them.

Reath shook his head and lit his lightsaber. Three Nihil raiders collapsed, but the rest opened fire on the Corellians, killing them instantly. Reath leapt, slashing away lasers as he flew through the air and landed, lightsaber first, on top of the nearest raider. The man screamed and fell, and Reath cut and sliced, clearing an open area around himself so he could get to the open boarding ramp of the cruiser.

More Nihil ran over, sensing a chance to outnumber one of the hated Jedi. Reath sent a group of them flying backward, then cut down one and a second and third as they ran screaming at him, blaster bolts flying in every direction.

He stumbled backward, barely able to take in the bodies already surrounding him, the sheer amount of death he had brought in just the past hour. This was not the time to dwell on that. A whole wall of blaster fire seemed to unleash itself at once, flashing out from the Nihil amid shrieks and laughter. Reath swung at a diagonal, lunging to the side, and flung most of the shots back at the attackers.

More death.

One bolt shrieked across his arm, another his shoulder.

Neither were direct hits, but they stung, then burned, and his clothes had to be in tatters.

Didn't matter.

All that mattered was protecting this ship.

Or destroying it, if need be.

More Nihil arrived, backing up the ones surrounding him, and they surged forward. It wasn't a coordinated effort, just a wrathful charge fueled by the sheer momentum of so many furious at being held off by one.

Reath pulled a thermal detonator from his pouch and sent it rolling past their feet, right into the middle of the attack.

FOOM! It blew with a vicious blast that sent Nihil flying in every direction and scattered the attackers. Something hard whipped out at Reath, smashed into his chest. Armor, or an armored body part. It sent him staggering backward onto the boarding ramp, and two Nihil who'd been gathering themselves nearby leapt into action.

Reath managed to regain his balance in time to slice off the gun hand of the first one, but the second fired at the same time, the bolt smashing into Reath's thigh.

"Hrrrgh!" he yelled, dropping to one knee, and then smashed the follow-up shot right back into the shooter.

The other attackers were rallying again, and Reath had to turn immediately around and whip away two more shots, then another and another.

They were closing in, yelling and jeering, and Reath didn't have much left in him. Pain arced through his leg like a thousand bolts of lightning, shredding him from the inside.

"You will not board this ship!" he yelled. And he meant it. Three raiders decided to put that challenge to the test, running past, just out of his reach. He called on the Force, yanking them back and sending them collapsing into the dirt beside him. He cut the closest one as the raider reached for his blaster, and then the next, who was scrambling to get up. Then the world did a somersault around him and a sharp throb erupted across his right arm.

He'd fallen, somehow. He'd been hit—shot, he realized, seeing the sizzling charred injury on his arm.

He blinked through the pain and sweat and exhaustion, trying to make sense of the world as boots streamed past him onto the ship. The ship he'd been defending.

No.

He would not be the cause of even more destruction. He struggled to stand. He would not let them hurt his friends. He—

Boots ran past again, but this time going the other direction. Screams filled the air around him as Nihil raiders scampered away.

Away from the ship.

Away from the ship?

Reath lifted himself onto his elbows and almost tried to run away himself.

Amid the smoke and dust, a gigantic figure emerged from the belly of the cruiser, clomping down the boarding ramp on huge metallic feet. Blaster bolts flung out from cannons lining its long arms.

Reath squinted through the chaos at . . . "Shug?"

"Afazeeeeeeeee!" the tiny Anzellan screamed from his load-lifter workframe. He blasted a few more Nihil, then stomped forward to where Reath lay, and looked down at him with a wrinkled little smile. "Weee are all athee Republic!" And then he was off, sprinting with huge, creaking steps into the battle, lighting up raiders left and right.

"Reath!" a very welcome and familiar voice called.

Ram jogged down the boarding ramp and knelt beside Reath. His eyes were wide with worry, which meant Reath was probably even worse off than he felt.

"Ram . . ." Reath mumbled, trying to smile.

"Are you . . . ? Can you . . . ?" Ram tried, but none of the questions he was clearly trying to ask made any sense, not really. Finally he just shook his head and helped Reath into a slanted kind of stand. Ram wrapped Reath's arm over his shoulder, and together they made their way up the ramp onto the cruiser.

"Remember . . . ?" Reath said. "Remember that thing I said about enjoying the thrill of battle, back on Starlight?"

"Oh, boy . . ."

"I take it back."

"Stop talking," Ram said, half-laughing, half-sobbing. "Just shut up, please. I can't carry you and giggle and cry all at once. It's too much."

"I take it all back! I want a full refund for my words, please."

Ram led them off to the right down a small corridor, then popped open a bench that turned out to also be a . . .

"You're *not*!" Reath gasped.

"Just for now!" Ram said. "You need to heal, and to heal you need to rest, and to rest you need to hide. There's *nowhere* safe right now. Get in."

"I'm *not* luggage," Reath complained, easing himself into the little crawl space.

"Stop fussing and let me look you over." Ram rustled through Reath's clothes, probably making sure none of the wounds was actively bleeding or life-threatening in any way. Judging by Ram's scowl, that wasn't a sure thing at all.

"Take this," Ram said, digging into his pockets and then passing Reath a few small bacta packs.

Reath held them up to his face. "Bacta? Ram, this is your whole supply! You can't—"

"Trust me," Ram said, already closing the lid over Reath. "You need it more than I do."

FIFTY-NINE

CORONET CITY

The Nihil just kept coming.

Kantam had never seen so many. Even as swaths fell in battle, more and more rushed into the field, literally crawling out of sewers, scurrying off that transporter, or dropping in from who knew where else. . . .

Kantam stood on the smoking charred remains of a speeder bike one of the raiders had charged them with. The battlefield was a sea of gas masks, goggles, helmets. Contingents of Nihil stormed through the shipyard, looking for a ship that hadn't been sabotaged. Soon they would realize the star cruisers wouldn't do them any good and they'd concentrate all their scattered forces on the Republic lot.

There were seven functional Longbeams.

From what Kantam could tell, the combatants defending them had dwindled down to about twenty-five. Both the Savrip and Wookiee were badly injured and had holed up inside a disabled MPO at the far end of the lot. Cohmac still fought valiantly, but Kantam wasn't sure how much he had left in him. Reath was off protecting the last MPO star cruiser, and Ram was probably helping the Anzellans dismantle its flight mechanisms.

There wasn't much choice left. Kantam got on the comms. "All Corellian defenders, this is Jedi Master Kantam Sy. New directive: destroy the Republic fleet. We can't afford to let it fall into Nihil hands. Repeat—destroy all the Longbeams. We must make a tactical retreat to the far end of the shipyard."

The only thing left to do was save as many lives as they could. But that had always been the mission. It was just that it had become a grueling slow-motion process of watching that mission fall apart, piece by piece. Still—they'd kept all the ships grounded thus far, and that was no small task.

Another Nihil loped toward Kantam, then fell in a barrage of laser fire. Kantam hadn't even had a chance to extend their lightsaber. "Thanks," they called to Fezzonk, the massive pilot who provided Crash her air support.

"Any time, Jedi! I'm going to go wreck some of these ships."

"Be careful," Kantam called just as a group of heavily armed beings floated over. "The Atchapats!"

"We said we would fight by your side," Barg'no growled, "and we meant it! To battle!" He led the whole family directly into an incoming Nihil assault, smashing it to pieces.

Kantam barely had time to appreciate the moment before someone yelled, "Incoming!" With a boom, yellow smoke covered the sky, the shipyard, the world.

"Blasted Nihil," Kantam growled, pulling on their mask. "Cohmac?"

"Masks on, everyone," a voice announced on the comms. "Grab one off a fallen Nihil if need be!"

"Here," Cohmac said emerging from the foul cloud near Kantam.

"We can't fight like this," Kantam said. "Our people are everywhere. The Nihil are even more everywhere." Kantam shoved away a sudden surge of panic. Everything was falling apart, but they hadn't lost yet. And the Force was with them. They took a breath of stale breathing-mask air, that rubbery smell.

A series of explosions boomed somewhere deeper in the Republic lot, sudden distant flashes lighting the fog. "Three ships down," Fezzonk announced over the comm. "Four to go."

That was something. Kantam glanced at Cohmac. "We clear the air here and call everyone to us. This is where we make our stand."

Cohmac nodded, exhaustion creeping across his face like a shroud. Together, the two Jedi raised their arms as Kantam spoke over the comms. "Defenders of Corellia! Master

Cohmac and I are clearing an area by the third Longbeam on the Republic lot. Come to us, and we will fight together. We must unite our forces."

What forces we have left, Kantam thought wryly. Then they quieted the rumbling doubts and fears, the many, many questions, and tuned into the Force. The gas had become more than a weapon; it was a calling card, an announcement. Everyone knew when those thick vapors surrounded you, the Nihil would come next—if you managed to stay conscious long enough to see them arrive.

Kantam and Cohmac reached out, and they pushed. The living Force surrounded them, flowed through them. Even in battle, in chaos, amid death, Kantam reflected, the Force was there; it was everywhere.

But they didn't have much time.

The first to arrive was Svi'no. She backed into the clearing, all four blasters trained on the fog. Ram appeared from the other side, his yellow lightsaber glowing like a beacon.

"And Reath?" Cohmac asked as Ram joined them on the boarding ramp.

"Injured," Ram said, "but I think he'll make it."

"You *think*?" Cohmac demanded. "Where is he?"

"I hid him in a storage bin on one of the MPOs," Ram said. "We were surrounded by Nihil, and it was the only way to keep him safe."

Cohmac seemed to steady himself, then nodded. "You did well, Padawan. Thank you."

Ram took over clearing the gas from around them as a few more masked raiders showed up—then Kantam almost shouted with relief when Zeen appeared beside a tall Weequay named Barchibar, one of Crash's team. "It's good to see you, Zeen," they said.

"Where's Crash?" Svi'no asked, her eyes already filling with tears behind those thick goggles.

"She's okay," Zeen said with certainty. "She went after Tralmat."

Svi'no didn't look convinced, but there was nothing else to be done.

A few more came—a Twi'lek Ram called Inspector Deemus, who seemed to have an entourage of troopers of her own. A Gamorrean and a delicate-looking Rodian.

"I'm not sure how much longer we can—" Ram was saying when blaster fire exploded out of the fog, shredding through Barchibar.

"Pull back to the boarding ramp!" Kantam ordered, thwacking away another couple of bolts. "Pull back!"

Zeen, Cohmac, Ram, and a few others ran past him. Barchibar was already dead, his body smoking on the permacrete.

Kantam glanced around. "We have to—"

A low rumble sounded nearby. Was that—

"That's a Longbeam taking off!" Ram yelled.

No. There was no way to stop it, Kantam knew, not with

their forces so torn up and gas everywhere. It had probably already lifted off, from the sound of things.

"I got it," Ram said simply, and ran off into the fog.

Kantam and Cohmac blinked at each other.

"Just hold the position," Ram called. "This one's mine!"

SIXTY

CORONET CITY

It was possible that Ram had been waiting his whole life for this moment.

It was also very possible that this moment would shorten Ram's life considerably and suddenly.

Yes, everything was terrible—worse than the Republic Fair even. Starlight was probably lost, many people had already died, and many more would soon.

But after all that subterfuge and caution, investigating and dressing up and playing roles, finally everything was very simple. Very straightforward.

The Nihil were taking a Longbeam to attack Starlight.

Ram had to stop them. Ram *would* stop them. No matter what.

He ran harder, shoving fog out of his way with the Force as he went. The Bonbraks, each wearing a tiny gas mask, chattered back and forth in his shirt. They knew what was coming. They were ready.

Up ahead, a figure ran toward Ram, mostly concealed in the chemical cloud. Could be an ally, but probably not. Ram kept running, extending his lightsaber. As he neared, the figure raised something—a bowcaster!—and Ram lopped off the front of it, shoved the attacker backward without even having to touch them, and kept going.

Everything was terrible, but the Force was still unstoppable. It was bigger than these disasters. Bigger than the Republic, bigger than the Nihil. And it was with Ram.

He could almost feel the ship calling out to him from the fog ahead. Its fierce song stretched along the fibers of the Force, beckoned Ram.

Was that thing imbued with the dark side somehow? Ram wondered, finally reaching the all-black drill-nosed starfighter and pausing to catch his breath.

No. That possibility seemed too simplistic by half, and entirely implausible. The starfighter did feel . . . alive, almost, and it thrummed with power, like the Force was a fire pouring through its circuits and gaskets. But that was, if anything, Ram's own perception of it, his excitement and the sheer, ferocious knowledge within him of what must be done.

What would be done.

No, this wasn't the dark side calling. It was the momentum of the galaxy, the simple, urgent truth that the moment beckoned, and Ram would rise to meet it.

He raised one hand and reached out with the Force. He felt his way through the labyrinth of gears and controls, the navicomputer, the astonishingly brutal and ancient weapons system, the thick carbon fibers that made up the shielding. Then he twisted his wrist, nodded once, and heard the engine rev to life, the computer system blip awake. He swung his arm up. The cockpit hatch clicked, shook, and then popped open.

Ram climbed inside, already feeling the hum of power surging through him, through the ship, through the whole galaxy.

The hatch slammed shut, turning Ram's world into a tiny dark sphere.

The control panel glowed with a dim sheen, but that was it.

It didn't matter. Ram didn't need to see—he needed to feel. And he felt *everything.* That dullness—the utter, terrifying emptiness he'd complained to Reath about—had been seeping off gradually since they'd learned about the Starlight attack, and Ram had felt strange surges of emotion rush in to fill the gaps where the emptiness had been. He had felt them, released them, felt them, released them, as he had been trained. As Ram piloted the small starfighter into a hover over the shipyard, whatever was left of that dull sense of nothing blew away. Emotion raged through Ram—grief, exhilaration, fury.

Ram was a Jedi, and the Force was with him. It had protected him this far and been his ally through danger, devastation, and ruin. One day he would become part of it. It seemed like today might be a very good candidate for that. But that was secondary. The Force was more powerful than all Ram's emotions combined. It was more powerful than death.

He breathed in, allowing the feelings to surge through him, and then exhaled, releasing them all into the thick air of the cockpit. The Eviscerator rose higher and higher, engines warming up after decades and decades of slumber, flight systems checking and rechecking, cannons whirling on their turrets, readying themselves to deliver abject destruction.

The emotions were back already, all of them. But the Force had never left, and it never would, and Ram knew what he had to do.

He pointed the drill-shaped nose of the starfighter toward the sky, directing it as much with the Force as with the controls, took another breath, and blasted off.

SIXTY-ONE

CORONET CITY

One ship. Less than two dozen defenders. Hundreds of Nihil.

This cruel, cruel arithmetic.

Kantam crouched behind one of the crates they'd set up on the boarding ramp—part of their final desperate barricade—and swiveled their wrist, using the Force to sweep yet another thermal detonator back into the fog. It burst somewhere to the left; the thuds of bodies and agonized screams rose in its wake.

If they tried to take off, the Nihil would simply blow them out of the sky.

As it was, the only reason the raiders hadn't destroyed the Longbeam already was the fact that it was the last functional one around, and they surely assumed they'd be able to overrun the defenders soon enough.

They were probably right.

The near certainty of their defeat was the one thing keeping them from being blown to bits.

It was that and, Kantam was pretty sure, the Nihil wanted to punish them for putting up this much of a fight. Killing them all in a fiery explosion wouldn't be enough. These raiders had come expecting a victorious boarding and then a simple flight through hyperspace to where the Starlight attack was already well underway, if not already won. Then they'd just smash away the survivors and aid workers.

Instead, they'd found themselves stopped in their tracks, slaughtered in droves, scattered and only now regaining their momentum. They were fueled by sheer indignant rage at finding a fight where they weren't expecting one. Kantam could see it in their sloppiness, the desperate charging attacks that would leave them flailing, suddenly limbless, and then simply dead. This wasn't the glorious raid on defenseless civilians they'd imagined. And they would find a way to make whoever was responsible suffer as much as possible.

"Down!" Cohmac yelled. Kantam ducked. More blaster fire splattered from the fog, ripping across the belly of the Longbeam and slamming into the makeshift barricade.

Kantam peered out, using the Force to shove aside some of the haze. Figures ran through it toward the boarding ramp, raising their blasters and spears. "Another charge coming."

Laser fire lanced out from inside the ship, over Kantam and Cohmac's heads and into the oncoming attack. Nihil collapsed to either side, and more sprinted forward, lunging over their fallen comrades' bodies. Those fell, too, and the row behind them opened fire. Bolts were flung back and forth between the two sides, and screams of pain rose all around.

"We can't keep this up much longer," Zeen said, racing down the ramp to Kantam and throwing herself against the barricade.

Kantam nodded. It was true. They knew it. There wasn't much left to do about it though. Already, they'd let one ship get away. "Do you have a suggestion?"

"If we can't let them take this ship," Zeen said. "Then we destroy the ship."

Kantam shook their head. "We can't make that choice for all those people who've shown up to help us."

"It's not going to be a choice for much longer," Zeen said. "We can have them evacuate and then—"

"There's no evacuation," Kantam said, trying to keep their voice even. "We're surrounded."

"I know, but . . ."

From somewhere nearby, a cheer went up. Then a rumble. Kantam and Zeen both glanced to the side. Cohmac was already shoving the fog out of the way in the direction the voices had come from.

"Oh, no," Zeen gasped.

One of the MPO star cruisers rose into the air and pointed toward the sky.

SIXTY-TWO

CORELLIAN SPACE

This beast had been made with two exact purposes in mind: speed and destruction.

That was it. And those were exactly the two things Ram needed it for; so for once on this awful night, something had gone some kind of right.

There were no viewports. A cranky rudimentary sensor system blurted out alerts, and matching flashes appeared on the control panels. That was about it.

Everything else was acceleration, more acceleration, turbo-acceleration, each with a corresponding version in drill mode, and cannons—presumably for softening up whatever spot you were about to go full turboacceleration drill mode on.

And then, of course, there was the Force.

Ram rocketed through an orbital layer of trash, past satellites and some civilian crafts, an abandoned freighter. He could feel all of them, their weight and rhythm. They popped up on the scanner as he zoomed by, only confirming what the Force had already hinted at within him. It almost seemed like the Force was functioning as a link between Ram and the onboard systems of the ship; but surely that wasn't possible—the ship wasn't alive!

It really didn't matter though.

All that mattered was catching up to that cruiser before it made the jump to lightspeed, which would probably be any second, if it hadn't already.

The navicomputer burped frantically at him just as he felt the weight and thrust of something directly above where he was flying.

Got ya, Ram thought.

A tiny readout confirmed it was indeed a Longbeam, and it was revving up its hyperspace engines.

Its hyperspace engines, which, when Ram quieted his mind, set all those screaming emotions to simmer, he could visualize. That wasn't the Force at all—he'd spent many nights poring over the brilliant logistics of these brilliant ships, the five-engine configuration, their hyperdrives. He could picture the alluvial damper plates sliding free of the emission chamber, the hyperdrive field folding out to encompass the ship in its bubble of space-time. It had only partly been because he thought it might come in handy one day—mostly it was just sheer fascination.

And he was about to lay waste to one, which would've felt like a shame if it didn't also mean helping save his friends.

Five seconds before the Longbeam's hyperspace engine is fully activated, his monitor advised him.

He needed only three.

Ram swung the Eviscerator into a sharp climb, thrusting all available power into the turbothrust engines. It jolted forward with even more juice than he'd expected, the massive star cruiser already looming in front of it.

"Yeeeeeeeeeeeeee!" both Bonbraks shrieked at once.

Ram barely had time to hit the drill switch before the ship slammed full force into the Longbeam's rear hyperspace engine.

"AH!" Ram yelled. Acceleration compensators redlined, transmitting waves of calibrated antigravity to cancel out the impact momentum that would have otherwise dashed Ram against his controls. The impact nearly tossed him from his flight seat.

But it didn't. And the only damage indicators showing up on his monitor were, well, none actually. He kept the drill going but slowed to a minimal acceleration mode. This ship wasn't going into hyperspace any time soon.

A horrific rending of metal sounded from just beyond his cockpit, and explosions rocked either side of the fighter. But he was okay. He had done it. Now he had to finish the job.

There was an entire ship ahead of him, and he was going to make sure it didn't fall into Nihil hands, hyperdrive or not.

Ram shoved the Eviscerator up through the rear engine bay, shredding metal all around him, jostled back and forth by more explosions, and then angled himself forward and down just a little, letting the Force guide his maneuvers.

There.

He'd lined up with the trajectory of the starship, which hung in space, probably smoking and sputtering but not fully demolished yet.

Ram closed his eyes and pushed forward on the accelerator stick, lurching the drill into a grinding path of sheer destruction through the central column of the Longbeam.

Vaguely, he was aware of living beings running for their lives, clawing desperately over each other to escape.

Some hid or made it to other parts of the ship. Others became one with the Force.

Ram understood his mission, and he knew it wasn't over.

"Kantam to Ram," they blurted over the comlink, pulling Ram from his meditation. "Kantam to Ram."

"This is Ram."

"Did you—" Blaster shots cut off Kantam's voice, and when they came back, they sounded out of breath. "Did you stop the ship?"

"Yes. Are you . . . ?" It was a silly question. Of course they weren't okay.

"Good," Kantam said, ignoring Ram's trailed-off question.

"Because there's another headed your way. It's an MPO star cruiser."

"I got it," Ram said. "Don't worry."

"I'm not," Kantam said, and Ram heard the pride in their voice. "Not anymore."

Ram ramped up the acceleration, smashing his way toward the front of the Longbeam.

"Ram." Kantam's voice suddenly sounded far away, sadder than Ram had ever heard it. "May the Force be with you."

Goodbye, they meant. Ram knew it. He blinked away tears, fought with his voice not to let that sudden well of sorrow out. He didn't want Kantam to die. Or any of his friends. He knew it just meant they'd join the living Force. He knew it was part of life and that he had no control over it. And still the sorrow washed through him.

Rage followed it, like lava rushing along a riverbed.

So many emotions.

"Balance," Ram whispered to himself in a pretty good imitation of Reath's voice. It was the only way. Lava heated the water; ice would chill that fire.

"What's that?" Kantam asked.

"May the Force be with you, Master Sy," Ram said, voice shaking.

Then he clicked off the comm and blasted through the last wall separating his ship from the bridge of the Longbeam, slowing to a stop as he did. Emergency bulkheads slammed shut in his wake, extending from the bridge walls, trapping enough atmosphere for him to exit.

He popped open the cockpit hatch and leapt out, lightsaber already extending in his hand.

"What the—" a Nihil screamed, rising from a pile of debris and raising his blaster.

Ram smashed away the first shot, angling his saber so it would deflect directly back at the shooter, who dropped with a throaty shout. The other Nihil who'd been piloting lay beneath rubble, dead.

Ram ran down the drill-shaped nose of his ship, careful not to keep his feet down for too long, as it would probably burn right through his boots, and leapt across an open area, landing at the control panel.

He didn't know the MPO star cruiser schematics that well, and he wasn't sure how long it would take to find and blast through all thirteen engines of the unique Drabor Configuration, much less which ones would be crucial for hyperspace travel.

But Ram had something else in his arsenal besides the punch and precision of the Eviscerator: he had a Longbeam.

He grabbed the main directional shifter and shoved it all the way to the front, lurching the ship into a sudden dive.

The whole fiery beast groaned and angled downward. The havoc he'd wreaked on the rear engines probably didn't help, but a few were still intact on other parts of the ship—enough to get them pointed back toward the surface of Corellia and . . .

. . . the approaching MPO, which had already climbed at a sharp incline so it could reach a safe distance from which to jump to hyperspace.

Not if Ram had anything to say about it.

SIXTY-THREE

CORELLIAN SKY

Everything hurt.

Reath's body was one gigantic throb of pain.

But he was alive. Which was . . . a surprise actually.

Except the world was dark, and whatever low roar had woken him up was still vibrating through everything around him.

Engines.

Big, powerful starship engines. Lots of them.

Ram! Ram had stashed Reath in a storage bin of some kind, under a bench. Where was everyone? Why were they taking off?

He kicked open the lid and heaved himself out of the bin, landing on the floor with a painful thud.

Everything hurt. Now it hurt a little bit more.

He pulled himself up and staggered out into the main corridor.

They'd only just taken off. He was sure of that.

Nothing seemed right. He stumbled toward the front of the ship. Somewhere there would be a bridge, and on that bridge would be either Nihil or Jedi or . . . He couldn't think straight.

That door up ahead though . . . that led to the bridge. He was sure of it. If he kept walking, he would get there.

The ship lurched to one side; it sent Reath sprawling into a table. Whoever was piloting wasn't used to star cruiser controls, which meant it was either a civilian, like Crash, in which case all the Jedi were probably dead, or the Nihil.

Reath drew his lightsaber, rising, and charged forward unsteadily.

The door to the bridge slid open.

Inside, four Nihil warriors swung their blades and blasters up to face him. A fifth turned from the control panel and smiled.

Sabata Krill.

"Ah . . ." Reath said. He was in no shape to fight off one opponent, let alone four with their weapons already raised.

"Ooh, a Jedi." Sabata giggled. "How perfect. You look wounded, poor dear."

One of the raiders approached gingerly, blaster rifle poised for a headshot. "Drop the saber, kid."

Reath retracted it and placed it on the floor, each muscle sending urgent complaints through his body.

"Do you want to watch your pretty little space station get destroyed?" Sabata asked sweetly.

"Reath?" Ram's voice sounded urgently in Reath's ear. "Reath?"

"Yes!" Reath said.

Sabata looked a little unnerved. "That was a little more enthusiasm than I was expecting, actually."

"Are you on the star cruiser?" Ram asked. "The one in flight?"

"Yes!" Reath said again. The raiders looked back and forth at each other, uncomfortable.

"Get off it," Ram said. "Right now."

"I . . ." Reath looked around the bridge, confused. Where was he supposed to go? Then he saw something through the viewport over Sabata's shoulder. Something huge.

He didn't have the energy to fight, but he was pretty sure he had one good push left in him. Reath put his hands out, called inwardly upon the Force, and shoved forward with all his might. The Nihil around him flew backward, smashed into panels and walls. Reath thought maybe he could see Ram's face on the bridge of the Longbeam as it zoomed toward them. It looked like he was standing on top of another ship *inside* the bridge—that ancient black starfighter from the yards.

Well, Reath hoped Ram knew what he was doing. If anyone did, it was that kid.

All Reath had to do was stay alive.

His lightsaber smacked into his open hand.

He turned around and ran like hell as the first explosion rocked the cruiser.

SIXTY-FOUR

CORONET CITY

"Kark!" Crash yelled as a flash of light blitzed toward her out of the darkness. It had to be artillery of some kind, she thought, diving out of the way. What kind of reckless clown would use artillery in a tunnel fight?

The Nihil, of course. She scrambled to her feet and pushed forward at a low crouch, using the dust cloud as cover.

This was pretty much how it had been going for the past . . . Crash had lost track of time since she'd split off from the others. It seemed like forever, at this point, as if time had closed in on itself in the dark and she'd entered some awful loop of slaughter and near misses.

Crash wasn't sure how many Nihil were up ahead, or how many she'd killed. They had kept a steady march forward through the tunnels. At some point the waterway had narrowed and then fallen off completely, and the worms said they'd meet her at the birthing pool on the other side, but void knew how far along that was.

It all seemed never-ending, yes, but Crash had a theory. A theory and, possibly, a plan.

She paused, then flattened herself against a grimy wall. Bright red laser fire surged from the tunnel ahead. At any moment, the whole Nihil party would come clomping past to deal with her once and for all. Crash could hear them rustling closer, the splash of their boots in puddles a few meters away, the swish of their clothes. This would be face-to-face fighting, and it would not be pretty. She tightened her grip on the blaster.

A Mimbanese raider in a tattered muni uniform stepped in front of Crash, glaring farther down the tunnel. Crash let him pass. Next came an Ithorian—that long loping stride, a hefty firearm raised in both hands. Crash let her pass, too. Then a tall bearded guy with a blaster rifle and breathing mask stopped in front of her. He started to turn his head. Crash opened fire. The man collapsed into a puddle, and Crash stepped over him and lit up the two who'd walked by as they turned to see what had happened.

Someone came swinging out of the darkness—a middle-aged human woman. She wielded what looked like an axle from some ancient vehicle. It thunked into a puddle, throwing her off balance. Crash dropped the woman with a spin kick to the face and kept moving.

"Stay back!" someone yelled as footsteps clomped farther down the tunnel.

Tralmat. Finally.

"Back, I said!" he called from up ahead. He wasn't far, and he sounded out of breath—his footsteps had slowed to an unsteady shuffle. Crash heard the anxious clicking of shaking hands prepping a blaster.

"You aligned yourself with the Nihil," she yelled, throwing herself against a wall as shots zinged by. "Against Corellia."

"It's *for* Corellia, you ridiculous girl!" Tralmat said, hurrying off again. "It's all for Corellia. The Nihil will save Corellia. This fool Republic will see us collapse under the weight of its naïve ambitions, with their Great Works and ridiculous beacons. Everything I do is for Corellia! The Nihil are just a means to an end!"

Crash pushed off the wall and broke into a run. There, about five meters ahead, Tralmat stood on a metal walkway, blaster out. "Stay back!" The dark water stretched out to either side of him.

"Was Prybolt a means to an end? Ovarto?"

"I didn't kill your men, Crash!" Tralmat shrieked, that suddenly high-pitched voice betraying the lie behind his words.

"No," Crash said. "You didn't pull the trigger or hunt

them down, I'm sure. But you made sure they wouldn't live to spill the secret of your alliance with the Nihil, didn't you?"

"I—"

"Didn't you?" Crash yelled. An unexpected well of sadness rose in her. Her friends had died, the rest of their lives snatched away from them, all so this man could protect his dirty dealings. When would it all end?

"I did what I had to do," Tralmat said. "They shouldn't have gone meddling where they don't belong! When the alarm let us know the outer door had opened, I told Sabata to hit me, in case it was one of those ridiculous gossip reporters who had somehow gotten through. Then I could claim I'd been attacked and that would be that."

Crash felt her blood turn to ice. "But it wasn't a gossip reporter. It was my friend."

"He had no business doing that!" Tralmat wailed. "Of course there were consequences! That's how the galaxy works. Of course I gave the okay to Sabata to do what she had to! That's how we survive! By doing what must be done. Someone has to. . . . But anyway, you . . . you're sworn to protect me, Alys Ongwa. You . . . you can't do this."

Crash shook her head. She thought this would feel triumphant somehow, but all she felt was sadness. "I'm done with all that. But anyway, I'm not doing anything. You did it all yourself."

Tralmat's look of confusion as tall shapes moved

through the darkness around him—that almost made it all worthwhile.

He whirled around. The towering form of Mother Fastidima rose from the canal with a gentle slurping sound. The beady eyes of the four younger Grindalids appeared at the surface of the black water.

"Mo-Mother Fastidima!" Tralmat gasped. "I . . . *we* have an arrangement! You have been well c-compensated for the use of your—"

"The arrangement," Mother Fastidima pronounced with an aggressive rolling of her *R*s, "was canceled when you admitted to having my son murdered."

"No! I—" was all Tralmat was able to get out before she craned forward and closed her jaws around his head. A sickening moist crunch sounded. The other Grindalids surged out of the water on either side, clamping their teeth around Tralmat's arms and legs and pulling what was left of him apart.

The slivering voice of Mother Fastidima rose over the splashing and chewing nearby. "We thank you, Young Ongwa, for bringing us the treacherous one responsible for the death of my son."

Crash bowed slightly, not taking her eyes off the worm arching over her. She tried not to flinch. Given what had just happened, she preferred the Grindalid not come anywhere near her head.

"And you are absolved of responsibility and we welcome you as a trusted guest in our lair, from here forward."

"Thank you. I just have a small request."

Mother Fastidima got up close, her tiny eyes twitching slightly; bits of slobber and muck dribbled from razor-sharp teeth. "Hm?"

"A ride to the shipyards."

SIXTY-FIVE

CORONET CITY

"Just lay down a blanket of fire when I give the signal," Kantam advised into the comlink. "And then run like hell." Another blistering crackle of laser fire came from the fog. Kantam and Cohmac rose as one, swatted it off together, and ducked back down, both panting.

"Okay, but why didn't we do this earlier?" Zeen asked over the comms.

"Because when we do it," Kantam said, "they'll realize it's not worth keeping this ship around with us in it."

"Oh."

"And then they'll blow up the ship."

"Right."

"So lay down fire, and then run."

"Got it."

The Wookiee, the Savrip, and most of their other wounded had been stashed in various ships around the lot—hopefully, Kantam thought belatedly, not in either of the ones that had taken off. So all that was left was to make it out with the people who could walk and then try to figure out how to launch a rescue mission once they were clear.

Of course, everyone was pretty banged up. One of Kantam's arms had been badly burned, and it made swinging a lightsaber almost unbearable. Cohmac looked ready to collapse. Most of their crew was either limping or in some state of shell shock. Kantam knew that making it out through the throng of surrounding Nihil was probably just shy of impossible.

Without question, they would lose some of their party, more than likely all.

But if they could provide cover for even one to make it through, it would be worth it. Anyway, it was better than hiding on this boarding ramp, waiting for a stray blaster bolt to finally claim them, one by one, or for the Nihil to rally enough to overrun them.

No. This was the only way Kantam could see.

They glanced at Cohmac.

Cohmac nodded.

More blaster fire slammed against their barricade.

Kantam looked back at the motley, harried crew of

Corellian defenders waiting at the top of the ramp. "Cohmac and I won't be able to clear the fog *and* fight," they said, "so we'll have to push our way through it best we can."

The fighters nodded, preparing themselves.

"We do this together," Kantam said, "for Corellia, for the Republic."

The Corellians seemed to rally some, their blasters raised, ready.

"For Starlight and life!" Kantam yelled. Then, quietly, "Zeen, now."

"For Starlight and life!" the Corellian defenders yelled, charging down the ramp as a burst of laser cannons exploded from the ship.

Kantam led the charge, Cohmac at their side. The first row of Nihil were completely wiped out by Zeen's fusillade. The rest quickly regrouped in the fog around them.

"I'm coming," Zeen yelled into the comlink as blaster fire erupted all around Kantam and the sound of incoming mortars screeched through the air.

With a horrific clap, the Longbeam collapsed, pummeled by blast after blast of Nihil artillery. Debris shot outward in all directions, smashing into Corellian defenders and Nihil alike.

Kantam and Cohmac used the confusion to cleave an opening in the nearest group of raiders. More emerged from the fog, already firing.

"Go!" Kantam yelled. "That way!" Corellian defenders

streamed past, directly into another cluster of raiders. The whole small foggy world became a mass of tangled limbs, locked in close combat; blaster bolts slashed through the mist, and bodies fell all around.

Zeen ran up beside Kantam, pushing both hands ahead of her and sending a charging Nihil Gigoran staggering backward. She pulled both blasters out and let loose with them. Another attacker hurdled out of the fog immediately behind Zeen. Kantam swung over her head, slashing in a sharp downward arc across the man's chest and then kicking him away.

Where was Cohmac?

Where was Zeen? Barely a second had passed, and she was already lost in the fog—maybe dead.

Someone ran at Kantam. Was it friend or foe? Kantam had no idea. They stepped back, felt a cruel burning erupt across their back, and spun. A figure with a blaster hurried away; it was too late to deal with them, but whoever had been running at Kantam was probably still coming.

They dropped to one knee, sensing something—*something*—swinging at them from nearby, felt the whoosh of a blade passing overhead, then stabbed straight out, felt the lightsaber rend a direct, fiery path through heavy armor, then flesh, then emptiness as the body fell away.

More attackers were coming; Kantam felt them all around. The dense hot smell of that burning ship came from . . . the direction Kantam had thought they were supposed to be heading in. But that couldn't be right.

Where was everyone else?

"Cohmac?" Kantam yelled into the comlink. "Zeen? Can you hear me?"

A cheer went up, and Kantam was positive it came from the Nihil. What had they seen? Then the familiar rumble of a ship's engines sounded from not far away.

"Kantam?" Cohmac said over the comms. "Do you see this?"

"Stand by." The Nihil fog was unyielding, but at least the fighting seemed to have paused for the moment. Kantam waved a hand and the sky appeared, but it was almost immediately covered by a massive trawler passing overhead. A contingent of Nihil must have slipped into the next shipyard over and taken one to attack Starlight. "Cohmac," Kantam called, already reaching a hand skyward. "Zeen. Can you . . . ?"

"Already here," Zeen said, appearing from the mist alongside Cohmac. Both were badly scratched up and limping, but both had that fire in their eyes, ready to fight. Kantam passed Zeen their lightsaber. Already the Nihil were grunting and growling around them, turning back to the fight now that they'd gloated over their victory. Blaster bolts lit the fog.

That ship would not leave, though.

Kantam would have to trust Zeen and Cohmac to keep

them covered. This would take every drop of focus. One hand raised, the Force flowing through each beat of their heart, each cell of their body, Kantam imagined the Force like a wind, sweeping upward, swerving through the sky and then clenching around the ship like a giant fist.

With a wrenching jolt, the trawler stalled directly overhead.

Kantam was dimly aware of fierce fighting raging all around. The tiniest flicker in their concentration would rip into a seam that would undo all of it. The trawler quaked, and Nihil shrieked with rage in the fog. Slowly, it began to angle toward the ground.

Lula.

The image of her stricken face flickered through Kantam's mind. She was in terrible, terrible danger, the station collapsing around her, a ravenous darkness closing in. But Kantam knew this. They had accepted it, and released. Accepted it, and released.

Up above, the trawler yanked itself out of the dive, trying to lurch away from the Force's grasp.

No!

"The lesson of Younglings we take on is one of the hardest ones for most Jedi to learn. To let go," Yoda had said all those years before. A lesson Kantam had been learning over and over since. And maybe hadn't learned at all.

In their mind, Lula's face became Yoda's became Lula's.

In truth, Kantam had released neither. They'd been

holding on to Yoda all along, to his memory, to the hope he'd return. And of course! Who wouldn't?

But the mind in battle could hold only so much. And Kantam's grip on the trawler was near to nothing as the ship crept forward and away into the sky.

No.

"I release you," Kantam whispered to the ghosts and memories of their Padawan, their master. "I let go."

The trawler plummeted several meters, and Kantam directed it away, using all their focus. Up ahead, the fog began to clear, revealing a mass of figures heading toward the battle from across the shipyard.

Nihil reinforcements.

Kantam could see them crawling from underground tunnels and launching forward, blasters raised.

They had come so close. So close to making it out, to stopping whatever had been planned.

"Don't stop," Cohmac growled, seeing the trawler start to pull off again. "We're not done yet."

Kantam nodded, blocking out the triumphant cheers of the Nihil all around, the flickering images of Lula, Yoda, Torban, Avar . . . blocking it all out and focusing only on the trawler.

Both hands raised, they called on the Force with every shred of their being, and then, very suddenly, the weight of it all became light, almost nothing, as something seemed to give way in the air all around them.

Without releasing their grip, Kantam blinked into the fog. The Nihil reinforcements still sprinted toward them; Cohmac and Zeen still beat back attacks on either side.

The remaining fog, all that was left of that foul yellow-gray cloud, was swept suddenly away as if a heavy wind had blown in from the harbor.

But there was no wind.

All around Kantam, warriors looked to either side, confused.

There in the middle of a wide-open area, the last bit of fog cleared to reveal a short hooded figure standing alone amid all that destruction and death. A bright green lightsaber extended from one hand; the other was raised to the sky.

Master Yoda.

"A hand, it seemed you might need," Yoda said. His eyes locked with Kantam's.

Kantam gasped, tears sliding down their face. The entire weight of the trawler was gone now. Kantam dropped their hands, panting.

Master Yoda made a single mighty sweeping motion, and the trawler above careened out of the sky, smashing directly into the charging Nihil horde with a fiery explosion.

The whole shipyard shook with the blast. Nihil and Corellian defenders scattered as debris rained down on them. But the fight wasn't over yet. Already, the remaining raiders began regrouping, forming tight clusters around the Jedi.

Kantam blinked through more tears as their master leapt

into motion, smashing his way through a sudden onslaught of attackers. The Nihil fell to either side, a collapsing catastrophe of severed limbs and lifeless bodies. More came, and Yoda leapt again, smashing directly into the leader feetfirst and then launching upward into a wild flip and landing in the midst of the rest of them, sending the lot flailing away with a single hand motion.

"For light and life!" Kantam yelled, finally finding Cohmac and then Zeen again amid the chaos. They spun into action, cutting down the nearest Nihil and leaping to where more were preparing to lunge at Master Yoda.

Yoda's battle mode was dizzyingly fast. He launched into the air, cutting through a crowd of Nihil as he went, and then landed amid another crowd of them and immediately sent them all flying with a flick of his tiny wrist.

"Master!" Kantam called as a tall, heavily armored raider bore down on Yoda with some kind of whirring buzz saw. Yoda whirled around, then stepped easily out of the way as the beast went roaring past. Kantam sent out a blistering shove with the Force and the attacker stumbled backward, arms waving, until a bright green lightsaber burst through his chest.

He collapsed with a screech, but more came, so many more.

"Stay close!" Kantam yelled. "We're not out of this yet."

The few reinforcements who had managed to get out of the way of the downed trawler were rushing into battle, and all the Nihil had the fury of a losing hand electrifying their every movement. This wasn't supposed to be a battle at all, and it certainly wasn't supposed to be a losing one.

"Gather we must," Yoda said as Kantam and Cohmac fell into line on either side of him, "and charge, to close this out for good."

The others soon appeared from the tangle of fighting: Zeen, and more of Crash's crew, and Corellians Kantam had never seen before. They were worn-out and injured, but the sight of this tiny kinetic green Jedi lit them up from within. They were ready.

Up ahead, the surviving Nihil had congealed into a swarm, blocking the only way out of the shipyard. Smoke rose from the shattered wreckage of that trawler. Somewhere far away, the Jedi of Starlight Beacon were fighting for their lives and the lives of so many others.

But Kantam was on Corellia, and so, somehow, was their master.

"I release you, Lula Talisola," Kantam whispered again. "But whatever happens after this, if you live, I will find you."

Yoda glanced up and down the lines of fighters around him. They stared back, faces set with determination and grit. He raised his saber. "For light and life!" Yoda yelled, his voice thundering across the battlefield.

As one, they charged.

"For light and life!" The shouts rose up all around as they ran.

"For light and life!" cried Zeen, blasting away with tears in her eyes as they neared the bristling horde of Nihil.

"For light and life!" yelled Kantam Sy, whacking one bolt and then the next away and then leaping forward into the tangle of bodies and blasters.

"For light and life!" called Cohmac, dodging an attacker and then using the Force to send him catapulting back into three more.

"For light and life!" yelled Svi'no, and Smeemarm, and Fezzonk, and . . . was that Crash? Crawling out of a utility hole and looking around, confused.

Yoda had led the charging defenders directly into the middle of the Nihil line, sweeping it away entirely. The remaining raiders were cut off from each other, fighting a suddenly desperate battle for their lives as the Corellian defenders and Jedi crashed through whatever was left of their defenses and sent them scattering into the darkness.

SIXTY-SIX

CORELLIAN SKY

Ram waited just long enough to see the Er'Kit girl stand up on the bridge of the star cruiser and open her mouth to scream.

Then he dropped into the safety of the Eviscerator's cockpit. The hatch slammed shut over his head just as the two ships collided. Ram gunned it, crashing out the front of one ship and then immediately in through the front of the other. Havoc and destruction spread to either side in his wake; explosions blasted all around him. Both ships were probably about to disintegrate.

"Where are you, Reath?" Ram muttered, reaching out

with the Force as he yanked the starfighter through a charred wall and away from the wrecked Longbeam. "Come on."

If Reath had any sense at all, which he did, and if he'd been able to, which wasn't certain at all, he would've airlocked himself. And that meant . . .

"There!" Ram yelled. A tiny, fleeting thread of life flickered in his consciousness. It came from somewhere over to the left and far below him. He slowed the Eviscerator to a gentle crawl, trying to pinpoint Reath's location and ignore the rapidly and loudly deteriorating situation behind him.

Then he dove.

The surface of Corellia would be rushing up toward them, and Reath was likely plummeting toward it.

Ram just had to go faster—that part was easy—and also not accidentally smack into his friend on the way past and splatter the poor kid all over Coronet City. That might be a little trickier. Then again . . . Ram kept his dive at a steady pace and popped open the hatch.

"Hold her steady," he told the Bonbraks. He climbed up to the top and poked his head out into the night sky. The wind whipped past him. The vast ocean spread out below, sheer darkness.

Reath had to be . . . Ram squinted through the night. Caught a glimpse of movement. A flash of pale skin.

"Faster!" he yelled. "He's still below us."

The starfighter lurched into a steep downward spiral

that almost sent Ram flying out of the hatch. "Easy," he said. "Easy."

Just above and off to the side of where they glided, Reath fell.

That would work.

Ram reached out with the Force, felt the sudden resistance rise up around his friend. Reath slowed. "Come here," Ram yelled, giving a small tug.

Reath blinked as he neared the cockpit. "I just had the weirdest dream," he muttered.

Ram rolled his eyes, grabbing the boy's clothes and hauling him to safety. "Yeah, yeah, yeah."

Up above, explosions rocked the night sky over Corellia.

Reath smiled, then wheezed, "Extremely . . . wizard," and passed out.

CORONET CITY

Most of the Nihil had been killed or captured when Ram brought the Eviscerator in for a landing on the airfield. The rest had fled. The fog of gas was gone. Kantam and Cohmac, then Zeen, ran over while Ram helped Reath out of the starfighter. They all looked pretty banged up, but they were alive.

"You did it!" Kantam yelled, grabbing Ram in a huge hug.

"You lived!" Ram said.

Kantam nodded, then stood to the side as a small figure with long ears stepped up behind them.

"Y-Yoda," Ram said. "Master Yoda, I mean."

The old Jedi nodded, smiling slightly. "Much to discuss, there is, but not much time."

"Yes," Kantam said. "We need to get somewhere safe so we can regroup and find out what we can."

"I know just the spot," Crash said, walking over with her arm around Svi'no and a huge smile plastered across her face.

SIXTY-SEVEN

THE GREEN

Sometime in the middle of the night, they felt it.

The endless splatter of laser fire had finally died away, along with the echoes of screams and groans, the smashing together of bodies clenched to kill.

So much death, so much life.

The Jedi had fought and they had won, against all odds, and then came the quiet slipping away, the healing, the letting go. Battle-weary and near broken, they had boarded ships and airspeeders that whisked them off to Baynoo's hideaway in the swamps outside Coronet City.

There they were joined by a strange figure swathed in

robes and bandages who had accompanied Master Yoda. "Much to explain, there is," Yoda had muttered, without explaining anything. Nobody bothered trying to get more answers just then. There would be time for that later.

They ate and bathed and let Baynoo fuss over them, and finally, fighting off endless cascades of worry and wonder about their friends, their home, they slept.

And then, in the darkness, each of them, all at once, felt the sudden plunging, the rending of steel, and the terrifying breathlessness of an explosion.

All of them had known it was coming. The knowledge of it loomed, larger and larger, became a certainty.

Still, they had hoped.

They had struggled, each in their own way, to find detachment, to breathe through the impending sense of loss, the fear.

Each had failed; each had tried again anyway, and then again.

This was the Jedi way. There was no other.

And then the crash came; it felt like an impossible silence, a sheer slipstream of emptiness, a mass grave that erupted from the inside out and covered everything.

For most of them, there was too much turmoil, too much pain, to sort out who had lived or died.

But for Cohmac, there was only a sudden unmistakable certainty.

"Orla," he said, sitting up from the pallet he'd been

sleeping on. The truth was, he hadn't felt her for a while. He'd suspected she might be gone, but something in the finality of the crash—Starlight Beacon had fallen, of that he was sure—crystallized it as truth.

Orla Jareni was dead.

He stood, a terrible calm settling over him as the reality of what had happened sank in.

There was no room for panic, no spiking anxiety or fear. It was simply true: so many were gone. And all he could feel was a sorrow so deep it had no name.

Still . . . with that sorrow came resolve.

Finally, finally, Cohmac knew what he had to do.

A quiet knock came at the door, but Reath Silas was already awake. He had felt it, too, Starlight's fall. They all had, he was pretty sure. He stood in the candlelit side room beside Ram. They'd both sat up in bed suddenly, as if the explosion had been right there on Corellia and not somewhere light-years away.

It might as well have been, Reath figured. The explosion had happened inside of them all as much as it had happened in the sky over Eiram.

Reath had no home.

A tiny thing, really, amid all the other tragedies, but somehow it was the only part of it he could wrap his head around.

"Come in," he said. His voice was steady.

He felt clearer, more together, than he ever would've believed himself to feel in such a moment.

Had there ever been a moment quite like this, though? It was hard to imagine.

Cohmac stood in the doorway, his face drawn and somber but somehow calm. *You felt it?* Reath almost asked, but that was silly. Of course he had.

"Come," Cohmac said. "Both of you."

Reath and Ram walked out into the cozy sitting room, where the dying embers of that cauldron fire still filled the whole cabin with a gentle flickering warmth. Yoda was there, along with Kantam and Zeen.

It is time to plan, Reath realized. *Figure out what to do. How to launch a rescue mission, then strike back.* But the others weren't talking; they just stood there solemnly.

They had to do something, right? Surely. Actions had to be taken, strategies discussed.

"Reath Silas," Cohmac said.

Reath held up his hands. "Wait . . . what is this? We have to talk about what to do next! Why is everyone just standing around?"

"Reath," Kantam said.

"We have to *do* something!" Reath was yelling, and he wasn't sure why. Nothing made sense. Not the tragedy of it, not the silence of it. It was all impossible. He didn't have a home. Suddenly, all that calmness he'd felt started slipping away. He'd thought he had at least some of it figured out. It had seemed so clear a few hours before.

When a Padawan laughs, the Force laughs harder, he reminded himself. And then he was laughing, but tears were streaming down his face, too, because Starlight was down, and so many had died, and nothing would ever be the same.

"Shhh," Zeen said, cocooning him out of nowhere, her own tear-stained face landing on his shoulder. "I know."

A few moments passed with just the crackling embers and the wild hoots and chirps of the swamp. Then Cohmac again said, "Reath Silas," and Reath finally understood. "Are you ready?"

No, Reath wanted to scream. *I'll never be ready. Not after this. Not after everything that's happened and whatever is about to. No.*

Reath shook his head. He'd pictured this moment many times. He used to imagine it happening on Coruscant, surrounded by all the ancient texts of the archive. More recently, of course, he'd envisioned the ceremony on Starlight, his home. He would be surrounded by his friends. He would glow with joy at what he'd achieved; he would begin the rest of his life.

But Starlight was gone, and many of his friends were, too.

"All this time, all this fighting, all this death," Reath said, his voice shaky, "and I haven't learned anything except how little I know."

Yoda made a thoughtful grunting noise. "The hardest lesson to learn, this is. One of the most important."

"The only way I could get out of my own way and move forward," Reath said, "was by realizing that there is no one path forward."

"That's right," Cohmac said.

"But that's not an answer," Reath insisted. "That's just a way to feel better about being lost."

Yoda shook his head. "Impossible it is, to be lost, when there is no path, hm?"

Cohmac sighed. "I told you, Reath, on the day you asked me to be your master, that perhaps you would be my greatest instructor in the Force."

Reath was pretty sure he was blushing. None of this was right; everything was turmoil.

"I only wish I had stopped to listen to you more. I have so much to learn, and I should've done it side by side with you." Why was he talking in the past tense, like it was too late for them to learn more from each other?

"I left Starlight with a hundred questions," Reath said. "Now Starlight is gone, and all I have are more."

"Being a Jedi isn't about having the answers," Kantam said. "It's about knowing which questions to ask. Even if some of those questions span centuries and generations."

"If all these Masters believe you to be ready," Yoda said in his warm, raspy voice, "think us mistaken, do you, hm?"

Reath had to smile.

He didn't feel ready, no. But somewhere, beyond the fear, beyond his own ego, he knew he was.

He stepped forward, looked his master in the eye, and nodded. "I am ready, Master Cohmac."

The slightest of smiles creased Cohmac's tired face.

Zeen stepped up on one side of Reath, Ram the other.

There was no path. And there was no being lost. As confused as Reath felt, he knew the Force had guided him to this moment, just as it would guide him to the next one.

Yoda stepped up beside Cohmac, Kantam on his other side. "By the right of the Council," Yoda said.

"By the will of the Force," Kantam said. Reath realized he was crying again, tears of both joy and sorrow. The Force had led him to this moment; the Force would lead him to the next. There was no being lost; there was no path.

"We name thee," Cohmac said, reaching out to gently pull up Reath's Padawan braid. He lit his saber, nodded at the others.

Then all three Masters together: "Jedi."

"Knight of the Republic," Cohmac finished, slicing through the braid. His saber went out. "I am so proud of you, Reath."

They hugged, Ram and Zeen both patting Reath on the back. When Reath stepped away from the hug, there was a lightsaber in his hand. Cohmac's.

"What . . . ?" Reath managed to say.

Cohmac looked suddenly like a human storm, like all the anxiety and grief he'd been holding back had surfaced now that the ceremony was complete. "I . . ." He glanced around the room, eyes wild. "I can't do this." Then his gaze locked with Reath's. "My saber is yours now."

"Cohmac," Kantam said, stepping forward. "That story . . . I wasn't trying to tell you to—"

Cohmac cut them off with a shake of his head. "This isn't a walkabout, or a pause." His face was ashen. "I am no longer a Jedi."

He traded nods with Master Yoda, then walked shakily out of the room and into the night before breaking into a run toward the dark tree line.

And then he was gone.

Missing, presumed dead.

The sky over Zeen was perfect—bright blue and dotted with puffy little clouds—and perfect was terrible. Everything was terrible.

Missing, presumed dead.

That was what the first official reports from the scene said about Lula, Farzala, and Master Torban.

And so many others.

Starlight had fallen.

Hundreds had died. The Nihil had unleashed an unspeakable horror on the galaxy, on the Jedi.

And hundreds more probably would've been killed if the Corellian attack had been successful.

Still.

Missing, presumed dead.

The words landed heavily on Zeen's tired mind every time she thought them. It was a terrible kind of weight—like they were dead things themselves. Dusty, and solid, and horribly lifeless.

Zeen sat up. She blinked at the bright day, the forest around her. Not far off, the others conferred on the porch wrapping around Crash's house.

Presumed didn't mean *definitely*, Zeen reminded herself for the four hundredth time that morning.

She'd lost track of time, lost track of her own racing heart and pounding head.

So much had happened so suddenly. And then, just as suddenly, it all had ground to a halt, and they were safe.

Well, they weren't being shot at. Safe didn't seem like a real thing anymore, not really.

Not with Starlight down and so many dead. And so many others languishing under that impossible deathlike label. *Missing, presumed dead.*

Zeen stood.

She was alive. That mattered. And so were Ram and Reath, Kantam and Cohmac. And Crash and most of her team. Impossibly, Master Yoda was there. Zeen still cherished the memory of him appearing like a phantom amid the vanishing mist, downing that trawler with Kantam, and then smashing through the attacking Nihil. She had felt the breath leave her, in that moment. She'd been absolutely sure she was going to die and was only hoping not to accidentally take someone she loved with her when she went. So much confusion, so much death.

She shook her head, touched her own face. It was wet. Again.

She wiped away the tears, blinking through the new ones that came, unbidden, again and again, no matter what she did.

Missing, presumed dead.

Presumed meant there was a chance. There was a chance. Lula and Farzala, and so many others—they might be alive.

Qort was. And Master Kriss. Many had survived.

If Lula and Farzala were alive, then Zeen would find them. She would get Qort, make sure he was all right, and then they'd be on their way. They'd find their friends and heal them. And then Zeen would never fool herself into thinking she and Lula were better off without each other again.

There: a plan. A way forward through this hell. A plan felt like a lifeline.

She let the sun caress her face for a few more moments, then stood.

Over by the cabin, Yoda and the others were readying themselves to head out.

Ram and Reath stood side by side, packing their bags and saying goodbye to Crash. Kantam and Yoda chatted quietly.

A little off to the side, that strange hooded figure sat, singing as always. They'd come with Yoda, Zeen had realized once everyone had disembarked and settled in at Baynoo's.

The figure never showed their face, never spoke to anyone, just sang a sad little ditty over and over in a raspy whisper: *"They'll do what they can. . . . They'll do what they must. . . ."*

It was time to go. There was no turning away from the Jedi Order, no running. If Zeen stood any chance of finding Lula, it would be with the Jedi by her side, the Republic at her back. If they'd let her, she'd enter their ranks—it seemed like certain ways of doing things were about to become irrelevant in this new era of their fight with the Nihil.

"But when they do find you . . . all you'll be is dust."

Lula was alive. She knew it in her bones. If she had died, Zeen would've felt it. It would have cratered her, no question. "I will find you, Lula Talisola." Zeen whispered her oath to the sweeping sun, the dancing blades of grass, the humming swamp all around. "Whatever it takes."

Balance, Ram Jomaram thought, gazing at Reath and Crash. *Somehow we made it through. So many didn't, but we made it through.* He felt strangely invigorated, like swinging right up to the edge of death yet again had zinged a firebolt of pure life into his veins. He had survived, and there was so much to do, so much rebuilding and revitalizing. There were mysteries to unravel and battles to fight. He might not make it far into whatever was coming next, but he'd be there to see as much of it as he could.

"I'm gonna miss you fellas," Crash was saying when Ram

blinked away from his daydreams, back to their conversation. "You turned out to be pretty all right."

"We'll miss you," Ram said. "I always knew you were amazing."

"What will you do?" Reath asked.

Crash let out a morbid little chuckle. "Oh . . . fight, of course." She tipped her head toward the house, where Svi'no, Tamo, Tangor, Fezzonk, and Smeemarm were plotting some exciting mischief on the couches. "Ovus has already made a move to consolidate power and claim none of this ever happened. As it stands, he has a good shot at doing exactly that, and then taking over Corellia entirely." She scowled. "I have no idea if we can actually stop him," she admitted. "But we're about to find out."

"I'll be there to help," said Deemus Abrus, walking out of the cabin.

"Deemus!" Ram ran over and hugged the Twi'lek before she made it all the way down the stairs. "I didn't know you'd come out here!"

"Had to say my goodbyes," the endangered species officer said with a smile. "And bring you this little one." A tiny lump squirmed along the sleeve of Deemus's uniform shirt, then two large ears popped out of the cuff, followed by Teetak's very adorable fuzzy head. *"Patachaclán!"* she squeaked.

"She wouldn't stop talking about you." Deemus chuckled. "I had to learn a bit of Bonbreez to figure it out, but she wants to go along with you, if that's all right."

"Of course it's all right! Fellas, come meet the newest member of our team!" Tip and Breebak crawled irritably out of Ram's collar—they'd clearly been napping—and eyed the younger Bonbrak. They glanced at each other, blinked back at Teetak. Then they both erupted into squeaks and chirps and laughter as they danced down Ram's arms and scooped her into a massive furry hug. All three Bonbraks zipped off together, chattering about new ways to take things apart.

"Ah, rats," Crash said wistfully, tossing some gork gork treats after them. "Anyway, we're happy to have your help, Deemus."

Yoda walked over from his shuttle and bowed to Crash and Deemus with a slight smile. "With you both, the Force will be, hm."

"Thank you, sir master," Crash said with unusual reverence. "What are you all going to do?"

"A new threat has arisen in the galaxy. The Jedi . . . are not safe. Return to Coruscant, we must," Yoda said. "All of us."

"The recall signal you asked for went out a few minutes ago," Kantam reported.

Yoda closed his eyes. "Much to discuss, there is. Difficult the way forward will be. But there is a way, hm? There is always a way. And young Reath has learned, make that way ourselves we must. For it has not been made yet. To do this, though, to forge our path to the future, guided by the secrets of the past, we will be."

ABOUT THE AUTHOR

Daniel José Older, a lead story architect for *Star Wars: The High Republic*, writes the monthly comic series *The High Republic Adventures*, where you can find out more about Lula, Zeen, and Ram. He is also the *New York Times* best-selling author of the sci-fi adventure *Flood City*; the upcoming young adult fantasy novel *Ballad & Dagger*, book one of the Outlaw Saints series; the middle grade historical fantasy series Dactyl Hill Squad; *The Book of Lost Saints*; the Bone Street Rumba urban fantasy series; *Star Wars: Last Shot*; and the award-winning young adult series the Shadowshaper Cypher, which was named one of the best fantasy books of all time by *Time* magazine and one of *Esquire*'s 80 Books Every

Person Should Read. He has won the International Latino Book Award and has been nominated for the Kirkus Prize, the World Fantasy Award, the Andre Norton Award, the Locus, and the Mythopoeic Award. He cowrote the upcoming graphic novel *Death's Day*. You can find more info and read about his decade-long career as an NYC paramedic at danieljoseolder.net.

ACKNOWLEDGMENTS

First and foremost, a huge thank-you to George Lucas, for creating this incredible galaxy that I have been playing in since I was three! It changed the world (and my world) for the better and helped send me on my path as a storyteller.

Second, thank you, Michael Siglain, for inviting me to come play in that galaxy and help develop this whole new era in *Star Wars* history. What an amazing adventure it has been, and a dream come true. He is the Jimmy to our Commitments—an absolute visionary, mover, shaker, consigliери, and capo rolled into one. Also, a great friend. Thank you for being unstoppable and helping us usher this gigantic story into the world.

And of course, to the crew, my fellow Lumineers: Claudia Gray, Cavan Scott, Charles Soule, Justina Ireland. It has been an incredible honor working side by side, sharing so much and learning so much along the way! Here's to all the greatness ahead. . . .

Thank you to my editor, Jen Heddle, and to Story Group and everyone at Lucasfilm, including Kathy Kennedy, James Waugh, Matt Martin, Jason Stein, Emily Shkoukani, and Kelsey Sharpe. Special thank you to Pablo Hidalgo for all his wisdom and miscellaneous nerdery about the Force and *Star Wars* tech throughout this process.

And thank you to everyone on the art team who has helped us put flesh and blood and cool technology on this era, including Phil Noto, Iain McCaig, Grant Griffin, Petur Antonsson, Phil Szostak, Leigh Zieske, Scott Piehl, and Jeff Thomas. And to Cristiano Spadoni, Ornella Savarese, and Gregor Krysinski for the terrific cover art.

Over at IDW, the editorial and art teams have also done phenomenal work in crafting *The High Republic Adventures* with me, where a lot of these characters first appeared. Thank you, Heather Antos, Riley Farmer, Elizabeth Brei, Rebecca Nalty, Kevin Tolibao, Pow Rodrix, and Jake M. Wood. And a huge thanks to guest artist Toni Bruno.

To Harvey Tolibao, who has been my creative partner on *Adventures* from the beginning: your incredible sense of humanity and breathtaking craft has infused a whole new life into this world, showed me new sides of the characters, and taught me so much about who they are. I can't thank you enough for the dedication and love you've given this project.

Thanks to the *Trail of Shadows* team at Marvel: Dave Wachter, Giada Marchisio, David López, Joe Sabino, Mark Paniccia, Tom Groneman, and Danny Khazem.

And thank you to Lyssa Hurvitz, Seale Ballenger and the whole Disney PR team for helping bring *The High Republic* to the world.

Without Joanna Volpe and all the great folks at New Leaf, Jenniea Carter, Jordan Hill, and Abigail Donoghue, I wouldn't be where I am today. Thank you, all—there's no one in the business doing it like you are.

I did a lot of research on diplomatic protection work for the Crash sections of *Midnight Horizon*, but nothing compared to hearing writer Shawn Taylor talk about his lived experience on the job. It was Shawn who described the whole process as a symphony and insisted I could give that notion to Crash, even when I told him he might want to keep it for his own work. A great mind and a great friend.

And a belated thank-you to Kara Scott, who was kind enough to give me insight into what it's like being a professional gambler, when I was writing *Last Shot*.

Brittany—my wife, my partner in crime, my co-conspirator, brilliant writer and reader, maternity fashion icon, absolute genius of the heart and soul—thank you. I love you.

To Tito, mi hijo, thanks for showing up in the middle of all this *High Republic* stuff and teaching me some real life lessons about love. A true Jedi, and you've only just arrived!

And thanks always to the rest of my amazing family, Dora, Marc, Malka, Lou, Calyx, Paz, and Azul. Thanks to Iya Lisa and Iya Ramona and Iyalocha Tima, Patrice, Emani, Darrell, April, and my whole Ile Omi Toki family for their support; also thanks to Oba Nelson "Poppy" Rodriguez, Baba Malik, Mama Akissi, Mama Joan, Tina, and Jud, and all the wonderful folks of Ile Ase. Thanks also to Sam, Leigh, Sorahya, Akwaeke, and Lauren.

Baba Craig Ramos: we miss you and love you and carry you with us everywhere we go. Rest easy, Tío. Ibae bayen tonu.

I give thanks to all those who came before us and lit the way. I give thanks to all my ancestors; to Yemonja, Mother of Waters; gbogbo Orisa; and Olodumare.